Buried By The Roan

An Allison Coil Mystery

Mark Stevens

People's Press
Woody Creek, Colorado

Buried By The Roan
by Mark Stevens

© 2011 Mark Stevens

People's Press
Minds Wide Open

PUBLISHED BY PEOPLE'S PRESS
Post Office Box 70 • Woody Creek, Colorado 81656
www.PeoplesPress.org

PEOPLE'S PRESS MISSION
Through its current and future publications and expanding distribution network, People's Press is part of this global, local community

PEOPLE'S PRESS EDITORIAL BOARD
Catherine Lutz
Mirte Mallory
Nicole Beinstein Strait
George Stranahan
Craig Wheeless

Library of Congress Control Number: 2011925590
ISBN: 978-0-9817810-9-9

Cover and Interior Design: Nick Zelinger, NZ Graphics

First Edition
Printed in the United States of America

This one is for Gary.

1

Allison Coil tugged the reins on Sunny Boy and the horse came to a stop with a labored sigh. His clock was punched. Allison stood in the stirrups and squeezed her shoulders back, the bones of her torso snapping and popping with exquisite release. Her day was done too.

"Do you want to go another half-mile and join the camp or make do in that stand of blue spruce over there?" Sunny Boy didn't respond or even look around. "Huh?" Allison said. "What do you think?"

Sunny Boy shook his mane, rattling his bit. Allison patted his neck and reached into a pannier for binoculars. She knew the hunting camp wouldn't be visible, a quarter-mile across Oyster Lake, but she might be able to see if anyone was out. She scanned the lake shore and everything she could view beyond. Nothing, nobody. She repeated the search, overlapping her fields of vision, probing for any movement. Zip. She was a few minutes from camp but she preferred to keep the night to herself. The men could drink their Wild Turkey and stumble around and tell their jokes without her company.

She would have all this ridiculous serenity to herself.

Allison smiled.

Make this my addiction, she thought.

Put this moment in a needle or a shot glass. Bake my brain with this intense calm, pack it with serenity. Fill me with this sensation of nature, of horse and lakes and woods. Of fire, smoke and stars. Somebody once said the average person has 60,000 thoughts a day—individual phrases that attempt to gel and form the substance of the story you are telling yourself about yourself. And of all that gibberish, 99 percent are repeats. Maybe that was city life, the world of commutes and deadlines and e-mail. Up here, Allison Coil calculated she must be down to two thousand thoughts a day—max.

Good thoughts.

Grounded thoughts.

"We're staying here," she told Sunny Boy. "I've got a bag of oats with your name on it. Tomorrow for breakfast, some hay over at the camp, okay? Special bacon-flavored hay, what do you say?"

A stand of Ponderosa pine beckoned like a sepia-toned picture-postcard. The trees stood a few hundred yards off the main trail at the base of a thousand-foot cliff that climbed to the high plateau. Allison pointed Sunny Boy off the trail and they picked their way across a scrubby meadow—bunchgrass and clumps of bitterbrush scattered by nature's definition of random.

The trees were tightly clustered. Allison found a flat spot for her pup tent. She hitched Sunny Boy to a tree and hung a bag of oats around his neck.

"Dig in," she whispered in his ear. "Well deserved."

Allison walked a few loops in concentric circles searching for tracks. There was no point in sleeping on a bear highway if she could avoid it. She would just be a snack. She had added a few pounds to her normal 110, but was probably just thickening for winter. Her stand of trees was nestled against the base of a cliff. From the top of the small rise to the south, the terrain rolled away into the misted distance. She spotted a darker strip of vegetation at the bottom of the next draw which should mean running water. She found old raccoon scat, but no tracks from bear or mountain lion. Finding an opening on top of the ridge, she spotted

Sunny Boy in the stand below and studied the sheer beauty and forbidding toughness of the landscape. Red, white and blue were honorable colors—but what would have been wrong with blue, deep green and another deep green for the stripes on the American flag?

Allison unhitched Sunny Boy and guided him over the ridge to the creek where he slurped and sucked with no apparent regard for the silence he was shattering.

Back at camp, Allison gathered a handful of dry sticks and found a gold mine for fire lovers—a dead spruce from a decades-old blow down. The tree trunk shed several armloads of branches as thick and round as an oatmeal carton. Her fuel supply was fully stocked by the time last light faded.

October weather was a tease. Daytime could mean comforting warmth, when there was no difference between skin temperature and the air, but at night the winter could bang at the door like a battering ram. There was no Katy Bar tough enough.

The fire roared to life and Allison unpacked a small pot and two bottles of water. She boiled the water for tea and to re-hydrate a packet of freeze-dried beef stroganoff. There was probably wild food all around for the harvesting, and if she was skilled enough she might pluck a trout from Oyster Lake—but these plastic packs made nourishment a snap. She would leave foraging to the animals and to her earthy, herbalist friend Trudy Heath.

Allison fed the fire a fresh supply of wood. The night air would be no match for a hunting guide's ordinary layers of clothing. If she was going to wake to warmth, she would have to utilize her trick of waking up every two hours to throw another couple logs on the fire. Sunny Boy would appreciate it too.

Her mental alarm clock was something she had picked up back in her city days, when she didn't trust digital hotel alarm clocks (no two the same) or the equally baleful telephone robots and their lack of heart. She had found it within herself to fixate on the necessary wake-up time in order to forego an electric prod.

It was still early. If she climbed into her tent now, it would be a long night. She was tired, but sleep wasn't the only salve. She pulled a flask from her stash and poured a generous splash of her custom blend—99 percent straight tequila, 1 percent triple sec, and a squeeze of juice from a wedge of lime. She had anticipated the first taste of this tart concoction, oh, about 963 times already that day. She took a few delicious sips, set the cup down and moved Sunny Boy around to a spot closer to the fire. She checked him for nicks and slid her hands along his shins and shanks, searching for injuries. All good.

"Too bad you don't like tequila," she told him. "It makes you think you're warm."

A coyote howled a mournful note, soft and low. No sense of urgency. Allison smiled. "Music," she said. "How about you, Sunny? Hear the wail?"

She settled by the fire on a rock she had rolled into position from a few yards away.

Okay, she thought—the alone thing.

The alone thing might need some work. She had been repeating that thought for months. She wanted to spark something, wanted somebody in closer, regular orbit. It didn't have to be anything on the road to permanentville, just something meaningful. Her straight, shoulder-length brown hair bounced loosely when it was not too smoked up by campfires. Her body had grown tougher with the years in the outdoors, but plenty of guys still circled around, so her feminine vibe hadn't completely gone underground. She liked being the hunting chick in the guys' world and did what she could to make sure her reddish-brown eyes, high cheekbones and Midwestern smile didn't lose their appeal. It was time to stop holding guys off and let one buzz closer.

The fire crackled and popped and she took off her hat, stretching her neck around in a post-horseback yoga twist. She took a sip of tequila mix and wondered if the contentment scale needed another notch.

The tequila went down tart and tasty. She finished her first and poured a second, starting to feel the aches of the day melt away. Two drinks would be plenty and she reminded herself to chug a few cups of water. You could never drink enough at this altitude.

A twig snapped in the meadow.

Not a twig—a stick. A stick with heft.

She estimated the sound was thirty yards off to her left, no more. Prickles flared across her shoulders. She stood up cautiously and stepped away from the flickering firelight, blocking it with her hand. She peered into the blackness, hoping her eyes would quickly readjust, and blamed the rare jolt of fear on city residue. The idea of joining the men in camp held appeal.

Allison back-pedaled until she was clear of the light. She circled out into the darkness and stared in the direction of the sound. A branch lying on the ground would not break of its own free will in a wide-open meadow. Something or somebody had put some weight on it. Would a bear be that careless?

She crouched and waited, trying to discern movement in the black. Would she prefer to be right—to verify that her outdoor skills were keen—or would she prefer to be wrong, so she didn't have to confront an animal? Or worse, a human being?

Nothing moved.

She reached into the pocket of her jean jacket. Her gloved fingers settled around a comfortable, friendly shape. She couldn't remember putting it there, but it was as welcome as a .45. She could flip the flashlight on, but that would make her a target. She glanced back at her camp, waiting for something to happen, a figure to bounce out of the night or a bear to slouch into the ring of light and give her tent a whiff. She moved cautiously toward the meadow, trying to see a movement or hear a sensation of an interloper.

She flipped on the flashlight and pointed it at the ground in front of her—scrub, grass and dirt. She aimed the beam horizontal, belt high, and considered holding it away from her side as a ruse, in case somebody out there was looking for a target. Unnecessary. No shot rang out, no lion leapt. Had she imagined the snap? The adrenaline taking a joy ride in her bloodstream told her otherwise.

She glanced back to check the fire and Sunny Boy, to make sure nobody was slipping in behind her. She stepped further into the meadow, stopped. She swept the light in an arc and anticipated the snap of a branch or the sight of a telltale print that might confirm her sanity—and her heightening panic.

Ten more steps, she told herself, and if there's nothing I'll call myself crazy. The swath of light across the meadow was so narrow and the beam so weak that the search was more a matter of self-satisfaction than self-protection.

Then she saw it.

The shape on the ground was so out of place that she had to suppress a laugh.

A baseball cap. It was as though somebody had walked to this spot, removed his cap, and placed it ever-so-gently on the ground.

She picked up the cap in her gloved hands. It was well-worn but hadn't been sitting in the meadow for long. There wasn't one piece of extraneous dirt, only a jagged stain where salt from the owner's sweat had leached from skin to fabric.

Her hands shook as she held it, knowing somebody was right *there*. The cap was practically warm to the touch.

Above the bill was a logo in a simple font, white on black, with the top line forming an arch.

The Colorado Rockies.

Tuesday Morning

The straining whine from the airplane engine was out of place. Allison wriggled her head out of the sleeping bag and sat up inside her tent, the morning sun filling the inside with a green glow. The noise was odd in the Flat Tops, particularly at dawn and never so close.

She zipped open the front of the tent, more than a little concerned that the plane might be coming from the west and would need elevation in a hurry. If it was coming from the east, it would be flying straight down a thousand-foot cliff. North or south, no major issues.

Front tent flap unzipped, she stood up outside and tugged her coat against a bracing gust of morning air. The plane was banking hard. It was a ridiculous-looking machine, a single-engine flying metal bug that produced a hearty whine like a lawnmower. She had no clue about small planes. The flying bug tilted steeply on a wingtip, and Allison held her breath. The wings snapped back level and tilted in the other direction as if the pilot had suddenly seen the insurmountable wall. The plane accelerated and zipped overhead. The engine coughed a hard, throaty complaint.

That was a first, thought Allison—a plane flying that low in the wilderness. Who would perform such a stunt? "I don't think it's legal either, is it?" she said to Sunny Boy, rubbing his head. "Are you okay, fella?"

The plane disappeared over the treetops. She wondered if it had a tail number, whether she could have spotted it. But then what? And so what? Had it done something illegal?

The engine faded as though the plane had dived into a hole in the earth.

"Maybe they were looking for a lost baseball cap," she told Sunny Boy. "That makes as much sense to me as anything else."

The Oyster Lake hunting camp was quiet. A puff of smoke drifted from the round metal chimney poking through the roof. The smoke was in no hurry, as if reluctant to leave. The outside of the tent looked reasonably sharp and clean—she took pride in keeping her gear shipshape, respectable. The time she'd spent scrubbing and drying it in the summer fields with Woolite and water had paid off. It wasn't a pup tent you could hide under the trees; it was a human barn large enough to sleep a dozen grown men and it spoke volumes about her outfit's quality and standards. She wanted any hunter or wildlife officer who saw it to think one thing: class act.

Allison hitched Sunny Boy to a railing where he could attack a bale of hay. "Have at it, big boy," she said. "Promise kept."

Inside the tent, it was good to see the stove was being tended by at least one of two men. One was sitting on a metal-framed lawn chair. The other was stretched out on a cot. The man sitting up was Colin McKee, one of her guides. It was odd to see Colin inside the tent midday in hunting season. It was even stranger to see him sitting down. Allison was sure every muscle in his body twitched with a need to roam outdoors, stalking deer or elk from a high ridge. He was part Daniel Boone and part Ben Affleck, and she had a shameless craving to see his muscles twitch in her direction with pleasure. But he was six years her junior and she didn't want to create what the city folks called a "hostile work environment" with one of her employees.

Check that.

Yes she did.

"Good morning," said Allison. "What's this?"

"Sick bay," said Colin.

"Since when?"

"Since dinner last night," said Colin.

Josh Keating rolled over with a faint groan.

"Sucks," said Keating with a dry grumble. "My guts feel like somebody is slicing them open with a hot, dull razor from the inside. And I had only one beer at dinner so it wasn't that."

"Suffering all night," said Colin.

"So if everyone else was okay, it wasn't the food," said Allison.

Keating was a quiet but imposing figure. His long face was sunburned, nicked and craggy. His hands bore the wear and tear of a caveman's. The owner of a buffalo ranch near Meeker, he was an experienced hunter who didn't need a guide. He knew how to survive in the outdoors. He asked no questions. He already knew the answers.

"I didn't eat a thing," said Keating, letting out a groan. "Another dagger right now. Christ."

Hangovers frequently felled over-confident hunters, particularly city guys who put the pedal down on the first night with a full bottle of Maker's Mark. Altitude also took its toll. Life at 9,000 feet, with hunting routes taking them to 11,000 feet during the day, could strain sea-level lungs so badly that their owners felt more punk than Joey Ramone. But this guy was local, like the others in the camp.

It was a bit unusual to have so many locals book a camp, but they had said they wanted some time away from the home routines. Plus, two of them had drawn bull tags and wanted to fill them in the heavy timber in prime mid-season conditions. Keating said he hadn't drunk much, so that couldn't be the problem, and everyone else had survived the communal chow. A natural cause? It was possible these symptoms would have been identical if the man was home watching football from the comfort of his couch.

"Nice of you to stay with him," said Allison.

"I couldn't imagine leaving him alone," said Colin. He shrugged his shoulders. "It wouldn't have been right."

"Jesse and Walt?" she said, trying to get a fix on the agenda for the day, which required her other two guides. Her mind spun through the options of how to care for Keating.

"Out with the others," said Colin. "One more hunter is coming in tomorrow, the one you're guiding in from Sweetwater."

"Guess I momentarily forgot the plan," said Allison. "Who decided which guide would stay?"

"I told the others to hit the road," said Colin.

Colin stood and went to the kitchen, the corner of the tent where the propane stove, dishes and pantry had been set up. The tables and sink were shipshape, another point in Colin's favor. Colin was up two points—the first had been awarded for staying with the wounded. Make that three points for the way he walked, confident and squared-shouldered. Allison could easily study the way his tight torso melded into his hips for a long, long time.

Colin returned with two mugs of hot coffee. "Black, right?" he said. Four points might be a bit generous for this early in the morning, but what the heck.

"Perfect," said Allison, thinking of Colin's thick brown hair, combed straight back to leave his everyday walking-around expression open and sincere. He had a strong jaw and one faint, raisin-sized freckle by his left eye. An interesting blemish.

The coffee was a blessing. Allison's sleep had been spotty after the prowling-visitor incident, and grogginess ruled the moment. One essential piece of equipment that Allison required in all her camps was good coffee. There was no Boy Scout merit badge handed out for enduring bad coffee. Girl Scout neither.

"Could it have been caused by bad water?" said Allison. "What did you drink yesterday?"

Keating opened one eye and stared back at her.

"The spring," said Keating.

"What spring?"

"I should have thought of that," said Keating. The words came hard. "Walt and I hiked down the west ridge yesterday. We had seen an elk in a clearing. We only had an hour of daylight left but we needed two. I was low on water and we came down the ridge faster than we should have. Ran smack into a spring. It had a thin sheet of ice on top. I jabbed my boot through the ice and dipped my face into the water, which tasted like a dream. I was parched."

"What about Walt?"

Keating gave it some thought.

"I think he still had his canteen water. I don't think he took a single drop from the spring."

A nasty case of giardia? Gastric pain—check. Nausea—probably. Allison was no doctor but she'd seen her fair share of sickness from sucking down standing water. Giardia cretins thrived in cold mountain water, though the symptoms usually took days or a week or more to wreak havoc. She'd picked it up herself last spring. The boxing-match of convulsions in her guts would never be forgotten. The doctors wanted to bombard her system with anti-parasite drugs, but her friend and now housemate Trudy had nursed her through the roughest days with Goldenseal, an herb like a buttercup that produced a bitter tea. During the battle, Allison had lost eight painful pounds and frequently fantasized about a stomachectomy.

"Was the water running or sedentary?" said Allison.

"Moving a bit," said Keating. "Walt asked the same thing before I put my head in it. If you're thinking giardia, I know all about it. Been there. Just doesn't feel quite the same. I've been light-headed too."

It didn't matter. The wrong water could cripple humans and animals, moving molecules or not.

"Do you want to stay here and try to shake it off, or catch a ride to a doctor?" said Allison. "If it's an intestinal attack, you might need a heavy dose of medicine. Or perhaps an herb man— or woman."

"Huh?" said Keating.

"Take it from me, nature's got a cure," said Allison.

"I'm staying," said Keating. "I'll be fine."

Maybe not, thought Allison, but it's your call. She respected his toughness, but didn't think determination alone would get him back on the hunt.

Keating rolled over, signaling the end to that line of questioning.

There was a quintessential stew of greasy smoke, sweaty men and stale canvas that rendered hunting-tent air one part locker room and one part slaughterhouse. Nobody would label it 'mountain fresh.' That was reserved for aerosol cans. Allison signaled to Colin and he followed her out.

The sun was burning away the overnight frost. Sunny Boy stood in his own personal spotlight. The horse chose that moment to lean forward and produce a massive whiz. Hello to you, too, thought Allison.

Colin filled Allison in on the first two days of the hunt. Bottom line: lots of spoor, a few sightings, no kills. They would need to go higher. There wasn't enough snow, and the temperatures had been too mild. What if the elk were getting smarter? This was Colin's theory. He respected the elk, knew how they thought. Allison wondered what the elk knew about October and human beings in orange vests. She wondered what they whispered to each other and how they communicated about hiding places. It was remarkable that one of the largest elk herds in the Lower 48 could disappear like experienced chameleons.

Because it was Colorado and because it was October, the odds were good that the weather and the hunting trend would change. All they needed was a twenty-degree drop in temperature and knee-deep snow.

"Did you by any chance see or hear an airplane this morning?" said Allison.

"What a racket," said Colin. "Noisy sucker."

"Right over my tent, circled around and then was gone."

"Probably scared the elk into next month," said Colin. "Isn't it illegal?"

"Dunno," said Allison. "Unusual, no question. But I'm no expert on altitudes."

As soon as she said it, she laughed. And Colin, who had been waiting to see if it was okay, laughed too. It wasn't a hard laugh but a knowing one. Of course she knew about altitude—she had felt the earth's tractor beam of gravity as few people had ever experienced it. Only, she was among the few crash survivors at LaGuardia. Of course she knew about altitude.

"Was it higher?" Colin asked. He had a sly, slicing smile.

"Higher?" asked Allison.

"You know, higher than you were."

Colin's eyebrows lifted. The distance the eyebrows travelled probably couldn't be measured, but they had moved.

"Where did you go to school?"

Colin's glance indicated this might be some trick. "First time I ever heard that question."

"Was it public school?"

"Of course," said Colin. "West Grand Elementary. Kremmling's finest. Moved to Buford in the fifth grade. All Meeker schools from then on, boss."

"Must have been some sharp teachers and please don't call me boss. No college?"

"Why would I have gone to college?" said Colin. "They don't have degrees in fun, do they? I didn't think so. But you're avoiding the question. How high was it? Or how high were you?"

Allison flashed on the memory of the jet that had almost killed her, a memory never too far away. The memory had carved out its own palace in her brain, the lone spot where no detail would ever rust or fade. The newspaper accounts said her jet had been airborne for seven seconds. Surely, a commercial jet could climb higher in seven seconds than the treetop flyer she had seen.

"Doesn't matter," said Allison. "Does it?"

"Only curious," said Colin. "Since I never saw it."

"Okay. I had another strange incident."

"What's that?" said Colin.

"Somebody was poking around last night. I was camped not too far from here—"

"Wanted a night by yourself?"

"I thought it was a good idea," said Allison. "Until I heard footsteps or, more accurately, heard a stick snap out in the clearing. Come here."

She led Colin over to Sunny Boy, who nickered hello. Colin was an old friend. Allison had snapped the adjustable hatband of The Colorado Rockies hat around a buckle on the flank cinch.

"I found this," she said. "Have you seen it on any of your customers?"

"Don't think so," said Colin.

"Your guys were all inside last night?"

"Tucked in and tuckered out," said Colin. "And well-buzzed except for Keating, who couldn't stomach the thought of whiskey. Probably couldn't stand the thought of anything."

The alone thing. It wasn't hard to picture sitting naked in a cramped claw-foot tub with Colin. There would be scalding water up to their shoulders and cold beers within reach. On ice. If there was one thing she wanted to see, and get used to seeing, it was that section from Colin's ribcage to his hips. Allison realized she could get used to his mischievous grin, no matter the age gap. She wouldn't mind seeing how this cowboy was put together— a nature boy, muscles and sinews and flesh the result of living and working in the outdoors, not from free weights or 24 Hour Fitness. She didn't know Colin that well, but she couldn't picture him in the city, standing on a concrete corner, waiting for the light to change. The image wasn't fish-out-of-water; it was fish-in-a-tree.

"Let me know if someone is missing a hat," said Allison.

"You bet."

Allison listened for any hint that he was answering employee-to-boss. But she didn't pick up anything.

A dull, soft gunshot rolled across the valley. The sound was muffled, flat and pleasing. Colin smiled. "Oh, yeah," he said. "Maybe our luck is turning."

Perhaps, thought Allison. It's possible.

Tuesday Midday

Back at the meadow, Allison hitched Sunny Boy to a tree and set a course back across the clearing, one steady step at a time. She had placed a couple of sticks on a bush near the spot where she had found the cap, giving her a mark to line up on from the trail. Her former campsite was the third dot in the line. She had returned the site to its original condition but it wasn't hard to spot the distinctive stand of trees. She wanted to retrace the intruder's route, assuming he had started on the trail. Perhaps he—certainly a he—had left another clue. She didn't really have the time for this detour. It was a full day's ride back to her A-frame cabin near Sweetwater Lake, just a stone's throw outside the wilderness boundary. The trail back from Oyster Lake was a diagonal southeast shot straight across the Flat Tops to the meadow she called home. Given the light now, the last leg of the return would be in the dark. The ride across the Flat Tops would be manageable but the trail down from the high plateau through the thick woods could have its tricky bits. Oh well. She had her headlamp, which would provide the occasional burst of illumination for reassurance, and Sunny Boy knew the way.

She stepped, stopped and scanned right and left. Step, stop, scan. Hardpack dirt hid its secrets. She kneeled to touch a possible impression, but wasn't convinced it was anything, certainly not from a boot or a shoe. Step, stop, scan. If she headed back and stashed the stray baseball cap in a mental drawer marked "miscellaneous crap," the drawer would have rattled nonstop of its own volition. She knew how her mind worked. That drawer had plenty of other business to digest and resolve. It didn't need another stray orphan from the universe of the unexplained. There were very few things that happened in the Flat Tops that could be stored in miscellaneous crap. Cities and their crush of humanity created pinball machines where people and their contraptions bounced off each other in zany configurations, generating plenty of miscellaneous crap. The result was everything from fender benders to burst water pipes. Up here, there were fewer pinballs. Even better, there were fewer people thinking that they were playing a game. Up here, it was you and nature. All the miscellaneous crap should have a reason to go with it.

Halfway on her step-stop-scan walk to the marker, she spotted a print. It was from a worn-out sneaker or some sort of crude foot gear. She crouched. No nifty tread pattern but a good impression nevertheless—more than a second-rate Renoir. The sun was well up, not good for tracking, but she could have spotted this print from atop a ladder. Mr. Mystery Man might have stood in this spot for a full minute because the print reflected equal weight from heel to toe. This print was a left shoe, but a stride length's away the right print was shallower, a faint echo of its brother. The stride was short. He had been walking. Or stalking.

Allison stood up. What else was there to do? She had proven to herself that a hovering UFO had not lost the cap. Now what? She followed the prints to her marker bush and set the sticks back on the ground where they belonged. She should get going. A cool breeze from the north suggested the balmy autumn might be in for a shock. The first Arctic Express was always the harshest. Nobody remembered from one winter to the next how a true freeze could crush all sensation to a fine powder.

Back on the trail, she unhitched Sunny Boy from the tree.

"I know," she said. "I probably looked like I didn't know what I was doing. I know, you probably think it was a waste of time. It's a long story."

She sucked in a sudden sharp breath. On the trail directly below Sunny Boy's nose was a footprint, a perfect match from the meadow. Only fresher. And there wasn't one lone print this time— there was a jumble.

Then she spotted the cinch where she had fastened the cap. The strings dangled free. No cap.

Tuesday Midday

Devo crouched in the woods. He was a long stone's throw from the trail and he had ample cover behind a tree. His bronze skin and dark beard were camouflaged by the drab palette of the undergrowth to the extent that he was just another brown smudge. He peered around the tree when the woman wasn't looking his way.

What could her name be? She seemed tough. She wore the cautionary orange vest, setting a good example even if she was staying on the trail where no hunter should be shooting. But you never could be too careful out here, especially with city hunters.

The woman was looking around. She leaned away from her saddle, the leather creaking, and did a careful scan of the terrain. But Devo was invisible. He had surreptitiously retrieved his cap from the horse at the moment she had stopped in the middle of the meadow, where she may have spotted his footprints. It hadn't been hard to slip away in the opposite direction.

She wouldn't be lingering anywhere for long. The morning had turned from warm to frigid, as if the sun was capable of shooting off shards of ice. This was no gentle coo in the ear, whispering that winter was around the corner. This was the whole wet Willie, straight to the hammer bone. It was screaming, "I'm here, I'm now, I'm real." It was only mid-morning but this Extra Chunky Extra Tough variety of cold sliced through skin and wrapped itself around your bones, going for the kill. Based on what he had learned to tell from the changes in the air and humidity, tonight would be hellacious.

The woman slid off her horse and kneeled to study his prints. She followed a few steps but then came to a stop. There was no clear direction to follow. Devo could have stepped out of the woods and said hello. He could have made contact. Last night, by the fire, he could have given her a real jolt by walking out of the darkness and standing there, unannounced. But he didn't want to frighten her. He had only been curious to get close, have a look. The fire was inviting. Hell, she was inviting. She was open to possibilities. Snapping the stick in the meadow had been an accident. Leaving the baseball cap as a calling card was not. He had not meant to scare her, only to watch and observe. He liked tracking hunters, observing people from the city and how they traveled in the woods.

Last night, he had come too close to breaking one of his rules, the one about minimizing human contact. Save for twice, he had been fairly successful: first when a hiker had stumbled across him last summer as he took an afternoon nap on the warm rock by Rim Lake and next when a hunter had surprised him high on a ridge near the Chinese Wall. In both cases, the encounters had been brief. Surely no one wanted to get too close, not the way he looked. Or smelled.

The contacts didn't hurt anything either. They were good fodder for his website. He was honest on the web and with his YouTube broadcasts. It was warts and all, including bloopers.

His experiment was devolution. A century earlier, any man or woman would have been able to survive in the woods. But today few could do it without a truckload of gear, the latest in microfiber clothing and a GPS linked to an orbiting satellite. He had been there. But now society had reached a breaking point. Soon, there might be no going back. Now, it was time to devolve. It was time for society to regress to its earlier ways when all men and women knew hundreds of skills for survival. Look at Teddy Roosevelt. Look at Lewis and Clark. Look at Shackleton. It was time to go back, time to reclaim the grit, time to devolve before it was too late.

And maybe the name Devo would go down in the books as a forefather who would call out the soft-bellied flock from their homes and their un-calloused lives and bring them back to life, back to reality.

The woman climbed onto her horse and peered around into the woods. This time Devo didn't duck. He had been caught off guard by her quick turn. He couldn't move. For a moment, he thought their eyes had locked and he had been spotted.

But then she turned away, gave her horse a cluck and headed off down the trail.

Tuesday Afternoon

Josh Keating sat up and took a deep breath.

"I think it's going away," he said, buckling over and wrapping his arms around his stomach. "I'll be fine."

"Don't push yourself," said Colin.

"The worst that happens is I keel over and die. Just quarter me up and pack me out, or dig me a hole and shove me in. It wouldn't be the worst thing to be buried in the Flat Tops."

Keating stood slowly and winced, took a tentative step to show he was doing better. Took a breath, smiled faintly too. "You still got six or seven hours of daylight left," he said. "Why not go do some scouting?"

"I suppose," said Colin. "If you're sure."

Already Colin was going for his gear—hunting vest, jacket and old Browning High Wall. The rifle was a beauty. The single-shot showed the guide's utter confidence. Colin had bathed it in PrOlix since just after breakfast, shining it within an inch of its life.

"What are you going to do?" said Colin.

"Flop around, keep the tent warm," said Keating. "And sleep."

Keating puttered in the kitchen, clanged a pot or two in the sink and dug in the pantry for crackers and peanut butter.

"No coffee for you, I would imagine," said Colin.

"No truer words," said Keating. "I think the stomach could use a few days of baby food."

"I don't think we packed any."

"A medium-rare elk tenderloin might do."

"I'll see what I can rustle up," said Colin.

"You need the elk first."

"Probably a good place to start," said Colin. "Good chance this Arctic blast will remind the elk that it's winter and time to come on down in search of warmer digs."

Colin was ready to go.

"Good luck," said Keating. "If I'm not here later, it means I rebounded all the way and headed out."

"Take it easy," said Colin. "Don't push it."

"Yeah, thanks," said Keating.

Keating waited five minutes to make sure Colin had completely departed. He scraped together gear—small backpack, rope, his knife, rifle, water and two energy bars. He nibbled on bites of a peanut butter and crackers snack, which tasted good. He was seriously hungry, but discarded any idea of staying to cook something. He had been convincingly sick. There would be others, no doubt, and the bad-water plague would make the news. It would work. It had to work.

But there was no point in wasting his cow tag or the day.

Keating stepped out of the tent. Cold air surged into his lungs. The only exposed skin was on his face, and he wished he had a bank-robber mask with the nose and mouth cut out for more protection. The temperature wasn't in frostbite territory, but the air came with a polar prick.

He strapped his Weatherby Magnum over his shoulder and loaded a backpack with water and tools, should he need to gut a kill. A dense ridge to the southwest was the fastest way to higher ground. He had seen the rounded print of a cow elk toe, at least eight inches long, up on the ridge the day before. The ridge dropped off to the north and was heavily wooded down the slope. It was perfect elk cover. He wanted to hang out in that spot and test his luck. He just wished he had a way to skip the next hour of hard hiking.

As he expected, his legs began to balk at the activity. The valley dropped away. The dull cold sky descended. A dense aspen grove gave way to beefy spruce. He kept a sharp eye on the farthest point he could see, worked to keep his profile low. He settled into a comfortable pace, and the trail carried him up.

He stopped, realizing that for the past ten minutes he had felt he was being followed. At first it was only a sensation—one that he hadn't fully absorbed. Then came the soft crunch of a footfall behind him. It carried the eerie echo of a footfall from one minute earlier. The first sound hadn't registered completely but the second brought the first back to vivid life. He hadn't seen a critter or anything else move for an hour. The birds were staying low, conserving energy. He stopped—suddenly—and heard nothing.

Funny?

Not so funny?

The sounds were no coincidence. Weird. He turned and peered into the woods, a thorough study with his shifting focus-point creating ample room for his peripheral vision to overlap. He gave it a full minute, just listening.

Nothing.

A brush of wind caught the treetops.

He regained his pace. It was another quarter-mile to the place where he had seen the elk print. He added some voltage to his radar, gazing into the woods on either side. He dug for some jerky in his pocket and gnawed off a wad to suck on. The salt and pepper in all that dried fat and protein cut through the paste in his mouth. He was feeling better.

He slowed as he neared the top of the wooded ridge. A black squirrel jabbered. A crow swooped down from the treetops and veered off into the woods where light went to die. He was stepping straight into a breeze. It was possible that there were no elk within a mile. But he had a hunch—and then the hunch materialized, as if he held clairvoyant powers. The elk stepped out of the woods a hundred yards up. It carried a decent rack of antlers—no prize, but decent. Ten seconds behind the bull elk was a cow and then another, ambling along. And then a third. Keating liked the third one best, plump and solid. She was easily six inches taller than the first cow. The light on the trail was marginal but it would do. Adrenaline seeped into his every capillary. The cow stopped, lifted her head and stood still. She was facing away from him. The other two cows kept walking. Keating pulled his Weatherby around, keeping the motion to a painfully deliberate creep. He sidestepped behind a thick fir, eased the rifle up to his shoulder and peered through the scope.

The crosshairs were square on her butt. She turned and flashed her fat belly and shoulder. She resumed her pace—her rear-guard duties complete—and stopped again. And turned. This time, full profile. A gift. Keating had the crosshairs frozen on her.

He was steadying the shot when something flashed in his left eye, but he forced himself to keep the concentration on the brown, tough fur through the scope. He adjusted a hair up. The sights were set to account for bullet drop and his shot was uphill. He squeezed the trigger. The cow buckled as if a zap of clear lightning had hit her. She leapt for the woods. The spared elk scattered. Keating stayed put. The cow was already dead but didn't know it. The shot had been perfect. Giving chase would spook her further into the woods. The blood trail that she would leave behind would be easy to follow.

Keating waited two minutes, most of the time spent staring at a spot off to his left. He had seen something—a flash—which he knew should not have been there.

The cow had fallen on a steep slope. Her belly faced downhill. Keating put a hand to her neck. No pulse. Her wound was underneath. He strapped on a battery-powered headlamp and unpacked his hacksaw and knife, a well-sharpened six-inch blade. He kept replaying the odd flash as the cow had dropped. What the fuck could it have been? Keating found himself looking around more than normal, shooting the beam from his headlamp off into the woods, trying to catch something out of place. Somebody.

He had his bearings and a good sense of the terrain, but it would take an hour until he had the carcass cut in quarters and the pieces strung up. He weighed a decision to start a fire—for light, in case his headlamp batteries failed, but also for heat. He checked his wristwatch. It was always darker in the woods. His toes flashed a warning. It was cold.

But he decided on no fire. It would take too long to build, and would be too distracting to tend.

Near the end, as he worked alone in the cold black woods, he reached under the elk's backbone between the ribs and pelvis and cut away a hunk of tenderloin. His hand came out warm and bloody. The boys would be glad to see him.

Tuesday Evening

Trudy Heath watched the afternoon turn from bright blue to dull gray. Wind slashed across the field in front of her house, whipped the far trees into a frenzy. The cold front had pulled a dark curtain over the Flat Tops. The windows by the front door rattled and the branches rustled with so much energy it sounded like she was standing at the bottom of a thundering waterfall.

She hoped Allison was warm and secure. The front carried a bite. The temperature inside the greenhouse dropped and the sky overhead turned gray as if somebody had a dimmer on the afternoon light. Trudy had been working on trays of basil and Italian parsley, but when the day snapped in two she retreated to the more secure confines of the main house. An overwhelming urge to clean and straighten came over her, not that either task was necessary.

Trudy's house was a year old. She had moved out of the over-sized, over-inflated monstrosity that her ex-husband George had built a mile down the valley. She had shed George's surname and reverted to her family name, Heath. The sale of the property was part of the divorce and the divorce had left George destitute. He now had the backing of the state, which would be monitoring his needs, if not his wants, for decades to come. Last she heard—and Trudy didn't care—George was headed to the place in the state best known for its experience with keeping killers locked up. That was Cañon City—a town she would never visit. The whole county, for that matter.

But she'd never leave the state. She would never leave this valley. It was, quite simply, too beautiful. The proceeds from the sale of George's property were beautiful too, and went into the construction of her house—a two-bedroom, one-greenhouse structure with a leaf-green metal roof and log cabin shape. She had sketched the plans on a napkin in under a minute, straight from her dreams. She had lived in this house inside her head long before it was even a remote possibility. The greenhouse was almost as large as the main house. The headwaters of the greenhouse, in fact, were in the oversized kitchen, and the greenery flowed from there—herbs and plants and flowers.

Allison had given her the land. Their houses were the sole structures in this patch of the valley. Standing in by the front windows, she could make out the porch light of Allison's A-frame. It was a glimmering beacon the size of a pinhole in the dark, cold universe. Allison never kept, knew or broadcast her precise itinerary but she was supposed to have been back for dinner, and Trudy had the feeling Allison was out there alone. She stared into the thick night, hoping to see the A-frame's lights blaze on, to see Sunny Boy stride out of the darkness.

Trudy stoked the fire in the front room, put the cast-iron kettle on top of the wood-burning stove for tea, sat on the couch with a copy of *Herb Life Today* and listened to the wind attack the valley. The cats moved in but they sensed she wasn't settled down. She had five cats—Smoke, Ginger, Thyme, Pepper and Razor.

They knew her routines. Trudy was certain that they knew the barometric pressure had dropped.

Five cats, down from fourteen. Any number over a dozen cats was not exactly a man magnet. In fact, it tended to send up an alarm: "Crazy old quirky lady in training. Run for your life."

Even five might have been pushing it. That seemed to be the message from Jerry Paige, the trim, earnest grocer. She thought his look was a good complement for hers—unadorned, down-to-earth. The confining days with George now past, she had dropped back to her high school frame, trim and sleek. She still kept her hair long, braids and ponytails hanging to the middle of her back. Her face was long and she had clear brown eyes, straight teeth and a small nose. She wasn't every guy's girl, but those who looked past normal surface glitz—she had none—sensed she was very much alive.

Jerry's store was her first steady customer for her line of pesto. "The Growing Season" did a steady business in downtown Glenwood Springs.

Jerry lived by himself. He was two years younger than Trudy, had an easy-going smile, and wasn't bothered by her minor splash in the waters of notoriety, given that she'd shot her ex-husband in the leg and that she had been married to a murderer who also, by the way, broke every hunting regulation known to the great state of Colorado.

It had all come out in the papers, complete with the story about her struggle with seizures, her surgery and recovery. She wasn't going to be trapped into a marriage all over again. Now she was free and safe to drive a vehicle and move around, even invite young, handsome retailers like Jerry Paige up to her remote house for an evening of lentil-walnut burgers, carrot-yogurt salad and organic red wine. Her greenhouse and dense trays of bursting basil enthralled him. He nearly licked the plate at dinner and then relaxed with her on the couch as they worked on bottle number two, listening to John Prine and laughing along to "Illegal Smile." But there were the cats.

He left that night with a kiss and warm hug, but later as Trudy had reflected on the night, she knew he had balked when she said the number "fourteen" out loud, as if it were no big deal. Well, it was. No matter how good the possibility of sex and the cooking at the center of it all, no man would ever say he was comfortable around so much feline fur. Five was reasonable, wasn't it? The other nine had been given to good homes, each separation more painful than the last. Five might still be an off-putting number but it wasn't cat-lady country.

Trudy went to the window and studied the black night. Allison's porch light stood as a lone sentry. If it weren't for the light, Trudy might have wondered if she lived at the bottom of a coal mine.

She retreated to the couch in the small front room, purposefully left the lights on, and stretched out. She pulled a couple of wool blankets up to her neck. A cat pawed around her feet for a warm bed. Usually, but not always, the cat was Thyme. As the cat nudged her toes, Trudy's eyes closed of their own selfish volition.

Tuesday Night

The taste of tenderloin indicated their luck was changing. The cold snap was brutal but had produced the results which were now being chewed.

It was nearing midnight. The bottle of Wild Turkey didn't stand a chance. Keating sat up in a collapsible camp chair near the stove. The whiskey coursed its way into the aches of his chest, overflowed the banks of his bloodstream and unhitched his head from its worries. He still had to pack out the meat—no problem— and drive home at the end of the day tomorrow.

"I'll go with you in the morning and help bring your kill down," said easygoing Max Hiatt, who always applied the brakes and stayed a drink or two behind everybody else. Max was round and short. His head appeared to sprout directly from his shoulders.

"I'll make the trips," said Keating. "You go hunting."

"I don't mind helping you," said Hiatt. "At least I'll feel useful."

"You came here to hunt, not to play pack mule," said Keating. He was worn out from gutting the elk and from stumbling back to camp in the dark. "I'll take a horse, make it easy."

"How far away did you say?"

"Two hours on foot."

"Southwest?"

"The steepest direction," said Keating. "Way up high. Strangest thing, though. Right as I was lining up the shot, I saw a blur, something moving out of the corner of my eye."

"Set of antlers?" asked Hiatt.

"Nothing distinct," said Keating. "Low to the ground. It was faint, but there. I had the shot lined up and by the time I looked over I didn't see anything. And I had to keep an eye on the cow and see whether I needed to give it a chase."

"That's weird," said Hiatt.

"Like a ghost," said Keating. "And I don't believe in 'em."

"To ghosts," said Hiatt, holding up his cup for a toast. "Are you going to switch to single malt when you sell those property rights?"

This topic was inevitable. Keating knew it would bob to the surface sooner or later. He was prepared to mislead. He could disappoint them later. He didn't want the fight up here, in close quarters.

"Single malts I can't say I understand," said Keating. "Cheap whiskey gets you to the same place."

"After you cash in, maybe you could pop for some indoor plumbing up here," said Hiatt.

"Aren't you selling some property too?" asked Keating.

"If I'm sitting on anything worthwhile," said Hiatt. "When are you closing your deal?"

Keating wondered who else might be within earshot.

Austin Rayburn was sleeping. Rayburn's presence in the hunting group was odd—any of his brothers would have fit in better. Austin was the least outdoorsy of the bunch.

The guides were nearby, poking around in the kitchen. Conrad Gray, the group's senior citizen and a tough-ass hunter, was two cots over, sipping whiskey and reading a book.

"I want to see the final offer," said Keating.

It wasn't much of a lie. He had already made up his mind.

"You've seen some numbers," said Hiatt.

The Roan Plateau, west of the Flat Tops, had found itself at the end of a rainbow. The natural gas reserves were a giant pot of gold and the riches were being rushed like California in the early 1850s. Estimates of its value ranged into the hundreds of billions of dollars. Depending on your location in the valley, and whether or not you owned both the surface rights and the mineral rights, even a medium-sized ranch had the sudden potential to make its owner feel like he'd won a lottery.

"Just numbers," said Keating. "They aren't real."

"Your wife's place?"

"Our place," said Keating, making sure he caught Hiatt's eye.

"Sorry."

"Her parents had no clue they were living on a gold mine," said Keating.

Loretta's parents, hardworking people with quiet ways, had missed a hairpin turn on Wolf Creek Pass during a snowstorm on their way to Durango. It was December. Their wreck was found in April. The ranch they left behind was located where the Roan Plateau's near-vertical north face eased off into a gentle grade on the way to the valley floor. There were lots of ways to pee on a stick, but doctors in this case didn't dispute the diagnosis. The land was pregnant with riches. Somebody needed to shove a straw down and start sucking out the special syrup. While on some properties the mineral rights were available as a separate deal, Loretta's parents owned everything that could be extracted straight down to the center of the earth.

"You're selling the rights." Gray said this without looking up. "All you're gonna do is sit there and cash checks, and not harm a thing."

"It's like a gift," said Hiatt.

"It's about to give even more," said Gray, putting down his book.

"Most likely, I suppose," said Keating. "The feds still have to open up that section over there for the mineral rights."

"They're going to do it," said Hiatt. "They're making a show of making a decision, but they know it makes no sense to borrow money from China to buy gas from the Middle East when we're sitting on our own supplies right here."

"When's the decision?" said Gray.

"I don't know for sure," said Keating.

"I hope Bostwick is there to see you cash in," said Hiatt. "You might want to invite him over for a cocktail and make a toast to the American way. Fucker."

"You got him on the run now," said Gray. "That was a sweet move."

"Who could have known about that particular legal maneuver? What was it again?" said Hiatt. "Adverse what?"

Gray abandoned his book, moved over to Hiatt's cot and poured himself a splash of brown liquor.

"Possession," said Keating. He wanted another drink, knew he was done. "Adverse possession."

Hiatt reached for the bottle, held it up and offered a pour. Keating ran a finger across his neck. He was done with this topic, was done with the greed that permeated Meeker. Hiatt poured enough to moisten the bottom of his glass.

"Bunch of geniuses came up with the phrase 'adverse possession,'" said Gray.

"You're doing the right thing," said Hiatt. "You're not having doubts, are you?"

"Please," said Keating, mocking them.

"You can't let that twerp tell us what to do," said Gray.

"He's getting the message," said Keating.

"Think so?"

"We've got his attention."

"How do you know?"

"Because he came over and told me."

"To your house?" asked Hiatt.

"Two days after the suit was filed," said Keating. "He was one angry man, but he couldn't let it show. He was shaking though, underneath."

"As if he had a right to get upset about anything to do with the land," said Gray. "As if he knows Colorado or knows how things work. Mister big shot from Pittsburgh."

"Philadelphia," said Keating.

"Whatever," said Gray. "It's not like he's been working the land forever."

Bostwick and his wife had moved to Buford to help his parents run the ranch. Their physical abilities had declined below the heavy labor required. Over the years, they had retreated to light household chores. When they moved out, the younger Bostwick hauled along his notions about how to run the world—and didn't mind shoving it down the throats of their new town.

"What did Bostwick say?" said Hiatt.

"He told me straight to my face that the suit was one of the meanest tricks he'd ever encountered."

"How come you didn't tell us he stopped by?" asked Gray.

"Some days I'm tired of talking about him," said Keating. "Plumb tired of him."

The idea for the suit against Ethan Bostwick had come from Stewart Exby, a lawyer. Almost a year ago to the day, Exby had knocked on Keating's door and introduced himself on behalf of a group of unnamed downtown businessmen. The lawyer stood five-five, wore a bolo tie with a rifle clasp and bullet aglets. Real bullets. Patches of gray whiskers covered his cheek and neck. Keating figured he was pushing eighty.

Like most of the town, Exby said he was sick of Bostwick and his one-man reign of "enviro policy terror." Exby had done some title work in the area where Keating had lived a few decades back. He remembered a path that cut across Bostwick's property to the White River. Keating knew the path—he used it regularly. The path sliced off a forty-one-acre chunk of Bostwick's turf. Bostwick had his own path down to the river, farther east. The forty-one acres were unused. They weren't farmed. There were no improvements. They just sat there. They could become Keating's property. In court, the land could transfer, slicker than fresh pork belly, to Keating. Why? Because Bostwick's acreage adjoined Keating's and Keating was the one who used the path, which in the eyes of this particular statute became the true border of his property. The trick to this bizarre, antiquated piece of law was simple: Keating had to assert that he had always intended to claim it.

That was all—tell a lie.

Exby's visit took place in November, just before Thanksgiving. The lawsuit was filed on Pearl Harbor Day; the newspaper coverage noted the irony of the "sneak attack" lawsuit. After motions and positioning, the depositions were filed on July 5, the morning after fireworks at the Meeker Fairgrounds. On Labor Day weekend, Bostwick had stopped over for the talk.

They shared a couple of beers. Bostwick was polite. He discussed big picture goals, talked about what could become of the valley, about water shortages and uncertainty over drilling methods. By the third beer, Keating knew the lawsuit wasn't in him. He didn't have the stomach for it. There was something fundamentally un-American about it. He had felt it all along. The lawsuit wasn't right and Keating realized he wanted to back away from the feeding frenzy over the drilling rights until things settled down. He loved Meeker and he loved the whole White River Valley just the way it was. In the weeks between Ethan Bostwick's visit and the hunt, he had sat on a powder keg. The trial date was set for December, still two months away, but he had told only one person of his decision. Even then, he had only hinted at his thinking, and he had done so with guaranteed confidentiality.

Keating reached for the bottle of whiskey, poured himself a couple of chugs.

"I mostly listened," said Keating. "That's all. I gave him a look and listened like a good neighbor, you know?"

"That lawsuit is more like a stake in the heart," said Gray. "Imagine it if were reversed."

"You can't turn down gifts from Mother Nature," said Gray. "Or a gift the legal system dropped on your doorstep. You're a two-time lottery winner, one from Mother Earth and the other from Daddy Law. Count your fucking blessings."

"Would you have done the same thing?" asked Keating.

"Bet your prize bison," said Gray. "Slam dunk no brainer."

"You gotta mess with him," said Hiatt. "Gotta get inside his head and muck around in there."

Gray held up his cup of Wild Turkey. "To mucking around," he said.

The three touched plastic cups, and Hiatt said "clink" to make it official. They drank. Keating told himself that was enough. The tent wobbled and the floor tilted.

"You gotta squeeze the fucker," said Gray. "Heel on throat. And keep stomping."

Hiatt and Gray bundled up and headed outside.

The whiskey fog in his brain was thick. Keating picked up a glass of the brown liquor and gave it a sip. There was nobody to toast, but Keating tipped the glass to the air. He would have some explaining to do down the road, but tonight he had his elk and the plan was in motion.

As he stood, he told himself it was a good thing he didn't have to drive anywhere in order to get outside for the pre-sleep whiz. He was one blasted motherfucker. The tent pitched one way and then the other, a canvas ship tossed by the sea.

Outside, the cold air smacked him like a brick wall. Hiatt and Gray stumbled from the darkness.

"Everything come out all right?" said Keating.

"We saw a couple polar bears on an ice floe out on the lake," said Hiatt.

"My pee froze on the way to the ground," said Gray.

Keating ambled farther out. He sucked in a few long breaths, as if oxygen might clear his brain and bring him back to the land of the sober.

The lake was a couple hundred yards away. Keating urged himself to go all the way. Some guys liked a bush or a tree. Keating liked taking a leak under a billion stars and the great wide open. This was a ritual. Up to the lake, try not to stumble, and hike back. Maybe it would clear his head. He might not look up at the stars tonight, in fear they might spin more than they should. Anyway, it was no time for real thinking.

He straightened his back and sucked in the frozen air. He

wasn't sure if he was close to the lake yet, wasn't sure how much time had passed, then sensed the ground rising and knew he was coming up on the lip of the lake. He let out a deep breath, reached for his zipper and tilted his head back.

A flashlight beam popped on and caught him square in the chest. The source of the beam was a few yards up.

Well, must be company. Good—he would have help stumbling back to the tent, a companion to make sure he didn't get lost.

Somewhere off in the corner of his muddled mind, he tried to do the math concerning who was where, and who this person could be. He assumed everyone was accounted for back in the tent, but he must have overlooked one of them.

One of the guides, most likely.

He hadn't paid much attention to those guys.

Good Lord, he was drunk.

"Yo," he said.

The flashlight nailed his eyes.

He spun at the beam's fierceness, nearly painful in his condition, and found himself staring at a series of white pipes laid out on the ground. All the pipes were the same length. Two sets were connected, two sets unconnected. PVC pipe. Was someone getting ready for some weird irrigation project? The pipes sat neatly on the rocks. They looked like outsized tinker toys. It was nothing his marinated brain recognized or comprehended.

"Okay, okay," said Keating. He turned back around. The light stung. "Who is it? Can't sleep?"

Keating held his hand up to block the beam. He could make out a vague shape of a man, but he didn't recognize him.

"Lower the light before I go blind," he said. "What the hell are these pipe things over here?"

The man holding the flashlight looked like the Michelin Man's brother, all puffy outerwear. Facial details were impossible to make out behind the light.

It was comforting to know he wouldn't have to walk back to camp alone, but Keating was starting to get pissed, especially at the silence.

The light came off his face and pointed to the sky for a moment, and Keating followed it out of instinct. Purple splotches clouded his vision and he was about to get angry at this mute jerk, who had stepped down to within reach.

There was a moment of trying to make sense out of it all. Keating wanted to spin the light on the guy's face and end this merry prank. The blow came from right field and Keating stumbled hard, his boots clipping a rock as he lurched sideways. The earth rose up and smacked him brutally on the face, and the jolt of wrenching pain on his skull was followed by a trip to a world where the light and dark all tumbled together with something wet and woozy, and he could smell his own blood and feel the whiskey and bile rising in one swirling frenzy of confusion as he plummeted headfirst into the void.

2

Wednesday Early Morning

"You didn't wait up?"

Trudy stood at the door in a sleepy, startled daze. She pulled Allison inside the house. Allison dived into Trudy's warm embrace, and wondered how Trudy felt hugging an ice cube.

"Where's Sunny Boy?" said Trudy.

"I already put him up," said Allison. "He was the living definition of a hungry horse."

"And then you walked over here?"

"I saw your light," said Allison. "It was either a short walk here to warmth or three hours of waiting for my wood stove to make a dent in the cold air."

The words came hard. Allison had not used her mouth much in the eight or nine hours since sundown. Maybe she had chatted to Sunny Boy or maybe the words of encouragement had all been inside her head. She couldn't say for sure. Either way, her mouth didn't move freely.

"What a night," said Trudy. "I can't believe you were out in that."

"Yesterday morning it was like summer," said Allison. "By noon it was like January."

"January in Nome," said Trudy. "How about some tea?"

Allison headed for an oversized chair near the wood stove.

"A gallon, please," she said. "And beer."

The thought of a cold beer had served as an upbeat focus point during the ride as Sunny Boy carried her down through the frigid woods. She yearned for the sensation of the soft carbonation on her tongue. It was a good thing she and Sunny Boy had practiced the after-dark horse ride. Five summers ago a group of oil executives from St. Louis had invited Allison and two other guides to ride up after dark to Johnny Meyer's camp for the best shrimp gumbo ever concocted in the state of Colorado. The group would get seriously liquored up and then Allison and the guides would ride back in the early morning. Since the horses and mules stayed sober, the risks were minimal. The animals knew every exposed root, every path, every turn.

Trudy returned with a cold brown bottle, a local brew.

"Vapor Cave India Pale, from Glenwood Canyon Brewing," said Trudy. "Tea on the way."

"Bit of an odd time for a product plug," said Allison.

"Sorry," said Trudy.

Everything Trudy did was related to Trudy's Triple Crown philosophy. Green. Organic. Local.

The beer was an elixir.

"Hungry?" said Trudy.

"Anything you've got," said Allison. What she wanted was a juicy cheeseburger as thick as a brick. Trudy would probably offer raw carrot sticks and garlic-red pepper hummus. Allison followed Trudy to the always-immaculate kitchen with its pungent, earthy aromas. Trudy's kitchen generated warmth and produced bounty.

She puttered around slicing bread and tomatoes, starting the toaster and opening a jar of pesto.

"What happened?" said Trudy.

"I got behind," said Allison. "When I arrived in camp Colin was there—"

"Your favorite."

"He wasn't alone," said Allison.

"Too bad for him—and for you."

"Well, one of the hunters was laid out sick as a dog. His guts were ripped up and Colin was tending to him."

"Sounds awful," said Trudy, pure anguish across her face. "But Colin—what a decent guy."

"He's all heart," said Allison. "I'm telling you."

Trudy didn't dislike Colin, but she thought he was just another mountain boy trying to get by on good looks while cultivating a tough-hombre image.

"Go on," said Trudy, "You were sorry you weren't alone—"

"I was worried about the sick guy. I didn't think he would be able to sit up straight on a horse if it came to escorting him down to a doctor."

"Did he eat something tainted? All that meat and all that whiskey, plus the altitude and living in close quarters is definitely not the ideal recipe for dynamic health and well-being."

"He said it was something he drank—he sipped some water from a mountain spring."

"So Flat Tops water makes you sick, huh?" said Trudy. "Hard to believe."

She turned from the counter and offered up a plate with a toasted sandwich. "Pesto, tomato and mozzarella. You'll never get sick if you eat this stuff. The allicin in the garlic is one of the most powerful antibiotics known. It's all in the enzyme. Antifungal too."

Allison took a bite of the tangy, gooey gift from the gods, not certain she needed anything antifungal.

"Jesus, that's good."

"You're my favorite customer," said Trudy. "But Jesus had nothing to do with it. Thank the ancient Greeks. This is one of the oldest sauces known to womankind."

"Somebody back then was a genius," Allison said with a full mouth.

"You need a bed."

"Might not hurt," said Allison. "An hour or two."

Allison glanced at the clock on Trudy's counter. 3:13 A.M.

"Or eight," said Trudy.

There was no time to tell the baseball cap yarn or about that clear, vivid, chilling sensation when the cap had been swiped from Sunny Boy, when she knew she was being watched. The less she thought about it, the less she would be concerned with the mysterious cap or the fact that she ought to feel afraid.

"I'm supposed to ride back up tomorrow—I mean later today—to bring in a customer who arrived a couple days behind his group."

"Back up so soon?"

"Pesto and a snooze will do me good."

"Be ready for the dreams," said Trudy. "Garlic does the trick every time."

"No time to dream," said Allison. "If I sleep as well as I think I will, a head of raw garlic wouldn't make a dent."

In the last hours of Sunny Boy's midnight ride, she hadn't been able to form a coherent, sustained thought, and that meant this whole conversation with Trudy was produced by a sham combination of adrenaline and manners. And now it was over; even the fumes from the tank were spent. She had resisted worrying whether Sunny Boy might step into a hole or whether she'd get knocked off by a branch. Her fear had gone straight for the jugular and it had taken every bit of effort to scold it back into a corner. Yes, she was cold but no fingers were snapping off. Yes, it was dark but Sunny Boy knew the way. Yes, it was only a matter of staying alert and conscious—of giving panic the cold shoulder. Mostly, Allison questioned herself for poor planning—for leaving camp late, for lingering on her search in the meadow, for not getting a move on. She had known all along she had to be back to meet another hunter—just a few hours away from now—and bring him back to the camp.

Trudy led her to the spare bedroom, a place where she had slept many times before, either too tired to walk home after hours of dinner and conversation or because she enjoyed sleeping under the same roof as somebody else—separate but together. Allison shed her clothes, pulled back the covers and wriggled under the puffy down comforter. Three hours, she told herself. You have three precious hours of sleep.

Wednesday Morning

"That wasn't three hours," said Allison.

"No," said Trudy, "it was three hours and twenty minutes. I called the barn. They're getting your horse ready."

"Not Sunny Boy," said Allison. "He needs rest."

"They figured as much. It's Lightning."

It was a good thing horses didn't grasp sarcasm. Lightning was a singularly plodding but sure-footed beast who knew Allison well. He was unflappable and loyal like a big old dog. He might take all day, but he'd get there. Maybe the mules had passed along a few tips.

"Good," said Allison.

"I've got a Thermos full of hot green tea for you, with flax seed bread, organic peanut butter and homemade plum jam. The plums were frozen last winter but they're fine. Your client from Denver is there. I guess he pulled in within the last hour. I told them to kill as much time as possible getting him fitted on the saddle and getting the mule loaded up. Apparently he brought more supplies than General Sherman."

The information came at Allison in a blur, not that she didn't appreciate every consideration. The next few motions all came hard—rolling over, standing up, splashing water on her face and getting dressed. Yesterday's gear would have to do. There was time to stop at her place but she didn't have the energy. She tugged on thermal long underwear, the lined flannel shirt, black fleece, lined blue jean jacket and her favorite inert object on the planet, Cruel Girl blue jeans. The jeans brought the whole package together with a boost of confidence. They hugged her legs like a lost friend. She tugged on her lace-up leather Roper boots with a helpful pair of grunts.

From their shared clearing in the woods in the southeast corner of the Flat Tops, just outside the wilderness area boundaries, it was a ten-minute drive up the valley to the barn at Sweetwater. Trudy reviewed precautions about the cold, and mentioned something about a dinner party and some new friends coming over. Allison slugged down coffee heavily cooled with milk. They rode in Trudy's new hybrid pickup, freshly decorated with colorful logos and signs on the door panels: "The Growing Season—Products by Trudy." Trudy had traded a catered party for ten, complete with wine, for the design and artwork. The logo featured three basil stems and their shiny, emerald leaves.

"Nobody else can do this run?" said Trudy.

"I told them I would," said Allison as she fiddled with a hooded scarf that she would wear under her cowboy hat.

"You're not even awake yet."

"Who said I needed to be? I wasn't awake last night on the way down."

"It might not hurt," said Trudy. "Just so you've got your wits about you."

"You sound like my mother, and I mean that in a good way."

Allison's eyes were open but her brain was still under the down comforter in the land of slumber. Thigh muscles called a meeting with her brain. Mutiny was the first topic on the agenda. Ahead, the barn stood stiff and beautiful, straight out of a diorama of a horse farm.

Standing outside the truck in the frosty air, Allison gave Trudy a hug. In return, Allison received a series of motherly admonitions about the cold and how to survive.

"Lots of perfectly healthy people get hypothermia," cautioned Trudy. The air was butt-ugly cold. "Their heating systems get overwhelmed. I can't help you with the fatigue factor, except don't eat a heavy meal. That will only pull blood from your brain to your stomach for digestion purposes and make you tired."

"Got it," said Allison.

"Back when?" asked Trudy.

"Not gonna say," said Allison, though she had no specific itinerary. "This cold might have a thing or two to say about how the hunt goes, and I don't want you worrying."

One more hug. Trudy's were the full-body version, pelvis to pelvis, not an A-frame of brushing cheeks.

Inside the barn, Lightning stood rigged and ready. He was a solid, beefy horse with a mix of blue and black roan. Allison said hello and gave him a scratch behind the ear. She hoped it was the hardest thing she had to do all day. "Yeah, it's cold out there," she said. "But we'll warm up." Lightning was one of her oldest and most personable horses.

Hitched nearby was Eli, sporting an intricate packsaddle and two well-stuffed panniers on his wide mule frame. Eli's demeanor was forlorn. It was a permanent state. He didn't know how to reveal contentment like a happy horse.

Allison introduced herself to Terry Zamora, who had been admiring the horseflesh down the line of stalls. Zamora's gear was catalog crisp. He took up a lot of room, even more than his six-three frame. He was bald and wore black-rimmed glasses. Freckles dusted his face. They were the only youthful features on a hardened, tired front. It had been a no-smile greeting. At first Allison had thought his eyebrows were up because he wanted to ask a question. But the eyebrow position was locked in place, and was a bit unnerving. Magoo, a dun quarter-horse with a bit of spirit to his temperament, would take Zamora up the hill. Magoo was a good choice, the biggest horse in the team. Allison would have felt sorry for any other horse drafted for this rugged assignment.

"You're catching up with the Keating crew, right?" Allison confirmed. It never hurt to double-check, like a surgeon marking the limb before cutting. It would suck to arrive at Stillwater Reservoir when you wanted to be by Trapper's Lake.

"Trying," said Zamora.

"Hunted before?"

"A bit here and there."

"Usually not this cold."

"I've dealt with worse," said Zamora. "Bring it on."

A couple of her ranch hands helped fit Zamora's stirrups while Allison went about her routines like a robot.

An iced-up robot.

An iced-up, zonked-out robot.

She went to check on Sunny Boy, who was splayed out on his stall floor like a Great Dane, lying on his side fast asleep. Hope you're feeling okay, she thought, and tried to remember if she had ever seen him so prone and so done in.

It had been an hour already and Zamora hadn't answered much other than "Okay" and "Fine" to various questions about his stirrups, tightness of the saddle and general well-being.

The two of them stopped by a creek and Allison jabbed a boot through the ice to give access to Eli, Magoo and Lightning. The jabbing took some work but she opened up enough of a hole so the animals could take turns, slurping noisily.

"So you work with Josh Keating or know him somehow?" Allison said.

"Friend of a friend. I've met him a few times. Nice guy. He had my family up from Golden. We went to his ranch and they cooked us buffalo steaks on a campfire down by the river."

Allison poured a mug of Trudy's tea for Zamora and hoped the conversation would keep her awake. The tea issued wisps of steam, tiny quarter-inch tendrils, before they were killed by the cold. Allison thought how the steam, now being set free deep in the woods, had been born by the flame on Trudy's stove. Given her bone-weary state, Allison was bemused by her feeble attempt at deep thought.

"I'm in meat packing," said Zamora. "I guess Keating's got plans to expand his buffalo herd up and down his valley. I think it's the wave of the future, buffalo."

"Okay with me," said Allison.

"There's no such thing as a confined animal feeding operation when it comes to buffalo meat, and once anybody tastes it, they know it's got that good unique flavor."

Trudy Heath had long ago spread the gospel about CAFOs. Her description of cattle being confined and fattened was enough for Allison to swear off grocery store ground beef, but she couldn't jettison chicken in the same painless-divorce fashion.

"Still, nothing tastes better than elk," said Zamora. "If you ask me."

"Especially if it's from the animal you hunt, and if it's meat you bring home," said Allison.

"That's what I'm here for," said Zamora.

"Most of the locals go for the late-season tags," said Allison. "Get a cow when the herds drop lower."

"Yeah, usually," said Zamora. "I know. Doesn't make a whole lot of sense to take chances during the hunting season, when your odds of bagging an elk aren't quite so good. But Keating and a couple of others wanted to try the whole real-deal hunting experience and a chance to get away, so we all went in to hire you and do it right, pretend we're all a bunch of flatlanders in for the big hunt."

Clients are clients, thought Allison. Whatever it takes.

"Toes okay? Fingertips?"

"Gloves from Cabela's, socks by Thorlo," said Zamora. "My wife thought I was going a bit overboard but it's all worth it now."

Zamora tossed his remaining swallows of tea into a nearby scrub oak. Allison winced.

"Not to your liking?" asked Allison.

"Raring to go," said Zamora.

"Been riding much?"

"Not a lot," said Zamora.

"Then you want to take it easy, believe me," said Allison. "Stretch when you can and keep the liquids flowing. If you don't have to ask for a pee stop, you're getting behind the hydration curve. At this altitude, the headaches can feel like somebody traded your brain cells for barbed wire."

Trudy would be proud of her speech on liquids, and to prove her point Allison stepped a few trees away, exposed herself to the brutal elements and squatted.

Back on their horses, Allison dug a Nalgene quart out of a saddlebag and passed it to Zamora. "Drink half and we'll start up," she said.

"You're serious," said Zamora.

"Dead," said Allison with an ever-so-faint smile.

Zamora unscrewed the cap.

Two hours later they came to the base of Shingle Peak and headed east, down the slope. The Flat Tops were quiet. The cold kept activity low, there were few birds out. Zamora had not spoken for an hour. Allison was in front, with Eli in the middle on a rope hitched to Lightning. Once without thinking about it, Allison let her eyes close. Mini anvils seemed to hang from each eyelash. She tasted the delicious sensation of sleep. Those taste buds were located in two black holes of nothingness, one behind each eye. The buds yearned for any morsel they could scavenge and Allison gave into their brat-like begging. Her willpower was shot. Her head bowed low in deep thanks. Her body treated every second of unconsciousness as if she were inside a world-class spa.

She blinked her eyes open and took a guilty look around. Zamora was clueless about her stolen nap. She did it a second time on purpose, setting a two-minute internal alarm.

So this was what it was like to be blind. She could smell the fir-and-spruce mix known as alpine, but the most powerful scent was eau de horse. The steady clop of hooves on the trail wrapped her in a warm cocoon of familiarity, her favorite white noise. Lightning must have sensed her distraction. He snorted. A weakling breeze tickled her cheeks. She inventoried other touch sensations—general ache in the butt, rein loose in her right hand, feet in stirrups, a wobbly sensation in her head due to utter fucking exhaustion. There was also a chronic crotch pinch that meant she was, in fact, on a horse.

It wasn't really sleep; it was a fragile nap. No matter how tired her eyes, brain waves crashed to shore. The combination of cold and fatigue must have injected a hallucinogen into her thoughts. She was suddenly Allison Coil walking to high school in Cedar Rapids, inhaling the Iowa winter air at dawn. The half-mile hike from their new subdivision to Kennedy High School, where her father taught English, gave the cold enough time to penetrate all the outer layers. The light was dim; damp fog hung over the street. She could hear the squeaky crunch of snow under her rubber-soled boots. Younger brother Adam walked silently beside her, shoulder to shoulder. Both their heads were down and scarves tucked tightly over their faces. She could feel the relief of making it to school, walking out of the cold overcast morning and into the welcoming warmth.

The memories of pre-airplane-crash Allison Coil lived under a separate steel dome. Sometimes the roof retracted and she could see the up-and-coming graphic designer taking computer and web courses in high school, starting to develop a talent, a knack and an eye. That Allison Coil would soak up four years at Drake University, majoring in graphic design, and then head straight to New York to look for work. At the time, living in the city was the appeal, the prize. That Allison Coil enjoyed the increasing densities and increasing complexities and increasingly smart, artsy boyfriends from Cedar Rapids to Des Moines to Manhattan.

A mental and physical rehab stretch on the ranch in the Flat Tops immediately started life in a new dome. In this one, metal, steel and concrete were at a minimum. Trees, greenery and wildlife were at a maximum. Sometimes it seemed as if she had been lucky to have lived two lives, lucky to have found her way to this spot and this moment, no matter how cold. Was it time that pulverized the pre-crash memories into something more manageable, something she could digest? Or was it the extreme scenery makeover? It was the same human heart that experienced both worlds, but looking back on the first experience had an anomalous quality, since it was devoid of both sentimentality and nostalgia, though she still loved her parents.

"You're sleeping."

The voice shattered layers of darkness, comfort and pure pleasure. It came from starboard and Allison snuck a peek. Magoo had pulled alongside Lightning, confirming her worst fears.

"Guilty," said Allison.

"Rough night?" asked Zamora.

"Just long."

"I saw your head slumped."

"It's a good thing Lightning knows the way," said Allison. She was still flashing on her parents, vivid at the front of her mind. She owed them a call. They worried the most during hunting season.

"Do you want to stop and make some coffee?" he asked.

"That would take too long. Plus, I don't have coffee with me."

"Nobody else could have played taxi driver?"

Allison straightened up, stretched her spine. "We're a small operation," she said. "I'm it today."

"Can we push on a bit faster?" asked Zamora.

"Horses with full packs don't run—mules either."

Allison pulled Lightning to a stop and Magoo followed suit, out of courtesy.

"What the hell are you doing?" said Zamora.

"Just going to close my eyes for a few minutes," said Allison. "Like pulling off the side of the road when you're tired."

"A nap? You can't sleep in this cold."

"Just a few minutes," said Allison. "It will have the same effect as a double espresso."

"Fuck." Zamora slurred the word, but it was clear enough. Allison ignored it.

"A brief rest stop," said Allison. "Unavoidable."

Allison dismounted. They were in the middle of a broad field. In five minutes, she had Lightning's saddle off and was rolled up in the saddle blanket, every functioning brain cell anticipating the nap like a strung-out junkie about to score.

Zamora stayed on his horse.

"You may as well give your horse a break," said Allison.

"I'm going ahead," said Zamora.

"You can't."

"Why?"

"Do you know the way?"

"Is it that complicated?"

"Complicated enough," said Allison. The wool blanket was stiff, thick and not exactly cashmere. But it was doing the trick. "There are plenty of ways to end up missing."

"Can't you tell me how to get there?"

"Not really."

"Map?"

"Didn't bring one," she lied.

"The hell," said Zamora.

"There will still be time to hunt tonight," said Allison. "Want some food?"

Zamora climbed off Magoo. Allison closed her eyes and let the fatigue rush in. A few minutes, she told herself, a few precious minutes.

Allison opened an eye and knew instantly she had been out too long. It was too damned quiet. She sat up in her stiff wool wrap. Her cheek, the only exposed skin, was numb. Lightning, tethered to a sage bush, looked around. Eli was rock still, maybe catching a few winks. Zamora was gone. Magoo was gone. Now it was her turn to deploy Zamora's f-bomb oath in a full-blown shout.

She stood up and did a quick 360, knowing what she would see. The landscape was lifeless. How long had she been asleep? She hadn't checked her watch when she crashed—what difference would it make now? Had it been an hour? Two? The light looked about the same. Hard to say.

She put Lightning back together with his saddle. She stashed all the self-loathing under "s" for selfish, stupid and another generous helping of stupid. She headed for camp.

It wasn't necessary to like your clients, but it helped if you did. It made the days go faster, but she didn't count on it. She had learned the lesson as a graphic designer in the city. It wasn't marriage or dating. It was work. You'd go broke if you expected every client to match your attitudes about life, art, God, food, music, style, politics, beer and UFOs. Allison understood every attitude about hunting. She couldn't post a pre-contract personality questionnaire on her website. Customers allowed her to do her thing, which boiled down to one essential combination: horseback and Flat Tops.

No, she didn't care for Zamora and his approach. He was too much bluster for her. But—going to sleep on a customer? This was a first.

Allison mounted Lightning with a sigh and followed Magoo's tracks for the first twenty minutes. Then the tracks were gone. Still trying to count the ways she had screwed up, she ran a mental inventory of what Magoo was carrying and how Zamora would fare if he lost his way. Recriminations piled on. She blamed it on Baseball Hat Man distracting her and making her late.

Allison realized she wasn't enjoying the ride. Funny how a monster case of self-loathing buried everything else. She tried to relax and take in the surroundings, the muted tans and flickering aspens lit up from the inside, but it was a half-assed, half-hearted attempt. Her brain wasn't capable of wandering off her core thought: *You are an idiot.*

About an hour from camp, the trail departed from a wide valley and plunged down through a stone outcropping.

Terry Zamora was bent over at the waist, hands on his knees. Magoo stood stoically nearby. Zamora was breathing hard.

"How far to camp?" moaned Zamora. "My guts are on *fire.*"

Wednesday Dusk

The camp was empty as expected. Daylight was fading. Allison helped Zamora to a cot, then tended to the horses and Eli. She found another blanket for Zamora, who seemed to be shivering, and fired up the stove.

She and Zamora had exchanged very few words on the ride in, although she had told Zamora about Keating's illness. When he could form words, Zamora told how he had scooped water from a pool up on a ridge. He had glassed a herd of elk and was trying to do a little solo hunting. He went after them, figuring he would stay within sight of the trail, but by the time he reached the clearing, they were gone. He thought the water appeared clear and "harmless," but ten minutes later he was reeling.

Heat from the stove was beginning to lift the temperature when the low rumble of voices skipped across the air.

Colin came into the tent first. "This has a familiar look," he said.

Zamora was stretched out on a cot and covered up, the same way Keating had been, but he took up more room.

Allison introduced Zamora, who mumbled a horizontal hello.

"Same thing?" said Colin.

"He was fine one minute and sick the next," said Allison.

"Two hours between the moment I left you and saw you again." Zamora said the words carefully, minimum energy expended.

Allison didn't want to think about how long she might have slept. Nearly an hour? Ugh.

"Left you?" said Colin.

"Long story," said Zamora. Allison felt a surge of relief. It would be best if her broad-daylight nap didn't become fodder for common camp jokes or gossip.

"Keating is better?" asked Allison.

"He shot a cow yesterday," said Colin. "All of us shared tenderloin last night."

"That's a relief," said Allison.

"I guess," said Colin. "He seemed in good health last night, drinking with the guys. But now we don't know."

The tent filled with three more hunters—Hiatt, Rayburn and Gray—and Jesse Morales, one of her guides.

"Don't know what?" said Allison.

"Nobody heard him leave this morning."

"And nobody has seen him all day," said Hiatt. Allison remembered Hiatt, the shortest and stockiest of the bunch, built like a bulldog.

Allison did a quick scan of their faces. The mood was hard and heavy. Tough-guy Gray, the older man with the boot-camp physique, was bristling with worry.

"Maybe Keating is up there quartering the kill," she said.

"That's what we thought," said Colin.

"Shit," muttered Zamora from his cot. "What a mess."

"But you did say Keating was feeling better?" said Allison. A mental flash connected Mr. Baseball Cap with Keating's absence. She suppressed a shudder. Should she tell them that story? Did it have any significance?

"What do you mean?" said Gray.

"Okay, why don't you start at the beginning?" said Allison.

"All of us saw him late last night right here in this tent," said Colin, who had slowly stepped around so that he was at Allison's side.

"We were buzzed on whiskey," said Gray. "Keating had brought down this nice elk steak and we were all into the bottle."

"Not all of us," said Rayburn. Austin Rayburn was a string bean. Even in his bulky hunting gear, he looked scrawny and underfed, with gaunt cheeks to match. Ancient acne scars dotted his face. Something about his manner indicated he had a rough time in high school. "I was sound asleep. When I'm like that nothing bothers me. Hell, I can sleep at a ZZ Top show—and did once."

"We're pretty sure we saw Keating head out last night to take a leak," said Hiatt, who ignored Rayburn's irrelevant boast.

"Positive," said Gray. "Not pretty sure. He was heading out when we came in."

"I was ripped, so I don't remember much," said Hiatt.

"Hey, Hiatt was ripped—mark it down," said Rayburn. "Did you have a whole sip of something alcoholic?"

"We were all buzzed," said Gray. "Again, except for Rayburn."

"But you don't know if Keating came back?" said Allison. "Did you hear anything?"

"I turn off my hearing aid at night," said Gray. "I never hear nothing."

Hiatt removed his jacket and sat down by Zamora's feet on the cot. Rayburn headed to a chair by the stove and sat with his rifle across his lap.

"We don't know for sure about anything," said Colin. "We've been over it a hundred times."

"I was going to help Keating pack out his cow this morning," said Hiatt. "Even though he said he didn't need or want help."

"Possible he left early and couldn't relocate the kill," said Allison. "I've seen it happen. Might be out there right now."

"We thought of that," said Colin. "Thought of every angle."

"He's having problems at home with a neighbor," said Gray. "We thought he might have gone to his ranch to deal with some issues."

"But—" said Hiatt. And waited.

"But what?" asked Zamora from his prone, doubled-up spot.

"All his stuff is here," said Colin. "Rifle, everything. He didn't leave a note about his intentions. Nothing like that."

"Where have you looked?" Allison said.

"We purposely split up today in different directions," said Colin. "Scouting and looking at the same time."

"Have you tried calling down to his ranch?" said Allison.

"Need to hike to a reliable ridge," said Colin. "We kept trying."

Allison didn't have to look outside to know it would be pitch dark within an hour.

"Did anybody check to see if he took tools or knives?" asked Allison.

"They're all here," said Colin. "We figure he's only got the clothes on his back—and we hope that's enough."

Allison had been placing her money on the idea that Keating had lost his kill, but if his tools were still here that would have been a sucker bet. Experienced pros like Keating knew how to mark a kill and leave a trail of breadcrumbs to find their way back. Allison's next favorite option was that Keating had made a side trip home, for whatever reason. There was only one way to clear that possibility.

"How long will it take you to find a cell spot?" she said.

"Half hour," said Colin. "It's straight uphill."

"I'll go with you," said Allison. She showed Hiatt and Gray the supplies for dinner, packed a few Fig Newtons and grabbed a bottle of water. This was not how the evening was supposed to evolve. She would rather be slipping out with Colin for a talk by the lake. Maybe there would be time for that later, if they got this Keating thing resolved.

Wednesday Dusk

Devo squatted on the rocks on the shore of Oyster Lake. He was a few feet from the dead hunter, the same man he had followed the previous night. The same guy who had shot the elk.

The man's face was an odd blue-white. Blood had pooled black on a rock under his skull. He had landed on his back with his head toward the lake. The man was down in a dip in the rocks, almost as if he'd fallen in a shallow grave. Devo hadn't seen the corpse until he was almost on top of it.

The man's hat had fallen off and come to rest a few feet away from the body. His legs pointed up the rocky shore in a V. He could have been in the middle of a jumping jack or trying to make a snow angel—or in this case a rock angel. His arms were extended. One eyeball spaghettied out over his cheek, perhaps the work of a magpie.

One thing Devo didn't need was to be spotted at this scene. He didn't need to get tangled up with the authorities.

The other hunters could find the dead man by themselves. This spot was only a few hundred yards from their camp.

Devo had a hunch the dead guy wasn't one of the big city softies who didn't know how to handle the wilderness. He'd followed him yesterday. This guy had acted like he owned the woods. The now-dead hunter had hiked at a good clip but he wasn't hard to keep up with. He had dropped a cow elk in one shot and gutted her. Devo had helped himself to a steak after the man left. He took enough for dinner, no more. He had pan-fried the meat over his fire back at the cave. Tasty. But how could a man so energetic and tough one day—

Wait.

Devo thought of all that meat up on the hill.

Who else would know it was there?

He remembered the man's crude rock marker, a mini cairn in the trail. How would anybody else find the strung-up elk far down the slope? It would be a shame to waste the kill. It would be cheating on the long-range goal of Devo's self-imposed mission to survive on his own nickel. Eating the dead man's already-cleaned elk would be a case of merely taking advantage of everything the wilderness coughed up. No different than coming across fresh road kill. You take what fate throws your way.

Okay—he had to concede it was cheating. But he sure would love another helping of that meat, and the supply wasn't very far away. With this cold, the meat might even be good for a few days.

Could he eat that much elk?

Another idea surfaced which made him smile.

He knew precisely what to do with the meat.

Wednesday Evening

Trudy's carrot-basil soup simmered gently on the stove. In the oven, barbecued tofu pumped out wafts of garlic, paprika and red pepper from a homemade rub. The tofu had marinated for a full day before being set in the oven to braise. She had perfected the rub from dozens of attempts, looking for the right rainbow of flavors, from brown sugar to cayenne. She thought she had a winner. It might become the second group of products in her line.

Trudy wore black jeans and a purple alpaca pullover. It was a rare treat to clean up and look fresh for guests, especially with the house in top shape. She drifted into the greenhouse, which was equally immaculate and stunningly green. The aroma was like inhaling the inside of a basil plant. She checked the table settings, tasted the soup again, sprinkled in a touch more sea salt, added a log to the wood stove and poured herself a glass of organic Cabernet Franc from a vineyard with biodynamic soil near Hotchkiss, in Colorado's fertile North Fork Valley. There was a trademark symbol next to every appearance of the word "biodynamic" in their brochures. The wine was rich and deep, full of tantalizing flavor. She liked the taste of hearty red wine but had never grasped what was meant by "hints of apple" or "cinnamon overtones." She liked the way it complemented good food, and she could make a single glass last an entire meal—sometimes even far beyond dessert.

Tonight, she might just drink. Really drink. She had a sense of the questions her guests would ask. Anticipation filled her with anxiety, hard and thick in her chest.

The first to arrive was Lilly Vernice, who owned a goat cheese operation on the far side of Carbondale and about halfway to Aspen. A plateful of samples was balanced on one arm. She was a small, round woman with neck-length, black hair and a permanent smile. She was prone to saying "Wow." Each cat she was introduced to got a "Wow," as did the greenhouse and the smells from the kitchen. There was nothing left from Lilly's first glass of wine when the second guest arrived, not much later.

Jerry Paige was a familiar figure. No house tour was necessary. He brought in two baguettes and a bottle of wine, and gave Trudy a warm hug. Trudy tried her best to return it, unsure whether a friendly kiss on the cheek belonged in the greeting scenario. He gave her a kiss but she was late returning it, so the moment turned awkward.

Jerry was slender and tall. He wore oval-shaped wire-rim glasses tucked in close to his eyes. They didn't look like bifocals but they never came off. He had short, straight gray hair, but despite the glasses and hair he projected youth and energy. He peppered every conversation with big-picture questions and smiled with a trouble-making gleam when he asked such things as, "If we could start today with a new system of government, what would we draw up?" He was a firm agnostic who said his conversations with God needed no corrupt institution to help with the translation. Scenes of Catholic priests blessing the weaponry during the Serbian war proved that the church was "just another hypocritical organization more interested in power than in helping needy people."

The third guest was Brad Grasmick, who brought a bowl of vegetables to be chopped for salad—tomatoes, cucumbers, arugula, sprouts and butterhead lettuce.

Trudy and Brad set about preparing vegetables, and Lilly made a dressing with supplies from Trudy's pantry. Trudy picked a few blue oyster mushrooms from her terrarium to toss in with the salad.

Her guests gabbed like long-lost triplets. Topics ranged from the cold weather to a rock that fell on the highway in the canyon, from the county commission elections next month to the price of gasoline and how it might help people put the cost of everything in perspective. Jerry stirred the pot with what-if questions lobbed like hot potatoes. Perhaps the questions were designed to expose everyone's true values but they were equally successful at keeping the chatter above the dreck of marginalia and gossip. Jerry wanted to know what each person was doing to cut fuel consumption, recycle, and promote a healthy environment. Somehow, his spiel wasn't retro. His words were cutting edge and fresh. He was on top of his data, policies, pending legislation, budget breakdowns, and voting records from the school board to the White House. Trudy listened in a haze, feeling the tightness under her breastbone growing in direct proportion to the relaxation of her guests. She began to think seriously about pouring herself a second glass of wine. The first was down to a drop of liquid.

"So as I was saying..." said Jerry. They had gathered at the table and everyone was digging in. Lilly had opened a third bottle of wine. Trudy let her glass be refilled and she took a full swallow as though it was fresh apple juice, wondering how she would react to what was brewing.

"Yes?" Lilly's chipperness was perpetual. "I heard something about a plan, and it sounds exciting. You know that I'm game for anything. What is it?"

Trudy inhaled involuntarily, hoped nobody noticed. How could somebody be up for *anything*? Trudy liked upbeat people, but Lilly's positivism was drawn from an awfully deep well. Trudy had agreed to this discussion in a moment of utter weakness. Perhaps her brain had been briefly abducted and reprogrammed by aliens.

"The idea is to put our area on the map, to set a new standard for the slow-food movement," said Jerry. "We need an educational campaign for the entire community. We need to head back to a time in history when crops didn't get shipped by train from Timbuktu just because we wanted a kiwi in February. There's no reason we can't set a goal as a community that we're going to dramatically cut the amount of energy it takes to put food on tables in Glenwood Springs, including lunches at schools for the students. I would like to propose that we form a friendly coalition of farmers in the area. I don't care how far out we reach— Carbondale, New Castle, Redstone, Basalt or even up to Eagle. Anybody who wants in, fine. We need to let people know what's produced here. We need to get them to compare a real, fresh tomato with a genetically altered tomato whose DNA has been reprogrammed so the skin is tough enough to survive a thousand-mile trip in the back of a truck, and sit waiting for a week on a shelf in a mega-market that offers every ingredient being used in Tokyo, Beijing, Rome, Buenos Aires and Bangkok. It's absurd."

"If you're talking about coming between people and their right to watch any show on the Food Network in the morning and match that same dish by dinnertime, no matter if it requires lemongrass or truffles, you may as well take away the keys to their cars too," said Brad. "There are those who will tell you to keep your self-righteous fingers off our processed food. They think high fructose corn syrup is natural."

Trudy saw a ray of hope.

"I'm not talking about overnight change," said Jerry. "I'm not even talking about lame-ass changes where the corporate grocery store claims it's green because it buys local peaches when they are fresh, or lame-ass commercials from Detroit that claim their cars are hip to efficiency because they resemble a small army tank and not a full armored personnel carrier. I'm talking about a complete and real transformation of the community through leadership, information and sustained effort over a period of years. I want to make a statement and get others to take notice. I want impact for every step wc take, every move we make."

"Wasn't that a Sting song?" asked Lilly.

"Police," said Jerry, "the whole band."

"Spooky tune," said Brad.

"Nothing scary," said Jerry. "I am just trying to inject reality back into this community's life. I can think of no better spot, no better place."

Jerry took a sip of wine. Lilly praised the tofu. Brad helped himself to more salad. Trudy's stomach rumbled and her head seemed to float away. Was it the wine? Didn't Brad have a rebuttal to Jerry's statement? Brad?

"We need an action plan," said Jerry. "We might consider going to City Council and getting a resolution to set some goals. We should schedule something with the school board. God knows where their lunches are shipped from, flash-frozen by your government and held in deep freeze for years before they drop processed cheese on your mystery goop. We could do an inventory of all the farmers in the county and go visit a few each week."

"Or call a meeting about organizing the group, and see who comes," said Lilly. Her wine glass was now in permanent orbit, with her smiling mouth as the center of the universe.

"You might be surprised at the interest we generate," said Brad.

"It's about the network," said Jerry. "We'll only be as good as our message."

"And our messenger," said Lilly, who turned and smiled at Trudy.

This was a conspiracy. Trudy sensed it. There was a script. They had it worked out right down to who would say what.

"Trudy would make a terrific spokeswoman for the campaign," said Jerry. "Every good campaign needs one voice—a pleasant, modest and unassuming voice of reason, calm and inspirational."

"And celebrity doesn't hurt. Not a bit," said Lilly. "Not one bit. Trudy Heath. The name means something."

In fact, one-time celebrity was more like it, but Trudy knew what they meant. She had been married to a murderer who had been running an illegal hunt-for-hire business behind her back. That had provided plenty of fodder for dramatic newspaper stories. The surgery to rewire her brain—and the surgery's success—triggered a new round of media updates and profiles. She had been a beneficiary of the write-ups when her pesto line debuted. Her story gave the new product a hook. She had consented to the interviews—four newspaper reporters, including two from Denver, and one television station—but she had turned down a couple of national television talk shows. She had consented to the media requests during the shock of learning about George's dark world. Half of her experienced enormous relief, wriggling free of George's bondage. Half of her felt shame for not realizing what George had been up to. And the third half commended her for taking the necessary steps to get away from the man. It was that third half that uttered the word "okay" when Jerry Paige suggested the idea of a grow-your-own, eat-your-own, local slow-food campaign. Ever since that overture had been made she wondered if her real self truly craved so much visibility and notoriety.

She stole a glance at Lilly, searching for a lifeline. Lilly's eyes were blinklessly wide above a frozen, glistening smile. Trudy smiled back and tried to turn her jumbled thoughts into a coherent response. Trudy's mouth opened slightly and she started to speak. The room grew intensely quiet.

"We don't want to exploit you," said Lilly.

"But I could sense your passion for the issue when we spoke at the store," said Jerry. "It's clearly part of who you are. I mean, sitting at this table feels like we're sitting in a basil emporium. You asked me what's local and fresh because you yourself are."

"It's true," said Trudy. "I don't mean to be a wimp. I do care. I like the ideas. And I do want to help. I think things have to change, that it makes a difference whether we eat food from down the road or across the country, whether we take responsibility, one community at a time, for how this country is put together."

The pace and resonance of her words felt satisfying. Was she going to commit? She still didn't know.

"These are things I ponder all the time," said Trudy.

"I don't think this is a big deal," said Brad. "Hasn't this push already taken place?"

"In a surface way," said Jerry. "Just lip service, a few tweaks to a few lunch menus at school, but what has changed? Whose lifestyle has been impacted—really impacted?" There was an uncomfortable sharpness to Jerry's tone.

"You can't mandate anything," said Brad.

Trudy found herself siding with Brad. "You can set policy, set high requirements for the issue you're going after," she said.

"And what are you going after?" asked Brad.

Trudy snuck a look at Lilly and the exchange of glances said, "Let the big dogs go at it."

"Whatever we choose. Pick one. City energy use. School lunches, vegetables imported from the other side of the world, anything that makes Garfield County the greenest spot on the planet."

"I'm not against trying," said Brad. "But I don't want to act like we're groundbreaking pioneers."

"All I'm saying is that the agenda has to be bolder, not the baby steps they've taken so far," said Jerry.

"I need specifics," said Brad.

"You'll get them." Jerry stabbed his index finger on the table. "This is the start. We have to decide how far we're willing to go, how hard we're willing to push."

"I would love to expand the minds of this community," said Trudy, "but Jerry, you're the one with the words, the vision. You have a store downtown, you're at the crossroads. I'm way up here in the hills. And I'm not much for the limelight."

"Exactly," said Jerry. It was if he had anticipated her statement. "I myself can't do it. It would be viewed as a self-serving grab for free advertising because I live down here in town. The message has to come in softly, from the side door, and it has to be wrapped in humility. Not cloaked, but genuinely wrapped. All the messages have to be honed, and all the public demonstrations prepared."

Trudy took a deep breath and sat back.

Why did everyone except herself have an answer for everything?

Wednesday Evening

Josh Keating's home number was scrawled in black marker on the back of Colin's hand, underneath his gloves. The numbers were courtesy of Austin Rayburn, who pulled Keating's info from a contact list on his cell phone. Colin had tried to find a signal twice on the way up to the ridge top, but no go. When they could climb no higher and were standing in line of sight with Meeker, the cell phone offered up a feeble, lone bar.

Colin let her punch the numbers while he exposed his wrist and read the numbers. She had to assume she was making contact, going by what her eyes told her. Inside her gloves, her fingers had been cold. Exposed to the air, they trembled. When she was finished dialing, she passed the phone to Colin and he guided her hands up under his jacket and put them up by his chest, furnace warm. They were each wearing a headlamp. The beams cut the night in jerky slices. Colin had pulled up his wool ski cap to expose his right ear. As close as she was to him, Allison could hear the phone ringing on the other end.

A woman answered. "Hello?"

"Hi, this is Colin McKee. I'm one of the guides on the hunt with Josh Keating."

"Yes?"

"We're calling because we're a bit concerned. Josh has been missing for awhile. May I ask who this is?"

There was a pause. Too long.

"Oh dear." Allison thought she heard a gasp. "This is Loretta Keating. Josh's wife."

"We just wanted to check. Obviously, he isn't there with you."

"No. Why did you think he would be here?"

"He wasn't feeling well yesterday. We thought he might have hiked out."

"Josh sick? Doesn't happen. With what?"

"I'm not sure—and he wasn't sure. I don't mean to worry you."

"How long has it been?" There was a rising panic in her voice.

"We haven't seen him all day," said Colin. "He was with us last night. He shot an elk when he was hunting. If he didn't hike out because he was sick, we thought maybe he might have gone back to pack the meat out today."

Again a pause.

"It's been so cold," said Loretta. "Pipes are freezing."

"We'll let you know the second he turns up," said Colin. "Okay? And we'll notify the sheriff."

"Please," said Loretta. There was a meek quality to her voice.

"Of course," said Colin.

Colin said goodbye and flipped the phone shut.

"Damn," said Allison. "Just damn."

"Something's not right."

Allison stepped closer to Colin, who wrapped his arms around her. She was chilled right through.

"We should call the sheriff now," said Allison. "It's been nearly twenty-four hours. That's like a week up here."

"9-1-1?"

"Might be easiest," said Allison.

Colin punched the numbers. Allison remained in Colin's warm grasp. Colin showed no indication of being cold. He could have been standing on a beach applying a dab of sunblock.

Where would the sheriff start? What questions would he ask?

Colin ran through the basics with Deputy Sheriff Travis Doyle. The upshot of the conversation was that this situation did not rise to the level of a national security threat, although it turned out that the officer was a friend of Mr. Keating's and he was definitely concerned. For now there wasn't much they could do. Deputy Sergeant Doyle jotted down their cell number, asked what camp they were using, and said he would swing by to check on Loretta Keating.

"We'll call again tomorrow," said Allison. "And hope we don't have to."

Allison projected ahead a day and imagined the searchers trying to draw a bead.

She was missing something. Something basic. Something right smack in front of her.

Late Wednesday Night

Jerry wasn't drunk, just feeling high. Before Brad and Lilly headed off, the group had cleaned up the kitchen together. Trudy had objected to the team effort but was forced to relent when Brad manned the kitchen sink and wouldn't budge. Jerry dried dishes with a towel, stacked them on the counter and poured more wine all around. Trudy put a hand over her glass, which still had a few sips left. Brad cued up a Van Morrison CD on Trudy's player, a countertop boom-box that had seen better years but still sounded fine. When they were finished cleaning up, Lilly said she had to go, and Brad followed. Trudy fully expected to be alone but Jerry made no move to the door. Jerry topped off his own glass, and Trudy agreed to another splash.

"Fantastic dinner, fantastic tofu and soup," said Jerry, who had sat down next to her on the couch with one blue-jeaned leg hitched up.

"Thanks," said Trudy. "I do have a spare bedroom if you'd rather not drive. Bed recently used by Allison, who stays over every now and then, but she's up on the Flat Tops tonight."

"Brrr," said Jerry. "Hope she's got a heater with her. Allison is the one who—you know—that one?"

"Yes."

The one who had rescued Trudy. The one who had found Rocky dead. The one who exposed the incompetent hunter who had shot the animal-rights protester. The one who uncovered the antler dust factory. Take your pick.

"Does she live around here somewhere?"

"Up at the end of this clearing. We're neighbors."

"And she still guides hunters?"

"It's in her blood. She loves the Flat Tops, spends as much time up there as the mountains allow. As soon as the trails open up in the late spring or early summer, she's up in the Flat Tops."

"Have you been up there?"

"A few hours by horseback. I got just enough of a taste to see why she's crazy about it."

"Hunters," said Jerry. "I can see the beauty of the outdoors, but all the testosterone, all those guns and the sheer mess of it all. I mean, dealing with the dead elk and guts and blood."

"Sounds like you're opposed to hunting."

"I'm opposed to stupid hunting," said Jerry. "I'm opposed to rip-up-the-forest hunting and high-tech hunting and let's-drink-whiskey-all-night hunting. It's the weird part of this country—making every event something rowdy, loud and obnoxious."

"From what I gather, it's not all like that," said Trudy. "Though I'm sure the Flat Tops has its share. Anyway, she's like a sister to me. And I see the satisfaction she gets from it."

Somehow Jerry had inched closer, had placed a hand on her knee.

"Aren't you from around here?" he asked. "I mean, you know, originally."

"All native," said Trudy. "Glenwood Springs High School."

"Did you ever leave town, go see the world?"

"Nope. My parents live outside of Tucson now. My sister Anna teaches in Colorado Springs, mother of two boys. She got the go-anywhere, do-anything gene. She likes people and activity and the city."

Jerry asked about her business, her plans. The evil "what next?" demon popped its head out of its cave every time she heard the word "plans." She was sometimes so afraid of not knowing what the consequences of the hundredth step would look like that she couldn't take the first. One way might be a yellow brick road. Another might be a vapor trail with no substance. Was that a demon thought, or in her dying days would she look back through the long tunnel of her life and wish she had done more, sought more, tried to accomplish more?

"Fewer cats," said Trudy out of the blue. "That was planned. Down to five."

"Seemed less like a zoo around here," said Jerry.

"And Pepper isn't doing so well. She is getting up there, I'm afraid. But I couldn't change her surroundings at this stage. That'd be cruel."

"Indeed," said Jerry. "So the flinch was visible?"

"Flinch?"

"Last time I was here you talked about the number of cats?"

"Fourteen," said Trudy.

"You saw it?"

"I could feel it," said Trudy. "I probably heard your flinch because I imagined how it sounded. Like there might not be room for you."

Jerry moved his hand back and forth across her knee.

"Is there?" he asked.

"I want there to be room." Trudy surprised herself with how confident that sounded. "I don't mean to be overly dramatic."

"You're not," said Jerry. "I think you have room. I also think your heart is rich and runs deep."

"Would you like to spend the night?" said Trudy. "Not in the spare?"

"Only if it's not too much of a rush, and if you've got coffee for the morning."

"Number one, it's not too much of a rush. And yes, coffee beans from your store. Flown in from Guatemala, I believe."

"Hey, where would the world be without Central America and South America? I'm not sure we can include coffee in the local food campaign," said Jerry. "There are some limits."

He tested a new stretch of her thigh with his hand, letting it wander. Trudy turned more to face him, grabbed the wandering hand between both of hers and gave his knuckles a gentle kiss.

"I have one question," said Trudy. "If I say yes to you, do I have to say yes to the campaign?"

Jerry mulled over the question, sat up and put his arms around her. "I don't mean to be overly dramatic about this," he said. "But the answer is no, you don't. Absolutely not. But I know you'll do it. I know you will."

Late Wednesday Night

Warmth beckoned. The descent in the dark had taken as long as the climb. Loretta Keating's thin voice lingered in Allison's head. Allison thought of the calls to her own parents. "There's been an airplane crash..." Didn't Rose Kennedy urge that all calls carrying bad news should wait until morning? It made sense.

Colin had tripped on the way back down and took a noisy header into the branch of a tree. The result was a lump on his skull, a beauty of a bleeder. After the initial gasp, Colin laughed, and the blood dried in streaks above his eyebrow. The trail was a chute in most spots and the pitch was perilous. Allison's shins burned. No horse-riding muscles came in handy here.

At the end, one path led back to camp. The other would take them south, past Baseball Cap Meadow.

Allison stopped. It suddenly dawned on her. It was as if her subconscious had been working on the question. Out of the chorus of women who stewed around in the muck of her brain, one had stepped forward and announced, "I've got something lucid to contribute to the real-people thoughts and conversations you're having. While you've been thinking about cute Colin and his inviting demeanor, we were working on the real problem and we unearthed a tidbit for your consideration."

"Colin," said Allison. "I've got a question."

"Shoot," he said.

"Who saw Keating last?"

"Hiatt said he saw Keating headed out of the tent."

"What for?" said Allison.

"Probably to take a whiz," said Colin.

"Exactly," said Allison.

"And?"

"And did you ever go out late at night with Keating?"

"You mean in that situation, for a last pee?"

"Yes," said Allison. "In that situation, on the first couple nights you were up here."

"You mean—"

"Yes," said Allison. "Exactly. Guys like to whiz together, don't they?"

"I don't know about all guys," said Colin. "Keating did tell me where he was headed."

"And that was where?"

"Up by the lake. He said he liked a big sky."

Ritual, thought Allison.

"Would a guy walk several hundred yards, say—"

Colin cut her off. "Yes, he would."

"In the freezing cold if he was drunk?"

"The drink wouldn't matter, most likely."

Allison let the idea linger. She spun her headlamp beam back up the trail toward the lake.

"Did anybody look up there?"

"I think Rayburn said he checked it out," said Colin. "There's a lot of room up there, though."

"There's lots of room everywhere up here," said Allison. "That's why we like it. Are you coming with me?"

They cut through the sparse woods and headed straight to the lake, flicking their headlamps from side to side, covering as wide an arc as the beams would allow. Nothing. They followed the rise to the lip of the lake, where the shore was wide and rocky.

Allison crouched down.

"By the shore?" she said.

"Probably any spot where the sky opens up," said Colin. "That'd be my guess."

Dark, jutting shards of rock defined the shore. The pitch down was about the same as a playground slide but twice as long. Standing on the lip, looking out over the void, you could be peering into the crater of a volcano. Colin stepped slowly down to her right, his light beam zigzagging on the shore's hard shell.

Allison stood still, scanned to the left. Her heart hiccupped. The dread needed no logic. It started somewhere deep inside and radiated out to every pore of her skin. She caught a whiff of something she had smelled before. Maybe at the sight of the jet crash. Or was that a trick of the stupid and oddly wired human anatomy?

They searched silently for ten minutes, fifteen, thirty. They climbed over rocks, took baby steps along the shoreline. There were many uneven spots where you had to look down between the rocks in order to make sure you hadn't missed anything.

Allison promised herself just one more minute of this wild goose chase, this hare-brained notion. Goose, rabbit. Take your pick.

"Shit." Colin's voice came out of the darkness with the blunt declaration. She knew.

Allison whipped her light around and found her partner stooped low with his beam of light pointed at the bad news.

Colin was practically standing right on top of the body. Josh Keating was lying on his back, staring at the cold stars.

3

The sun cut through the morning chill and painted heat on Allison's cheek. The warmth wasn't enough to thaw out Josh Keating, still lying on the rocks. Three Rio Blanco County sheriff's deputies formed a ring around Keating. Two crouched; one stood. The oldest of the deputies worked close to Keating's body, studying the evidence and taking pictures. Keating's hunting companions lingered in gloomy and shifting clusters.

The whole night had been sad. Allison hadn't slept; how could she? Spreading the shock around camp, watching the men absorb the news, sending Max Hiatt and Conrad Gray to the ridge to call the sheriff, waiting for their return, imagining Loretta and the deep rush of grief, trying to figure out what might have happened– it was all too much.

Gray had been the most conversational during the previous evening's long lament. But he had grown talkative only after an hour of composing himself. He tried to keep things in perspective and took deep breaths before saying anything. From his sick bed, Zamora had been the most shell-shocked and out of sorts. Rayburn was a portrait of the word "stunned." He barely moved. After they had come back from the ridge and whiskey was being passed around, Hiatt hung his head low and sobbed.

They had gone up to the lake together to take a closer look before the sheriff's crew arrived. The long night hadn't changed a thing. Contagious waves of anger, confusion and grief were passed around like a bad germ.

A chipmunk skittered across the rocks near Allison. It stood up on its back legs and squeaked.

"Did you see anything?" Allison asked. "Hear anything? Got a secret to tell me? Was there somebody wearing a Colorado Rockies baseball cap who had something to do with this?"

The chipmunk hopped in a flash over a rock and was gone. Allison turned to the rising sun and closed her eyes, trying to think of all the things that needed to be figured out. Did this death have something to do with Keating's sickness? Was it too much booze? They'd had a few drinks, sucking down whiskey neat and in quantity. If Allison had to guess, having been around her fair share of late-night camps, Keating would have had a drink in his hand for many hours, and his brain would have been deeply marinated by the time he headed out of the tent. Blame the whiskey and whatever germ or virus had invaded his system the day before. The events of the last day had left Allison feeling jumpy. But it wasn't the unsettled feeling. This was worse. This was ugly worse, awful worse, sad worse, maddeningly worse.

Two of the deputies started to pull the hunters and guides aside one at a time. Each deputy had a palm-sized notepad. They gripped pens in leather-gloved hands. Allison's turn would come. She walked up to the spot where the men were being debriefed. The tones of conversation were sullen, matter-of-fact. She stood within listening distance of Conrad Gray.

"He was fine," said Gray. "Heck, he had hiked way up over the ridge and shot an elk."

"When did he come back?" said the deputy.

"I don't know," said Gray. "Sometime after dark is all I know."

"If you had to estimate?"

"I don't know, seven or eight. I do know he was healthy as a horse, proud and smiling."

Allison stepped closer. Deputy Ken Durkin wore an oversized

green parka. He had a ruddy complexion. Red hair curled in un-gainly fashion beneath the fringes of his kerosene hat. From what Allison had gathered, the trio of deputies had set out before dawn for the three-hour horseback ride from Trapper's Lake. The quick response was impressive. Allison had a better feeling for the Garfield County staff, but the Rio Blanco County Sheriff's Office couldn't have more than a dozen law enforcement types in all. The county had more deer and elk than people by tenfold. There was always the possibility that the Colorado Division of Wildlife might come sniffing around and the National Forest folks too, even though the story was likely to be nothing more than a straightforward accident. Sad, but straightforward.

"You say he had been sick the day before?"

"Something got to him," said Gray. "He missed a day of hunting, which doesn't happen. Not with Keating."

"Did you see anybody else when Mr. Keating headed out?"

"You mean that night? The last time we saw him?"

"Was he alone?"

Gray searched the ground.

"Well, it's not pretty but it's the truth—we were all lit up. But I don't think anybody could have been out there—everyone else had crashed already. It was me, Hiatt and Keating at the bitter end. Rayburn was sleeping and the guides had crashed."

"Why didn't the three of you go out together?"

"I'm not sure," said Gray. There wasn't an ounce of tension or worry in Gray's voice. "Like I said, we were lit. We weren't think-ing in those terms. Two of us headed out, one didn't. No reason, but that's the way it happened."

Durkin knew Allison was listening, but he didn't seem to mind. There was no steam to his questions, as though he had already drawn a conclusion and there wasn't much to figure out.

"Did everybody get along well up here?"

"Yeah," said Gray. "Great."

"Does anybody know Mr. Keating's situation down at home?"

Gray returned this question with a shrug. "Everyone knows about the stuff going on."

"I suppose," said Durkin.

Allison perked up.

"What stuff?" she said.

"Nasty squabble with his neighbor," said Durkin. "New guy from Back East, wants everything different."

"Like what?"

"Like how people live," said Gray. "The whole enviro thing. Real pushy."

"His neighbor?" said Allison.

"There wasn't anybody else up there," said Gray, seeing where this was headed. "Where would they have been hiding? What would they have been doing? Waiting out by the lake for one certain guy to come along and take a whiz? In that bitter cold? Not likely. Anybody with half the sense that God gave grass was inside and hunkered down."

It made sense. Josh Keating goes out for a late-night leak. He decides to walk all the way to the lake, perhaps in an attempt to sober up. But it's dark. He's drunk. He reaches the edge of the lake. The edge is hard to spot. Maybe his eyes are on the stars and the toe of his boot catches on a rock and the next second the earth rushes up and smacks his face like a speeding train. And he's out. Dumb hunter tricks. Dumb drunken hunter tricks. This could be another chapter in the book about how hunters spend large sums of money to go out in the woods and hurt themselves. Look this up under former vice president Cheney, subcategory "joke." There was only one problem. Keating was no fool. He was too grounded, too tough, too real, too much of the mountains to make such a mistake. On the other hand, as sad as Allison had been and as much as she still ached for the loss, shit happens. She was sure of that.

"Ms. Coil?"

Another deputy. This one was taller with a disposition that implied he couldn't chitchat if his life depended on it. He had longer sideburns than fashion or regulation allowed, if Rio Blanco County was concerned with sideburns. His nose was razor straight and long. He was wearing dark sunglasses tight against his face like a swimmer's racing goggles.

"Yes?" she said.

"Deputy Chris Dale. I was wondering if you can show me Mr. Keating's things."

Allison shrugged. "Sure."

She led the way back toward camp. The open sky and sun vanished as the two stepped under the canopy of pines between the lake and the tent, where a deeper autumn chill lingered.

"Any initial opinions?" said Allison.

"What do you mean?" said Dale.

Conrad Gray and Durkin were following a few paces back.

"Just wondering about your take on what happened," said Allison.

"Is there much debate?"

"Not that I've heard. Did you know Keating?" said Allison.

"Some. Not well."

"Did you ever see him drunk?"

"Didn't socialize with him."

"Did he have a reputation?"

"Not like that."

"Then like what?"

"He lived outside of town," said Dale. "Couldn't tell you much more than that."

The tent was in sight. Allison wondered whether a guy with less experience getting hammered might be more likely not to know his limits, might be prone to a wicked, ill-timed stumble. What was there to sort out? Tests would be run and no doubt the cause of death would be listed as rock-to-head, with gravity the main accelerator.

"Hey Conrad," said Allison. "What's this?"

Allison was standing in front of the tent and staring at a bundle blocking the doorway. It was wide and oddly shaped. Lumpy. Big as a stew pot. It was wrapped in a loose, discolored sheet.

"No idea," said Gray.

Allison gave it a gentle kick. Whatever was inside had some give.

"What the hell?" said Dale.

The sheet was tucked underneath but was no more secure than a sheet on a teenager's bed. Allison gave it a yank and lifted it up. She got a whiff of meat before her eyes registered elk carcass. The chunk was a front quarter with four ribs.

"Damn," said Deputy Dale. "Looks good. Recognize it?"

"Hell no," said Gray. "Nobody in our group got one, except Keating. And his kill is a long way up …"

"Wait," said Allison.

A paper fluttered out of the sheet. She snapped it from the air and held it up.

The paper had seven words at the bottom: "Your friend's elk. Sorry about your friend."

Above the words was an X next to a drawn square with a roof, like a child's first drawing of a house. "You are here" was written in small letters. A dotted line pointed "SW" toward the top of a ridge where another X marked "kill here." And in smaller letters accompanied by an arrow: "Red cloth in tree."

Allison passed the sheet to Deputy Dale and turned around slowly, trying not to give anything away.

"The meat is Keating's," said Allison. She looked around, every nerve telling her they were being watched at this very moment.

Thursday Morning

Devo sat by the fire at the front of the cave. Another elk steak sizzled on a stick. He had taken only a small slice for his second helping. After all those bugs, it was satisfying to have his teeth sink into food he could chew to keep his weight from slipping down too far.

He was in dangerous territory as it was. The latest cold front had cut right through his system. Moving swiftly in the daytime kept his temperature up but he wasn't prepared for these winter conditions. He had kept the fire going for days. He figured he had lost twenty pounds. He had gone into the Flat Tops at 180 pounds, purposely bulked up, storing fat. Last spring it had been bitingly cold on some nights when his system wasn't used to the rigors of living in the wild. He had snared a lot of rabbits but their meat was too lean. Men were known to fade away eating nothing but rabbit, which can bring on a nasty digestive breakdowns and diarrhea, which could be deadly. Fat was his most critical need. He had killed a plump beaver in a figure-four deadfall. The Flat Tops were rife with beaver. Mackinaw Lake and Mud Lake had coughed up a few. He had even caught a couple muskrat, which he hadn't been trying to trap. He had killed a small doe in a deadfall, partly for the practice. Stalking deer patterns and digging the hole and planting the stakes had consumed a week. Bugs were full of fat, but grubs and moths got old. The elk meat helped. He could feel his system relishing the protein, which he was careful to thoroughly chew. After all the fungus, berries and bugs, it was a welcome mouthful.

"The cold," he said aloud. "There is only a brief escape around the fire. But you can't stay by the fire forever. And you can't bring the fire with you when you go look for food. I got lucky with this elk steak. I stumbled across a hunter's kill …"

He had rigged up a DV camera on his right hip. A metal socket in his leather belt allowed him to screw in a hollow metal rod. At the tip of the rod was the camera on a customized mount. As long as he kept his belt tight—he had to cut notches in the leather as his waist shrank—managing the slightly lopsided weight was easy. Remembering not to rush through narrow gaps, like the space between two tight trees, took getting used to. The camera kept him sane. It was his friend. Twice a month, Devo picked up a shipment of fresh batteries. The batteries arrived via ultralight. The plane landed in a clearing near Sheep Mountain on a regular schedule. Devo never made contact with the pilot, a long-haired ex-hippie named Ziggy who lived outside Paonia. Prior to dropping off the grid, Devo found Ziggy through a hiking club. They met at hot springs just near Redstone and discussed Devo's idea and needs. Ziggy was game from the get-go. At first, Devo thought the supplies would be brought in by foot to the drop point and his used-up batteries and filled-up video cards would go out the same way. After the second week, he started noticing the buzzing plane and where it was headed. Apparently the ultralight didn't need much of a landing strip to land or take off. Batteries—and blank video cards—were the only outside technology Devo would use. He didn't shoot video all day, only snippets here and there to show his transformation, and to document the hunt for food and the effort to improve his shelter. Ziggy edited the clips and uploaded them to Devo's YouTube channel and Facebook page.

Devo turned the steak and tested it for doneness by pinching it with his fingers. The meat was still a bit soft. "You want to eat the meat just past raw—medium rare to rare. You'll get used to it. All meat is more nutritious raw than well done, which cooks out all the good stuff. Remember, well done is another stage on the way to ash and by that time, nothing is left."

Devo had his episodes all planned and Ziggy had the rough script outlines, too.

"Get Back" would cover how to liquidate your possessions, what you would need to survive, and deciding where to head back to nature.

"First Days" would talk about making the mental adjustment to life in the woods and taking stock of all your resources.

"Settling In" would focus on getting used to the routine of life in the woods, and adjusting to a new diet.

"Assessing Dangers" would discuss how to evaluate your habitat, how to figure out if you're sharing the terrain with bear or mountain lions. All about tracking, trapping and snaring.

"Bugs" would feature everything to do with eating insects—the good, the bad, the bitter.

"Moccasins and Mittens" would cover woodland fashion, from preparing hides to stitching cured skins.

In reality, of course, the video production was beyond his control. He had the original plan, but that plan was now in the hands of Ziggy and any of his compatriots on the topside. That's how he thought of civilization: the "topside." He was down in the lower decks with the grunt workers. The sun might shine but he couldn't return to the city and a high-tech studio if he was going to continue to devolve. That wasn't a process you could temporarily halt. Returning to your down pillow, mega grocery stores and clogged highways would instantly undo the mental and physical progress. And thus the irony—he would be counting on the world of communications technology to encourage and inspire others to reject the same.

Somewhere out there Ziggy was building and showing his journey on the web. If all went as it should, he would be gone for a long, long time. He was the devolving guinea pig, and he could not hold back or pull up short. The truth was that the specialization of mankind could not continue. Most workers were trained to do one thing and one thing only, like operating one piece of software or fixing one kind of appliance. Drop a modern father from suburbia into the wilderness today and he wouldn't last more than a few days—or few hours—depending on the month. A hundred years ago? No problem. A man would hunt, fish, find shelter, build fires and find a way out. Certainly the trend was wrong. The trend would render human beings useless.

The steak was done and Devo took a bite, chewing for the camera. The meat was hot and tasty. He stood next to the fire, nibbling. The dead hunter might be a problem.

After he had dropped off the elk quarter and the crude map, he watched from the woods as the sheriff's deputies questioned the other hunters. Devo had a hunch there was something more to the whole deal than an accident.

Something was out of kilter on the Flat Tops.

He had an idea what it was.

And he hoped it would not force him to go topside.

Thursday Late Morning

The more Jerry talked, the more Trudy felt a subtle lift of confidence. There was a quiet strength in his point of view, an earnestness that grew from his core values. He had a firm belief that world change began with the right ideas and the right people. He was provocative in a good way. And, judging by one night, he was a terrific lover.

Jerry sat across from Trudy at the kitchen table. Large cups of steaming green tea sat between them. Jerry had slowly eaten two whole-wheat blueberry pancakes and bacon. The bacon was thin tofu and had been sautéed with liquid smoke, sea salt and a splash of soy sauce.

"I've gotta go," said Jerry.

"I guess you do," said Trudy.

"But I don't want to go."

"The store? Is that what you're thinking of?"

"I'm thinking about you. The staff will open the store. I'm sure it's already open. It had better be, anyway." He laughed. "I'm always there."

"Then you gotta go," said Trudy, knowing he wouldn't move. Hoping he wouldn't move.

"Time to leave," said Jerry. "I feel like I'm doing something illegal."

"Have you ever done something illegal?"

"Once or twice. Got behind the wheel after too many drinks, fibbed a bit on the old tax form. Same as everyone."

"Not everyone."

"You were always an angel?"

"Always. Chronically good. Never did anything bad."

"Except last night?"

"Last night? Who, me?"

It was already a joke between them. Last night he had told her with a smile that he was surprised to find she had a naughty side. She had responded with her most mischievous gaze. The comment had come after a warm, affectionate round one. She was expecting a semi-drunk attack from a horny guy. Instead Jerry was a patient man who wanted to make out, chat, grope a bit and slowly undress. They must have spent fifteen minutes lying side by side, topless but with underwear on and talking. They had touched each other everywhere and she knew he was hard, but he didn't rush. He had taken long minutes to kiss and nuzzle her breasts and every inch of skin between and around. Away from the politics and the action plans, he quizzed her kindly about her views, her dreams and her favorite things. He may have been buzzed but he was polite and made her feel comfortable.

He had a strong, sinewy body but he was relaxed and unpretentious. It could have been their tenth or hundredth time, not their first.

"I gotta go," said Jerry, followed by a slow sip of tea.

"You better hurry," said Trudy.

"I don't want to go," said Jerry. "I like it here."

"You're welcome to stay."

"What would I do all day?"

Trudy liked the way Jerry's mouth moved. He talked with a minimum of wasted motion. She liked that. It looked efficient. He had interesting ears, too—flat and close to his head. Again, no excess.

"I'd think of something," said Trudy.

"Something to do with basil?"

"Most of my days move in that direction," said Trudy.

"And nothing to do with what we talked about last night?"

"You mean what the *group* talked about last night?"

Jerry smiled, let that question linger. "Yes, the table talk, not the pillow talk. Much as I'd like to relive every second of the latter."

"There's no time for that," said Trudy. "You gotta go."

"I know. Here I go," said Jerry. "So what are you thinking?"

"About the big-idea stuff?"

"Yes, that stuff."

There were times. Well, there were seconds. Well, there were nanoseconds over the last eight or ten hours when the idea of Trudy The Confident flashed in front of her eyes. She was there in various strobe-brief moments, this vision of Trudy The Confident. The role was within her capabilities. She was standing on a rock for that one nanosecond, a mountain of granite. And the next second she was out there floating in space between the moon and the North Star without a spacesuit. It was a long, long way to solid ground and the air was being sucked—hard—from her lungs.

One minute she was sensing a newfound posture and imagining she could step up to the challenge, the next she was shrinking back and wondering if she could rewind last night's conversation and this time tell the assembled friends to take a hike, that it wasn't going to happen.

"How do we get the ball rolling?" said Trudy. Damn, she thought, do you know what you're doing to yourself? All she could figure was that a part of her so enjoyed last night she didn't want to create any reason for Jerry to not come back.

"Really?" asked Jerry. "That simple?"

"You'll have to help me," said Trudy. "And when I said let's get the ball rolling, what I meant was, how do you do it?"

"What do you mean?"

"How do you know you're going to get anywhere?"

Jerry gave it some thought, took a sip of tea and bobbed his head from side to side in slow motion, rolling the question around.

"Well, I don't suppose you really know if you're going to change things."

"And how do you get up the nerve?"

"The nerve?"

"To speak out. To tell other people what to do, how to live."

"It's community stuff," said Jerry. "That's the way I view it. It's being an active part of the community. It's not putting up with things the way they are. Somebody's out there pushing an agenda and it may as well be me."

Was it that easy? That natural?

"You'll have to help me."

"You've already said that. And don't worry. These kinds of events and messages are all scripted. We'll practice 'til we're blue. We'll imagine questions and come up with answers, so we'll know what to say. Get the whole campaign locked down."

Jerry grabbed her left hand and she felt … sensed … connected with that corny, out-of-the-blue whiff of crazy brain fumes that suggested she could do this, she could really do this.

"So what exactly is first?" she said. "Where does it start?"

"I don't know," said Jerry. "I've gotta think about it. Plus, I gotta go. It's late."

"Okay," said Trudy, wondering if that gentle lift of confidence would evaporate the moment he left.

Jerry stood up. The tea was gone. They hugged, kissed and she stood looking out her front window while he gathered his coat and things.

"I've been thinking," said Jerry. "I've been reading about this guy over in Rio Blanco County who is shaking things up, working on these same issues. I thought it might be a good idea to go pay him a visit and see how he's getting all the good publicity."

"Who's that?" asked Trudy.

"Ethan something," said Jerry "I think he moved out here from the East Coast. Ethan Bostwick, that's his name. He's making a splash—a splash like a cannon ball."

Thursday Midday

The red cloth was easy to spot. Allison, Colin, Hiatt and Zamora walked down the slope four paces apart. Deputy Durkin followed close behind.

"Let's go slow," said Durkin. "Look for anything out of place. Anything."

The pitch was steep. The air was icy in the shade, but in patches of sunlight it might have been spring, with all the hope that came with it.

They were silent. Twigs and dry underbrush shook and snapped underfoot.

The mood on the ride up had been somber and sober. There had been long stretches when it seemed a giant vacuum in the sky had sucked up every word they knew. The horses grunted. Silence bred more silence.

"There it is," said Hiatt.

Elk quarters dangled from a tree twenty paces further down the slope.

"Stay here," said Durkin.

Zamora gave a shrug of the shoulders and a skeptical *whatever* roll of the eyes. Durkin studied the ground and inched his way forward like he'd cornered a snarling dog. Allison appreciated the effort, but couldn't imagine what signs or evidence were available to find. If anything, he might find tracks from scavengers drawn by the easy elk pickings.

Durkin scanned the undergrowth, squatted once and then again, taking a long moment to look at the ground. One slow step at a time. Finally Durkin gave them a wave and they joined him at the oversized frozen tree ornaments, hunks of elk carved by a pro. One front quarter was missing a few ribs. Zamora cut the ropes and lowered the pieces. Allison stood back as the men assigned tasks and knew what to do without so much as a syllable uttered between them.

"The cold kept these puppies in good shape," said Zamora.

"Worth the effort," said Hiatt. "It would have been a shame to waste this."

Colin stood, knife in hand, and caught Allison's gaze. Fatigue hammered his face; his eyes sagged.

"What are you thinking?" said Colin.

"Just trying to figure out how Keating was followed," said Allison. "It doesn't seem right."

"Doesn't seem possible," said Colin, "that a good hunter, a damned good one, wouldn't know he was being followed. By the way, what was going on when we found the butchered meat by the tent?"

"What do you mean?"

"You were looking all over the place."

"I was?" said Allison.

"You know who left it?" asked Zamora, a note of accusation in the air.

Allison paused long enough to know she would have to start at the beginning and would have to enlighten them all about the baseball cap—its discovery and disappearance. She told the story with as few brush strokes as possible and a just-the-facts approach, no drama.

"Strange," said Hiatt when she was done. "Keating told me he thought he was being followed."

"When?" said Durkin.

"That night after dinner. Just before he left the tent," said Hiatt. "He said he had seen some kind of blur or motion out of the corner of his eye when he was getting ready to take the shot that killed this cow."

"What was it?" said Durkin.

"I don't know," said Hiatt. "I don't think he knew."

"Why didn't you mention this before?" said Durkin.

"Just remembered it now. I'd forgotten."

"And why just now about the baseball cap story?" said Durkin, turning to Allison.

"Don't know if it is connected. But, no real reason."

"But you had the cap on the horse one minute and it was gone the next?" asked Durkin.

"Like ten or fifteen minutes, but yes," said Allison, feeling her throat tighten.

Zamora shook his head. "I'm not sure what it means, but I still don't think anybody would have chosen to be outside that night.

Hardly a ripe time for foul play—midnight in the dark by a lake on the coldest night since God invented ice. Not what I would call prime time for a trap."

"But there's somebody out there who knows something," said Durkin. "I think we've got what we like to call a person of interest."

"Be a good idea to find him, I don't disagree," said Zamora." But most likely Keating tripped, and that was that."

Durkin shrugged, considering it all. Allison replayed the last few days in her mind. She hadn't thought much about the buzzing airplane since it happened. In fact, she hadn't thought much about airplanes for a couple days, and that was always a good thing. Then there was Keating's odd illness, Keating's death and the gift chunk of elk and a map. Keating's death, of course, dominated all the other quirky events. Allison tried to block out the death and envision how the other pieces connected, but it was like thinking only about a solar eclipse and ignoring the sun.

Back up on the trail, they strapped quarters of meat on the horses for Zamora and Hiatt to load out. Allison took the head, complete with Keating's tag on the ear. Even if the kill belonged to a dead guy, you followed legal procedures. Durkin was the last one up the slope and on his horse.

"I'm going ahead," he said. "I need to get back down and round up some folks to help me find this sneaky weirdo. I need a few more supplies than we brought—and some ideas. I know an old outfitter from Craig who can follow spider tracks by moonlight. I want to see if he can lend us a hand."

"I'm with the deputy," said Zamora. "If someone is out there messing around, I say we find him. You can't stay hidden forever in the Flat Tops." He sat on his horse with a pained look on his face. Somewhere inside he still hurt.

Zamora's assertion hung in the air. Allison mulled a response but opted not to say it: *Anyone who can slip into a camp overrun with hunters, guides and cops—and manage to dump a package of elk meat on the threshold of a tent without being noticed—probably knows how to avoid being tracked down.*

The Flat Tops were tailor-made for hideouts—dense woods and rolling, rugged terrain with an ample supply of caves, canyons and cover. The hunt for the mystery man might be harder than tracking a raindrop after it hit a lake. It wouldn't hurt to quiz Baseball Cap Man and Elk Delivery Man, if they were one and the same person. He must know something. Maybe "sorry about your friend" meant "sorry I killed your friend." What if he'd been coming for her on the night she found the cap in the field? The odds of setting a trap or tracking the slippery figure were close to zilch, but Allison welcomed a tough tracking challenge.

The other questions that occurred to Allison were whether the hunters would call it quits, how soon the Rio Blanco County authorities would determine what caused Keating's demise, and what she could have done to prevent it. In addition to policies limiting the amount of weight carried to a campsite, and requiring every hunting team to carry a GPS, a map and a compass, she wondered if she should insist on a buddy system for late-night pee trips.

"What next?" asked Zamora.

He had stopped to let Allison catch up. Lightning and Magoo picked their way down the narrow trail with care, hooves clacking on the occasional stretch of stone. Deputy Durkin had headed off and disappeared down the trail. Allison had hoped to let Zamora and Hiatt sprint for home while she stayed behind to think things through with Colin. One thing for certain: The desire for intimate time with her favorite employee hadn't been put on hold. It was right there, undiminished by events.

"I think 'next' will be up to what the sheriff's men have in mind when they all get back up here," said Allison. "What are you thinking?"

"I'm thinking all of us need to head back down and be there for Loretta," said Zamora. "And I'm also thinking I want to help the deputy find the slippery fucker who left the meat and the map."

"Going to be tough," said Allison. "But I know we've got to try. How are you feeling?"

"Accelerating out of the curve," said Zamora. The look behind his black-frame glasses was all business. "Unimportant compared to any of this."

"What about the hunt?"

"What about it? I don't care about an elk at this point. The sneaky dude who left the meat was right there—maybe one hundred yards away while we were out by the lake."

"Pretty close," said Allison.

"He must have seen us with the cops and either knew exactly how many of us there were, or took a risk by coming into camp and making his delivery. The guy knows *something*. He has to."

"Do you think the others want to head down too?"

"I don't know. What if we see if we can find this guy? It would be a hunt of sorts."

Hiatt and Colin were already waiting at the bottom of a long switchback.

"We could try to pick up a trail," said Allison. "But I think he's pretty wily."

"Everything that moves leaves tracks." Zamora sounded like he was scolding a child.

"I'm going to look," said Allison. "Believe me."

Organizing a noisy, angry posse wasn't the way to find Waldo of the Woods. You went small and you went stealth.

"You don't seem very optimistic," said Zamora.

"I think he knows how to hide. He's proven it."

Keating's death could have been an accident, she wanted to say.

"Are you a professional tracker?"

"I can hold my own," said Allison. "And thanks for not mentioning my trail nap." The wash of guilt. Again.

"You're welcome," said Zamora. "Nice to have you owing me something." A faint, sarcastic smile came with the statement.

"Keating was a tough hunter," said Allison.

"Really capable," said Zamora. "He was a quiet-strong, stoic type. Ran a big buffalo ranch, but practically did it all by himself. The ranch work, housework, vegetable garden, fences, chickens too, and some goats and ducks. And then there's his wife."

"What about his wife?"

"She doesn't do much around the ranch. She stays in the house, from what little Keating told me. Reclusive, I guess. Don't know how she's going to cut it now that he's gone."

Allison let the comment hang. She needed to gnaw on everything. She cared about Josh Keating and chalked his death up as a personal failure. But she also knew there was a place in her head where Keating's name would join with dozens of others, most of them from her airplane crash. All the names on that list could be given the same tombstone. No pithy, meaningful quotes were needed, no parting words from the deceased—just a lone punctuation mark.

The trail hit a series of steep switchbacks on its last pitch down to the valley floor. Allison stopped and, being the lone woman, asked the others to go on ahead. She relieved herself behind a tree and tried to calm her restless thoughts. She stretched, gave Lightning a quick check and climbed back on. Oyster Lake slipped into view, and Allison enjoyed the few moments of solitary thought. She could make out the spot where Keating had been found. The lake had been restored to its natural state, no dead body splayed out. No quizzical cops.

Somebody was on his knees on a rock near the shore.

He was near the spot where they had found Keating.

The sun lit up the cliffs beyond the lake with a soft glow. Allison found her binoculars and stopped Lightning, who stood like a granite statue.

The man's back was to her. He took a slow step on his knees and his hands went down. He was crawling carefully. He straightened up and peered around like an anxious prairie dog. He was too far away to discern facial features. He was a shimmer, a smudge of dark green against the tan, black and brown rocks.

Allison scanned to the right and down to the lake. Dead rocks, nothing. Scanned left. Ditto. The man was alone. Then she drifted back to the man. But he was gone. She looked up and down the shore. He was gone.

She squelched a burning desire for a warm stove, a hearty meal and a week without any weird shit. Why was somebody out on the rocks acting wary and wanting to be alone? Something about the figure suggested he wasn't old enough to be Conrad Gray. And something suggested he wasn't Jesse Morales, who always seemed focused on the group's needs around the camp. Was that a cop out there? Or was it Elk Delivery Man? Maybe it was somebody from one of the volunteer mountain rescue outfits. They never missed a chance to get involved.

A switchback down, Colin was waiting for her on his horse.

"Knew you'd come eventually," he said.

Zamora and Hiatt were long gone. Lightning quickened his pace ahead.

"I saw somebody out on the rocks," said Allison. "Out on the rocks where we found Keating."

"What?" said Colin.

"On his hands and knees, crawling around."

"Who was it?"

"Even with the binoculars, I couldn't tell."

"Maybe somebody dropped something when they were all out there with the cops," said Colin.

"Maybe."

"Is he still there?"

"No—a minute later he was gone."

Colin pointed his horse down the trail. "Are you going down with them to Meeker?" he said.

"I suppose I should," said Allison.

"What are the rest of them going to do?"

"We gotta wait and see," said Allison. "But the elk hunt may be over for this camp. Zamora wants to hunt for Meat Delivery Boy."

"Probably a low-percentage deal right there."

"Tell me about it."

"The guy is slippery," said Colin. "I saw no trail."

"Did you look?"

"Of course," said Colin. "All around the spot where he dumped the meat. Nothing."

"I guess we've gotta give it a go," said Allison. "

"I'll go with you to Meeker first, if you want," said Colin, and she caught his studious gaze.

Now here was a bright side. Allison knew precisely nobody in Buford or in Meeker and therefore she would need a place to board Lightning. A motel room with Colin had a certain appeal. Although she knew there were concerns in the city that introducing romance between boss and employee might be viewed as creating a hostile work environment, she thought the only risk here was the usual black fear: simple rejection. That would have been a risk worth fretting over ten years ago, prior to her plane crash, when she inhabited a different body also named Allison Coil. But she knew for a fact that the reward had a tremendous upside. And the opportunity would answer the question of whether she and Colin might be compatible.

"Don't see why not," said Allison. "I'd love your company."

At camp, Zamora and Hiatt already were removing the elk quarters from their packs. At the rear of the tent the two remaining deputies were huddled, preparing to head down. A travois, like those Allison had seen in history books about Plains Indians, had been fixed to one of the deputy's horses. Typical travois design fanned out in a triangular shape, probably to create more carrying space, but on this one the wood slats were parallel. It was a clever rig. On top was Keating's body, wrapped in a bag and lashed with a web of ropes. Not that the passenger would notice, but it would be a bumpy ride.

"If we had found him before he was frozen we would have been able to drape him over a horse and carry him out that way," said Deputy Dale. "If you get the body when it's still limp, it turns into a stiff in the right curvature. But it wasn't possible."

"All of you look pretty tired," said Allison. "Are you gonna make it down before dark?"

"We should make Trapper's Lake," said Dale. "We'll have to see when we get there whether we drive to Meeker tonight."

"Leaving soon?"

"Momentarily," said Dale. "Your guide Jesse is packing up some provisions."

"You got headlamps?"

"All of us."

"Colin and I are coming with," said Allison.

"Fine," said Dale. "We could use the help."

"How's that?"

"To make sure Mr. Keating stays on the travois, and to make sure we stay on the trail."

"Colin's from outside Buford," said Allison. "He knows every inch of the trail."

"There are a couple of real rocky spots where it might be too gnarly," said Colin. "But I know where they are."

101

"We'll have to figure it out when we get there. We requested a helicopter but they were all booked up. We got our hands full with this load, so we could use the help."

In her head, Allison kissed goodbye the thought of a bowl of steaming beef stew and some blissful shut-eye. On the other hand, she could be sharing a couple of beers with Colin at the Trapper's Lake Lodge in a few hours—or perhaps down at the Ripple Creek Lodge at the bottom of the hill. The thought gave her a lift and she scolded herself for thinking about anything other than the issues at hand.

"I'll steal a few things from the pantry too," said Allison. "Give me a sec. Colin, what can I get you for the ride? Do you have enough water?"

"I'll come and get some in a minute," he said.

A snack or two would do—and some liquids. It couldn't be more than a five-hour trip down. Given the dragging travois and tight turns in places, it might be six. Allison did what she could to ignore the sensation that her soul, heart, brain, eyes, nerves and spinal column were all starting to fly apart. Internal clock, fried. Hands, wobbling. Thoughts racing all over the place. The prospect of not being able to crawl into a hole and sleep for a week was surely a bad joke. Even now, the lift of being with Colin wasn't enough to counteract the revolt from her bones. "Mind over matter" was a concept best employed after eight hours of sweet dreams followed by a hearty breakfast—not when you were running on fumes.

The tent was pleasingly empty. She sat down on Keating's bare cot. She kept her feet planted on the floor—made a point of that—and laid back. She tested—tested—to see if closing her eyes would deliver that delicious sensation of nothingness that had been pestering every productive thought for hours.

"Allison!"

"Huh?" She jerked to a sitting position. "What?"

She had been out cold. Ten minutes? Longer?

"In here," she shouted, hoping it wasn't Zamora.

"It's me," said Colin.

Colin stepped into the tent with Jesse Morales draped around his shoulders. Gasping for breath, Jesse looked like he might have just been keelhauled. He was holding his stomach with his left arm, the one that wasn't clutching Colin.

Jesse let himself down gently onto a cot on the far side of the tent.

"I was out there with the cops," said Colin. "Getting stuff packed and our horses ready. Jesse came staggering up the trail like a wounded drunk."

"Don't tell me," said Allison.

"Yep," said Colin. "Said he was scouting and found a running stream under some ice. He'd gone way up high, looking for clues. Hadn't packed enough water, knew the stream—"

Jesse moaned.

Allison took one of Jesse's cold hands in hers and felt his knuckles. They were mini knobs of frost.

Jesse shuddered, quaking inside.

"Where were you?" she asked.

"Up east of here, just off the top of the ridge."

"Did you stop by Oyster Lake on the way back?"

"No," he said. "Why?"

"Get some rest," said Allison. "We'll stay right here with you."

Allison pulled the wool blankets around him. Her heart ached like a tooth being extracted with dull pliers and no gas. One of her clients was dead—and now three in all had turned up ill.

Jesse's presence eliminated him from the scene on the lake shore. She still couldn't understand how the nimble figure could have been Conrad Gray, who was tough for his age but didn't move easily. She was sure the man was too loose and too limber to be anyone over the age of creaky knees—say, sixty.

Allison turned to Colin. "Have you seen Rayburn?"

"Outside with the others," said Colin. "He was making sure the cops and their cargo got off okay."

"Have they left?" she said. This might be her first clue about how long she had been conked out.

"Ten minutes ago," said Colin. "We'll catch up. Won't be hard."

"I'm looking for Austin Rayburn," said Allison.

"Why?"

"Because of the man I saw by the lake."

"You don't think it could have been cops taking pictures and measuring stuff?" said Colin.

"It didn't look that way," said Allison. "Didn't look official, you know? It looked like somebody scrambling, searching."

Allison found Austin Rayburn outside, watching as Gray and Hiatt packed empty coolers full of elk quarters. Rayburn was standing nearby, a disinterested observer.

"Is Jesse real bad?" asked Gray, who didn't stop working.

"As bad as the others," said Allison.

"Then he should recover in a day or so if the way Keating and Zamora rebounded holds true," said Hiatt.

"I'm glad I didn't go with Jesse," said Rayburn.

"Were you thinking about going with him?" said Allison.

"He asked if I wanted to go scouting," said Rayburn. "I probably would have drunk some of the same water, and we'd have had a whole hospital ward here."

"What was going on around here?" said Allison. She tried to make it sound like a casual question but there was something too convenient about his decision to stay behind twice. He had chosen not to help with retrieving Keating's elk, and he had chosen not to help Jesse Morales on a scouting trip.

"I just hung around the tent and helped the cops build that sled to drag behind the horse," Rayburn said. "I made some coffee, laid down for awhile. I don't know what it is about the air up here, but I'm tired all the time. I can't explain it. After we got Keating's body back here I don't think I was more than ten yards from the tent all day."

Rayburn gave a shrug as if he didn't have a care in the world. "I could use some coffee, as a matter of fact," he said. "Anybody else?"

Thursday Dusk

The man with the towering backpack was a black dot weaving through the woods. He was moving quickly. Devo was right on his tail.

Hunter? Definitely not. Camper? No. Hiker? No.

Devo didn't like him from the get-go.

Devo had been checking a squirrel trap when he saw the man, a trim six-footer with an effortless gait, moving purposefully near Shingle Lake. Devo caught up with the man in thirty minutes but kept his distance. He guessed the pack weighed fifty pounds, but it didn't slow its carrier. The pack was a custom job and looked ungainly. It started at the guy's hips and climbed straight up, box-like, so it obscured the back of his head. No bungeed-up sleeping bag or tent. No Nalgene bottles bouncing off the back. The hiker didn't wear any orange.

It was nearing dusk. Bashing through the woods took much longer than hiking in the open. Twice the man stopped abruptly and Devo had to scramble for cover. They came to Coffin Lake, shaped like an elongated teardrop. It was shoreless and ringed by woods. At the pointed tip, the man plunged down into the trees. He moved too nimbly to be a full adult. There was something childlike in his gait. Devo scurried along the thin shore, exposed. If the man suddenly reversed course, Devo was dead meat.

The lake drained to the south, feeding a narrow, docile creek. Devo found a spot by the shore where a fallen snag provided cover. He took a long drink from the water in his wineskin. The water had been skimmed from a high spring near the cave that he had grown to trust, that his body had learned to accommodate. He had boiled his water during the first month, but the process took too much time. He had paid the price with bad water once, a bout of stomach agony that lasted two full days, but he knew he needed to convert his system over to one that could drink unfiltered water and not worry about parasites. He needed to be able to drink alongside animals.

At the lip of the lake, Devo stopped. The lake was iced up but water gurgled quietly from an underground exit below his feet. Nature had fashioned a culvert. The slope down was treeless. Tufts of brown grass jutted from the rise. Forty yards down, the creek entered a square pool the size of a boxcar. The man squatted next to the pool. His pack was on the ground, its guts opened up. He reached inside and pulled out a bottle. He used both hands to lift it, and steadied himself in a crouch to help with its heft. He set the bottle up on the rocks at the edge of the pool. It was gray metal, the size of a propane canister for campfire gas grills. He used a wrench to unscrew the top.

A marmot whistled. A rock wobbled.

The man jerked around, stared upslope.

The man stood with the open canister in his right hand and a surgeon's mask covering his mouth, a bright white square in the gathering gloom.

4

Friday Morning

The brown metal heater under the window generated a white-noise hum. The yellow shades over the window glowed. The clock said 8:32. Allison's bones hadn't moved all night. She had slept for six straight hours. Pure joy.

Allison climbed from beneath the covers and peeked outside. The day was bright. The view east to the wide valley floor was gold and rust. The parking lot was lifeless. A flatbed semi full of hay bales rumbled past on the highway, downshifting for the slower speeds of tiny Meeker.

She knew her reason for being here in Meeker was valid, but she wondered if she ought to be picking up the trail of the mystery man instead.

She dressed and freshened up, then went to look for Zamora and Hiatt.

A knock on their motel room door went unanswered. She knocked harder to make sure, but got no response. Hiatt's black Jeep was parked in the lot. The front of the parking lot was taken up by a modest café with a brown-gold stucco exterior. She found the men inside, sipping coffee. In front of Zamora sat a plate of huevos rancheros with steam rising from the chunky green chili and soft, buttery eggs. In front of Hiatt, hot blueberry pancakes covered the plate underneath. Hiatt was preparing to drench them in maple syrup. A plate of bacon took up the tablescape between them.

"What did I miss?" said Allison.

"Ordering," said Hiatt, scooting over in the booth to make room. Zamora didn't budge. He took up his half of the booth by himself.

"Nothing that we know of," said Zamora.

"Sleep felt good," said Allison, instantly realizing this was not a good topic to bring up around Zamora. "Word from anybody?"

"Nothing from the cops or the coroner," said Zamora.

"Any change of plans?"

"I'm afraid not," said Hiatt. "We gotta go do it."

Allison ordered oatmeal and coffee from a waitress with long dark hair and a calm presence. The oatmeal came in the time it took to walk to the kitchen and back, never a good sign. The mush was bland. She wondered what delectable morning nibble Trudy might be preparing.

The caffeine worked. It surged to Allison's brain like a hit of oxygen. Hiatt recognized the oatmeal issue and pushed the bacon her way, then loaded a hunk of pancake on a spare plate. The day was coming to life.

They headed out to the Keating ranch east of Meeker. Hiatt drove. Allison had crawled into the rear of the Jeep. Zamora was too large to sit anywhere but shotgun. They retraced their late-night route back toward Buford and Allison ran through the previous day's last few events in her head—leaving Colin behind to tend Jesse, catching up with the cops and their travois an hour out of camp, riding quietly for the next three hours, turning the body over to the coroner (who was waiting at the trailhead), making the long drive into Meeker, and sitting in Zamora and Hiatt's motel room toasting Keating with a few beers from the cooler in Hiatt's Jeep. A pounding hot shower had preceded a final stumble to bed.

As they headed back upriver in the daytime, the ranches and grassland in the fertile valley southeast of Meeker spread out on both sides of the road. The cattle lay low. Giant cottonwoods sucking water from the White River marked the path of the farmlands' main source of nourishment. In the distance, the ground rose gently toward the Flat Tops. She thought of Colin, pictured him tending to Jesse. She pictured the mystery man and squelched a growing fear that she was in the wrong place and had chosen the wrong course.

The valley grew tight in spots, then broadened, opening itself up to stunning tracts of ranchland. Some of the homes were trophies, better suited for an overlook along the California coast. Others were clearly the centerpiece of hard work and grit. Twenty minutes later, as they wound into tighter and tighter valleys, Hiatt turned down a road that was paved for a short stretch and then switched to gravel and dirt.

Hiatt let out a sigh. "This is going to be rough," he said. Nobody disagreed.

The road to the Keating ranch was lined with cars, pickups and government vehicles. There were people leaving the house and headed to their cars. Others were just pulling in. The ranch house was two-story white clapboard with dark green shutters on the second-floor dormers. A wide wraparound porch added weight to the house's profile. Billowing cottonwoods guarded the west flank, and fences raced off from a nearby barn into broad fields of breeze-blown pasture. Dozens of buffalo dotted the landscape with their unlikely silhouettes, all heft and imposing power.

Mourners clogged the porch. Cowboy hats bobbed in the swarm. Arriving guests carried tins and plates covered in aluminum foil or plastic wrap. Departing well-wishers were empty-handed. Allison hung back as Zamora and Hiatt plunged into the mini throng, then followed them while she had the chance. Hiatt was the familiar face. He knew everyone, and Zamora seemed to nod knowingly at a few people, too. Words like "terrible," "sad" and "tragic" floated above the greetings. Allison was a stranger, invisible, the new awkward kid at a new school.

The low chatting on the driveway and porch gave way to hushed, mumbling tones as they moved into the house. The inside was just as jammed with townsfolk, friends and relatives. In the living room, most were seated, including one man in sharp, crisp sheriff gear. Loretta Keating occupied an oversized chair at one end of an enormous braided rug. Daylight poured through a large picture window. The living room was spare, functional.

Loretta Keating reminded Allison of a librarian. Her pallor was dull and tired, weighing down potentially attractive features. Allison guessed her age at forty. Her hair was thick and golden, brushed tight to her head and pulled back in a taut ponytail. She had strong cheekbones and a handsome if plain presence. Her head hung as she listened to the sheriff. Loretta smiled briefly at something the sheriff had said, up close and personal, and Allison saw a flash of straight, solid teeth. The widow clutched a handkerchief tightly, a clump of white cotton billowing from her fist.

The people who comprised the inner circle of sympathy sensed the arrival of fresh visitors on the periphery, and a trio of women on the couch stood up, each in turn giving Loretta a brief handshake or a pat on the shoulder or a tender hug. Hiatt led them closer into the living room and suddenly Allison was standing next to the new widow, who was still focused on the man in the gray-green uniform.

"It was just one of those things," said the sheriff, who was inching up out of a nut-brown armchair. He stood, revealing a sizeable frame. The sheriff looked forty but could have been a fit fifty. He was dressed in a snappy uniform and held his sheriff's hat in his hand. It was hard to miss the gun bulging from his belt along with the handcuffs and other gear that dangled from around his waist. If the Meeker equivalent of D-Day was tomorrow, he was ready.

"Thank you so much for coming over," said Loretta. "It means so much to me."

Allison suppressed an urge to follow the sheriff out the door to find out what was new.

"Loretta, Max Hiatt. I'm so sorry."

"Thank you," said Loretta. She was either tired or inured to the emotion, given the parade of well-wishers. Her tone was dry and matter-of-fact.

"You know Terry Zamora... "

"Yes, indeed," said Loretta.

"My condolences," said Zamora.

"It's overwhelming," said Loretta. "All this. All these people all at once. All this support."

"Loretta," said Hiatt. "This is Allison Coil. She owns the guide service."

"The one Josh was with?" said Loretta in a slightly recriminating tone of voice.

"I'm so sorry," said Allison.

"I didn't mean to sound accusatory," said Loretta.

"Not at all."

"I wasn't implying that this terrible incident had anything to do with your business."

Allison often wondered if she herself would be able to utter a complete word if a loved one died suddenly or tragically. It was odd that Loretta Keating was apologizing for a subtle implication of a word choice—or that she even recognized the possible slur.

"You're with the young man who called me the other night, when he was missing?" said Loretta.

"Yes," said Allison.

Loretta's eyes were a drained swamp, oozing and moist but dead.

"Nice of him to call," said Loretta. "Supremely kind."

"He wanted tell you what was going on," said Allison.

"I was worried right then," said Loretta. "In fact, I didn't … " She stopped and stared, took a breath, started daubing her eyes before Allison saw them pool up and the tears overflow onto her cheeks. Utter sadness. Hiatt reached out, put a hand on her shoulder as she buried her head in both hands.

Loretta's grief exhumed every old bone of grief within Allison. The quantity of deaths from the airplane crash might have increased the misery quotient, but they were all individual deaths that just happened to share a crossroads. Loretta's loss brought shards of emotion to the fore in high definition. It was one of those moments when you realize what matters and what doesn't.

"It's okay," said Loretta. "I didn't think this was a good year to be going." Her chin quivered. "For him to go hunting I mean. I had a bad feeling. All the hassle with that crazy neighbor."

She paused, sobbed, took a breath. "It's like there has been a dark cloud over the valley ever since he moved here," she said. "Everybody is on edge. The cloud might go away for a few days, but it always comes back."

The words were composed quietly and with care. She was still crying, but the tears weren't having any effect on her tone of voice, which carried a timid quality.

"I hope he had the good sense to stay away today," said Hiatt.

"Oh, no," said Loretta. "You wouldn't believe it, but he was here earlier, knocking on the door all by himself."

"Bostwick came here?" said Zamora.

"A card would have been fine," said Loretta. "After all the miserable stuff he heaped on us. Most of it was aimed at Josh— or maybe at the whole town."

"Did he stay long?" asked Zamora, still incensed.

"Not really. He probably couldn't stand being on a real working ranch, one with bison. He was in and out. I'll never see him again if I have anything to say about it. His first time here was his last."

"I can't believe he had the guts to come by," said Zamora. "At a time like this."

"One of them things," said Loretta. "Just one of them things."

Zamora offered to help in any way he could, and Loretta thanked him and appeared to be truly reassured. The deep emotion of a minute ago had evaporated like a teaspoon of water on the hood of a car parked in Death Valley. No doubt sadness would ebb and flow for weeks and months to come.

It was time to go. There was a natural, unspoken protocol to these things. One must not monopolize time with the widow.

They bid goodbye one by one and drifted into the dining room, where the table strained under a crush of casseroles, tureens of soups and stews and chili, plates of cold veggies, and trays of brownies, cookies and assorted breads.

The sheriff was holding court with a group of men in the far corner of the dining room, a giant mug in his hand. The women had retreated to the safe and familiar hubbub of the kitchen. Allison could imagine this going on all day.

Hiatt and Zamora waded into the thicket. Allison peeled off from the mingling crew and headed back outside. The gentle hills stood serene. The sky was cloudless. A breeze from the south was cool but lacked a sinister edge.

Allison leaned on the porch railing and studied the buffalo scattered in loose clusters. For all their size and power, the shaggy brown animals projected peace and majesty. The pleasing aroma of grass, dirt and livestock came in waves. Allison couldn't shake the uncertainty lodged in her gut. She wondered how Colin and Jesse were doing. Rayburn and Gray had stayed behind and she wondered how they were doing, what they were doing. She could imagine a letter asking for their money back or a partial refund. With the visit completed, Allison itched to get back to camp.

Zamora and Hiatt emerged from the throng and joined Allison at the railing.

"Pick up anything?" said Allison.

"According to Sheriff Christie, no word from the coroner yet—might be later today or tomorrow. Every indication is it's your garden-variety stumbling accident, aggravated by alcohol. But apparently that Deputy Durkin is trying to put together a search party to go after our mystery man. Sheriff says if the examination comes back that it was all an accident he won't authorize the search—budget crunch and all."

"Most people are still buzzing about Bostwick making an appearance," said Hiatt. "If lynching wasn't outlawed there would be a mob on his porch right now."

"Just for stopping by to pay respects?" said Allison.

Zamora and Hiatt exchanged a glance that told Allison she was not plugged in.

"This was war," said Zamora. "You don't rush over and console the widow at the first light of day, not when you've been lobbing hand grenades over the fence."

"It's astonishing that he came at all," said Hiatt. "I mean—send a card, for Chrissakes."

"Or never send nothing," said Zamora.

"What about Loretta?" said Allison.

"What about her?" said Hiatt.

"Does anybody know what she's going to do with all this ranch?"

"I hear she wants to figure out a way to keep it going, pour the money from a gas lease into ranch hands or something," said Hiatt. "But it's early."

"Way too early," said Zamora. "Let the dust settle."

"So Bostwick has the whole valley on edge?" asked Allison.

"On fire is more like it," said Zamora.

"It's like a form of slow-motion terrorism," said Hiatt. "Coming in here and telling people what to do, like a bully. Josh Keating was sitting out here taking a beating. He was the number-one target, the bull's-eye. Bostwick probably thought if he could rattle Keating he could shake the whole town."

"Then why the hell would Keating do anything to put himself at risk?" said Allison.

"Put himself at risk?" said Zamora. He said it sharply, like he didn't understand.

"Why take any chances?" said Allison. The idea had been gnawing at her. She was surprised to find herself turning the thought into words. It hadn't been a fully formed idea until now. The seed sprouted without her knowing.

"What are you suggesting?" said Hiatt.

"It doesn't make sense. He was careful, smart. He had climbed off a sick bed to stalk, kill and quarter an elk. Look at this place, this ranch and think how capable he was."

"It was an accident," said Hiatt. "Nobody means to trip in the dark after a few too many Wild Turkeys."

"Sometimes you don't know how much you've had," said Zamora. "You're right. It doesn't make sense. It's stupid, and it happened, and you can't go back and tell him to be careful. You wish you could, but you can't. It was late—stupid late—and we were all seriously messed up. My brain wasn't working. It was sauced. I didn't even stay up to make sure he came back okay."

Allison had been there.

All the would-haves.

All the could-haves.

All the picayune decisions that go into choosing what to do on any given day, at any given time, including choosing a flight or choosing a seat. You were choosing, in a way, but then you were always choosing something—what to do, where to go, what to think, how hard to work, what to eat, when to eat and on and on. How did you know one choice would lead to survival while people right next to you would perish? Who knew that one decision about a flight, about a particular airplane, would change her life?

"It was an accident," said Hiatt. "A dumb accident."

Friday Evening

Driving through Glenwood Canyon was an unadulterated act of faith. The highway in this stretch consisted of giant slabs of concrete cantilevered out from the wall, their grip on the steep sandstone a mystery. A Nebraska cornfield or Utah desert might be a good place for four lanes of interstate, but Glenwood Canyon was a spot for a horse trail, not ribbons of concrete hurtling back and forth high above the river, boring through buttes and cliffs with disregard for the sharp turns, and a dramatic plunge toward Glenwood Springs. Trudy slipped behind a pickup truck with Arizona plates moving at an easy pace and let him take the abuse from grinding big-rigs and speeding cars.

Tonight, as she got off the highway and looped around past the Colorado Hotel and crossed the river onto Grand Avenue, she saw the whole city, her hometown, in a new light. What had she been thinking? What could they really change?

Jerry's grocery was off a side street, a block from where the bridge over the Colorado River dropped into the heart of downtown Glenwood Springs, built where the Roaring Fork and Colorado rivers collided.

Lilly Vernice, Brad Corwin and Jerry were there, huddled in a booth, one of four that constituted a mini-café inside Jerry's store. Brad gave her a kiss on the cheek, Lilly gave her a quick hug and an air kiss near the cheek, and Jerry gave her a warm, welcome hug that amounted to a full-body massage.

There was a possibility they had become a family of sorts, a network. It had been Jerry's idea to celebrate Trudy's commitment to the cause and he offered meals and wine at his store as an incentive. It was after hours; they had the place to themselves.

Trudy wondered if Brad and Lilly could tell that anything was different and Trudy felt a brief flash of embarrassment, which she tried to shake off. Weren't they mature adults now with the option of sleeping together? In some ways, no big deal, right? Of course she had packed an overnight bag.

"Here he is—Ethan Bostwick."

From the seat next to him, Jerry grabbed a copy of *High Country News* and plopped it in the center of the table.

"Cover story," said Jerry. "Doesn't get much better in terms of media attention. *High Country News* goes all over the planet, reaches the right people. They treat Bostwick like a hero. No reason we can't borrow his political roadmap and aim even higher."

"But how much would it take to make changes in Meeker?" said Brad. "The town is cute and all but it's nothing more than a wide spot in the road."

"That's the point," said Jerry. "He's getting all this attention, and Meeker is a tenth the size of Glenwood Springs."

Trudy stared at the portrait of Ethan Bostwick on the cover of *HCN*. He stood tall in a golden light and cast a long shadow as he leaned on a fence. Buffalo grazed behind him. Bostwick wasn't smiling. The pose had caught him in an odd grimace like he was in some mild pain. The headline on the cover was "Shaking Up The White River Valley" with a smaller "No Stone Unturned" beneath.

"He's got *cojones*," said Jerry. "This says he signs up for every public hearing, town council meeting, school board, county commission, you name it. Says he made friends with a reporter out of Steamboat Springs too, and the paper there published a long profile about his plans to build a wind farm up on Rabbit Ears pass. He figures there's enough steady wind to keep all of

Meeker juiced and maybe have enough power to sell some of it to the grid, though I guess there are problems with moving the extra electricity across the system."

Trudy stared at the cover and wondered: Is that what they want me to do? A queasy feeling stirred in her stomach.

Jerry led them back to the deli and they dug in—free-range barbecue chicken, fresh hot tomato soup, local cheeses, whole-wheat baguettes and some of Lilly's goat cheese and homemade pear chutney. Trudy asked for a helping of the chicken and tarragon salad with grapes. She tried to relax, no longer the rookie drone in the hive. She tried to settle into the warmth and comfort of a new circle. She tried to think about what it would feel like to start a more purposeful life, to help shape the world around her.

"So are we getting together to eat and drink or are we going to do something?" said Lilly. "Sorry to get down to business. You know me—work, work, work." She laughed at herself, part silly teenager and part adult deep into her Shiraz.

Trudy wondered if she had ever felt as unselfconscious as the vibe Lilly exuded right then.

"I say we start with the schools," said Brad.

"The city," said Jerry. "The schools have been done and done. No offense, but that's not edgy enough. All the city expenses—the electric and gas bills alone—and there's so many things they could do better. We've gotta get the city to establish code require-ments, insist that people build houses that treat every ounce of electricity as a precious commodity and every trickle of water like a stream of liquid gold."

"But schools are a soft touch—doing it for the kids," said Brad. "Find a school and get the kids involved with gardens or changing the lunchroom meals they serve or doing more with recycling."

"I like the schools too," said Trudy, surprised to hear her own voice and even more surprised to find that it carried weight. "The schools might be a good first step, a quick win."

"Trudy," said Lilly. "You go."

Lilly took a moment. "We can't let the schools off the hook with lip-service buzzwords and baby steps," she said..

"The schools have been done to death," said Jerry. "They have already made changes and milked it for lots of PR."

"But not well," said Brad. He began a speech about the difference between "surface stuff" and making changes that affect the organizational culture. It seemed Brad had a script prepared about companies that acted with a conscience and those that operated only to be perceived in the right light. Jerry listened attentively. Lilly was zoning in and out. Trudy chimed in with the occasional idea or two, felt Jerry's gentle hand on her leg under the table, and enjoyed the sensation of being part of something. The notion of moving a whole community still seemed as improbable as altering the course of the Colorado River, but the others acted as if this kind of organizing was routine.

"I still want to go over there and see how this Bostwick dude is getting all the attention," said Jerry.

"We can do our thing," said Brad. "Set our own standards. It looks to me like Bostwick pissed off some of the town, alienated them to the point where there's no dialogue. Some people are dumb enough to react to that sort of pushiness and they start being more wasteful, more lackadaisical. You can't scream and yell at a junkie because they grab the closest needle and start looking for a vein."

"We'll take the high road," said Jerry, "but not the slow road. We gotta move."

A fresh bottle of wine materialized from the ether. All their glasses were topped off amid a sudden burst of silence. Jerry took a deep breath, smiled at Trudy and spoke.

"Good," he said. "We're a team. We'll add as we go, build as we go. And we have a good place for a coming-out. There's a school board meeting next Wednesday night."

Saturday Morning

Allison squatted in the dirt, studying a tangle of shoe and boot prints where the trail came into camp and dissipated into the beaten-down, high-traffic ground. There were prints distinct enough to identify, but she knew that the idea of tracking the mystery-meat deliveryman was virtually hopeless. It would have been difficult seconds after the elk ribs were dropped on their doorstep. A couple of days later? She couldn't fathom the chances, but they were low.

"It's not gonna happen, is it?" she said, studying the soft brown whiskers sprouting from Colin's upper lip. Days of hunting were taking a toll on his shaving schedule.

"Everybody leaves a trail," said Colin.

"True," said Allison. "If I were part Ute we might have a shot."

"Or part bloodhound," said Colin.

"We need a seed scent."

"How's your nose?"

"Not as good as my eyes. Yours?"

"Not as good as my instincts," said Colin.

"What are they saying?"

Colin glanced up, as if the treetops might hold an answer. Was he checking to see if his instincts would generate a tangible thought or was he working on his retort?

"My instincts are saying boola-boola," said Colin.

Allison laughed. "I knew you were onto something. What is that? Polynesian?"

"It's Hollynesian. As in Buddy Holly. In the movie. It's what he says when his girlfriend gets on the bus, leaving Lubbock and there's so much uncertainty about what's ahead. Boola-boola."

"That could mean anything," said Allison.

"And it probably did," said Colin.

"Do you watch a lot of movies?"

"My dad does," said Colin. "And he loves old rock-and-roll. I think he's watched *The Buddy Holly Story* a hundred times. Myself, about three."

Allison had watched the movie post-airplane crash. She had tried to steel herself to get through to the end. She knew it involved a plane crash but she had no idea whether the movie showed Buddy going down, whether it showed panic in his face, whether there were any scenes inside the plane on his last flight. She didn't remember the "boola-boola," but she recalled the growing sense of dread and the tears when Buddy sang "True Love Ways." The movie had been a test to see if she had gained perspective. She failed in a flood of tears, stopping the movie long before the last concert in Clear Lake.

"Sad movie," said Allison.

"Way sad," said Colin. "The Crickets—my dad told me that name inspired The Beatles. The day the music died, right? Airplanes and rock-and-roll don't mix. Ricky Nelson, Lynyrd Skynyrd, on and on."

Lots of people and airplanes don't mix, thought Allison, whether they strut on a stage or not.

"Back to your instincts," said Allison.

"Like I said, boola-boola. Whatever. Meat delivery guy knows his stuff, skipping in and out. He's been in the area awhile."

The thought struck a chord. Allison hadn't tried to mentally profile a man who drew maps, delivered raw elk and stole back his own baseball cap.

"You think so?" she said.

"I think he knows his way around. I think he might be living up here."

"Living?"

"Somewhere."

"You don't think he's somebody from another camp?"

"It's possible," said Colin. "But most of the city lugs I know wouldn't have been able to do what this guy did. I doubt I could have snuck in and out of camp in broad daylight like that."

"He lives up here?"

"Seems like it," said Colin.

"In a tent somewhere?"

"Or cave."

"I've heard of Spring Cave and a couple others. Any near here?"

A coy look.

"Care to tell me?"

"Care to let me show you?" he said. A flicker of mischief flashed across his face. There was no accounting for a preoccupied brain.

"I want to take a look at something up on the shore," Allison said. "Won't take long."

"After that?" he said.

"Where do we go?"

"I think I can find it about three hours from here. It's on a ledge in a cliff, kind of tucked off the shoulder of Crescent Peak."

"Do we have time today?" said Allison.

"If we leave now."

"Don't think we should take the cops?"

"Thought you said they might not put together a search—money problems."

"But they might. For all I know, they might be here any minute. I know if Deputy Durkin had his way, they'd be here now."

"But they're not," said Colin. "We can do a bit of work on our own."

Our own. A nice ring to it.

"What about Jesse?"

Allison had checked on Jesse when she first returned to camp, but he had been sleeping.

"The others can watch him," said Colin. "He's tough to begin with and he's coming around."

It was true; all the others were back in camp. There was some talk about hunting tomorrow.

"Can you tell me something?"

The tent was out of earshot, but Allison started walking toward the lake. Colin followed.

"Try me," said Colin.

"What were Gray and Rayburn up to while we were down in Meeker?"

"You sound like one of the cops when you ask it that way."

"Well?"

"Gray puttered around, helped me brush down the horses and clean up around camp. He went scouting this morning while you were on your way up from Trapper's."

"And Rayburn?"

"Not much," said Colin. "Read a book. At one point last night, they were both sitting around reading. Jesse was sleeping, I was sipping whiskey. Practically a goddamn library in there. Quietest night I've ever had in a hunting camp."

"And the rest of the time?"

"Rayburn was busy, cleaning and poking around. Nothing specific, I guess."

They walked for a minute in silence, moving out of the woods into the clearing. The lake was ahead. A gray jay bounced ahead of them, leading the way.

"What the hell is going on?" said Allison.

"Wish I knew," said Colin. "Bad water."

"And a whole lot more."

Allison gave a snapshot overview of her thoughts, how Keating was an unlikely candidate for a careless death.

"Good points," said Colin, his eyes calm.

They were on the shore of the lake, looking down at the allegedly guilty rocks. The stones were mean enough, squared off and sharp. How many times had Keating come to this spot?

Clusters of footprints lingered on the icy crust of the lake where the cops had trampled around while the body was being studied. The footprints were a handy marker on either side of the spot where Keating had fallen. It was as if Keating's body was still there.

"The guy I saw through the binoculars was looking down in the rocks," said Allison. She creep-stepped across eight boulders, stopped. Colin followed. Allison got down on all fours and crawled, examining the tops of the rocks and the dark gaps between them.

"Was the guy as big as Zamora?" said Colin.

"Zamora was with us."

"I know. Just wondering."

"I'd say smaller. Smaller and busy. Very busy. Looking for something. He was practically sniffing every rock."

"That's odd."

"It was the intensity factor. The out-of-place factor. The what's-he-doing factor."

"You couldn't tell who it was?"

"Otherwise I'd go ask him."

"You would?"

"I might."

"It had to have been Gray or Rayburn," said Colin. "And the cops were still here."

"Unless it was somebody not with us—somebody else."

"But he did look suspicious?"

"Suspicious enough," said Allison.

"You thought he was looking for something?"

"Definitely."

Allison pulled a rock up for the heck of it, making sure it was a small one that she could budge.

"Guess it's possible he found what he was looking for," said Colin.

Allison let the rock thud back into place.

"But why was he looking over here? We're ten yards from where we found his body."

Colin lifted a rock twice the size of the one she had lifted. Allison clambered over to peek underneath.

"What if somebody comes out here now?" asked Colin.

"I hope he won't."

Colin let the boulder drop.

Allison tried to recall every frame from the movie in her head, the minute-long reel through the binoculars titled "Wary Man On Rocks." Had she read too much into it? Could she remember the exact spot where he had been searching? Could she count the rocks between the spot where Keating had crashed and the spot where the stranger had been searching? She crawled to the next rock and peered into a dimly lit mini-cave.

The brown leather strip sat in the shadows. It was jammed into a crevice. Weak light was enough to catch the buckle's gold, which was too shiny to be anything that had been out in the weather for any length of time. The leather strap attached to the buckle disappeared below ground. Allison had her fingers around it and felt the extra heft, a few more ounces than she had anticipated. The watch came up, lightly frosted with crumbs of sand and soil.

"Holy—" she muttered.

"Holy what?" said Colin.

"I remember this. It's Keating's," said Allison. "I was looking at it the other day, when he was sick. The watch face. It's the flip side of an Indian Head Nickel."

The hour and minute hands of the wristwatch were thin, black and tipped with arrows. The coin had been fused to the body of the mechanical part of the watch underneath. Clever. She held it up to her ear and heard a faint *tick-tick*.

"You know the old coin I mean," said Allison. "The one with the buffalo."

They packed and checked their horses. Tandem pairs of hands worked in sync. Lightning was still rigged and ready from the morning ride up from Trapper's, but Allison rechecked his tack. She helped saddle Merlin, a dirty roan. There was nothing magical about Merlin, only stamina. Allison found Jesse in the tent breathing steadily, asleep. From outward appearances, the worst was over.

Rayburn said he would do some scouting with Gray. Both were still melancholy but not fully forlorn.

A new level of uncertainty hung in the air like a foul mist. The unchipped, unscratched and neatly buried watch with the buffalo relief could be explained—if you believed the watch unbuckled itself mid-air as Keating was falling, if you believed the watch hurtled itself to a spot between two rocks, and if you believed it burrowed itself in the sand like a skittish crab.

"Do you think the cave is a crap shoot?" asked Allison.

"Worth a look," said Colin.

They were near the tent. They were speaking clearly and slowly on purpose, to make their intentions known.

"How long a ride?" said Allison.

"Two hours," said Colin. "Plus the climb to the cave."

"And no waiting for the cops?"

"Do you see them anywhere?" said Colin.

Colin packed a bag of food to share—dried fruit, nuts and Fig Newtons. The basics.

"I'll put some chili together for dinner," said Rayburn, who had come out to see them off. "Expect you back."

"We'll be here," said Colin. "No question about that."

"Stay away from the water," said Rayburn. "In case you haven't figured out that much."

Allison wondered briefly if she had ever seen Rayburn smile. His sad head was slightly cocked. She studied his dark green jacket, oily in spots and a few sizes too loose for his skinny frame.

Within an hour of leaving camp, they were crossing a wide expanse of calf-high scrub oak. They were drenched in sunlight. Like most Flat Tops trails, the path was single-file for hikers, let alone horses. Lightning led. Merlin worked to keep up at a good huffing clip. Allison appreciated the sense of urgency, even when the pitch forced the horses into a lower gear, their heads swinging side to side with each trudge. The trail pulled them up the spine of the ridge, one vertebra at a time, before it plunged down into a valley already sunk in shadows.

The woods were dead. Blown-down trunks of less hearty timber were scattered about. The undergrowth was toddler stage, still immature. Allison imagined a slow-motion camera shooting one frame a day for the next five decades, sitting on a tripod capturing the regeneration of the forest, sapling by sapling, leaf by leaf, branch by branch. She wondered if one of those frames would show a deer up close, nibbling leaves in this very spot. Or an elk drifting by, or an entire herd. Or a bear. Or a hunting guide, flat on his back, his shirt pulled up and jeans around his ankles on a warm spring day with her—yes, it was her—crouched over him with her bare legs squeezing his chest and all the fun parts doing their thing and putting a silly grin on his face. A breeze would cool their skin. Daylight would reveal every nick and scrape, every interesting fold of nature. Their sounds would carry through the woods, no thin motel walls to worry about. The guide would flip her over and the leaves and grass would be smooth and soft and she would lose herself in the moment.

Allison shook her head to snap out of the daydream.

Who controlled such thoughts?

The thoughts were fine, and as harmless as a hummingbird,

but cells in her brain were relentlessly insisting she gaze in the mirror at her feeble, unremarkable and virtually nonexistent sex life. And no—solo gigs did not count. Yes, the outcome was the same, and they were dependably exhilarating at the top, but if anything the ride down from the peak only reminded her that this was a sensation to be shared. Besides, nothing could compare to an honest-to-God real penis with all its many (two) moods and functions, especially a penis attached to a stunning cowboy, particularly the one on the saddle right up there.

Jesus. Allison shook her head again as if a bee were trying to alight—ousting the intense and distracting images and trying to focus on the mission at hand. If the brain would cooperate, so would she.

The trail plunged down through the woods past patches of dull meadows and frozen ponds rimmed with brush and brown grass. If amateur and professional and student painters waited every afternoon to enter one lush garden in Giverny, why didn't they come here? No crowds. Everybody could spread out. Giverny might have Claude Monet to make its reflections and colors famous, but there was enough variety in the Flat Tops to provide a painter plenty of work to capture an ever-rotating show of texture, light and color. The Flat Tops also kept a mix of scenery in its bag of tricks. Lakes nestled in deep bowls. Giant swaths of open, flat scrub at high elevations. Every wildflower exhibited more nuance and color options than a paint store.

Hiking around the San Juans or the Elks, where 14,000-foot peaks loomed high overhead, you felt as if you were missing something by not going for the summit. In the Flat Tops, the idea of a summit was moot. You could hike to the top of Derby or Turret—and the views were spectacular—but the peaks were humble and low-key, like the friend who drives out to the airport during your two-hour layover at 1 a.m. only to say hello and give you a hug. These were mountains without the machismo.

Colin stopped. They were at the base of a cliff. The top was bathed in mid-afternoon light, the bottom two-thirds cloaked in shade.

"Good place to tie up the horses," said Colin, dismounting. Allison followed suit.

Wind brushed the treetops. A whiff of something like grandma's fine linen closet floated on the air—cedar and allspice. Colin stepped close and Allison found herself inhaling even more, hoping for a lung full of him.

"Just gotta hike back along the base of the cliff, and there's a ledge you can follow that takes you up," said Colin. There was something a touch savage about him—steely and inscrutable— that added to his wild factor. It was an ability to decide, to just do.

The Grand Canyon would have laughed at this cliff. The Matterhorn, being Swiss, would have scoffed politely. But it was a cliff, not quite sheer but a steep wedge of thick limestone that jutted up and leaned back from the forest floor.

"Fig Newton?" said Colin.

"My weakness," said Allison.

"Didn't know you had any."

"There's a long list, I'm afraid. Tequila might even have the edge over Fig Newtons."

"Want some?" said Colin.

"I know you packed well," said Allison.

"Always prepared."

Allison studied Colin's face. Not a wisp of sarcasm ruffled its way across his eyes.

"Not right now," said Allison. A daytime buzz could lead directly to an overwhelming desire to take a nap, especially given her nearly empty tank.

"It'll keep," said Colin.

The trail was flat and meandered back in the dense woods. The cliff face and its intimidating disposition loomed overhead to her right. She didn't look up. She could feel its presence, taunting her. The trail ended abruptly at a collection of stone and rubble, almost like tailings from an old mine. The only way to keep moving on foot was to step from dirt trail to a rock ledge. Ledge, in fact, was a loose term. At its most comforting, the stone foothold was two feet wide and offered plenty of room to stand. But from the section of shelf that Allison could see before it disappeared up and around the gentle curve in the cliff's face, two feet frequently narrowed down to half that much. A squirrel might step carefully. It would be like climbing a jagged, irregular staircase—and, of course, these "stairs" were banister-free. The ledge was pockmarked and jagged like it had been shelled by mortars. For a moment, Allison hoped Colin was kidding. Walking up would require full body contact with the cliff at all times, but Colin started climbing without hesitation. Apparently he had taken Allison's assurance about comfort with heights as fact.

Silly boy.

Colin was ten strides up when Allison took her first steps, keeping a wary and worried eye on the ground, which rapidly went from ankle-sprain-if-you fall height to severe-head-injury-if-you-fall height to you're-probably-a-goner. Colin motored up. The steady scraping of his feet faded in her ear.

She was close to being alone.

She would not be looking up.

She would not be looking down.

She wondered what sort of strength it might take to pound a hole in the cliff with her fists so she could fashion an instant handhold when the need arose. If her knuckles were rendered useless for life, it would be worth it. By now the earth, the last surface that provided assurance, was a faint memory.

The light shifted and Allison had the distinct impression that she had climbed higher than the treetops. A glance over her shoulder would confirm this, but she let her instinct serve as proof. Colin had floated up as if he were skipping along a sidewalk, and Allison wondered if savage genes also meant mountain-goat fearlessness. Every bit of science told her she had plenty of support. But it was damn hard to suppress the notion that a crazy internal congenital bad wiring of her leg muscles might suddenly propel her into the void. There was also the possibility that time would choose this moment to send the cliff face tumbling into the history of erosion on the Flat Tops.

The ledge turned a corner and traveled upward. Colin was standing on the ledge, relaxed.

"Doing okay?" he asked.

"Apparently I don't love heights," said Allison.

"You don't have to love them, just survive them. It's mind over matter."

"The mind says turn around."

"We're nearly there," said Colin. "And the ledge widens. Check this out."

Colin turned slowly so that his back was pressed to the cliff. His arm came around Allison and he pulled her close in a one-arm hug and pointed a couple of feet ahead where the rock ledge gave way to a brief patch where the stone was crushed and soft. A clear shoe print sat in vivid relief. It was the front of the sole but a stride ahead was a whole print. The first was a right, the second was a left.

"It matches," said Allison.

"Matches what?" said Colin.

"The one in the meadow, day after he tried to sneak up on me when I was camping. Same size, same print."

"And it's heading up," said Colin.

"What if he's here?"

"Then he can answer our questions. But I don't think he's here."

"Why?"

"You get into the cave where the ledge widens out. He would have heard us by now."

They stepped over the shoe print, reluctant to leave their own tracks. But there wasn't any way to conceal their presence—the surface of the ledge was sandy.

The ledge grew wide and the pitch eased. They stepped around a corner and stood on a sheet of solid rock. Allison's heart rate searched for neutral gear. She wasn't about to dangle her legs over the edge, but a bit of comfort wormed its way into her system. Treetops clustered like fuzzy bushes far below.

The entrance to the cave was an oval gap, Hobbit-sized. A ring of blackened rocks and a stack of firewood sat a few feet from the opening, ready for use. Allison couldn't imagine how he carried all the wood up here, unless he had access to a helicopter.

Colin knelt by the entrance.

"Hello!" he called sharply.

They waited, listening.

"What are the wilderness laws about breaking and entering?" asked Colin.

"It's not like he owns this place," said Allison. "He's a squatter."

Colin pulled a flashlight from his jacket.

"Well?" he said, and ducked inside. Allison followed.

The opening gave way to a much larger vestibule, but there wasn't room to stand up. Allison followed his beam as Colin crouch-walked. The footing was loose rock and sand. The passage led them up a few natural stair steps. The stairs ended in a rock that came up to Colin's chest. He grabbed it with both hands like he was parachuting out of an airplane, palms reaching for leverage on both sides, and kicked himself up. He turned around to give Allison a hand.

Allison stood up next to him as he swung his light around.

The room was jagged and uneven. The rock ceiling dipped and rose precariously. One wall was flat and tall, ten feet high. The opposite wall was rough and the space in front of it was low. You would need to crawl on your hands and knees to make use of it. A bed was there, piled with grass and fresh pine branches. The empty space was intensely quiet, the air stale and musty.

Three sticks leaned against the wall. Two were hefty, like walking sticks. The bottoms of both were worn. They looked like older models that had reached their mileage limit. Allison gripped the natural handhold on one, and concluded that Waldo of the Woods wasn't too tall and had small hands. The third stick was like a green wand that had been in a fire or two. It had been turned into a skewer. Allison picked it up, sniffed the tip, caught a whiff of meat, squirrel or rabbit. Next to the sticks was a hardwood slab, like a small cutting board. It was worn and charred in spots. Another whiff. This time, fish. On the ground was a pile of rabbit skins, a dozen or more, and nearby a large skin, probably elk, being prepared for rawhide. A flat, wide stone sat nearby and it was obviously used to scrape and clean the skins.

"Check this out," said Colin. He was kneeling in a corner. Amid all the survival gear he had found a plastic tackle box, duo-tone tan and brown. He unsnapped the latch. Inside was an assortment of discs in square plastic cases—smaller than a compact disc and bigger than a silver dollar, but not by much. There were custom batteries for a specialized camera—and some cables, cleaning cloths, small screwdrivers, pliers and a strap.

"Looks like our boy has a split personality," said Colin.

"Think these are blank or used?" asked Allison, holding up a disc.

"No clue," said Colin. He was repacking the tackle box.

"What do you make of this guy?" Allison said.

"He's neat—that's for damned sure. And he's keeping things

as simple as possible—nothing wasted, nothing stored long term. I'd say this was a base camp, but he might have others. What about you?"

"What about me?" said Allison.

"Any ideas?"

"If we wait long enough, I think we can have the conversation with him that Zamora wants."

"Maybe he stays here only when he's in this neck of the woods," said Colin.

"What's up with all the secrecy?" said Allison. "All the slipping around?"

"Just somebody taking the hermit thing to the limit, I suppose," said Colin. "Damn good job of it, if he's been living out here for any length of time."

"Could you do it?" asked Allison.

"Do you mean live with just the bare essentials?"

"Looks like no essentials," said Allison.

"If I had to, I suppose," said Colin. "But I can't think of a good reason to go to all the trouble—I mean you're pouring energy into scrounging for every morsel. You can probably never get ahead. In the thick of summer or early fall it might be okay, but it ain't easy, I'm sure of that."

"Anything else we need to do here?" said Allison. The cave air was closing in.

"Want to leave him a message?"

"Saying what?"

"Asking him if he knows anything about what happened to Keating."

"Got anything to write with?" said Allison.

They patted down pants and jackets. It didn't take long. No dice.

"That wasn't exactly planning ahead, was it?" said Allison.

Colin led the way back. Waldo would know he had been invaded.

Allison imagined riding back tomorrow and leaving a well-marked note at the bottom of the ledge. They could bring Zamora along, and he and Waldo could go toe to toe. The wristwatch burned a hole in her pocket, burned a wormhole in her brain, burned up every bit of logic about an accident and too much to drink. She'd need to get the watch to the sheriff, dreaded the thought of the time it would take to go all the way back to Meeker.

The descent from the ledge was equally unnerving. Allison tried to keep pace but Colin scurried on down, oblivious to the layers of danger all around. He waited at the bottom of the ledge and offered a hand as she hopped off the last step, her throat dry and heart doing double time. Allison figured ninety minutes had passed since they had left the horses. It was hard to tell down here, under the thick canopy, how much of the day was left. They would return to camp in the dark, Allison guessed. She flashed on putting a hefty dent in the tequila supply.

The walk down through the woods was brief. Merlin and Lightning were asleep.

"Good job on the cave hunch," said Allison.

"Lucky guess," said Colin. "Can't imagine what it's like to call that home, giving up all the comforts."

"Do you think he can make it through the winter?"

"Only if he's a helluva hunter and eats bugs by the bushel."

Allison unhitched Lightning, gave his head a hug, his brow a scratch. She spun him around, checked his saddle straps in preparation for mounting but pulled up short and let out a gasp.

Tucked neatly into Lightning's saddle straps was a sheet of rumpled paper. Allison didn't touch it. She didn't need to.

"You found me. Somebody is poisoning the water. We have to find out who. And why."

The handwriting matched that on the note with the map to Keating's elk kill.

Again there was a map. Three stars formed a rough triangle.
"You are here / My Cave."
"Your Camp / Oyster Lake."
"Poisoned Pool Below Coffin Lake."

5

It was the perfect time to be at the Glenwood Hot Springs—on a freezing night in the fall. Steam billowed and rolled above the ridiculously long pool. Trudy had an annual pass to the springs and she made good use of it. She went every week, incorporating convenient visits among her errands. She knew the low-key off hours. She could sense the peak times and, once she was in the pool, could drift away to find an isolated spot to zone out. Even a brief soak would lift her spirits. She loved seeing new tourists gasp at the size of the pool and dare each other to try the hot side. She liked to imagine that some of these travelers were from Kansas or Oklahoma, and envisioned them back at home remembering their magnificent dip in that beautiful pool, surrounded by high mountain ridges, and how they would tell their friends about their hair freezing in the cold night air while they enjoyed one of their most relaxing nights ever. She wanted every dip to be that special. She liked a spot out by the lap lanes where she could float alone and tell herself she was deep in the woods at a secret pond. Except for the occasional downshifting semi on the interstate nearby or a train whistle across the river, the fantasy worked. With your head tipped back and ears under water, the sound was muffled. Her body loved the heat. Her body ached for it.

"Do you come here often?" asked Jerry.

She was leading him away from clusters of families in the shallow end. Something was gnawing at her and she needed to put the issue on the table.

"I do," said Trudy. "I love this place. It's one of a kind. The sheer size of it. I can get lost here if the steam is right. You?"

"I like it okay," said Jerry. "But I don't go out of my way. I never acquired the soak gene."

"I didn't know there was one," said Trudy. Jerry circled his hands around her waist from behind as she did a slow-motion breaststroke. "I thought it was like the watching-a-campfire gene. Everybody's got it."

"I dunno," said Jerry. "I always felt like an overcooked noodle afterward. Guess I never got the point."

"There is no point," said Trudy. "It's widely known to be good for you—the Native Americans knew it way back when, and the Japanese, of course. Enough said. Look at their longevity. I think it's a connection with the volcanoes—all that energy, the sulfur and the power right from the earth's core."

"So there is a point."

"The point is to tap into what's right here in our backyard."

There had been brief exchanges like this all day.

Small disconnections.

Trudy tried not to be sensitive about it. They weren't comments that represented major rifts.

After the meeting, she and Jerry had headed back to his house, a small bungalow in downtown Glenwood Springs, four blocks from his store. Trudy had a brief, drunken tour of the house, a three-room affair that was "purposely tiny" for minimal energy waste and minimal care. The house had a wood-burning stove and shelves jammed with organic-themed cookbooks in the kitchen. The furnishings were minimalist too. A round oak dining table snuggled up against a small window. Two simple chairs and a pint-sized coffee table flanked the stove. The bedroom was plain, a bed and a small side table. Sex was in the air from the moment they were inside. Jerry made a move, turning to give her a wine-flavored kiss, and within minutes they were tumbling and exploring and Trudy lost herself in a whirlwind of sensations and found a magical space where her busy brain went blank and carefree. She gave herself over to the moment, to pleasure, to being alive. Jerry had rubbed her back with mint-scented body oil and praised her sincere style and core values.

She woke the next morning to Jerry cooking French toast. It was over the third cup of coffee that he brought up the 9/11 line of thinking, that the country had been "shocked and stunned" but hadn't fundamentally altered its lifestyle. It was a bit of a rant about "W" and the privatization of homeland security and how the president had misused a chance to inspire a change that would have amounted to a "wholesale shift" in the American lifestyle.

"That's what we need," he had said. "To shock Glenwood Springs." He said it with a wild look. "*A shock.*"

Trudy found an empty gap along the wall of the pool. Nobody else was lingering out here. She put her back to the wall and turned to face Jerry, who was nuzzling her neck. He pressed his hand further down her back and gently squeezed her rear.

"You are stunning when you roll out of bed," he said. "You don't need a drop of anything artificial." He pressed himself against her. "And you have a powerful effect on me. You are so giving, so generous."

"And gun shy," said Trudy.

"Not with your body," said Jerry. "Holy cow."

"That part has always been easy," said Trudy. "People should worry more about their minds and less about their bodies."

"So what do you mean about being gun shy?"

Jerry's digging hands eased up a bit. He backed away.

"About this shock idea."

"Shock and change," said Jerry.

"I need to know what I'm signed up for," said Trudy, edging away. "I thought I had signed up for an information campaign, but this morning it sounded more radical."

Jerry didn't move but Trudy could sense him recoil.

"Maybe a touch more than passing out pamphlets," he said.

"You said *shock*," said Trudy. "Take your pick—electroshock, toxic shock, shock therapy—they all mean a jolt. Shock implies pain."

"I didn't mean it like that," said Jerry.

"You said shock and stun."

"I did."

"I don't like others telling me how to live," said Trudy. She let the statement hang there, the words coated with steam.

"I don't want to tell anybody what to do," said Jerry.

"Then how does the shock work? Are you out to make suggestions or point fingers?"

"Are you having second thoughts?"

Trudy anticipated the question and she wanted to be firm. "Not yet." It was dark, but light from the pool's edge was ample enough to highlight Jerry's sincerity.

"I'm going on how I feel," said Jerry. "I'm going on the fact that I know someday we will all be living very different lives based on food, energy, cars and our relationship to the planet. Sometimes I get carried away or caught up, or both."

"But it sounds like you've got drama in mind, like street theater."

"I have change in mind," said Jerry. "All I can say for sure is that I want to be a part of moving the conversation forward, and I guess I was trying to get everybody's attention all at once, something that would grab people."

Jerry's tone shifted from worried to calm. The fire had died. "There are moments when I see it all—the entire transformation."

"You don't think it's already happening?"

Jerry swung around and leaned against the side of the pool so that they were shoulder to shoulder. "I think there's a difference between a change in advertising messages—you know, buying spray cleaner that has been declared green for some mysterious reason, and deciding to reduce your driving by a significant percentage—or deciding to never again buy food produced by the industrial system. Most of the revolutions going on today are glossy, surface changes—minor tweaks to the American lifestyle. And most of them are the result of commercial enterprises inserting themselves into the dialogue, trying to hold onto their part of the marketplace with superficial changes."

"But it didn't get that way overnight," said Trudy.

"I take it you're implying that it's not going to switch back right away either," said Jerry.

"Something like that."

A young couple floated past in the billowing steam. The woman was on her back, eyes closed, guided by a man who had his hands under her back. The man—young, football-player arms, dark eyes—gave Trudy a faint smile.

"And you don't want to be a part of something splashy?" asked Jerry.

"Not if it comes across as 'we know better' or anything like that," said Trudy. "It's fine to show people what's possible without being obnoxious."

"Changing ideas need publicity," said Jerry. "To gain traction you've got to find a way to drive the messages into everything we encounter—television, newspapers, advertising, the web. Door-to-door and polite suggestion doesn't work. This guy Bostwick is doing it, he's instigating reform, pushing an agenda. The right agenda."

"Perhaps," said Trudy.

"Seems to be."

"What if he's making a lot of enemies along the way?"

"People get stubborn, think they've got a God-given right to drive a Hummer as if gasoline was one of the things found in the Garden of Eden."

"And so?"

Was she being too sharp, staking out ground too firmly? Did she know what she was talking about?

Jerry studied his turf. "So you've got to meet these embedded habits and culture with something clear and definitive."

"Which brings us back to the shock thing," said Trudy.

"Tell you what," said Jerry. He put his arms around her in a hug and lifted her. There was a sly smile and a twinkle in his eye. "Why don't you go there and see what he's up to, see how he's getting it done."

"Go where?"

"Meeker," said Jerry.

"Me?" said Trudy.

"Yes," said Jerry. "Ask him about his campaign, ask how he's doing it and how it's going."

"By myself?" The idea of a school board meeting was daunting enough.

"Bring him some herbs—or see if he wants to help you break into the Meeker market. He's bound to have connections."

"Why don't you come with me?" Trudy felt a bubble of anxiety pop in her stomach, flooding every capillary.

"I could," said Jerry.

"Who says he's doing it the right way?"

"Nobody," said Jerry. "But he is prompting change, he's having an impact."

"He was in the paper this morning," said Trudy.

"He's a machine."

"But it wasn't for those reasons," said Trudy.

"When did you have time to read the paper?"

"There was a copy in the women's dressing room here," said Trudy. "In fact I was thinking about Allison because the same story mentioned her outfitting business. One of Allison's hunters was found dead. Very sad."

"What do you mean *found*?"

"They found him by a lake. They think he'd gotten lost and couldn't get back. They don't know."

"Sad," said Jerry. "Wow. What's the connection?"

"He was Ethan Bostwick's neighbor. Bostwick and the guy they found by the lake had not been getting along, like feuding families."

"Are you worried about Allison?"

"Always," said Trudy. "When she's up there, I'm worried. But I know she can handle it. She can handle pretty much anything."

Whenever she thought of Allison up in the Flat Tops during the late fall, she ran the same film clip in her mind—a woman sitting tall on horseback, swallowed whole by a whiteout as she rode into the teeth of a brewing storm. Trudy knew to avoid imagining what Allison might or might not be going through—Allison always walked out of the dark storms intact and nonplussed. Compared to Allison's tenacity, Trudy felt like a meek recluse. For a flash, Trudy pictured herself in a quiet chat with Ethan Bostwick, pictured herself cool and comfortable and jotting down a few notes, absorbing the recipe for change to bring back to Glenwood Springs. It was brief, but the image lingered pleasantly.

Jerry pulled her close, fell backward and took her under the water, rolling her slowly and pressing his chest against hers. Trudy wrapped her arms around his neck as he took a few underwater strokes and she was flying, weightless and free and warm.

When, after all, was true character revealed? And how? Was it over time? How much? Here she was at the starting line of another relationship, and what did she know about the other human being who was starting to occupy the space around her and was angling for the right to see if there was something there that would click and sustain itself beyond the first flurry of infatuation?

They sat on the steps leading down into the hot pool. The

lengthy side of the vast pool was composed of underwater steps, like bleachers at the side of a gymnasium. Pick your step and decide how much skin to submerge and how much skin to let cool in the night air. Jerry sat with his waist beneath the surface. Steam poured off his exposed back, and he smiled a characteristic smile of ease and comfort and openness.

"So what should I ask him?"

"Are you going alone?"

"Unless you want to join me," said Trudy. "It might seem more like a delegation, even if it's an unofficial one. It might give us more clout."

"You don't want to go by yourself," said Jerry. His toes touched hers underneath the water, then he slipped down and turned over so his body stretched up the stairs and he was completely underwater except for his head, which still generated steam. Jerry kissed the top of her thigh, a quick peck on the outside below her hip bone. He gave her another smile. "Well?"

"I'd rather go as a team."

"We'll call him in the morning," said Jerry. "All we need is an hour of his time. Takes an hour to get there, another hour back. What better do we have to do?"

"Better?" said Trudy. "What do you mean better?" She tried on one of her own giving smiles.

"You can't fuck all day," said Jerry. He mouthed the verb.

"You can't?"

"I guess if you take one of those drugs then you might have a chance," he said.

"Poor men," said Trudy. "Needing drugs."

"Does that mean you'll spend another night?"

"I've gotta go home and check on the cats—but it doesn't mean I have to go right away. We can go to Meeker on Monday."

"Then I'm the luckiest man alive."

"No more talk of shock treatment?"

"None," said Jerry.

"Are you sure?"

"You know, you're kind of assuming that I'm the leader or something," he said. "Who's to say I'm not the one learning from you?"

Trudy slid down into the scalding heat. The frozen night air had iced up her wet hair and she went completely under to melt the icy chunks.

Sunday Morning

It was dawn. Seven horses waited outside the hunters' tent. She was in there. If Devo knew her at all, she'd be on a mission to Coffin Lake. He had no idea what foul substance the spooky backpacker had poured into the pool below the lake. Devo had circled back later and sat by the pool in the dark. He had cupped water in his hands and could smell the poison. His anger grew. It had been awhile since he'd been angry about anything out here in the wilderness and he recorded a seething video by the fire outside his cave. He wanted his complete version of events recorded as soon as possible so time wouldn't blur his memory. This was war. He had been attacked. This was knife-to-the-heart stuff. The smell of the water in his cupped palm had been instantly noxious. He didn't even like the fact that he'd put his hands in it, concerned that it might start to sting.

He had spent a nearly sleepless night trying to imagine the reason, wondering if there was any connection with the dead hunter, and thinking about how to track the man with the backpack again and—what? Several possibilities occurred to him, but they were based on such long-misplaced emotions that he wasn't sure what to do with them. Survival transferred his focus and energy to other needs, like food and warmth.

Not being around other humans had altered his mental state. The issue was self-consciousness. In the beginning, during the first few weeks alone, he was conscious of recording every thought. His inner voice pounded him hard. The voice second-guessed his every decision. For the purposes of the video diary, and remembering the days and keeping track of what he was learning, it was good to have the brain in full-alert mode. But something had happened after two weeks. The nerves calmed down. He realized he actually could accomplish this. He was no longer anxious. He had stripped his life down to basic needs. His mind shut up and his body took over. On his most productive days, his senses lit up. He would work hard for three hours and realize he'd been living in a dead zone, a vacuum of thoughts other than "dig this hole" or "set this trap" or "sharpen these sticks." The first time it happened, he was building a trap on a deer trail. The work netted a small doe on the first day. The doe kept him nourished for three weeks as he slipped further down into being at one with his surroundings. It wasn't as if he had forgotten the elements of city life, but they no longer held any relevance. They were parked on a shelf, gathering dust.

No more.

It was full dawn now, that gentle half-hour that invited introspection. Devo stood up and stretched, pulled a hunk of smoked elk from his pocket and gnawed on the dry meat. He kept his eye on the hunters' tent but moved out of his hiding spot in the woods to squat by the banks of Oyster Lake, not far from where the man had died.

After he had drawn a mental map of the drainage from Coffin Lake, he chipped through the ice with his Becker TacTool knife. He sniffed the water first, but detected nothing. A horse nickered in the distance, the sound muffled by the thicket of woods around the camp.

Devo moved closer to the camp. One of the hunters was standing by a tree a hundred yards away and taking a piss. The hunter was staring right at him, but Devo knew he was invisible. The hunter finished and zipped up. He was bigger than the man who had visited his cave with the woman. He was a few inches taller. He was older and walked with a determined gait.

By the time the hunter was back at the spot where the horses were hitched, the woman was there with the same man who had been at the cave. The man couldn't be very old, but he seemed completely comfortable out in the woods.

Low voices sliced through the morning air. No words were discernible, only distinct grunts. The men were talking. Puffs of air popped from their mouths. The woman stepped away, went to the other side of the tent and emerged a minute later with a cluster of bags draped in her hand—feed for the horses. All the horses ate together. Devo thought about the hunters' camp—city life in microcosm, right down to the horse feed and creature comforts for the hunters, liquor and other extraneous goodies. As if on cue, a fourth figure emerged from the tent carrying pots and cups, pouring coffee all around. They stood for a few minutes sipping, then the woman and her companion went to retrieve saddles. The hunter with the coffee pot headed back inside. Devo put his nose to the air and caught a pleasing whiff of brew.

The smell brought back memories of his work as a barista, where he had survived a whole nine months. It was one of his better gigs, an independent coffee shop in lower downtown Denver. He was Nick Timms then, back in another life. Back on the topside. He had learned everything there was to know about French roast, Italian roast, lattes, cappuccinos and Americanos. He had learned to make swirl patterns in the foam—lips, stars, diamonds and fancy squiggles. The women loved that as well as his memory—mixing their drinks the moment they walked in the door, extra shots of espresso with the Guatemalan blend for this customer, decaf hazelnut soy for that customer. It was during this job, after a series of not-so-successful stints at everything from bicycle messenger to pizza cook, that he realized how specialized the world had become. Also, how silly. Everybody wanting their coffee fixed a certain way, everybody saying his name, knowing his name, treating him like a coffee god because of his ability to line up drinks in all their myriad forms. For each of his customers, he was on center stage for forty-five seconds each day and it felt good. It stroked his acting ego. He had performed with local theater companies, had kept his eye out for television-commercial auditions, and for scenes in Denver involving Hollywood productions. But he never got anything beyond bit-part roles.

And then in walked Karen, applying for work to brew and pour coffee following her fifteen minutes of national fame as the runner-up on a national reality show which threw twenty men and women into the wilds and let them scrap and claw and try to survive while the cameras watched. Each week, a contestant was voted off after another round of major group psychodrama and athletic competition. Karen's show was shot on an island in the Maldives. She had survived until the final vote. The whole country had watched her prance around on the beach, negotiating interpersonal political deals with the ever-shrinking group of contestants. From the first episode, her small, provocative and increasingly loose-fitting red bikini made her hard to miss. The whole country knew every contour of her body. It was no longer a question that her boobs were surgically enhanced—they were the only parts of her body that looked the same at the beginning of the show as they did by the show's wrap. Devo was envious of the easy path to fame for the whole cast. They were "stars" on a TV show about surviving, and the producers actually preferred it if you didn't know too much, for instance, about starting a fire without matches. How was that for proof that specialization was taking over?

Karen had survived by playing nice, helping out, being low key. She had won a fat check, but not the million dollars. And now here she was in the coffee shop where Devo worked, learning about drips and grinds. The coffee shop was getting mentioned in the local newspaper and on TV, and Devo could see new customers in line. Most of these customers turned out to be only one-timers who pointed and gawked at Karen, their reality-show prize catch. It was like a zoo.

And then something clicked. Devo considered it magic that he had put two and two together. If the reality version of "surviving" was a ratings bonanza, what about a real reality show for the web about surviving, about somebody who tested the outer limits of life in the wild? About devolution. About taking society back in time to an era of individualism and self-sufficiency.

Devo sniffed the air again for a whiff of coffee.

He laughed.

Was he some sort of wine snob, looking for the subtle flavors in a ten-year-old cabernet?

The sheer fact that he had tried to identify the scent, that he wanted to put a name on it, was absurd. The brain reflex slammed him back to city life, such a distant concept that he knew now how much he had been transformed down deep inside.

He laughed again.

And tried to catch himself.

Too late.

The three people by the horses were staring straight at him.

He was no longer invisible.

They were coming his way and they weren't walking.

They were running.

Sunday Morning

Caveman. Meat Delivery Man. Waldo.

Him.

Allison knew it the second she spotted him. Her eyes found the sound. The sound came from a dull brown face. The morning light hit the face like a tailing spot. The comprehension came in a split second and Allison was running, flinging her coffee cup aside. Her boots thudded on the tamped-down dirt near the tent and her steps went soft but hardly quiet as she moved into the trees.

Colin passed her in a blip. She thought she heard Colin utter something like "Got him," and then there was a good-sized gap, and all Allison could see were Colin's legs cutting around the trees. The terrain rose at a steep angle but Colin could have been running on a perfectly groomed Olympic track in ideal conditions.

"Holy crap," said Zamora, pulling up behind her as she slowed to a walk, her lungs burning.

"See him?" said Allison.

"A blur," said Zamora. "It was our visitor, right?"

"Who else could it be?"

"The fucker had better come clean."

Allison pushed herself to keep running. The two were suddenly on a steep slope like climbing stairs. Nobody could run when the grade was this steep, but clearly the grade hadn't bothered Colin. Add sprinter to the list of his abilities. Who would have guessed?

Allison's thighs burned. They climbed through a dense stand of aspens, then the slope became more forgiving and finally went flat and the trees gave way to a meadow thirty yards across. The bead they had drawn was now gone. Allison dropped to her knees and looked for a disturbance in the ground, her heart beating hard and her focus slipping. Zamora came up behind her, near death from the way he was wheezing.

"Anything?" he gasped.

Allison answered by standing up, her gaze still on the ground. She stepped away a few paces and squatted down, putting her hands up to shield the morning light. There. A pattern of chopped-up grass and leaves, pockets of shadow lined up and pointed the way.

"Let's go," she said.

"No need," said Zamora, gazing across the clearing.

Out of the woods came Colin and Caveman. There was no sign of coercion, no rope around Caveman's wrists. They could have been two buddies out for a hike, except one buddy was your basic Colorado cowboy, and the other was part troglodyte.

Caveman's face was bronzed, edging toward black. Underneath his Colorado Rockies baseball cap, his hair had gone to dreadlocks, clumps of brown knots dangling down to his shoulders. His sunken cheeks said everything about his physical condition. His body and frame wouldn't take up much space in the world even if he spent the next month on a diet of grandma's home cooking. He was shorter than Colin. He was wearing furs and leather that overlapped and flopped as he moved, although the cutting and stitching indicated the clothes had been tailored to his body. He was a pint-sized Sasquatch who had raided Daniel Boone's used clothes. The look on his face was flat, but Allison detected uncertainty and fear in his black, tired eyes.

They were within a few feet. Colin had been keeping a distance between himself and Caveman, and now Allison understood why. A thick brew of stink preceded Caveman's arrival. Allison flashed on Pigpen from *Peanuts* bearing a cloud of reek.

"Holy..." muttered Zamora behind her. Allison could think of several appropriate words to fill in the blank. "Cow" wasn't the first that came to mind.

She didn't know what to feel on finally seeing Caveman, but

she spun through the options from anger to bewilderment to satisfaction.

"He stopped on his own," said Colin. "Otherwise I wouldn't have caught up."

"Greetings," said Allison.

"To hell with the pleasantries," said Zamora. "Why the fuck did you kill our friend?"

"Whoa, whoa," said Caveman. "Not me. I found him on the rocks before you did, but the last time I saw him alive he was shooting his elk."

"You were following him," said Zamora.

"I saw where he hung up his elk," said Caveman. "I got myself a little dinner. Took some meat and went home."

Caveman's gaze pleaded with Allison to bail him out.

"Why did you come back to our camp the next morning?" she asked him.

"If I had anything to do with it, I'd still be running. In fact, I never would have come around."

"Did you leave the meat and the map?" demanded Zamora. His voice still had an angry edge.

"Yeah," he said.

"Look," said Allison. "Let's start over. What's your name?"

Caveman took a moment to look around, then sighed.

"They call me Devo."

"Devo?" said Zamora.

"Like the band?" said Allison.

"I suppose," said Devo. He shrugged, flashed a slight smile.

"Back in the eighties," said Colin. "My dad liked them. They had a version of the Stones song, 'Satisfaction.' You know, 'I Can't Get No.'"

"That's what we need," said Zamora. "Satisfaction."

"Some people thought they were a joke," said Colin.

"I'm not," said Devo. "Devo is my YouTube name. I've got a channel going—26 episodes so far. A quarter-million downloads."

Allison had spent less time on the Internet than a cloistered nun, but she knew that was a plump number, which meant Waldo-Caveman-Devo had a following. Or a flock. How Devo managed to know his own web-traffic numbers was a curiosity that scampered to the top of her long list of questions, including the one about the neatly buried buffalo wristwatch.

"So you say you followed Josh Keating the other day when he shot the elk," said Allison, trying not to sound as confrontational as Zamora.

"Yeah," said Devo.

"Why in the world would you do that?" said Zamora.

"I like to keep track of what's going on out here," Devo said. "Practice my tracking skills."

"Why him? There's hundreds of hunters up here."

Devo looked as if this might be a good time to return to sprint mode. His gaze landed on Allison. She thought she spotted a touch of remorse.

"Only because of her," said Devo.

"Her?" said Zamora, jacking a thumb at Allison.

"You don't see too many women up here pitching a tent in the wilderness. I came back to get my hat and then, well, she was different."

"Is different," said Allison.

"Didn't mean nothing," said Devo. "Yes—is."

"No problem," said Allison. "I'm flattered. I didn't know I was a caveman magnet."

Devo smiled a caught-off-guard smile and Colin laughed. Zamora looked around confused.

"I thought you might be a recruit," said Devo.

"A what?" said Allison.

"A recruit. What's your name?"

"Allison—and this is Terry and Colin."

"Nice to meet you," said Devo, who was staring at her. "You look so capable, so comfortable in the outdoors. I thought you might want to join me on the ride, showing people in the city how to get back to the earth. The invitation is open." There was a flash of excitement in Devo's ragged, recessed eyes.

If the ride meant no tequila, if it meant living in the same zip code as this foul-smelling human, if it meant no cotton sheets, and if it meant never sitting at Trudy's table and enjoying a bounty of fascinating food creations, then it wasn't a decision at all.

"No, thanks," said Allison.

"Always an option," said Devo.

"But why follow Keating?" asked Zamora, getting back to brass tacks.

"Same reason as I do it during muzzle-loading season, and archery too. Meat. Most hunters do okay with gutting out the kills, but sometimes they leave edible scraps lying around."

"Did you see anything?" said Colin.

"Anything about how your friend died, you mean?" said Devo. "No, I saw him on the rocks—already passed away. I am very sorry for your loss. So you don't know what happened either?"

"There are various theories," said Colin.

"He might have tripped," said Allison. But she didn't sound convincing.

"Tripped and died?" said Devo.

"It was late at night," said Zamora. "Tripped, knocked out and froze."

Which wouldn't explain the wristwatch. Frozen dead guys don't take off their watch and embed it neatly in the soil. Allison hadn't mentioned the watch to Zamora or anyone else. After she and Colin had returned to camp the previous night, she had turned in, aided by a blue pill that dragged her to sleep. All she noticed before she lost consciousness was that Rayburn kept close to his supplies and Hiatt tried but failed to get a conversation going. Their scouting had been fruitless, she knew that much. She needed to get the watch to the cops, and explain where and how she found it.

"What's this about the water?" said Allison. To Devo, Colin and Zamora didn't exist. "We found your note."

"That's why I stopped," said Devo. "You are my first human contact other than a couple of accidental encounters during the last six months. But now I need help. I saw somebody pouring nasty stuff into a pool. A fast-moving guy with an oversized backpack. He was completely out of place."

"And he stopped at Coffin Lake?" said Colin.

"Like he knew exactly where he wanted to hit," said Devo. "I was thinking later about the way he moved. He went right past a few other lakes, some other ponds and creeks too. He was on a mission, and seemed to know exactly where he was going."

"I thought you said you were trying to avoid human contact," said Zamora.

"I didn't like the way he moved," said Devo.

"Did he see you?" said Zamora.

"Yeah, but then I was gone. I just took off."

"Nobody's going to catch Devo if he doesn't want to be caught," said Colin. It was one sprinter praising another, like a couple of Olympians hugging on the stand.

"I've learned how to move fast," said Devo. "Especially in thick cover."

"I'll say," said Colin. Devo and Colin exchanged mutual-admiration smiles. "This dude is one quick mother."

Add diplomat to Colin's list of skills. The scant smile he had extracted from Devo took the tension down a notch. Even Zamora relaxed.

"So you haven't reported anything about the water?" said Allison.

"I did," said Devo. "To you three. That's why I stopped. I don't like anyone messing with the Flat Tops."

A man after my own heart, thought Allison. She wasn't crazy enough to say it out loud, to give him another reason for any connection he thought they might have.

"Did you know Keating was sick—real sick—the day before he died?" asked Zamora. "He said he had drunk from a spring."

"I didn't know that, no," said Devo. "How would I?"

"You know everything else," said Zamora.

"Only what I see," said Devo. "I wish I did know something about your friend but I don't. You gotta get somebody up here to find out who is messing with the water."

"And why," said Zamora. "That's sick."

"Who and why," said Devo. "That'd be good. And now, I gotta go."

"Why?" said Allison.

"Overstayed already," said Devo. "I wanted to make sure you knew the note was for real, and that there was urgency. So I broke my own rules."

"How long are you going to be up here?" said Allison.

"Don't know. Long time, I suppose."

"Food?"

"You can see a whole chapter on YouTube. Barbecued squirrel. Making bark nutritious. Hidden nuts and late-season berries. It's all there."

"Warmth?"

Allison found herself worrying for his safety. His mission was risky.

"If I could make it through last week, I can make it through anything," said Devo. "It might have cost me another pound or two, but it only makes me tougher for the next go-round."

"And you have somebody up here taking videos too?" asked Zamora.

"Of course not," said Devo. "I take them myself."

"But no video of the guy at Coffin Lake?" asked Allison.

"I wish," said Devo. "Mostly they are video diary kinds of things I shoot back at the cave, especially now in the cold. The camera doesn't like being outside the cave. And that day I had to run. I would have left it somewhere anyway. It's not an easy rig to carry when you're crashing through the woods. Really—I gotta go now."

"Wait," said Allison. "What about recharging batteries, what about tapes for your camera—and how does your stuff get out of here?"

Devo thought it over, clearly unsure if he was revealing too much.

"Come with me and I'll show you," said Devo.

"I don't like any of this," said Zamora, whose vibes were obvious. "My friend is dead and we're talking about YouTube videos. And Devo here knows nothing? He followed Keating when he shot the elk, and he was there the morning after. He's all over the fucking woods and he knows nothing about how Josh died? I say we let the authorities sort it out."

Zamora made a move toward Devo. It was a small step, but given the size difference between them, Zamora's move was King Kong-esque.

Devo took two light hops back. He stopped. He was staring at Zamora. His expression was blank.

"Somebody's poisoning the water," said Devo. "Find him. If I see something move, I'll let you know."

Devo inched back a few more steps. Zamora strained forward like a bird dog waiting for a signal to be released.

For a moment the four of them were motionless. Colin was a bystander. Devo and Zamora were locked in a staring contest.

Devo had decided to take the meeting, as they said in the city, and he would adjourn matters on his terms.

"Stay in touch," said Colin. "And by the way, you've got every bit of my respect, hanging around out here the way you do." If Colin had a drink in his hand, he might have offered a toast. Allison couldn't imagine two people with more contrasting body languages than Colin and Zamora—the latter like a hyper bulldog, the former a trusting and relaxed sheepdog.

"Find him," said Devo. He took two steps backward, turned confidently, started walking toward the woods and then slipped behind a tree and was gone.

"Jesus," said Zamora. "Probably never see him again."

"Doesn't matter," said Allison. "I think he was telling the truth."

Sunday Midday

Allison lifted her cupped palm from the icy pool below Coffin Lake. She put the water to her nose and inhaled. Next to her, Colin did the same.

"Smell anything?" asked Allison.

"I don't know," said Colin.

Was there something acrid, something off? Or was that her imagination? She closed her eyes and took another whiff. There was a faint hint of something impure.

Colin lowered a Nalgene bottle into the pool and filled it up. "Maybe the poison doesn't linger, gets flushed out after a day or two."

"Do you know this drainage?" said Allison. "Where it goes?"

"North," said Colin. "It must end up at Trapper's Lake, one way or another."

"Is there any point in following the creek down?"

"That would be thick and slow going," said Colin.

"Any payoff?" said Allison. "Another sample from downstream?"

"I think it would be diluted," said Colin. "I wish we had a sample of whatever Jesse drank on the same day he drank it."

"Is this the area where Jesse said he got sick?"

"Same area."

"Do you believe Devo?" said Allison.

"Why wouldn't I?" said Colin. "Sounded like he knew what he was saying. And he seemed determined to alert us."

"It's hard to believe."

"It would explain a lot, though. I didn't know you were suspicious."

"Just thinking. Trying to see if we've got one-plus-one equals three."

"Or if we've got three separate ones that should not be added together." Colin flashed a thin smile, showing his eyeteeth, white and prominent along with their well-formed neighbors.

"Three?" said Allison.

"Three," said Colin.

"Keating, one," said Allison. "Bad water, two."

"Keating and his neighbor, Bostwick," said Colin. "Three. Everybody in the valley knows it's ugly."

"Ugly enough?"

"Enough to mean it might not have been an accident," said Colin. "We're talking enemies."

"What's it all about?"

"Two different ways of seeing the world," said Colin. "Whether Meeker and the West should be more environmentally aware. And now there's this lawsuit that would grab some of Bostwick's land. Retaliation, I would guess, to bully Bostwick out of town."

"Where does Rayburn fit in?" said Allison.

"What are you getting at?"

"Is he well known?"

"I know he spends a lot of time out at Keating's ranch, helping out. Drives a dump truck for the city. And every year he's in the event when they reenact the famous bank robbery from 1896. He plays the robber named John Law."

"John Law? You are kidding."

"Law dies like his other two robber friends, although it takes him longer to kick the bucket. He was running toward the river when they plugged him. I guess he was alive for an hour but nobody tried that hard to save him—or couldn't. All the money was recovered. It was pretty cool."

"But where does Rayburn fit in with the neighbor feud?"

Colin shook his head. "All I know is it's old versus new, black versus white, wolverine versus bear."

"That's not a pretty picture," said Allison.

"You get the idea."

They scrambled back up the rocks toward the shore of Coffin Lake where the horses were tied.

"I saw a wolverine once," said Allison.

Colin stopped. "You did not."

"Did."

"I'm dying to see one."

"I'd like to see him again," said Allison. "Been back to the spot many times. Nothing."

"Where was it?"

"Over by Stillwater Reservoir. It was about dusk. Coming back over the ridge. He popped out of a bush, stood up on his back legs like a small bear with a raccoon face. Like an evolutionary mistake. You talk about ugly and mean looking. And then he was gone."

"No doubt?"

"First and only thought was 'wolverine.' The whole sighting lasted about ten seconds."

"I'm jealous," said Colin. "Big time."

"I can show you the spot."

"I don't want to see the spot, I want to see the wolverine."

"We'll go camp there," said Allison. "You and me. Set up a wolverine blind, take pictures …" *And I'll spend the nights licking your teeth*, she thought.

What was wrong with her? She should be adding up one plus one plus one, but she was more concerned about tugging the boots off this ever-present distraction. She now knew the meaning of the word *fixation*. That's when a relentless thought coated your brain in a thick goo that dripped down over the inner eye and the inner ear and the part of the inner brain that decided what to think about, and conveniently modified every sight, sound and incoming message.

"So the feud between Keating and this guy Bostwick, was it that bad?" asked Allison.

"Nasty, clenched teeth. A ton of anger."

"Does Bostwick have any support?"

"Not much. I don't think people around Meeker saw any need for what he was selling—or pushing."

"Nobody?" said Allison.

"Maybe they saw the need to make some changes, or understood why change might not be a bad thing," said Colin. "But they hated being told they must change. Meeker ain't Boulder."

Allison bashed surface ice on the edge of Coffin Lake with the heel of her boot. Colin dropped rocks on the ice nearby. Merlin honed in on the water from where Colin's rocks had broken through. Lightning showed no interest.

"After all my work?" Allison admonished Lightning. Standing next to him, she gave his rein a gentle tug, but she might as well have been tugging a skyscraper.

"Lightning must have heard all this talk about bad water," said Allison. "And I still can't understand why Zamora didn't wait for us to come back with the sample."

Zamora had taken a horse down to Trapper's Lake and was bound for Meeker on the double. He wanted the sheriff involved. There was no waiting. He was revved up and pissed off. His actions were disconnected from Devo's grounded, calm account. There was something so slight and impish about Devo that she couldn't picture him getting the upper hand with Keating, drunk or sober.

"Speaking of which," said Colin, "should we go down tonight and be ready to turn this over first thing?"

"You and me?" she said. She smiled, perhaps a touch more than necessary.

"Yeah," said Colin. "You and me. We've gotta get this water tested—the sooner the better."

"Might run smack into Zamora."

"Zamora's got theories. But we've got something they can actually use," said Colin. "Something to test. We can stay at my folks' place."

"Or a motel," said Allison. "Right near downtown."

The look on Colin's face suggested he wasn't about to ask, "One room or two?"

Sunday Afternoon

Allison's debilitated hunting guide Jesse was awake, propped up a few inches past full horizontal. He made reassuring comments about feeling better and offered proof by eating a cracker with peanut butter in her presence. Hiatt led a cleanup campaign. The tent's interior was spiffy, shipshape. It didn't take much for a bunch of grown men to make a hunting tent look like a Saturday night at the frat in *Animal House*. This tent could have been used for a catalog shot from Cabela's. Hiatt and Gray were the frenzy twins. Allison chalked it up to boredom. She and Colin paid compliments to the effort. They were making a final push with the kitchen supplies. Allison brought Jesse a cup of hot tea.

"Are you well enough to head down and see a doctor?" she asked.

The calculations in her head added up to quiet time with Colin and a six-pack of beer by nine p.m. Three hours to Trapper's Lake, an hour to load Colin's truck and get the horses put up, and then a couple hours down the hill and into Meeker.

Finding Jesse a doctor and explaining everything would add time. But Jesse's suffering made her ache and she had a strong urge to insist that he head down if he could.

"I'll tough it out," said Jesse. "But my record for sitting up is only twenty minutes. The guys want to go hunting."

"They do?" she said. Hiatt was repacking a storage bin with dried foods. Gray was scrubbing a frying pan.

"We're heading out as soon as we're done here," said Gray. "We were waiting for you and Colin to come back and figured we'd fill the time by doing something productive."

Allison did the math in her head. Carry the two, divide by infinity, multiply by the number of motel-room occupants. The loneliest number was one.

"I'm glad you think it's time to hunt," said Allison. It was all she could do to muster the words.

"We can't wallow around here another day," said Hiatt. "It was either call it a season or do what we came here to do."

"It was Jesse who suggested it," said Hiatt.

"In one of his more lucid moments," said Gray. "In between fevers."

Hiatt laughed. "Mostly he's been a lump—"

"Hey," said Jesse. "I'll trade stomachs and intestines with anyone right now. I'll even skip the anesthesia to give them to you."

"Like I said, a complaining lump," said Hiatt. "But then he suggested we get on with the show, and even thought he might lead us—but that was all talk."

"At least I got you off your duffs," said Jesse, rolling over. "And got your sorry asses out of my face."

It didn't take a doctorate in psychology to know that the faux put-downs meant Allison had missed a round of the all-American sport of male bonding. Jesse must have stepped up his game in this arena, because he was usually so mild-mannered and lived on the perimeter of social interaction. This was a side of him she hadn't seen before.

"Zamora's long gone?" said Allison.

"He headed down a few hours ago," said Hiatt. "He'll be chewing on a cop's ear any minute now."

"Do you think they'll listen to him?"

"The man makes a compelling argument, particularly if somebody is purposely wrecking the water supply," said Hiatt.

Allison had a hard time imagining where the cops would start, but finding Devo and then getting on the trail of the guy he had spotted might yield a few breadcrumbs. She wasn't sure exactly how they would do that, but there was plenty of reason to get organized and do something. The quality of the water supply was everything—the same as anywhere. The folks in Meeker and Buford were sucking from the same straw and the straw was shoved down into what flowed off the Flat Tops.

She found Colin out by the horses, checking their coats and feedbags.

"Got a coin?" she asked.

"What for?"

"We're flipping for which one of us gets to stay here."

"What gives?"

She was looking for it and there it was—a flinch of disappointment on his face. They were standing between Merlin and Lightning in their own private horsehide chamber.

"Work," she said.

"What do you mean?"

Allison put a hand on Colin's shoulder. She could sense his change-of-plans droop.

"I mean if you got a coin we can flip for who gets to guide the hunt, and who's heading to Meeker. The boys want to hunt."

"Today?" said Colin, dumbfounded.

"Now," said Allison. "Rifles being cleaned up as we speak. I saw Hiatt getting his Weatherby out a moment ago."

Colin sighed. "What a messed-up deal."

Her hand was still on his shoulder, a few inches higher than her own.

"Gotta keep the customers satisfied," said Allison. "As much as that sucks right now."

"They ought to be two miles from here by this time of day, with a good spot scoped out," said Colin. "Unless we get lucky and stumble onto something, today will be just for show."

"Or scouting," said Allison.

"Even the places to scout you can barely reach before dark," said Colin.

"They want to feel busy, I suspect," said Allison. "Keating managed a kill between lunch and sunset. All I know is they paid for a guide, they expect a guide, and it's going to be either you or me, as much as we'd both rather head down the hill."

"Speaking of which," said Colin, "who are you planning to give the tainted water to?"

"I haven't figured that out yet," said Allison. "I thought I'd let the sheriff know, and then the health department. It should be easy to find somebody who wants to test it. But Meeker isn't exactly my turf."

"And the wristwatch?" said Colin.

"I don't know what to think about the watch."

They had long ago agreed to keep the existence of the wristwatch from the others in camp.

"If Zamora gets his way, the sheriff and his men will be scrambling up here to find Devo at dawn," said Colin.

"If," said Allison. "I've never known a cop who loved being told what to do or how to do it. Somebody will want to test the water, especially when the bad stuff is upstream of where they live. Are we going to flip for it? Gray and Hiatt probably got all their orange gear on by now."

"No need to flip," said Colin. "I'll stay. I know one spot to check, off to the east in the direction of Stillwater. We'll need to get going."

"You can search for wolverines," said Allison.

"I'm always on the lookout for wolverines," said Colin. "But we need to get going."

As if on cue, Gray and Hiatt emerged from the tent with rifles in hand. Allison gave Colin a quick, light hug. She said softly, "I wish you were coming with," and then let him go. He smiled. It was slight, but he smiled.

The sky was blue but bony fingers of blackish clouds sliced the sky from the west. Allison would have to hurry to get all the way down to Meeker before the world closed in.

She checked one more time on Jesse, who offered heaping reassurances, despite his lack of interest in moving about. She prepped Lightning, the Nalgene bottle of bad water safely stuffed into a saddlebag. Allison climbed up on Lightning and steered him around to the spot where Colin and the hunters were huddling, checking their gear.

"Follow your noses," said Allison.

"Today's our day," said Hiatt. "We're feeling lucky."

I wish I could say the same, thought Allison.

Monday Morning

Jerry drove his Prius, a rare sight in the land of behemoth pickup trucks and SUVs. The gray Prius seemed hatched from an alien mother ship sent by a world where beauty held no sway.

The drive to Meeker was beautiful. From Rifle, a short drive west of Glenwood Springs on the interstate, the road followed a long slow climb to the north. The steep faces of the Roan Plateau soared upward to the west. The Flat Tops were to the east and the pitch wasn't quite as dramatic along this stretch, a bit more disorganized and unimpressive than towering, sharp-edged Roan Plateau. The highway split the two. Driving precisely the speed limit, they were twice overrun by trucks loaded with drilling rig gear. Roaring semis loaded with pipes tailgated them when there wasn't room to pass. Everyone was in a hurry except them.

The road rolled north through a scrubby landscape dotted by old working ranches alongside trophy houses, preposterously oversized structures with fancy architecture and look-at-me finishes.

"A colossal waste of energy," said Jerry. "They have no solar, some of these, and they aren't even positioned the right way to do passive solar. Think of the cost of heating those suckers way out here in the middle of nowhere, with two residents at most and five thousand square feet of space to keep toasty. That's a mind-set that has to change. It can't last forever."

Jerry dialed an iPod to a John Hiatt CD into the player, "*A Thing Called Love.*" A red-tailed hawk fell from its perch on top of a telephone pole, then hit the brakes and hovered for a second before darting away in a brown blur. A line of aspen trees guarded the edge of the ridge on the Roan, easily a thousand feet above the highway. Was it possible to imagine the geological eras and eons that it took to create the folds and cliffs and thrusts in that formation? Could you grasp time in that context? What was the impact of their meager crusade by comparison? Probably nothing more than a new dimple on Jupiter. Trudy envied people who could go about their work and their lives and their loves without a blink in the rearview mirror or a burning need to know what was around the next bend, those who went out and did what they did because that's who they were, because that's where they were born and rooted.

The core of downtown Meeker took up a few square blocks. A stone church and school flanked a simple park rimmed by understated businesses—a hotel, a café. This was a town that served its own. It neither screamed at nor depended upon outsiders.

Jerry slowed the barely humming Prius into a grocery store parking lot east of town. The vibe was friendly and cozier than the mega-chain grocery stores in Glenwood Springs, where the aisles were wider than a fire truck and stretched to the horizon. Trudy asked for a manager and was greeted by a tall, fit man wearing a spotless white apron with a permanent marker poking out of a well-starched pocket. The pocket was embroidered with neat block stitching: Brett Merriman.

One glance at Trudy's sample basket—herbs in their pert bundles, carefully wrapped and tied (no plastic clamshell casing) and Trudy barely had to say where she was from before they had a handshake deal to start carrying her line. "I think people here will like your goods," said Brett. "I get lots of complaints about bland basil from the national chain and thyme that's lost its zip."

Brett Merriman, it turned out, recommended a distributor who made a daily run up from Glenwood Springs delivering fish, specialty deli meats and sometimes cheeses. He led her to an office near the rear loading dock and jotted down the distributor's name and number.

"He's very reasonable," said Merriman.

"Thanks for everything," said Trudy. "I only dropped into the store on the off chance, you know."

"You came up here for some other reason?"

"As a matter of fact, yes," said Trudy, realizing that she hadn't planned to bring up the subject of Bostwick.

After they had entered, Jerry had stayed by himself near the community bulletin board by the front doors. As a fellow grocer, though one with much more specialized food, he didn't want to be seen as complicating or confusing Trudy's business. She was alone and she started to feel that rising, foamy rogue wave of panic that could throw her off keel. Who knows what anyone in this town really thought of Bostwick? There could be a dozen local hidden entanglements, and her next words might set off a series of alarms on every block in town before they got started. "We were doing some research. We've got an appointment today to see—"

"Ethan Bostwick," said Merriman.

Trudy stopped.

"Don't look so worried," said Merriman. "There hasn't been anybody around Meeker for a long, long time who has attracted so much outside interest—reporters and people from national foundations. Lots of outside interest and even more from inside. Bostwick is an interesting enough fellow. Nobody has tried to impose his principles on the natives so fiercely since Nathan Meeker tried to convert a horse-racing track to farmland, causing the Utes to rise up."

"We all know what happened to him," said Trudy.

"Indeed we do," said Merriman. He was now leaning on the front of his steel, industrial-strength desk. Trudy studied the clear whites of his eyes and soft brown eyebrows arched neatly above. The look contained no judgment. "There's probably still some residue from that disaster," said Merriman. "It's hard to forget the lesson around here. We're constantly reminded. Is somebody out your way doing something like Bostwick?"

"Something like that," said Trudy. "Probably not the same— not really," she added.

"Noble cause. The guy is a genius in a lot of ways. You'll see. But motivating a whole town, even a dinky one like Meeker? You need more than public relations skills to change lifestyles." Merriman leaned back in his chair, let the thought settle. "Are you meeting him at his place?"

"Yes," said Trudy.

"Head out toward Buford, and if you spot the buffalo, that's the Keating ranch. You'll see a lot of activity around there because of what happened to Josh, about as sad a loss as this town has dealt with in a long, long time."

"We heard about it," said Trudy.

"We're still reeling," said Merriman. "It hasn't settled all the way in. It's one of those real shockers that makes you stop and think about everything. And I mean everything."

Merriman walked her to the front of the store and they shook hands. "You'll enjoy meeting Bostwick," said Merriman. "He's one of a kind."

Jerry drove east a mile out of town and followed a fork to the right. The road skirted the edge of a broad, flat valley. Trudy could make out clumps of leafless cottonwood trees on the far side of the plain where the river cut west. Cottonwoods were thirsty suckers and often marked the course of water. At the end of the valley, the road tucked around the corner of a low, flat butte and followed the river more closely. The canyon narrowed and widened, over and over, each secluded valley a home to its own stretch of river, its own ranch or series of showy houses. Jerry spotted a pair of deer grazing in a field. The river sparkled. Near one ranch, a cowboy on horseback patrolled the fence line. His brown horse glowed in the sun like a freshly roasted chestnut.

Trudy kept the conversation with Merriman to herself. She

didn't want to rehash it with Jerry. She felt as if she had been regurgitating the same thoughts for days, and didn't need to keep the cycle going. The ride back to Glenwood Springs would be jammed full of their reactions and analysis of Ethan Bostwick, and right now she needed a break. Jerry looked for ways to crack open a conversation, but she didn't bite. She put a hand on his leg and requested that they just enjoy the ride.

The buffalo were bunched together, an elongated diamond-shaped herd of the odd beasts. They didn't scatter randomly like cows. They were family. Across the field was the Keating ranch house and as Merriman had predicted, a cluster of cars surrounded the house as if it was a popular roadside restaurant. Trudy made out two men talking between a pickup truck and a police car. Jerry slowed past the Keating ranch as the road took a gentle turn where a wire fence separated the properties. The fence ran perpendicular from the road and all the way to the river. Around the bend was the Bostwick property.

Jerry slowed and pointed the Prius down the gravel driveway, which turned twice in a perfect capital-S shape on its way to the clapboard ranch house, a dark green square that sat close to the river, a quarter-mile from the road. The house, which looked like it was built in the 1950s, was functional and plain. The windows were small, the simple trim and fake shutters smack out of suburbia. A two-car garage was attached to the main structure. The house served the purpose of simple shelter, not showcase. As they came around the final curve, they could see where a large section of field had been marked for a garden, now dormant in the harsh fall. The scale of the garden was impressive—Trudy guessed a quarter-acre. She could make out the corner of a greenhouse jutting off the back of the Bostwick house.

If they were expected, there was no indication, no welcome mat or welcome feeling. It was mid-afternoon but not one interior light flickered, even though the house was already in shade from the butte across the river.

Jerry led her to the door underneath a small, functional portico which covered the concrete steps. He knocked.

"Ten minutes past three," said Jerry. "Right on time, as far as time goes in the country."

The door opened slowly.

"Damn," said a voice. "You're the two from Glenwood Springs."

"That's us," said Jerry.

Ethan Bostwick stepped outside and pulled the door closed behind him.

"Goddamn cops," he said. "Wouldn't you know? They called an hour ago and I guess they're on their way out here, for Chrissakes. Pure utter, pardon my French, but fucking pure goddamn harassment. That's it. I'm done swearing, but I've been storming around inside the house for the past hour and, man, it's pissing me off."

Bostwick took a few steps away from the house. It was clear they weren't going inside for tea and cookies and a philosophical chat about the future of the slow-food movement.

"My mom is sleeping on the couch," said Bostwick. "Afternoon nap every day. She's eighty-eight. Tries to help out around the house but always crashes this time of day for an hour while Dad watches *Jeopardy*. I let them watch an hour of TV every morning, every afternoon and evening. That's it. Any more is poison—just poison. What was it you two wanted?"

Bostwick stared up the road. Trudy wished they could turn around and head back to the car. She had a thought that was clear and succinct: This is a waste of time.

"We were looking for advice on how to get the ball rolling in terms of a campaign to make changes over in Glenwood Springs," said Jerry. "The kind of thing you've been doing here."

Bostwick caught Trudy's stare, then gave Jerry the once-over.

"Christ almighty," he said. He took a breath, puffed out his cheeks, glanced again at the road and then toward the Keating ranch. If Ethan Bostwick had earned a reputation as an imposing threat to Meeker and the surrounding valleys, it wasn't from his physical presence. He was slight, only an inch or two taller than Trudy. His shoulders were narrow. Although Trudy sensed an inner toughness, he could have been the kid in seventh grade who moved away over the summer and nobody noticed until one day at lunch in the cafeteria when somebody said, "Whatever happened to so-and-so?" Bostwick had deep-set black-bead eyes in a narrow face, permanently dialed to serious.

"You said something about improving school food and how the city wastes energy," said Bostwick. His tone was clipped and condescending. Again Trudy thought this trip was a huge mistake.

"We think we've got the issues," said Trudy. The disdain she felt for his personal style converted into a feeling of urgency to get out of here. "We want to learn from your experience with tactics on how to approach the whole thing."

"Well, if you want to feel the extreme sense of isolation I've managed to find, you've come to the right place," said Bostwick in a wry tone. "But I haven't changed one policy and I haven't helped put one new law on the books. I've just stirred the hornets off the hive. And now because good old Keating here found himself a case of drunken hypothermia, the police are on their way out to mess around with me, to make me sweat, to tighten the screws. They claim they're just covering all the bases. Yeah, right. A man keels over by a lake up in the Flat Tops at some godforsaken hour in the middle of a deep freeze, and it's like I'd have anything to do with it, for Chrissakes. I can account for every night, every moment. When I'm not downtown at a meeting or getting supplies, I'm taking care of my parents or stuff around the house."

"So today might not be a good day to talk?" asked Jerry. Maybe he sensed Trudy's feeling about this. She followed Bostwick's gaze up the road. They could see flashing lights from a police car coming around a far bend. No siren, just lights.

"Putting on a show," said Bostwick, reading Trudy's mind. "Letting the valley know they're on the case. Christ."

"Should we come back later?" said Jerry.

"Look, there's nothing I can tell you. You're going to decide how big a risk you want to take. I've got no magic formula. It's great that you want to get in there and mix it up. We all know the changes to date are minuscule, that decades of self-indulgence and exploitation aren't going to flip around to self-sufficiency overnight. It's that whole Charlton Heston bumper-sticker mentality—you ain't changing my lifestyle until you tear it out of my cold, dead hands. That's triply true out here in the hinterlands, off the interstate. Everyone thinks because they've got a bit of land and can see for a hundred miles, there's plenty of everything. But there isn't."

The police car made its way around the first curve in the S. What were the lights for, Trudy wondered, to warn the Keating buffalo?

"But this ain't about better food or using a few less kilowatts at home," said Bostwick. "These fuckers—sorry, there I go again—are all salivating over the Roan. There's enough oil and natural gas in the Piceance Basin to put a few countries in the Middle East out of business and everybody here wants a piece of the action. That's what this is all about—and I'm the freakin' fly in their precious ointment. Any of us who think that destroying the Roan Plateau for a few years of continued limitless pleasure—well, we're all dirty flies that need to be swatted. That's the real crusade. Finding the fuckers like the great, great Mr. Keating who are ready to cash checks—huge checks—and then stand back and enjoy the slow-motion rape."

The tires of the police car crunched softly on the loose gravel. Red lights flashed against Bostwick's house.

"Here's my only tip. Think big. Think impact. Don't go for small potatoes, the low-hanging fruit. Decide on your biggest issue and then don't flinch, don't budge."

They heard the police car come to a stop. Trudy turned with Jerry and Bostwick, who put his hands under his armpits and didn't inch a single step toward the visitors.

"They'll do anything," said Bostwick. "They'll do anything—even take your fucking land."

The car doors opened with weight, in unison, and two officers climbed out. They strolled up like they owned everything in sight and then some.

"Officers," said Bostwick, "can you give me one minute to say goodbye to my guests?"

Guests? Suddenly they enjoyed elevated status? Bostwick had an unctuous air.

"Please," said the taller of the two cops, who stood ramrod erect, a black leather-bound notebook clutched at his side.

"Let me show you something," said Bostwick, gesturing to Trudy and Jerry and walking fifteen steps away from the cops. "Follow that fence line all the way down to where it hits the *T*. See where the buffalo are gathered? That's the spot."

Bostwick was talking loudly. This was for everyone's benefit. Trudy wanted to ask if he was doing himself any favors or whether he wanted to tone down the vehemence, since he was under a faint cloud of suspicion. She felt her heart rate climb with the dark vibes and agitation in the air. She wanted to leave.

"My property runs clear to the water, despite the fence that runs parallel to the river. The fence is for the Keating buffalo. It's all private access to the river. An old Colorado law called *adverse possession* lets the late, great Josh Keating stake a claim to my river

Mark Stevens

frontage because he used it for a couple of decades. A well-worn path cuts through my side and heads down to that clump of cottonwoods by the river. This is a killer stretch for fly-fishing—the cutthroat trout in the river are legendary—and Keating had been allowing access along my side for years. So, to mess with me, he put in this adverse possession claim. He wanted to take forty-five acres out of my hands by a trick, a fucking legal trick. Poof."

"Jesus," muttered Jerry. "I didn't know they could do that."

"They," said Bostwick. "That's it. *They*. Them versus *me*. So that's my tip of the day, kids. Find yourself some friends if you can. Make sure they're in high places and do what you can to save the Roan. If we lose the Roan, you may as well kiss the West goodbye."

Bostwick offered a wistful smile and turned back to the waiting cops.

176

6

"A sample of the allegedly bad water?" asked Deputy Durkin.

"What we don't know is whether the poison was still strong and effective when we pulled the sample," said Allison. "But it's from the same pool where a man with a backpack was seen pouring something into the water."

"That's what Mr. Zamora was trying to tell me earlier this morning when he gave us the whole rundown, running into this Devo guy and everything," said Durkin. "But now that we've actually got the water, there's a chance the health department can tell us what in the world might be going on."

The brown Nalgene bottle sat on the corner of the steel gray industrial desk, which sported a calendar decorated in spiral-theme doodles, three side-by-side-by-side telephones, a charger box that was home to an imposing walkie-talkie and a tan-shelled computer with its companion keyboard. The office was a forest of brown and blacks, no primary colors allowed.

Durkin, clearly the doodle artist, tapped the ink end of a red Bic pen on one of his recent creations. Allison stood behind one of the two plain wooden chairs that faced the desk. Terry Zamora, fidgeting like a two-year-old, sat in the other.

"Since Mr. Zamora was in here the first time this morning, there are two bits of news that have developed," said Durkin. "The most important things need to come straight from the horse's mouth and he's around here somewhere."

With that, Durkin picked up the walkie-talkie. He leaned back in his padded swivel chair, which issued a bristling squeak, and held the walkie-talkie sideways to his mouth like a corn cob. He replaced the radio after the fastest exchange of indecipherable verbal code Allison ever heard. He tapped his pen twice on the calendar.

"Big cheese?" said Zamora.

"The sheriff himself," said Durkin. "He's pulling up outside."

"About time," said Zamora. "I've been trying to light a fire under him all day."

When Allison had arrived at the motel at five minutes before midnight, her body ready to implode from hard-core fatigue, she had left a note for Zamora. The note asked Zamora to wait to go see the sheriff with her because she had the sample. But clearly Zamora felt compelled to start the ball rolling before she managed to roust herself after eight delicious hours of sleep. He had returned to the motel and waited for her to emerge from hibernation.

A back door crashed. Zamora shook his head, reeking of impatience.

Sheriff Christie sported the same sharp uniform from Loretta's house. He looked tired and drawn.

"Good afternoon," Christie said with a half smile, quick and businesslike. He issued a few polite greetings at the introductions but plainly appeared to want to skip any small talk.

"The coroner ran all the tests," said Christie. "He has ruled Mr. Keating's death a case of hypothermia, nothing more and nothing less. Brought on by a blood-alcohol level that the coroner said rendered him impaired. Extremely impaired. He probably fell over and drifted into unconsciousness."

"No traumas?" asked Zamora. "He's sure?"

"One bruise on the back of the skull, exactly in the spot where his head landed," said Christie. "Another on the back of his left shoulder, which probably took the brunt of the fall on the rocks.

Both contusions are consistent with a fall on the rocks, nothing else. Neither one would have needed medical attention beyond a bag of ice and a Band-Aid if he had made it back to camp."

The sheriff moved over and leaned against the wall by his deputy's desk. "In that weather, he didn't stand a chance," said Christie.

Durkin's pen tapped on autopilot. Zamora broke the silence. "There's gotta be more to it—the fact that he was sick. That's why you guys have to get up there and investigate."

"This is a sample of the water that Miss Coil says may be tainted," Durkin said to Christie. "I told her we would get it over to the health department."

"I heard about the water," said Christie. "No trace of anything appeared out of line in the rest of the tests on Keating."

"I've got another guide at camp with the same symptoms," said Allison.

"And I got sick," said Zamora. "Painful sick, guts-on-fire sick."

"We've had a few others too, five or six from other camps," said Christie. "Really sick."

"Stomach related?" said Allison.

"Every one," said Christie. "We've got all sorts of people heading in to run checks on the water—state and feds, everybody with a say or a stake."

"And we've got a witness who saw somebody pouring some shit into the water," said Zamora. "I don't understand why you're not up there trying to track him down."

The sheriff pondered the comment with some care. "I know you're frustrated," he said. "We have relayed everything we know to the Forest Service and the Division of Wildlife. And we are interviewing everyone who knew Keating and his neighbors."

"Allison here knows where Devo lives, if you want to find out what he saw," said Zamora.

"You found him?" said Durkin, eyes lighting up. "How the hell—"

"He was around camp," said Zamora. "We spotted him and chased him down."

We? Allison flinched. Zamora could take any story and try to make it his own.

"He let himself be caught," she said. "He was fast and long gone, but wanted to let us know he had seen somebody up there, somebody pouring stuff into the water."

Christie sighed, shook his head. "Then we got problems. It might be a separate deal, but then we got problems. Might need to push the budget regardless. Think you can find him again?"

"He found us," said Allison. "He allowed the meeting."

"We can sure as hell try," said Zamora. "With his smell, shouldn't be hard."

"Have you seen the videos from your caveman friend?" asked Durkin. He spun the computer screen around and clicked the mouse. The screen flipped over from a photo gallery screensaver of swimsuit models to YouTube—the Devo Channel. The screen was filled with eight letterbox-shaped snapshots, each with a freeze-frame image of Devo in a variety of settings—by a campfire, kneeling by a lake, holding up barbecued rodent of some unknown variety on a stick, and sitting inside his cave.

"Another wannabe Internet celebrity," said Zamora.

"My kids love him," said Durkin. "They have a service with e-mail that tells them when new videos are posted. I've watched a few with them. They think he's wild. We had no idea he was right here in our own backyard."

"Big star," said Christie. "Our town librarian read an article about him in *The New York Times*. Kind of ironic that people are getting interested in his back-to-nature idea while sitting in their wired-up houses. The story said his website is pulling in advertisers—outdoor gear suppliers. Mr. Devo may not know it, but he's making a ton of good old-fashioned twenty-first century money by plunging himself back in time."

"Somebody is helping him," said Allison.

"Clearly," said the sheriff. "He has a delivery service—somehow he gets batteries for his video camera. He sure as hell ain't plugging a charger into a cave wall out there. He's getting his videos out to the world somehow. There's even a video here where he responds to questions from fans. So he's got help."

"The airplane," said Allison.

"What airplane?" asked Christie.

"Before all this started," said Allison. "The same morning after I heard him skulking around in the meadow, I woke up when an airplane buzzed my tent."

"There's no runway in the Flat Tops," said Durkin.

"This was one of those smaller ones, like a tricycle with a wing. Not much to it."

"An ultralight," said Zamora.

"Exactly," said Allison.

"Those things don't need much of anything to land on," said Zamora. "Patch of flat scrub is all."

"I heard the Forest Service say they had a report from campers worried that it was a plane in trouble, but there were no reports of any planes or pilots missing."

"Is he doing anything illegal?" asked Zamora.

"If he's taking game without a license or out of season," said Christie. "That would be a problem. Those Abert squirrels you can only take from mid-November to mid-January, I believe it is, and jackrabbits from October through February, something along those lines. You could check with the DOW on that. And there's only certain ways you're allowed to catch them. No snares, conibears, leghold traps. Those kinds of things have been banned. And you can't establish a permanent camp longer than fourteen days unless you're an outfitter leaving some cache, if I recall correctly."

"That's what our permits allow us to do," said Allison, "and we pay good money for them."

"So, yes, illegal," said Christie. "But you gotta catch him first. And then prosecute a folk hero."

"Too damn bad there's no video of the guy pouring crap into the pool by Coffin Lake," said Zamora.

"If there's something going on with the water we'll be putting a small army of people together to figure it out," said Christie. "You don't mess around with the Flat Tops, and you especially don't mess around with our water."

"I have no doubt what the tests will show," said Allison. "We know Keating and my guide Jesse had precisely the same symptoms. And then there's the mystery man Devo spotted. There's no need to wait."

"Good point," said Zamora. "That's what I've been trying to say. I don't think these guys realize how sick Keating was."

"How sick Jesse has been," said Allison.

"It's bad," said Zamora. "It's some nasty shit."

The sheriff and Durkin exchanged glances. Allison knew the next response would be the political reaction, the one that would send her a message about how cops could or could not help, about whether her concerns were appreciated, about whether she might or might not possess an analysis worth hearing and whether they were open to it. Allison felt she could have made more headway without that bulldog Zamora in the room, but at least his fangs weren't bared.

"You're dead-on right," said Christie. "I try to stay open to changing my mind."

It wasn't a shine-off. It was said with conviction. Allison felt that pleasant lift, like seeing the grade A circled on top of a term paper.

"Bravo," said Zamora. "Every minute counts."

"Let me get on the horn with the national forest folks and Division of Wildlife," said Christie. "I'll see if we can come up with a plan. Can you show me on a map where you found Devo's cave?"

Sheriff Christie escorted them to a cramped conference room lined with maps—Rio Blanco County, the town of Meeker, the state of Colorado and the Flat Tops Wilderness Area. The maps hung in simple frames and hadn't been updated in years. But the Flat Tops hadn't changed significantly in ten thousand years, so what did it matter? Allison followed the trail from Trapper's to Oyster Lake, then southeast on a trail over the ridge where Colin had escorted her. From there, it wasn't hard to spot the area where the lines on the topo map were stacked tightly, practically one solid blur of skinny brown stripes. Devo's cliff. She put a finger on the spot.

"There's a cave right here," she said. "That's home. Rest assured he'll smell you coming. It will be his choice of whether or not to make contact."

"Would it help if one of you were there?" asked Christie.

"It's all up to him," said Allison. "If I were you, I'd low-key the fact that you are who you are until you've got him talking."

"Do you think he'll cooperate?"

Allison doubted it. If anything, Devo would probably dive further into hiding. He had barely talked with them. He would vanish if it was authorities in uniform.

"Depends on the day," she said. "And how you approach it."

Allison showed them Coffin Lake and the ridge where they had found Keating's elk. She answered questions about riding time and the terrain. The borderline with Garfield County only left Rio Blanco County with the northwest wedge of the Flat Tops, but the cave was well within their turf. There was a brief discussion about jurisdiction and possible crimes and who would contact whom with the state and the feds, if needed.

"I appreciate your taking this seriously," said Zamora. "That means a lot."

"One more question about the coroner's report," said Allison. The thought was in her head before she had given it much consideration.

"Of course," said Christie.

"Let's say the tests from the water find something wrong, a chemical. Will the coroner be able to go back and see if there were any significant levels of that chemical in Keating's system?"

"Not possible," said Christie. "The coroner could go back to the tests he ran on Keating's blood and tissues, I suppose. But he's already found everything to be normal. Besides, Mr. Keating's body has been released back to his widow, and I believe the services are set for the day after tomorrow."

"At one of the churches here in town?" said Allison. She was being certifiably nosy now. Why did she need to know?

"No, out at his ranch," said the sheriff. "I believe he wanted his ashes scattered among his prized buffalo."

Cremation was the practical way to go with dead bodies. Allison imagined it like a second death. She found the utter finality of it appealing—no chance of lid-popping coffins by not-really-dead corpses—as well as the aspect of saving space in the environment.

"Is he already at the mortuary?" asked Allison.

"I think he's in an urn," said Christie. "At least that's my understanding."

"What if we can get Jesse Morales down to a doctor and get him tested?" asked Allison.

"Might not hurt," said Christie. "We need all the information we can get. Every scrap."

Allison counted back the days in her mind when Jesse had turned up ill. That had been the day they had found Keating's elk. Then there was the trip to visit Loretta Keating. Then the cave trip. Then the Devo encounter.

"It's been four days, so it might be all out of his system by now, but we can see," she said. If she could raise Colin on his cell, she could have them heading down pronto. What were the chances of that? Zero and zilch. She might be able to get back at Oyster Lake tonight. Another dark trudge on horseback could be in her near future. She yearned for normal routines, yearned for a warm stove in a tent, a cribbage board, a plastic coffee cup filled with over-priced tequila and some city boy's sexist jokes. It was already early afternoon.

She fondled the wristwatch in her pocket. She couldn't bring it up in front of Zamora. She'd have to circle back, perhaps, if Zamora let her out of his sight. She didn't want Zamora to think she had anything extra. But she wasn't getting a feeling of hustle and drive out of Christie, either.

"I'm going back up," said Allison. She was walking Zamora along the highway toward the motel, where she planned to check out and take Colin's truck back to Trapper's.

"It's going to be late," said Zamora.

"I'm fine," said Allison. She preferred solo. The thinking time would be relished. She needed to head back.

They were across from the motel. The highway was empty except for a lone car rounding a gentle curve far to the west.

"I think I should go with you," said Zamora.

"Why?" said Allison.

"Safer, isn't it?" said Zamora.

"It's just a matter of retracing my steps, and it's an easy trail up from Trapper's. No tricks at all," said Allison.

They waited for the car to pass.

"Are you sure?" asked Zamora.

"I could do it in my sleep on a moonless night," said Allison.

The car was too close to start crossing. Allison stared at it and muttered a command for the damned vehicle to move faster. She wanted to get on with her trek to Trapper's, and on to Colin. She had a goal. She felt a renewed purpose. The car slowed to a crawl. It was one of those new hybrids, low-slung and designed by committee. An odd cousin from the city lost in the land of pickups. A man was driving.

The car came to a complete stop. The passenger-side window rolled down. Allison assumed the occupants needed directions.

Except the woman in the passenger's seat wasn't a stranger.

"Trudy?" said Allison. "What the hell are *you* doing here?"

Monday Afternoon

Catching up on everything took a thorough ten minutes. The odds of their encounter seemed impossible at first, but they came down when Allison explained about the water, Devo, the hunter's death and the need to talk with the sheriff of Rio Blanco County. Trudy couldn't imagine coming across a dead body, the overwhelming heartache alone if the body belonged to a stranger, let alone someone you had been talking with, an otherwise healthy and regular grown man, the day before. "Horrible," said Jerry. "Just horrible. Trudy saw the story in the newspaper."

Allison was on edge. Her body language was capable of only one word: impatience. Trudy would have preferred to relax and catch up, but she knew their encounter would be brief. Allison said twice how she needed to get back to camp.

They were huddled in the motel parking lot. Zamora paced in meandering circles, looking up and down the highway. He glowered and guzzled his coffee, poured from a pot that had been simmering in the motel lobby.

"I think one of Jerry's friends was talking about Devo," said Trudy. "He had seen his videos on the web."

"Devo told us where to get the water sample," said Allison.

"Is it true?" said Trudy.

"Hell if I know," said Allison. "He was convincing."

"What's he like?"

"A man with a mission."

"A freak of the woods," said Zamora, who had circled back to eavesdrop.

"So what's Bostwick like?" said Allison.

"Focused," said Jerry.

"Very," said Trudy.

"And a bit agitated," said Jerry.

"What do you mean?" said Allison.

"Yeah," said Zamora. "Just how agitated? As agitated as the rest of us about seeing Josh Keating die?"

"Bostwick had some points to make," said Trudy. "Let's put it that way."

"The cops came out to chat with him too," said Jerry. "Not a normal day."

"Probably not the best day to judge him," said Trudy.

"He deserves every bit of harassment," said Zamora. "From the way I hear it, he's been messing with the whole valley."

"He's made a name for himself," said Jerry.

"By tossing hand grenades," said Zamora. "By stinking up the place."

Trudy glanced at Allison and caught her look of mild exasperation. Trudy took a step back from the others. Her boots crunched in the motel's dirt lot. The clouds had lowered. She was no expert forecaster but she could feel the humidity in this surge of new weather.

Allison followed her away from the guys, who seemed to be trying their best to have a civilized exchange. Jerry could revert to his polite grocer mode when needed.

"I gotta get going," said Allison.

"I know," said Trudy. "I'm really sorry about what you've been through—sorry about Keating."

"It's been strange," said Allison.

"He just died out there?" asked Trudy. Allison had never seemed distracted or distant—she was usually focused and listened hard. But now it was as if she were watching a movie in another room.

"There's no indication of anything else," said Allison. "According to the experts."

"What else would there be?"

Allison's normal expression—the handy smile, the heartfelt eyes—had drooped. But she started talking, her pace calm and clear. She explained about seeing the man who had been searching for something at the lake. She told Trudy about finding the wristwatch, showed it to her on the sly, and said how she was puzzled by it.

"Are you sure it wasn't in the same spot where Keating collapsed?" said Trudy.

"Dead certain," said Allison. "I don't know if it has anything to do with either, but Keating got sick from the bad water the day before he died. Flat-out ill. Then he got better, shot his elk, drank too much, and fell on the rocks."

"It all sounds too odd," said Trudy.

"I can't put it together. What did you make of this guy Bostwick—what did you really think of him?"

"That he's bigger than his britches, a bit of a blowhard. I'm glad the time we spent around him didn't last a minute longer than it did," said Trudy. "It's probably me but I can't stand people who think they can push the world around."

"I couldn't agree more," said Allison. "By the way, I am impressed with you coming all the way here to Meeker. And if I'm picking up on the right signals, something's going on between you and your grocer friend."

Trudy thought of herself as Allison's dependable anchor and she appreciated the fact that Allison never prodded her into venturing out. They had shared boyfriend tales and Allison was always frank about her entanglements and tumbles. Trudy had grown to enjoy the three-dimensional detail and the bond it created between them. Plus, it added to Trudy's fun, hearing about hunters and guides and other men who made various degrees of progress cornering this interesting, smart, city-turned-country hunting guide. Trudy knew there was nothing to hide from Allison.

"I haven't been home in days," said Trudy, flashing a smile. "Jerry works hard, has lots of ideas but loves to lounge around."

"And play around," said Allison.

"Lots," said Trudy. "I'd forgotten that feeling of counting the number of times in a twenty-four hour period—wondering if you could spend that much time doing one thing."

Allison beamed on her behalf. "Was it his idea to come to Meeker?"

"It wouldn't have been mine," said Trudy. "You know that."

"I do, I believe," said Allison.

"But I gotta get back tonight and check on the cats. What about you?"

"Heading back up to camp. Got some cats of my own I need to check on."

A siren sliced through the air and Trudy flinched as if she'd been shot. Allison turned around as though the sound was the most normal thing on earth. How did she stay so cool? Three police cars flicked by on the highway at a speed that would have been reckless on an interstate, let alone downtown Meeker. *Pffft. Pffft. Pffft.* The cars were alien creations on warp drive, an unwelcome reminder of the city.

Trudy followed Allison a few paces across the parking lot. Zamora had pulled out his cell phone, a stern look on his face as he listened. "What's the call about?" Zamora said into the phone. "What do you mean you won't tell me?"

They were standing at the side of the parking lot, watching the cars scream away in the distance. Another police car pulled up, not in such a rush, and Zamora flagged it down by stepping into the road.

The passenger window rolled down and Zamora approached the car like an old friend. Some people thought they owned the whole world. The cop riding shotgun had thinning red hair and a boyish expression. He could have been Deputy Durkin's brother—or cousin.

Trudy felt Jerry put a gentle arm around her back. She wrapped an arm around his waist, and he pulled her close. She couldn't hear the information being exchanged, but the conversation didn't last long.

The car revved hard and took off. Zamora turned around. He closed his eyes and winced.

"God bless it all," he said. "Four buffalo shot at the Keating ranch. All dead."

Monday Afternoon

By the time she climbed behind the wheel of Colin's truck, Allison was five minutes behind the sheriff and his deputies. She had bidden farewell to Trudy and Jerry. Trudy had shed tears for the dead buffalo. "Those beautiful animals," she said. Allison had hugged her as if she was the last real person on earth. She gave Jerry a squeeze too. The moment had been equal parts tender, meaningful and extremely awkward, although Allison could still feel Jerry's sinewy, powerful grip on her body. Trudy was doing well.

Allison pressed the pickup to the limit. In the rearview mirror another car with flashing lights came up fast, and she slowed to the speed limit as it zipped past. Then another, same thing— same steely, focused expression on the cop behind the wheel too. Allison backed off the gas pedal as the road turned into the canyon, but she still felt the pickup lean hard on each turn.

A plan was forming. She thought back to images of standing on the porch at the Keating ranch. To the west, downriver, was the Keating land. To the east, upriver, the Bostwick spread. But that seemed too obvious a location to slaughter four penned buffalo, unless somebody had skulked onto Bostwick's land to set him up. To the north, the snaking road formed the edge of the Keating property. The open road was a highly unlikely location from which to fire shots. That left the river and the woods across it. Excellent cover, no more than a couple hundred yards' shooting distance to the buffalo. Allison remembered a bridge across the White River. Driving all the way to the road up to Trapper's Lake now made no sense—it would take her too far out of the way.

One thing was clear—the Keating-Bostwick feud had reached the boiling point. The slaughtered buffalo would put Josh Keating's death back under a screaming question mark.

The sheriff cars were parked down close to the ranch house by the time Allison came up on Keating's place. Another flashing light, this one on a truck, bore down on her from behind. She pulled over to the shoulder so the truck could join the other vehicles of authority in the gaggle of emergency overreaction. There were six police cars and trucks—a decent, quick showing as far as the outskirts of Meeker were concerned—and soon there would be more. Allison knew the search for Devo would fade to a faint winking light on the cops' radar. Killing four grazing farm animals took every single rule, law and social covenant and smacked it in the jaw with brass knuckles. Two men in a bar fight and one gets killed? Hey, he had it coming. Shouldn't have drunk so much. But four animals being raised for their meat are not prey, not ducks on a pond.

Allison knew her concern about hunters with bad stomachaches might wait a day or two since the sickness was debilitating but brief. Yes, one of the guys later died of his own stupid inability to recognize that an off-the-charts blood-alcohol content did not mix with walking on the boulder-strewn shore of Oyster Lake. But before tripping on a rock in the frozen dark, he had recovered from the stomach attack enough to hunt and field dress an elk. Not much of an issue, was it? The wristwatch created a troubling wrinkle, but it would all wait, compared to four freshly slaughtered buffalo.

Allison came to a stop on the road beyond the Keating ranch and studied the scene. The truck that had followed her was now barreling down the driveway, kicking up a pillow of dust. Past the ranch house, four inert brown masses dotted the pasture. Two of the dead buffalo were a few paces apart. Another was smack out in the middle of the pasture. The fourth dead buffalo was close to the fence by the Bostwick property line.

An utter waste. Allison didn't know where to direct the anger she felt.

She gunned the pickup back to speed. The bridge was where she had hoped it would be. The canyon narrowed, the road climbed to higher ground. An unmarked road plunged down to the right at a sharp angle. Allison bounced along old pavement that hadn't been patched in years. At the bottom of the hill, the road bumped left and Allison guided the pickup onto the one-lane wooden bridge, feeling the planks give and the truck wobble. The long hill coming toward her was in deep shade. The sky was preparing to close down and let the snow fly.

The wild-goose aspect of this whimsical pursuit was plain. If she had covered a mile of riverfront from the Keating ranch to the bridge, finding someone across the river was unlikely. And give that someone a two-hour head start? Forget it.

But covering this side of the river appealed to her instincts, odds be damned. The road cut back along the river and penetrated a series of hills, swerving inland. Old snow packed the road in spots and tire tracks cut the white patches. The road rolled through a thick scrap of forest, aspen interspersed with fir. The river was far below, and she caught a glimpse of the water, iced over in spots.

She dialed in her internal odometer. Why hadn't she measured the distance from the Keating ranch to the bridge so she could match it on this side? Allison kicked her inner ass and heard her voice fill the cab of the pickup with a short, sharp "Fuck!" She couldn't see across the river and had no idea if she had gone too far. She sped up as if that would help her get smarter. The road plunged down and turned toward the river. She braked to a stop where the road edged close to the water and slid out of the truck to get her bearings.

She looked down a gentle bank to the river, narrow in this stretch. She could hear the water flowing over rocks in the main channel. Snow was starting to drift down, thick and chunky. It was a windless snowfall, as if the storm had tiptoed its way up the valley saying, "Pay no attention to me." She was still upriver from her target, but not by much. She could see the distinct outline of the Bostwick ranch house a quarter-mile downstream. Propelled by pure hunch, Allison stepped down to the riverbank, her eye on a spot a hundred yards distant where the bank rose up and might offer a better view. The path down was dotted with shrubs and tamarisk and the shaded north-facing bank here held onto old patches of snow, though most of the footing was hardpack dirt and rock. If this was a waste of time, nobody would know. The proverbial tree falling in the forest becomes the proverbial hunch flopping in the forest.

Either nothing was connected or everything was connected. Either Keating and Bostwick were at war or this was all a whacked-out series of flukes. It wouldn't have surprised her to see Devo right now, sitting on a rock by the shore.

Allison reached the base of the mini-bluff and headed up. The earth yielded bare spots of dirt amid clumps of tufted wheatgrass and windblown rabbit brush. The first bootprint was in the snow. It was the front sole—no heel. It was pointed up the slope. It was small. A woman's? It wasn't a cowboy boot, but a boot for all-purpose needs. The tread pattern was a nest of octagonal shapes. Allison poked the soil next to the bootprint. The ground was firm, didn't give easily. She conjured an image of a small man or medium woman. The print had to be fairly new, with all the off-and-on snowfalls. Flakes were being snagged by the octagon indentations. She stood up.

Another bootprint. And another. She was on top of the knoll with a clear view to the Bostwick spread and the Keating ranch. Bostwick's was in the foreground. She followed another thirty strides alongside Mr. Bootprint Maker into a patch of ankle-deep snow. Despite being leafless, the aspen trunks were crowded enough to block the late fall sun. The snow revealed that Mr. Boot-print had stood around on this spot for a long time. The messed-up, oddly shaped circle of disturbed snow was the size of a large tent. Allison skirted the area, studied it. She saw only one set of prints. None of them extended past this point on the bluff and, after a minute of searching, she found the trail of prints that led back in the direction of her truck.

The view to the Keating property was the equivalent of an amusement park shooting gallery. Were it not for the four slaughtered buffalo and the huddle of police cars and emergency vehicles, she could have been standing in the most idyllic snow globe souvenir ever created—one that a loving five-year-old girl had shaken gently and returned to her bedside table for a long stare. Only this wasn't the end of a storm, it was the beginning.

The buffalo across the river—the survivors, now huddled in a far corner of their fenced-in grazing land—were essentially fish in a barrel for anybody with a decent rifle and scope. The shots would have passed over Bostwick's land. It was a perfect setup. A sour taste grew in Allison's throat as she pictured the first buffalo dropping to its knees. Allison squatted beside the mess of prints— perhaps the area where the shooter had waited for the buffalo to graze over to a prime location. One clear print was in her focus. This whole scene would soon be buried in snow. Should she run to the truck and see if there was an old paper bag or something she could use to sketch the boot pattern? She might not beat the snowfall, which was putting a fresh coat of fluff over every dimple and ding in the earth. She blew softly over one of the prints and the flakes of snow briefly levitated. She couldn't keep blowing all day. She studied the view again. Were these the prints of an innocent? A photographer, perhaps, or birdwatcher? Her gut screamed *no*, and she focused on memorizing the octagon pattern.

Late Monday Afternoon

The run back to the truck and drive to the Keating ranch took a few minutes. She was processing everything, trying to let details gel. The snowfall was thick. There seemed to be more flakes in the air than space between them.

The official-looking government vehicles at the ranch had multiplied during the two hours she had been gone. One buffalo was being gutted to salvage the meat. The workers were probably working their way around, one carcass at a time.

Allison waded into the milling throng. Cell phones were being flipped open and dialed. Uniforms and badges crowded together as at a Boy Scout Jamboree. Allison stood for a minute on the outer orbit of the activity. There were a few others in this ring of Saturn who didn't belong in the power circle—neighbors, perhaps, or looky-loos. Allison plunged into the center of the authority gaggle looking for a familiar face. She stood for a minute as if she belonged and then spotted Sheriff Christie on the porch. Loretta Keating was sitting on a chair, covered in blankets. Four men surrounded her. Her head hung low as they offered condolences. No doubt she was hearing familiar refrains. Allison took a breath and sensed the agonizing hurt that she was being asked to endure, the overlapping waves of loss. Why Loretta would want to watch the investigation was beyond Allison. She wondered who else might have heard the shots—or who might have seen the shooter scrambling along the far side of the river.

The group on the porch was breaking up. Sheriff Christie came down the steps.

"Looks like we got our hands full," he said. "News trucks already rolling out of Grand Junction and Denver. And you've got a look on your face."

"I want to show you something," said Allison.

"What now?"

"Around the other side of the house," said Allison. "It'll take a second."

"Related to this—or the water?"

"To this," said Allison, reaching inside her jacket for the pair of binoculars she had found in Colin's glove compartment.

"Whatcha got?"

"Have you figured out where the shots came from?" she said.

"The crime scene guys are out there now, recording every entry wound. Look, I don't mean to be rude, but I don't have a lot of time for questions. The whole valley is in shock."

Allison walked briskly around the house, pointed east and south across the Bostwick land and the river to the knoll, which wasn't as clearly defined as she had expected, especially through the snow. She looked through the binoculars and found a red bandanna she had left dangling on a tree branch. She passed the binoculars to Sheriff Christie.

"I see the bandanna," he said.

"That whole area—somebody was tromping around there recently," said Allison. "And it's a perfect spot."

"What do you figure, three hundred yards?"

"But the angle from up there is a whole different deal, looking down. It would be a clear shot, and your targets wouldn't be moving. It'd be a snap."

"The last shot—maybe not."

"What do you mean?" she said.

"Mrs. Keating heard the first shot and looked out the window and saw the buffalo in a mini-stampede. That's why the four are scattered all over. Those are edgy critters, you know, and who can blame them?"

"But still not too difficult a shot from there."

"Buffalo at full speed?" he asked. "Not a horse, exactly, but those legs can move. Let me ask you this—what exactly did you see over there?"

"A mess of bootprints in the snow—most of it in the shade."

"One person?"

"Only one set of prints."

"Anything else? Bullet shells?"

"Just the prints, but it was like somebody had been standing around for a long time—you know, biding his time. And then the prints headed right back upriver to the road."

"Once we've got the caliber of the weapon, we'll see if it fits with a long-range rifle."

"Did Mrs. Keating see anything at all?" asked Allison. "Could she tell which direction the shooting was coming from?"

Sheriff Christie was giving her a look that said, "Whose investigation is this?" He let out a nearly imperceptible sigh. "No," he said.

"But you think Bostwick is behind it?"

"It sure smells that way," he said. "One of the possibilities, put it that way."

"Why would a guy who promotes sustainable living and healthy food have anything to do with slaughtering farm animals standing around in a field?"

"That's a problem with the theory," said Sheriff Christie. "The bigger problem is finding Ethan Bostwick so we can ask him some questions."

"But he was at home earlier," said Allison.

Sheriff Christie gave her a sideways, puzzled look. "We know that because we had deputies out to see him earlier. How do you happen to know?"

"I bumped into a friend right after I left your office. I was walking back to The Rustic Lodge. She and another friend had been out to talk with Bostwick."

"A friend of yours," said Sheriff Christie as if it was an indictment.

"A friend in the organic herb business," said Allison.

They drifted back around the house where the police activity thrummed. Two TV news trucks were parked nose to tail on the highway. A mast on one truck was at full extension, an out-of-place periscope searching for a satellite. The trucks must have been nearby for something else—it was a full two hours to Grand Junction. They were an odd bit of city technology in the remote canyon. A cop had been deployed to keep the media at bay. A video camera and tripod were camped on the road beyond the fence, zooming in on the dead buffalo. The story was exotic and would remind all the city dwellers on the Front Range that they still lived in a state that was a part Old West. Viewers tonight would mumble quietly and knowingly to themselves—the slaughter was the work of a drunken idiot, or else somebody who was mighty pissed off. Most people would prefer it to be the result of a nasty feud. It would be juicier that way. It would put Meeker on the map.

"The media boys can consider this a practice run for later in the week," said Sheriff Christie. "Now that they know the way here."

"What do you mean?" said Allison.

Sheriff Christie looked at her as if she had stepped off a rocket from Venus. "Don't you know?"

"Obviously not," said Allison.

"Some big shot undersecretary from the Department of Interior comes to town this Thursday. Some folks are saying the secretary himself will be here. He's looking at a decision to unlock an enormous stretch of land from the outskirts of downtown Meeker clear out toward Rangely, the whole valley down to the foot of the Roan Plateau, and in some cases up on the flanks of the Roan itself. Geologists say the drilling possibilities would make an OPEC sheik drool. In the meantime, every human being within a 300-mile radius who has the slightest leanings toward environmental protection is planning to show up to state their case. The federal government has the chance to make a lot of people terribly rich or terribly disappointed. It's what you call a 'pressure situation.'"

"And one of those people is Mrs. Keating," said Allison.

"But she's not alone, believe me," said Sheriff Christie. "This whole town is looking at the payday of a lifetime, if the feds play along."

Late Monday Afternoon

Allison drove to Trapper's Lake in a daze. The snowfall held steady. The afternoon light matched her dim view of the world—vague and in-between. The road dead-ended at the cluster of cabins at Trapper's Lake. A radio station out of Grand Junction reported the slaughtered buffalo at the top of the news, and that authorities were looking for neighbor Ethan Bostwick.

The forecast on the radio said it would snow heavily across northwestern Colorado, possibly a harbinger of a wet winter. She found Lightning in the corral and saddled him up. His jaw remained clamped shut during the entire process. She ordered a sandwich from the lodge kitchen—roast beef and cheddar—and had it wrapped up for the road. She bought an extra large bag of oats for Lightning from the lodge manager, Nora, who was less enthusiastic than Lightning about outbound trips right now. "You only have an hour of light left," said Nora. "That includes the very last candle watt of sun."

"Lightning knows the way, and so do I," said Allison. "One hour of light, two hours of not."

"And the cold?"

"At least it's cloudy, that keeps the temperature up a bit," said Allison.

"Can't it wait?" Nora was small-framed and feisty. She could smile like Julia Roberts. "Why don't you sleep on the couch here by the fire? No charge."

"I've got too many things to think about," said Allison. "And clients too." The offer was tempting, but lacked one crucial ingredient: Colin.

Allison pulled out her cell phone and dialed. It rang six times and flipped over to voice mail. "It's Colin. It's hunting season. You know I can't answer this. Leave a message."

"Colin, this is Allison. It's Monday afternoon. I'm headed back to camp. Try me if you get this."

An idea had been brewing in the back of her mind, and she tried Trudy too. Trudy did not do cell phones. Push-button dial, okay. Cell phones, no. Trudy's number rang twice. Allison stood in the lodge, looking out across the dirt road and the jumble of cabins—no two the same—wedged haphazardly into the hillside. The cabins looked as if they had fallen off a truck and were scattered at random. Frank Lloyd Wright never worked here. In the distance stood an undersized deck with a group of hunters huddled together in the glow of a battery-powered fluorescent light, like a classic kerosene-fueled hurricane lamp minus the charm. A plume of collective cigar smoke was thick but not enough to shield them from the snow. Allison supposed they had an elk being processed somewhere. She envied their success, their routines and their carefree moment.

"Hello?"

"Trudy?"

"Are you okay?"

"I'm fine."

"They're looking for your guy Bostwick."

"I heard that on the news. We stopped in Rifle for a bite. By the time we came out, it was all over the radio. Practically a manhunt."

"You just now got home?" said Allison.

"Jerry dropped me off—yeah," said Trudy.

"He's not staying?"

"We're taking a break—it's been pretty intense. I think he was more fascinated with Mr. Bostwick than I was."

"Do you think Bostwick could have done it?"

"I can't figure out why he would shoot the buffalo now," said Trudy. Allison pictured Trudy wandering in her kitchen, a concerned look on her face. "Why now after Keating is gone?"

That was exactly the right question. Was there something that could have been said or done to provoke Ethan Bostwick after Josh Keating was found on the rocks of Oyster Lake?

"I don't know," said Allison. "I was wondering if you would mind coming back up to Meeker."

For a second Allison thought she'd lost the cell signal.

"I can't go up in the woods with all the hunting going on," said Trudy.

"No, not with me."

"And I'm supposed to go with Jerry to this school board meeting on Wednesday night."

"It doesn't have to be tomorrow," said Allison, drawing a line in her mind on a map from where she was standing to Trudy's kitchen. It might take three hours to drive around the Flat Tops, even though they were only fifteen miles apart.

"I'm not sure I want to do that school board thing anyway," said Trudy. "If I'm telling the truth."

"Well, there's a big-deal announcement from the federal government later this week, something to do with drilling leases. Apparently Josh Keating stood to make a bundle. And there's the lawsuit Keating slapped on Ethan Bostwick. I don't want to put you in the middle of anything—I just want you to do some research."

"I'm in," said Trudy. There was confidence in her voice. "I need to deliver some herbs up to the store in Meeker anyway—the store where they agreed to start carrying my line."

"Great," said Allison.

"Do you want a copy of the lawsuit?"

"Whatever you can find out about it," said Allison.

"Done," said Trudy.

"And another thing," said Allison. "Keep an eye out for anything to do with the customers I've got up at camp. Do you have something to write these names down?"

Allison waited while Trudy rustled around for a piece of paper and pen.

"Go," said Trudy.

"Okay—Terry Zamora, Max Hiatt, Conrad Gray and Austin Rayburn. Though Zamora—you probably won't come across him. He's from Denver."

"He's the one I met, isn't he?" said Trudy. "Big guy, bald?"

"In the parking lot, yeah, that was him."

"I didn't care for him."

"Not a cuddly one," said Allison.

"How do I get hold of you to let you know if I find anything?"

In the distance, the smoking hunters were now in the process of rigging a tarp over the deck, apparently so they could continue to smoke cigars outside. The snowfall was dense.

"Leave a message on my cell phone. I'll get up to a ridge and check the messages. And it's possible I'll come back down again tomorrow or the next day. Stay in that same motel if you need to remain overnight, the one where we were talking in the parking lot today. You can leave a note there. What's that school board thing all about?"

"Something Jerry wants me to do. I'm not sure it's going to happen. This is so much better."

The trail was covered in snow, and as darkness settled in it occurred to Allison that she ought to turn around and postpone this journey. She had brought batteries for her headlamp and kept the beam on, though it made the falling snow look menacing and thick. In her mind she could see the page in the guidebook that covered horse-riding safety. Riding at night? Bad idea. Always stay in the open where you might pick up some light; never plunge into the woods. Don't ride alone unless it's absolutely, positively necessary. Unless it's a matter of life or death.

Lightning plodded along as if it were midday. Allison swung the headlamp beam around, wondering if she might spot Devo on her flank, or a mountain lion sitting like a cat on its haunches, licking a paw and waiting for a treat. In her private tunnel of trees, the view was like the repetitious background of an old cartoon rotating on a continuous loop, moving steadily and relentlessly toward her.

She turned her head from side to side, flicked the beam into the woods. A hiccup of alarm flashed through her chest. Steady, she told herself. Easy. She should have found a minute or two in the last week to call home. Did she really know how many weeks slipped by between phone calls? She pictured her father seated in his brown leather armchair, grading essays on *To Kill A Mockingbird* or *Lord of the Flies*. Bob Coil read every word of every essay, wrote neatly in the margins. He always found something good to say. He would read until the late news, watch the headlines and then turn in, happy with routine and satisfied with his station on earth. She pictured her mother knitting or sewing, doing a bit of spot cleaning or making phone calls for her church group or an upcoming school fundraiser. Lois Coil enjoyed mint tea and was obsessed with frugality. Allison could never remember her once verbalizing a dream, a wish, a want.

The sandwich in Allison's pocket tempted every fiber in her appetite, as if a few tasty calories might suffice to calm her down. She took two bites and put it back, and told herself to concentrate on the trail.

Trail?

Suddenly Lightning was walking between two trees that were closer than any two trees on the trail. Allison whipped her head around and felt the night and the blackness swallow her up. She shook off the memories of her parents. It was as if she had been sitting in the living room with them, relaxed and warm, and not paying attention to her riding.

The view ahead was trail-less.

The distinct extra-wide gap in the woods, the way forward, had disappeared.

She was someplace unfamiliar in the Flat Tops. Lightning might have inadvertently detoured from the main trail ten steps ago, or a thousand. Allison had an urge to blame the horse, but decided that would be unproductive.

Shit.

She dismounted and hitched Lightning to a tree, gave him a reassuring pat on the rump. "My fault," she said. She retraced the direction they had come, an eye cast to the left for the opening, something that said *trail* more than the way Lightning had chosen. Everything looked the same. Every tree. Every snowflake. Every probe of her headlamp into the white void.

She felt her breath shorten, her heart knock on the door to her throat. It was the moment when you know you are entering a situation that could become an entertaining story or could become something much, much worse. Would it be possible to backtrack to Trapper's? Should she try? The light, fluffy and quickly falling snow offered no possibility of holding even a trace of Lightning's hoofprints. A soft wind caressed Allison's cheek. Fuck you, she thought. She trudged through snow that came up to her mid-calf, stepping around trees, looking for a channel, an indication of a gap that screamed, "Trail right here!" The woods gave her nothing to go on. Her boots shuffled through snow with the same airiness as Styrofoam peanuts. She left no tracks. The trees took a giant step closer together, the wind turned up a notch, and in one slow 360-degree turn with her headlamp flashing off the trunks, she realized that she was not even certain of the way back to Lightning.

Monday Evening

Trudy knew who was calling. She knew it in her bones, and wasn't sure she was ready for him.

She dusted potting soil off her fingers above the trays of sorrel and walked back into the kitchen on the fifth ring. Three cats were perched on the counter like stoic sentries. She held a finger to Pepper's gray nose. Pepper immediately began to lick the sorrel-dusted fingertip with her coarse tongue.

"Hello?"

"Hey there," said Jerry.

"You just left."

"Longest three hours of my life. I can't believe you wouldn't let me stay."

"That was a mutual decision."

"You talked me into it. I caved too easily."

"We agreed," said Trudy.

"I know, I know. I just wanted to hear your voice."

"Are you at home right now?"

Trudy stirred a block of frozen vegetable stock, now melting in a pot on the stove.

"Yes indeed," said Jerry. "Empty home."

"Just for a night or so."

"Or so?" asked Jerry. "The school board meeting is Wednesday night. I've already put your name on the sign-up sheet. We might have to hang in there for our chance to speak, though. There's a big group of parents signed up because a popular principal is being let go, and the reasons are hush-hush."

"Allison called," said Trudy.

"More on those dead buffalo?"

"She wants me to look up some court records in Meeker tomorrow. She had to go back to camp."

"Are you going?"

"Yes. And thought I'd make a delivery to the grocery store while I was at it."

"Board meeting starts at seven. You'll be back in time?"

"I don't know," said Trudy, uncertain how disappointed to sound.

"You're not on board with us?"

"I still think we're moving too fast."

"Glad to hear you say 'we.' That feels good."

Trudy stirred the block of brown frozen stock sitting in a shallow pool of its own liquid.

"You're our spokesperson," said Jerry. "I've already talked to Brad and Lilly. They are fired up."

"If the idea makes sense, the idea will sell itself. Maybe we should meet with some district people first rather than make a big public splash. We could get a feel for how we'd be welcomed and how our issues would go over."

Trudy was surprised to find the words roll out of her mouth. She hadn't even articulated the strategy adjustment to herself, but the ideas must have been brewing somewhere. She felt calm saying it. The approach felt humane. Felt right.

"You're backing out?"

"If I can get home in time, I'll come along," said Trudy.

If the others started their public campaign without her, that would be perfect. They'd be off and gone. If they were successful, she wouldn't be needed anyway.

"You're part of the team," said Jerry. "We need you. You're the lead-off hitter."

She let silence build on the line.

They had talked extensively about their reaction to Bostwick during the drive back. Trudy had mostly listened. Jerry had been impressed with Bostwick's zeal but not enamored with his style. When she saw a drilling truck on the road now, she understood it was part of a larger, mad scramble that was splitting western Colorado in two.

"But why do it in public? What's the point?"

"To send a message," said Jerry. "Let them know we're here, let them know the community cares about this issue and that we want to raise the bar. If you go in for a meeting at their offices, they just take a few notes and nod their heads and shine you off. But if you step out in public, they have to sit up and take notice."

"First we need to get inside a school and see what's going on," said Trudy. "Our first step out the door, as a group, is so important. It sets the tone for everything, the whole relationship with the school district."

"Glad to hear you say 'our.' But you sound pretty certain." There was a deep note of resignation in his voice.

"I'm going to Meeker tomorrow," said Trudy. "You do whatever you think is best. That's my feeling at this point."

The Meeker trip was full of unmapped territory, but it had its purpose. Trudy decided she would pack a bag and make sure she spent the night away, no matter what white lie she had told Jerry.

"We don't want you to say anything outside your comfort zone," said Jerry. "We don't all have to say the same thing or in the same way. One chorus, different voices."

Having been given the opportunity to gently back up a step, Jerry had inched forward. There was a faint but clear note of stridency in his voice. She let him hang fire, let him see if he could hear his own words bouncing around in the growing, uncomfortable chasm.

"Trudy?"

A tear ran down her cheek.

"I'm here," she said.

"I still want to see you."

"Everything will be fine," said Trudy. It was the blandest

statement she could come up with. She walked back out to the greenhouse. During the last few minutes it had started to snow. The last thing she needed was a slick, treacherous drive out to Meeker.

"Okay," said Jerry. "I'm going to hold you to that."

They said good night and hung up. Trudy let out a sigh. The relief was overwhelming.

Monday Evening

"'I want to live deep and suck out all the marrow of life, to cut a broad swath and shave close, to drive life into a corner, and reduce it to its lowest terms, and if it proved to be mean, why, then to get to the where and genuine meanness of it, and publish its meanness to the world.'"

Devo spoke the words into the camera, slowly and with conviction. A quote from Thoreau, the original devolutionist. It was night and he knew the snowfall would be dense. It was dark outside. It was cold. He wasn't feeling very well. The snowfall had come full-bore and it was thick. This snow arrived with its teeth bared. Due to the darkness, the snow would appear dense and sinister, obscuring the image of his face on the video.

"Thoreau talked about riding the railroad," said Devo into the camera, hoping the snow was collecting on his beard. "He wondered if people rode the railroad or whether it rode them, changing their lives, increasing the levels of expectation. Out here, there is no railroad. It's you. It's what's around you. But mostly it's you. And it's survival. In a snowstorm like this, you have to keep your wits. Yes, it's snowing. Yes, it's dark. When I snap off this video camera, it's going to take my eyes a minute to completely readjust to the pitch dark. I won't be able to see much. But here's the deal. You've got to break down this moment into parts. Night won't kill you. The cold might kill you if you aren't prepared. Hypothermia is a possibility. You have to maintain your core body temperature. You have to realize that you are standing here right now, and you are fine. You can feel the cold, but you are well protected under layers of clothing. Your feet are warm."

This was a bit of a lie. He was queasy and he hoped his fear didn't show.

"I had some venison jerky an hour ago, before I set out. It's important not to eat very much because it might make you feel good and give you too much comfort. You have to develop an accurate fuel gauge, to know when you're on empty. You have to 'stay hungry,' as they say."

Devo wasn't going to talk about the real reason he had ventured out.

"So my system is burning fuel. I'm not on the edge. The night can't kill me unless I walk into a physical object and hurt myself, perhaps knock myself out. The snow can't take me down by itself. In fact, the snow can provide protection and warmth. You can hike in the snowfall all day if you're prepared for it. Look at Lewis and Clark in the Bitterroot Mountains of Idaho. Up to their waists in snow and still moving. It's all breaking it down to the basics. It's your head. It's staying cool and collected. I have lost my way a bit now, but I know I'm not too far off course."

Devo slowly rotated the camera away from his face, presenting a complete panorama of the woods, the tiny light throwing only enough wattage to dent the darkness, like one birthday candle with a feeble wick. Most importantly, he had turned the camera away in time so that it didn't capture his flash of anxiety. He felt a negative surge flow through his system, a tremendously alone sensation that he hadn't felt since the first couple of weeks. Weird! Where had it come from? Maybe it was his brief contact with civilization at Trapper's Lake, seeing people inside their cabins, watching them eat and drink through the plate-glass window of the lodge. Because of the big burn area, the lodge sat exposed on a high dirt knoll. It was like a massive hearth of warmth and comfort. Devo had been able to make out Allison standing near the window, talking on the phone. Allison. Clearly a soldier's soldier. Clearly a do-it-right sort. Devo had found a safe place near the jumble of cabins where he could watch for the return of her truck. From his view above the small buildings—no two cabins alike—he could see foot traffic coming and going from one particular building. The building had no windows, and a few of those coming and going were carrying towels. Dry towels in, wet towels out. It didn't take Sherlock Holmes. The thought of a hot shower, of a real toilet, was an enormous temptation. It made Devo feel like a drying-out junkie who had been asked to the guard the evidence locker for a narc squad. He imagined himself standing inside the shower stall, steam and hot water spraying parts of his soiled flesh that seemed fused to his clothing. But he didn't want to scare anyone—although by midday the traffic to the building was nonexistent—and he didn't want to scare himself.

He waited all day. He watched the lodge staff making their rounds, cleaning cabins and changing sheets. He moved around as they did, but he always stayed on the opposite side of the camp as they worked. He had stumbled across a food cooler and couldn't resist a peek. The lid squeaked like an angry cat caught in a trap but he helped himself to two slices of premium roast beef, two slices of Swiss cheese and four baby dill pickles. Lunch and dinner. Plenty. He found an outdoor faucet and drank heartily. He was losing hope that Allison would return that day, when her truck suddenly came cruising back up the hill. She had gone into the lodge, called somebody on her phone, and re-rigged her horse. The light was on its last legs. Snow had started weak and thick, then shifted to threatening and thick. Keeping up with a rider on a horse had its challenges but he had managed, knowing the trail and knowing the direction. He didn't need to stay too close.

He had followed her.

He had followed her too long.

Now was a moment to suck the marrow. Because she was lost. And so was he.

There had been a few *uh-oh* moments since winter had set in for good, but nothing like this. Somehow he had gotten turned around. He had lost his bearings. A first for him. He stood in the darkness. He could hear Allison somewhere ahead. He could smell the earthy odor of her horse. He liked to think he could smell Allison too. That didn't matter now. He had no idea which way was which. He had reduced life to its lowest terms. He could be positioned near the main trail, or way off the trail—it didn't much matter because he didn't know which direction to look for it.

Now it came down to disassembling the moment, understanding the threats and reviewing the options.

Devo acknowledged to himself that his toes had lost their battle with the cold, over an hour ago. There was no turning back on cold toes. They were seeds that would soon sprout and send cold vines climbing up his ankles and calves.

Devo snapped the camera on again. If it still worked, why not share the agony?

He let the snow fall in the camera light's beam, gave it a minute for everyone to feel the moment, suck the marrow.

"Thoreau talked about walking to his cabin at night, about how his body would find its way home if its master would forsake it. He compared the walk to his own hand moving to his own mouth without assistance." He paused, peered around. Who knew how long the battery would last? Who knew what the next eight or ten hours would hold? He tried to wipe any trace of fear from his face. But why? This was real. This was very real.

Devo screwed up his courage, thought of his video fans, thought of his purpose, and tried to break down the moment into its smallest parts, tried to review what he knew about building snow caves. He wondered if the camera battery could be jumped to create a spark that could be used to build a fire. But with what wire? Into what tinder? And with what tools might he strip wire from the camera?

"I wish I knew where I was. I know roughly where I am, but that doesn't mean I'm close to shelter or warmth. That doesn't mean I'll survive. I need my wits about me. I need to stay calm. I need to take a quick inventory of my resources and come up with a plan."

He took a deep breath. And another. His chin had gone numb. His bones ached. His energy was low. Allison was up here somewhere. Devo imagined he could still smell the horse.

"This could be the roughest night yet. I'm not sure what's going to happen. I'll keep you posted."

He clicked the camera off, peered into the darkness in the direction he had last seen Allison. She had to be out there and it couldn't be any easier for her. Suddenly his ankles were numb. He was standing on stumps. The ankles had been eaten alive. They were gone. He tried to take a step but the snow on the ground came flying up and slammed the side of his face.

7

Monday Night

What was that?

She thought she heard a muffled voice, then a soft whump. Something falling in the snow.

In the farthest corner of Allison's left eye a dim white light had flashed. It was a pinhead dot burning through the falling snow. Then it blinked out.

Lightning nickered. He had nickered earlier, thank God, and gave her direction back to his big resilient self.

She stepped forward carefully, thinking she was close to where the light must have been. She held Lightning in tow, the horse a welcome weight on the rein, a friend. She stared at the spot where the light had been.

"Did you hear something around here?" Allison said.

A garbled, pleading moan was dead ahead. It was a sound from the depths, guttural and heavy with agony.

Allison's heart rate intensified. She slowed her pace, taking a full rest between each step.

She flicked her head up and down, the lamplight struggling more and more to burrow into the darkness. She stepped, paused, stepped.

"Anyone there?"

The moan again, much closer, and she felt a jolt of adrenaline that prickled the skin on her nape. Maybe the sound was a fluke, two trees rubbing together or a forest form of black magic—

gentle wind and old tree trunks bending. Maybe it was a Douglas fir bass clarinet, the wind cutting through the trees just so.

But this sound was human.

"Goddammit," said Allison. "What the hell? Who is that?"

She squatted down and peered ahead, searching the outer edges of the headlamp beam. There. A human shape lying awkwardly between two trees. It was white on top, but facing her was a swatch of clothing, a cape, and she knew immediately it was Devo. She moved forward and put a hand under his head, lifted it and swept his face clear.

"Hang with me," Allison said.

She dug into her jacket pockets first. She owned four silver tubes, waterproof cases of wooden matchsticks—strike anywhere—that followed her around in various packs and coats and panniers. Her hand gripped the silver tube. Fire would be a challenge, but she should be up to it. Shelter might be a different story, depending on whether Lightning had thought to pack a hatchet. And she still had her sandwich. But the main issue was reviving Devo and raising his core temperature.

She pulled her knife from its sheath. She remembered an aspen tree a few paces back. Aspen were never alone, their complex root system capable of studding land in densely packed groves. Her headlamp flicked from tree trunk to tree trunk. She debated— dig a hole or build a base for the fire with deadwood? The answer came in the form of aspen trunks. All dead. Gifts. They pushed over easily. She wedged them between two trees and snapped off a batch of four-foot lengths. They cracked apart like fireworks. She hustled them over to a spot a few feet from Devo. She scanned for other trees and branches that might work for a shelter. First things first. The snow was dense, but she felt the surge of energy that comes with having a life-saving purpose. She built the top layer with the dry sides of the wood facing up, but they instantly sprouted a layer of snow.

Time was not a friend.

She trudged into the woods, grabbing dead branches. Inside the cloak of a bushy evergreen, she scored a six-foot bough thoroughly dried, well covered and protected by the tree's outer skirt. Several tempting branches were too far out of reach. She would come back in an hour when the snow was higher. She returned to the base with an armload of fuel, then put her knife to the bark on an aspen, first slicing then shredding. Tinder. She stuffed a batch into her jacket, then made another. This could be dicey. This could fail. This could fail miserably.

Back with Devo, she knelt and cleared snow from his face.

"Hang in there," she said. "Please, please hang in there."

After clearing a spot, she placed a loose ball of tinder on the wood base. She put her back to the wind and lit a match. The flame hung for a second, a mini sun draped on the end of a stick. The tinder took. Match to fireball in seconds. Allison started with twigs, went to sticks and then to small branches. One branch snuffed out the progress and she yanked the offender away. The heat grew. She let it cook while she searched for more fuel. She silently thanked Lightning for getting lost in the woods rather than a broad meadow where fuel would be as scarce as one-dollar shots of Patrón.

The fire threw light on a tree. Allison turned her headlamp off. She led Lightning closer to the fire, placed him where he could serve as a windbreak. Snow melted in an ever-widening ring. The first layer of the base burned through and the fire nestled down, issuing a plume of sparks and the accompanying crackles and pops, a satisfying sound. The snow around Devo started to melt and she pushed him closer, first scissoring his legs up one at a time and then dragging his upper body. It was possible, she supposed, that his core might warm up and he would still remain unconscious. She needed to get some broth down his gullet, but had no pan to boil water. And no broth.

Next, shelter. She spent a half hour gathering wood—six-foot sections for a lean-to and any deadwood she could harvest to keep the fire going. The sucker was voracious. She had built a monster that needed food. She was deep-down tired, not to mention hungry. She rested by the fire to eat half her sandwich which went down like a chewable elixir.

She finished the shelter, borrowing bits of leather strap from Lightning's saddle to lash the crossbeams to two trees, then laying branches from the crossbeam to the snowy ground for the crude lean-to. She filled a Nalgene bottle with snow and set it close to the fire to melt the contents without damaging the plastic. She packed more snow in and repeated the step, generating two cups of warm water. Devo had been making good guttural noises. She imagined his subconscious backing away from the brink, but she had no clue as to what was going on. His clothing wrap was now free of snow, and she had built the lean-to around him so the heat would gather behind him, to work on him from both sides. Pulling on him, she sat him up, crossing his legs in front. He was tangled up with a metal brace around his waist, a video camera attached to one end of a pole that protruded at an angle from his body.

"My friend," she said. "I'm here. You gotta help me." She spoke at full volume. "You have to drink this. It's water."

She pressed the lip of the bottle against his sealed mouth, tipped it to his crusty lips. Water dribbled onto his bearded chin. Even in the cold, his body emitted a potent stench and she found herself minimizing the volume she inhaled. She turned her mouth into her jacket.

"Come on, buddy," she said. "Can you feel the fire? You're okay. I'm okay." She smiled at the echo of the self-help book. "Want to the write the sequel? We'll be rich and famous. You're already famous. Come on, Devo. Work with me here."

She gave the water another try and this time his mouth parted. She heard a low, internal groan—a faint stirring.

"That's it," said Allison. "I need you. I need you now. You gotta help me."

She gave him a gentle shake.

Both eyes cracked open.

"What the—"

"Drink this, it's warm water."

"Fire," said Devo, drawing it out as if it was a four-syllable word.

"We've gotta get you dried off underneath."

"Can't believe—"

Devo bent at the waist, still sitting, and bellowed like he'd stepped in hell. "My fingers! I can't feel my fingers!"

"We'll get them warmed up," said Allison. "The fingers will come around."

Devo shed a glove, a thick wrap of hand-sewn leather. He stared at his fingers in agony. They were blue. He was cold to the core, with no body fat as barrier.

"Where are we?" His words came in slow, heavy chunks.

"Somewhere between Trapper's Lake and my camp," said Allison, noting that her own fingertips were in pain. Toes, too. "I got off the trail, but I'll need daylight to find it again."

"And me?"

"What about?"

"How did I get here?"

"I assume you were following me," said Allison. "Then you must have collapsed."

"I could have died."

"We aren't out of this yet," said Allison. "In fact, I need to make another run for wood."

Having explored every direction and gleaned the easy pickings, she chose a direction at random and plunged into the forest. Her headlamp lit only healthy, green saplings and their healthy, green parents. She wormed her way into a few evergreens, hoping for deadwood underneath their white skirts. The tips of branches dipped into the deepening snow. The space inside the trees felt warm, close and insanely quiet. The payoff was a kind of internal calm that Buddhist monks spent decades trying to achieve.

Allison returned to the fire with a full load of wood—another hour's worth. The key was to keep the fire small enough for the necessary heat but no more. As much as she loved a raging bonfire, she would not have time or fuel to keep it stoked. It was a matter of balance.

Devo had moved close enough to hug the fire. He bent over, studying his frozen paw. His camera contraption flopped and wobbled about like a separate life form.

"Are you okay?"

"My hand," said Devo. "It's throbbing."

"A good thing that you can feel it."

Allison fed a few branches to the shrinking fire, and the flames spit and spattered in thanks. The new, wet food was barely edible. Within a minute the fire went back to the business of gobbling it up. The fire felt good, but it would be hours before she was completely warm.

She remembered her sandwich, her brain tipped off by her empty stomach which had been shrieking for attention for the past hour. She retrieved what was left of her sandwich from Lightning's panniers and tore it in two hunks. She handed the larger piece to Devo. His mouth opened as if he had used super glue for lipstick and snagged a flap of dangling roast beef with his teeth.

"Good stuff—fresh bread," he said. "Long time."

"Eat up," said Allison. "Or I'll have yours too." Inside, her chest shuddered and shivered against the cold.

"What are you going to say?" said Devo.

"About what?"

"About me."

"What about you?"

"Finding me in the snow like that."

Allison pondered Devo's sunken eyes, the knotted tangle of hair and whiskers that covered his face. He was two parts caveman, one part raccoon. Maybe a Rasta raccoon.

"Who cares?"

"You won't say anything?"

"Who would I say anything to?"

"Your friends," said Devo. "Hunters, guides, anyone."

"I hadn't thought about it."

Allison finished her bites, took a drink of water, and realized she hadn't needed to pee since Trapper's. She couldn't afford to get dehydrated.

Devo was still massaging his fingers over the fire. A faint shudder wracked his body.

"You have to help me," said Devo.

"By not saying anything?"

"Exactly," said Devo. "This whole project—everything—would go up in smoke."

"Because you met your limit?"

Devo sighed, rubbed his hands.

"People would laugh." He said it with a sharp snarl. "The story would be finished. Kaput."

Allison stood up, poked the fire, tossed another branch on the orange-red circle of heat. The original base of wood was now thoroughly consumed. The fire had created a space that kept snow at bay. It had stopped snowing. It was midnight or later. She had no desire to undermine Devo and his growing cult. It was absurd to think man could devolve, could forget, could shake off industrialization or the modern world. Wasn't there a happy middle ground? Simply move back to the country where everyone had to multi-task, get gritty and down to earth? She had no interest in dimming Devo's mission, and clearly he'd been upset by the tainted water. His heart was in the right place.

"Couldn't you use it as a story—a hard lesson learned, that sort of thing?"

"Doesn't work," said Devo. "It's a deal-killer. It would be like Lewis and Clark having fresh vegetables dropped from a helicopter on their way across the Bitterroots."

"Even though that's what happened with you?"

"Even though," said Devo. He turned to look at her, a pleading look in his eyes.

"Okay," said Allison. "I don't have anyone to tell anyway. And we still have to make it out of here for this to make a difference."

"We'll make it now."

"What makes you so sure?"

"I can tell," said Devo. "It's your confidence. You practically reek of the stuff."

"You're easily misguided," said Allison.

Devo arched his back, held one hand over the fire. "You pulled out of it," he said. "Kept your cool."

"I guess," said Allison. It hadn't been a choice. "Do you want to take shifts sleeping until it gets light? Are you well enough?"

"I need to stay as close to the fire as possible and stay alert—you get some rest."

Allison eyed the lean-to longingly. If only she could move the fire over—the mini-shelter was outside the prime heat zone. She could curl up next to the fire, but she was after that pup-tent sensation too.

"Anything new on the tainted water?" said Devo.

"They're testing it," said Allison. The question slammed back a batch of information that she had cryogenically frozen for the past few hours. "Now the big question is who slaughtered four buffalo on the ranch owned by Josh Keating, the hunter who collapsed on the rocks." Allison gave Devo an overview, but didn't have the energy for detail. She was whipped. She wanted to sleep, now that the prospect had been raised.

They argued for a few minutes like an old married couple. Devo wanted her to sleep as long as she could. Allison insisted that Devo wake her in an hour to trade the fire watch.

She brushed snow from Lightning, turned him around and took off his saddle, laying it on a clear spot by the fire. She dug into the panniers and found dry but edible Fig Newtons, split them with Devo.

Allison made one more run for wood. She hit a small jackpot with a long-dead snag she had missed twenty paces from the fire. The snag pulled over easily, a thirty-footer. She returned with an armful that was so high she had to navigate back to the fire by peeking through the pile on her chest.

Exhausted, she wedged her butt into the lean-to and fashioned a makeshift pillow from an extra fleece pullover she had found in a pannier.

She lay down stiffly, tried to get comfortable. Warmth was an abstract concept. Parts of her felt reassured, others down deep seemed unconvinced. Her fingertips refused to thaw.

Devo's request still rubbed her wrong. His insistence on maintaining his mythology pissed her off, especially the fact that he was more concerned about his reputation than the fact that he had come very close to joining the *Into The Wild* drifter as an anti-civilization eccentric whose body had to be chipped out of the tundra come spring.

The only difference with Devo was his attempt to deliver a blow-by-blow account of his daily regression online. Allison felt no compelling desire to wreck his fantasy, but the way he had extracted the pledge of silence was bizarre. Allison knew that embarrassment wouldn't be the first thing on her mind if she herself had come to within a few minutes of devolving all the way to the cemetery.

Tuesday Morning

Allison popped an eye open and took in a frozen, calm scene that involved too much illumination. An Abert squirrel, jet black, was sitting casually on what was left of the lengths of snag that she had brought to the fire. It was munching on a chewy piece of bark. Allison realized it was the squirrel's snappy chattering that had pierced her sleep. The bad news was the fire, or lack thereof. It now issued only a thin, useless wisp of smoke. Allison knew instantly that Devo was gone.

She took a quick reading of her body, noting the tight muscles and cold hips and toes. She stood up with care, not wanting to shock her deep-slumbering system. The fire smoldered but a gentle kick revealed a plate-size pool of happily-baking embers. She placed two pieces of wood on top to catch fire.

Stupid.

She kicked the logs off where she'd placed them. The urge to build the fire was instinct borne of a regressive Girl Scout DNA she had never owned. She had no food to cook, no water to heat. She would relish the heat, but starting a good fire would consume a half-hour or more.

Dawn delivered a flat, still light but it was enough to indicate the direction of sunrise. Allison got her bearings, saddled up Lightning, promised him a double bag of oats back at camp, and picked up Devo's trail in the snow, which made a beeline for the heart of the Flat Tops. No thank-you note, no nothing.

So much for bonding.

Tuesday Morning

The doors to the two-story sandstone building in the middle of the town square in Meeker opened at 9 a.m. Block letters above the government-issue glass and steel-door entryway said "RIO BLANCO COUNTY." Gray linoleum-covered steps led up to the office of the court clerk at the top of the stairs. Doors to a courtroom were open, and three lawyers had huddled on a bench in the hall outside, briefcases balanced on their knees. One wore a black cowboy hat. The light was fluorescent, the mood functional but cheery. Every surface gleamed sharp and clean.

Trudy took a breath. She had been anxious on the drive up from Glenwood Springs, but had kept a lid on the anxiety by telling herself that she was helping Allison. The drive included its share of ice and slush, more treacherous than the first trek up. The ride into Meeker had been an uneasy blur of caution.

Standing in the outer hall of the clerk's office, she felt as if a spotlight tracked her every move. She felt seriously underdressed, too casual. She wore a green turtleneck, blue jeans, a jean jacket and zippered boots. An off-stage voice seemed to announce her arrival to everyone for blocks around. "Stranger in town," chanted the voice. Trudy's chest fluttered; her breath came short.

The woman tending the clerk's office was tall, slender and more polished and city-like than Trudy expected. She could have been working in a Denver office tower with her long pleated navy skirt and a plain-Jane but sharp white blouse. Her name was Anne. Her hair was short, straight and cropped close. She sat at her desk behind a wide L-shaped counter. Trudy asked for the case and the woman returned after a few moments away in the metal bookshelves behind the counter.

"We've had Denver reporters up here to make copies of that file and poke around town. We post these reports on the Internet now," she said. "That could have saved you the trip."

"That's okay," said Trudy, suppressing a mild shake in her voice.

"It doesn't matter to me," said Anne. "A public document is a public document, but I know there are all sorts of reporters out there calling themselves all sorts of different things nowadays and working for more than television and newspapers."

"I'm not a reporter," said Trudy.

"No notebook," said Anne. "And you don't look the type, whatever that is. Jaded, I suppose."

"Thanks," said Trudy. "I had to come to Meeker anyway."

"Copies are ten cents a page," said Anne. "So the lawsuit itself will cost you four-fifty. Wait a couple months and the file will be a few inches thicker from all the new motions and filings. Consider yourself lucky and a lot less broke."

Trudy thanked her again and gave the papers a quick flip-through on the counter, but Anne told her it was fine to take them to the wooden bench in the hall.

Trudy had seen few original legal documents, so it took awhile to find the meat of the story. The lawsuit was filed by Josh and Loretta Keating against Stanley and Ruth Bostwick, Ethan's parents. Ethan was running the show but his parents had their name on the deed. In their lawsuit, the Keatings laid out a long history of how they had used, accessed and enjoyed a significant chunk of what was technically Bostwick land. They laid out point after point that the use of the land was "actual." The "actual" idea was apparently critical. The Keatings cared for the land, using a footpath through it for access to fish the White River. The lawsuit pointed out that this use of the property had been going on for twenty-three years, well beyond the minimum eighteen years needed to claim adverse possession under state law. The suit cited several cases with unusual names—Suwansawasdi vs. Palmer Ranch, and Schoenherr vs. Campbell. The lawsuit walked through "the underlying principles of adverse possession."

Clearly the law required the Keatings to show that they had used and maintained and walked through the property as a hostile act. From everything Trudy could gather, the Keatings could not have made the claim if they had awakened one morning and suddenly realized they had been mistakenly wandering beyond their own property line for years. They had to show purposeful intent and that it was a "hostile" act, long planned.

Trudy could feel the sting. She knew the land was beautiful. The thought of seeing the land ripped out from underneath you would make you ill. She imagined Ethan Bostwick receiving word of the lawsuit for the first time and having the whole concept explained to him. She could taste his nausea.

Now with the buffalo slaughter, Trudy realized that Allison was in the crossfire of a nasty feud, and her mind raced to her friend, picturing Allison in a tent or on horseback with these men and not knowing she was with people who had already pulled out all the stops. If there were friends of Keating's in that camp, they must have been part of the war. You don't file an adverse possession claim unless you are extremely angry or a major league sociopath. You have to feel pure hatred in order to use a legal trick to steal your neighbor's property.

Trudy returned to Anne at the counter, paid for a copy of the paperwork to take with her.

"It's strange that under the law a person has to claim that he was intending to grab the land all along."

"That's why the whole state is freaked out," said Anne, lowering her voice. "Everybody is thinking about their land, and thinking about what their neighbors are thinking."

"Who is this Stewart Exby?" said Trudy, flipping to the last page. "I mean, I know he's a lawyer."

Anne didn't look down at the paper.

"He's been the main man in this town for decades, lawyer wise," said Anne. "And the Keatings' lawyer on that case."

"And people think this has a chance, yanking the land away?"

"Apparently," said Anne. "Look, I am saying too much. It isn't my place to comment. I shouldn't weigh in, not that the whole town isn't buzzing like a nest of angry bees."

"You've been very helpful," said Trudy. She paused, not wanting to come across as eager or desperate. "Do you think this Mr. Exby would talk to me?"

The question pulled Anne up short. She walked away from the counter. "As long as you don't mind paying his hourly fee," she said. "Bring cash—I heard he doesn't take checks."

"I'm curious," said Trudy. "How are they going to prove that they intended to take the property—that they had that plan all along?"

Anne turned around again and headed down into one of the stacks.

"You've read the suit." Trudy could hear the disembodied voice, clear and sharp. "But you didn't ask for the depositions."

Depositions?

Two hours later, Trudy turned the last page. She sat up straight and stretched. Her spine and neck creaked. She'd been frozen in place, rapt. It was as if she had been watching a movie. The story came in fragments from different parts of the plot, like shards of glass falling into place in a kaleidoscope and finally revealing a pattern. Ten minutes into reading the depositions, she had started taking notes—names and dates. The main thread wasn't hard to follow. It was a rope thick enough to tie up the Queen Mary. Reading the various grillings, Trudy had the sensation of listening to a secret audiotape from a fight club. She felt sick.

Light-headed, she stood up and returned the pile of folders to the counter.

She needed fresh air. She walked in a daze outside into the park that surrounded the courthouse. The park sported a fresh dusting of snow, just a spritz from the clouds. The sun was out and the blinding reflection of the white coating over the town was like a jolt of electricity, fingertips to the eyes. Her vision blurred. She bent over to let blood work its way back to her head.

She drove to the motel and checked in, to make sure she had a place to stay and to force herself to not hightail it down the highway. She wanted to stick around and help. Ethan Bostwick might have been assertive and abrasive, but her heart went out to him. He might have made himself a bull's-eye, but nobody deserved a hundred arrows when one would do.

A nap was tempting. Food was more critical. She was famished and thirsty. She went into a café across the street and settled into a wooden booth. She ordered a mushroom omelet, happy to find a place that served breakfast at lunchtime, and herbal tea. The omelet arrived quickly. The white toast was soaked in butter. The mushrooms were fresh and the eggs were fluffy. Trudy sipped tea and took out her notes.

There had been seventeen individual depositions. One was with Ethan Bostwick, another with his wife, Jennifer. One was with Josh Keating, another his wife Loretta. The other thirteen were with people who knew Josh Keating, who had spent time on his property, who had fished the White River, who had been told they could fish the entire one-mile stretch of water, who had been reassured that the length of the river was under Josh Keating's control, or who had been expressly informed that while the river in that section might be under the neighbor's control, it didn't matter because the neighbor didn't use it. Several had testified to hearing Josh Keating state plainly and clearly that he intended to take the property soon through adverse possession. All testified to the fact that Josh Keating's motivations had nothing to do with philosophical differences over lifestyle or environmental concerns with the neighbor, Ethan Bostwick. They had all sung in unison. Their answers in the depositions were carbon copies.

Trudy went through her notes. She had scribbled pages, but as the depositions grew repetitive, she had written less and less. The last five were one word—"ditto." The only other key information she had written down concerned how long they had known Josh Keating and where they lived. Sipping a second cup of tea, she wrote a simple spreadsheet of the names of those who had given depositions in support of Keating. When she was finished, she pulled out the list of names she had jotted down when Allison had called. One name overlapped:

Austin Rayburn.

Tuesday Midday

The sun was up, the tent stood quiet. Allison sensed its emptiness. Zero horses at the hitching rail substantiated the theory. At least Jesse was in better health. Allison sat on Lightning studying the scene. Hunger for food and a craving for caffeine competed in her head like a bickering couple. She refused to take sides. Both had strong cases. Five or six inches of fresh snow formed a white apron around the tent, with boot tracks and horse tracks in messy crisscrosses like fingerpaints.

Allison slid off Lightning with a weary thud, her knees barking in pain, and walked the horse to the rail.

She was back with civilization. There was every reason to call for a bone-deep, pour-it-on celebration, yet a surge of relief won the day, not joy. She had been there before—wet and confused and miraculously among the conscious bodies in Long Island Sound, airline parts and overhead bin detritus bobbing and sinking in the water all around. Nearby, people were dead. Just like that. Because of where they had been sitting.

After the shock of the accident had worn off, a weeks-long process, she could hear the festivity—not a rip-roaring kegger, just a champagne toast and honest-smiles party. She could hear it. But she could never reach the room where the survival celebration was being held. She wouldn't allow herself to walk up to that door and step inside.

The previous fifteen hours had generated their share of I'm-in-deep-shit thoughts, but it wasn't until this moment of walking into camp that she could acknowledge she had come damn close to punching her ticket straight off the planet. Again. The fact that this occasion was self-inflicted made no difference.

She parked Lightning in the sun and found him oats and water. Inside the tent, a stale warmth lingered. The stove could be touched, but only to a count of one. Wouldn't Colin have come looking for her? It was possible Colin knew not to venture out in the whiteout snowstorm and had also figured she was smart enough to change her mind and knew enough to stay at Trapper's overnight. Silly boy.

An inch of coffee at the bottom of the blue-flecked camp stove pot was warm and muddy but held enough liquid to fill a cup. She swallowed it down. The pantry coughed up bread, peanut butter, dried apricots and a Hershey's bar. Heaven. She stood by the stove and chugged a bottle of water, sipped at another. She kept thinking she might find a note. Her head throbbed and she raided the medicine kit and dug out four extra-strength Advil. Never send a boy to do a man's job. She curled up on a cot and rolled out the red carpet for a real sleep, her bones cold and fingertips tingling.

The stove ticked. A crow cawed—one lone cry. It sounded like disapproval. The stove ticked again. A chipmunk chattered with a relaxed lilt, making conversation. Allison peered off the cliff into the blackness of unconsciousness, but she couldn't make the leap.

The rhythm was off. It was morning, after all. The canvas walls were too bright. Devo was somewhere stuffing his face with nuts and elk jerky. Colin was leading Hiatt and Gray toward a grazing elk. Her brain was Grand Central Station for tracks that led nowhere: now departing from Platform A, the Loose Ends Limited. Today you're riding the bullet train for extra speed on the trip so you can get nowhere even faster.

She willed her body to a sitting position, used the momentum to keep moving. What she was looking for she had no clue. What she wanted to find was nothing.

Maybe.

But she knew for sure that her next move would be a conscious act, being a snoop. She wasn't sure whose stuff was whose, but she started with the pile that was closest. She recognized one of Zamora's shirts from the first ride up. She began searching in Zamora's belongings, not worried about putting things back in the proper order. Jeans, flashlight, medicine kit, underwear, wool socks, disposable camera, water bottles, aspirin.

Boring.

She found "M.H." in permanent marker all over Max Hiatt's stuff—backpack, jeans, T-shirts, sweaters. The detailed labeling reminded Allison of summer camp—the lakeshore and woods, her first overnight out in the wild long before she knew the outdoors would become her home.

What was she after?

Hiatt's things came with a musty whiff of dankness. At the bottom of his backpack was a palm-size Bible, print tiny and blurry. A teenager with good eyes could read it, but certainly no adult could. What was it good for, evoking emotions? Thou Shalt Not Everything—but when had that stopped anyone? At least Hiatt hadn't been pushy about it. The chipmunk chattered again, this time with more excitement. Hurry up.

A zippered pouch at the top of Austin Rayburn's pack included his wallet. A faded driver's license in the plastic window showed his stringbean face. It was a sad mug shot, at least five years old. Eleven dollars, one credit card, slips of meaningless paper, a receipt from a liquor store, nothing special. Rayburn's backpack was a mess, a demerit factory. A stern camp counselor would have had a field day. Dirty socks, crumpled-up T-shirts, crap piled upon crap. Depressing. If his house was like this, she would flee. Mom must have had a lost cause on her hands. The backpack was taller and wider than most. It could have been a hamper for dirty laundry. She plunged a hand down into the pile and groped around, then noticed extra firmness to the sides. She detected a hidden vertical compartment, sealed by Velcro flaps on each side.

She pulled back the flap and found herself staring at the ends of plastic pipes, jammed in tightly. Holding down the backpack with one hand and yanking hard on a pipe in the middle with the other, she slowly coaxed it up.

The plastic pipe was hollow, white and about three feet long. The surface was new but was scraped and cut in spots as if a beaver had gnawed on it to test for taste and texture. She found four pieces with the beaver chew marks. On these pieces, tiny snags of plastic jutted up like hangnails. Most of the pipes were smooth, tip to tip. They were light but as inflexible as steel. A roll of quarters might have slid down inside, but there wouldn't be much clearance.

The pipes were odd—and that was all she could think. A flutter of panic seized her chest as she thought of somebody walking in on her. She shoved the pipes back down, crammed the clothes inside, stood up and stepped away.

Outside, she checked Lightning, who had polished off the oats and put a sizable dent in the weed-free hay. He was sleeping. The day was quiet, cool. Snow was beginning to soften where it caught the sun. A loose thought was forming in her head about the pipes, but she couldn't connect the stray ideas. She doubted anyone had slipped down the trail past her while she had slept at her impromptu camp. In the end, she had been only thirty yards off the main trail. But given her exhaustion, she might not have heard a thing. She'd slept through Devo's departure, after all.

She circled the tent, the loose idea starting to find traction. Two sets of tracks detoured to the back of the tent. She followed them around to the shade, where the edges of the tracks held firm. The prints here were completely clean. The return trip had smudged them. The tracks stayed tightly together. Tandem. They dead-ended near the corner of the tent.

The two persons must have spent some time padding around here, but for what? Side-by-side whizzing? There were no matching holes, no "writing" in the snow. Most of the prints pointed toward the tent. Allison squatted down for a better look.

The stitching in a two-foot section of the tent was new, although dirt appeared to have been rubbed along the edge so the white thread didn't glow. But it was clearly new. The stitches were hours old. She could see where the knots had been tied off in a jumble of over-lapping loops. She pictured one man holding the fabric, one man sewing. But why was she so certain there had been two men?

She stepped back to the spot where the tracks were most clear, and found a clean left-boot print. She studied the symmetrical pattern on the sole. She found a matching right print, then searched for anything that didn't match. Nothing. It hadn't been two people back behind the tent, it had been one, and he had needed two trips to finish the work.

She didn't need to go inside the tent to see the location where the stitches lined up.

Stringbean.

Tuesday Midday

"Is it a trick? You can call the legal maneuver a 'trick' if you want to call it that," said Brett Merriman. "You wouldn't be the first. Plenty of folks around here thought it wasn't playing by the rules."

Merriman leaned back in his chair, shaking his head with a look of contempt.

"And they knew those depositions were—"

"A bit of a stretch, let's say."

"A bit," said Trudy. "Reading the depositions, you could tell."

"Is it that obvious?"

"I'm an outsider," said Trudy. "And not a lawyer."

"The word on the street is that they used identical language from that case down in Boulder, the one that gave Stewart Exby the idea," said Merriman.

"It was like they were reading from a script."

"It wasn't a fair fight to begin with," said Merriman. "Bostwick didn't do himself any favors the way he came in here with moral guns blazing. But if you're thinking somebody is going to step forward and cry perjury, you got that all wrong."

"The town will hang together behind him," said Trudy.

"Tight like only a small town can manage," said Merriman. "Keating must have been willing to try anything to send Bostwick a message."

"Not a pretty message," said Trudy.

"Probably not the way it was taken, either."

Merriman spoke with conviction. Trudy felt a kindred spirit, not the least because her first shipment of herbs had sold out and he had already given her a recipe for barbecue tofu with a paprika-based rub that sounded spot-on.

"Whose side are you taking?" she said.

"I try to not take sides," said Merriman. "I can't afford to in a town like this. I got all sides walking in that front door and I don't want any one of them thinking we got a stake in this. This store is Costa Rica when it comes to town politics."

"But what about you, Brett Merriman?"

"What about me?"

"What are your personal feelings?" she said. "I get this feeling you're holding out on me."

"What are you up to?"

"I'm worried about my friend Allison. She's up there with some of those people. Your store may not have to take a stand, but you could be a big help if you know anything that would help me provide information to Allison, to let her know whether she's dealing with more trouble than she suspects."

Merriman slid a drawer back, found a toothpick and popped it into his mouth. "Bostwick is around."

"Aren't the cops looking for him?"

"I believe so," said Merriman. "I'm not sure he's got much to say."

"Why do you say that?" Trudy surprised herself. It wasn't her nature to pry. But concern for Allison trumped all other concerns.

"It doesn't fit with what I know," said Merriman.

"And what do you know?"

Merriman leaned on his desk, forearms propping him up. The whites of his eyes were as spotless as fresh cream.

"You want to hear it straight from the horse's mouth?"

"Hear what?"

"It," said Merriman. "The straight scoop."

"From who?"

"From Bostwick."

"Where is he?"

"Staying with me."

Tuesday Afternoon

The accident scenario was on a sprint, running the other way.

Every life comes with a clock that's winding down toward its last tick. As soon as you're old enough to understand that fact, it's game-on. It helps to be born into a station of life that allows you some control of the ticking speed, but Keating's clock hadn't run its course on its own. Deep anger in camp had erupted like a volcano. The eruption was timed and planned. The cold snap made the plans that much easier, but any October night in the Flat Tops would have worked fine.

Allison stood on the shore of Oyster Lake. Each rock below came with its own white crown. The sun had melted part of the snow, but not enough to test a theory. Perhaps by nightfall the rocks would be dry. The sun had four more hours to work. The rocks needed to dry naturally if there was going to be anything to see—brushing the snow off with her hand might remove the evidence she was after.

A muffled, distant whump of gunfire broke Allison's thoughts. The echoing shot was followed by another. Somewhere, someone was hunting. It was possible it was her guides and clients. Whether they were in two groups or one, there was no way to know. Whether the others knew Austin Rayburn, really knew him, there was no way to know. Maybe they had missed each other in the early morning. Maybe a group had made it down to Meeker looking for her. Not likely.

The trouble was here.

Options? Waiting was pointless. She wanted a consultation with Colin. She needed to list all the facts and see how they took shape on paper, see how the pieces of the puzzle fit together or whether the pieces even belonged to the same damn game.

Allison looked down on the rocks, and knew they wouldn't give up their secrets until the snow had melted.

Tuesday Afternoon

Devo had chased him all day. Stalked him. Waited. He'd seen him go by while Allison slept. He hated leaving her, but didn't have a minute to lose. He had summoned every bit of energy to keep up. His stomach felt like a transplant, his inner store of energy was nearly nonexistent. There was no way to leave a note. He had felt famished, exhausted, exhilarated. As long as Allison kept his secret, he would be fine. He had learned a lesson, had pushed his limits too hard. But if it all led to this, it was worth it.

The man with the backpack had hiked up the trail at dawn. Devo had heard the footfalls, a soft pattern of thumps. His keen hearing woke him in time to see the square box bobbing through the snowy branches.

The man had made three stops, released batches of his poison at each pool or stream. At all three Devo had been too exposed to approach. Twice Devo thought he had been spotted, but the man only turned and stared, tried to ferret out Devo's face from the woods, but Devo knew his camouflage was better than the fucking Green Berets. It wasn't camouflage, after all, if it was you. Devo was the background. He could just as well be a movable bush.

The direction of his route began to grow clear. The first three stops he hit were in a rough arc, and Devo guessed at the fourth. The first three fed streams that flowed northwest. The man was on a run to Coffin Lake. It was a milk run. A sour milk run. These were stops. He was seeding and reseeding the poison. Each delivery made Devo sick to his stomach. He was still weak and hurting but managed to keep up. Sheer will was the main engine. Disgust was a pumping piston.

The man with the backpack was well-fed and strong. He had done this before, so he knew what he was up against. But even the tough ones needed food, and here at the third delivery stop he finished pouring the canister of crap into the hole he had punched through the icy crust, and then dug out a cube of Tupperware and a bottle of water. Devo was close enough to hear the seal on the bottle crack open. Clean water, thought Devo. *Fucker.*

The lunch break was Devo's chance. He dropped down the gully. He needed a twenty-minute head start. The footing was slick and the undergrowth was dense, forcing Devo up and down, losing time. He was estimating now, feeling the distance to the drainage out of Coffin Lake. He lost more elevation than he wanted, was bounced off his bearing by thick stands of scrub. He made up lost time scrambling upward along an open chute, imagining the gift to Allison—making things whole. He owed her. Owed her a mountain.

The pitch was steep enough to earn a black diamond on a ski run—the steepest rating. The grade left Devo's heart pounding. He tried to think like a goat, bounding from rock to rock, watching his step in the snow.

At the top, Devo smiled. His radar had worked. Another hundred yards up and to the southeast was the pool below Coffin Lake. If all had gone right, he would be in time to wait—and ambush his prey.

Tuesday Afternoon

"Glenwood Springs," Ethan Bostwick said flatly, as if stating Trudy's name.

He was sitting at Brett Merriman's kitchen table behind a mug of black coffee. He was rumpled and tired. He wore a washed-out flannel shirt with black and red checks. "Where's your friend?"

"Stayed home," said Trudy. Bostwick looked like a stray dog.

"Too bad." Bostwick turned his chair. "He's missing big drama. Have a seat."

Merriman heated some water for tea, put a few boxes of herb blends and a jar of honey on the table. The kitchen was cluttered, fussy—and spotless. Interior design by a committee of grandmothers. Bostwick's earthy presence was entirely out of place. Merriman's large family lived in a two-story Victorian three blocks from downtown Meeker. All the kids were school age. His wife had stayed behind at the grocery store while he brought Trudy to meet the semi-fugitive.

"You made it sound like you were a complete loner," said Trudy.

"Sometimes you don't know your friends until the going gets rough. But all this craziness is about to stop."

"Do you know something I don't?"

"The news is all over the Denver stations," said Merriman.

"The Flat Tops water," said Bostwick. "Turning up foul."

"From the fracking," said Merriman.

"The what?" said Trudy.

"A process of injecting a special formula into the ground to drive the natural gas up," said Bostwick. "It splits apart the rock, the gas is released. The drilling companies have all sworn on their mother's Bibles it's harmless."

"But now these hunters and guides are turning up sick," said Merriman. "Violently ill. About a dozen at last count."

"My friend Allison said Josh Keating was sick before—"

"Before he died," said Bostwick. "That was in the newspaper too. The hospital has a bunch of cases. Every water expert in the state is coming in."

The look on Bostwick's face wasn't smug. It was confident and satisfied. Trudy felt a lift. She was with the winning team, the team that had known the risks and sounded the alarm. Could it be that simple?

"There are some of us who don't believe in all the greed," said Merriman.

"What about the buffalo?" asked Trudy.

"What about the grab on my property?" asked Bostwick.

"Who shot them?"

"Hell if I know. But it was your classic Old West setup. I wouldn't even know how and couldn't imagine hurting one of those critters. I might have opened the gate and set them free. That occurred to me once or twice. But nothing worse than that."

Merriman poured Trudy a cup of hot water. She picked a Zen Mango teabag from the assortment. "I read the depositions," she said.

"Then you know," said Bostwick. "It's ugly."

"Somebody retaliating on your behalf?" said Trudy.

"Or trying to set me up."

"But you won't talk to the cops."

"Hard to trust folks around here," said Bostwick. "I'll talk to the state, I'd talk to the feds. And I've got to talk to them before they announce whether this fracking technique is as safe as the energy boys would have you believe or if it's time to give this drilling white dream a reality check. As long as the streams coming out of the Flat Tops are churning up poison, my hunch is the federal government will do the right thing. What do you think?"

Bostwick spit out weird energy, dark hues. Should these men be her allies?

"Since you won't answer that one, let me ask you another question," said Bostwick. "What's your deal here? I thought you were deciding whether or not to take on the powers in Glenwood Springs, which I think you should. But what are you after now?"

Trudy pulled the notepaper from her pocket. Would these names mean anything to them? Trudy gave a quick rundown of everything that had happened and then read the names aloud: "Terry Zamora, Max Hiatt, Conrad Gray and Austin Rayburn."

Merriman and Bostwick exchanged a glance of understanding. Bostwick shook his head with a look of disgust.

"I know all of them except Zamora," said Bostwick. "And didn't I see his name in the paper this week? Was he one of the men quoted about Keating's death?"

"They were all on the hunt with my friend's outfitting business. My friend Allison Coil."

"Your friend."

"Yes."

"An outfitter—for hunters?"

"She's very good," said Trudy. "The best. Very conscientious."

"Don't get me going," said Bostwick. "All I know is Josh Keating didn't need an outfitter."

"Seems strange to me he'd pay anyone a dime to show him where to go, let alone what to do," said Merriman.

"Agreed," said Bostwick. "That whole thing stinks right there."

"But Allison is still up there with them."

"Hiatt and Gray are straight shooters," said Merriman. "Good eggs. Good Meeker folks. Heck, Conrad Gray is one of the unofficial town leaders. He's been around so long he's held about every position from mayor to dogcatcher."

"Good like old-school good," said Bostwick. "But greedy as the next lip-smacking profit hound."

"Okay," said Merriman. "But they wouldn't hurt a fly—"

"—but don't mind raping the Roan," said Bostwick.

"How about Rayburn?" said Trudy.

"You read the depositions," said Bostwick.

"They were over the top."

"You think?" asked Merriman.

"Too perfect," said Trudy. "Too neat. It must hurt you, reading that stuff."

"Like a punch in the teeth," said Bostwick. "Rayburn is a shit."

"Who is he?"

"A nobody," said Bostwick. "A shit nobody, who saw a chance to play hero for the case."

"Why Rayburn?"

"Because he spent more time at Keating's ranch than Josh or Loretta Keating."

"He drives a dump truck for the town," said Merriman. "But he picked up some side work for the Keating ranch, running errands and doing odd jobs."

"There are rumors," said Bostwick. "I've seen his pickup parked out there for hours on end. Late on weekends and evenings when all the chores should be done."

"So he is credible," said Trudy.

"Shit," said Bostwick. "Not one word in those depositions is credible. All of this is a masterpiece of buffalo shit being fabricated by that Stewart Exby, the tight-lipped lawyer. This is a legal lynch mob. They think they've got their noose tied and the biggest oak tree and strongest branch all picked out."

Bostwick locked eyes on Trudy's. She glanced at Merriman, whose coffee cup vanished inside a bear-claw grip.

"I come in to town and ask a few questions about the way things are being done. A few simple questions. You would think I had lit the town on fire and was caught with a jug of kerosene and the matches. They are trying to run me out of town with their *adverse possession* mumbo jumbo, and now every one of them suckers is waking up to realize the whole deal may be off, that their dreams of hitting the big all-American jackpot went *kablewie.* They also might be realizing that I was right—that this so-called perfectly harmless means of tearing up the Roan Plateau comes with a price. Just because you can't see the damage they're doing underground doesn't mean it ain't damage and there ain't consequences. The gas has to go somewhere and it will inevitably start seeping into other systems where it doesn't belong."

Bostwick sucked his coffee, put the cup back on the table with a thud. "Perfectly harmless," he said, the first two fingers of each hand flicking down with each word. Air quotes. "What they said. Over and over. But it's so perfect and it's so harmless that they won't even reveal what's in their fracking formulas. Or should I say their fucking formulas. They think it's some secret sauce. But no matter what they're injecting, what comes out is methane—and methane sure ain't something you want in your drinking supply, believe me. Taking a shower will clean out your sinuses, drinking a glass will wrack your innards."

Merriman shrugged. "I'm just a grocer," he said. "I don't know about politics and drilling for natural gas. What I do know is when you step back and look at what they're saying, it can't really work that easy. And anyway, why not leave the Roan Plateau alone and figure out a way to change the way we live? Reduce the energy we need. Ripping up the Roan will only delay that step, not eliminate it. I say we face it now."

"Amen to that," said Bostwick. "People should know Keating and I might have had our squabbles, but he was not the bad guy."

"It was his lawsuit," said Trudy.

"He was the front," said Bostwick. "The town's anger poured through him, that's all. Josh Keating was a decent guy and given the chance he would have done the right thing. He was getting egged on by others. Egged on but good."

Tuesday Afternoon

Every nook and cranny explored, every plastic container opened, every flashlight unscrewed and opened, every cot flipped over, every toilet kit ripped through, every hidden, zippered-up pocket of every pack and every duffel turned out. Allison was a combination FBI and CSI with a tenth of the patience. There was one thing missing from her theory and that was the connectors to join the pipes, to make them long enough to confine Josh Keating. To make them deadly.

The guts of Rayburn's backpack were strewn at Allison's feet in a heap. Rayburn might notice later but let him make a move, do something. React. Was he alone? The question pounded away inside her.

Conrad Gray's belongings next. His stuff was old-sailor ship-shape, every pant folded in sharp creases, T-shirts neatly compressed. No wasted space. Nothing out of place. Nothing that didn't belong. Everything had a purpose.

Allison bashed through the kitchen, searching every tub of dry goods—pastas, cereals, bagels, crackers, cookies, granola bars. The coolers. The larger supply tubs. The tub of pots and pans, the spices, the coffee, the liquor, the box with paper towels and TP.

Would the sun have melted the snow on the rocks by now? She considered a trip to Oyster Lake but didn't want to get caught studying the spot if the boys returned.

She was one step outside when a mental photograph snapped, developed itself and rushed to the surface. The rifle cases. Sitting there all lined up. In her mind the cases were plumper than they should be. How many rifles were out on the hunt? One per man, most likely. So, five. There were a dozen or more cases in the tent. No labels here, no permanent markers needed. A Remington, a Weatherby, a Sako, another Weatherby, a Browning and a Kimber. A few empty cases. A couple hardbound cases, some soft-sided. And one that had plumpness but not enough heft. The zipper was secured with a three-dollar hardware store padlock.

She weighed the case in her hand, gave it a shake. There was no rifle inside. She flashed on Rayburn's backpack, remembered a side compartment, a small ring with what could have been toy keys. She felt close but no closer, sensing the day slipping away.

The inside of the case might contain harmless contraband like

Fig Newtons or a porn magazine. Each side of Rayburn's pack sported a zippered pouch like a catch-all office drawer—weathered packs of matches, chewed-up pencils, old maps, receipts, stray papers, plastic corkscrews, broken sunglasses, a bottle of bug spray, a bottle of fox urine, sunscreen, lip balm and, finally, the key ring.

The key fit. The lock popped open.

The whistle stopped her cold. It was faint, but audible. Human, clear, beckoning.

The lock dangled loose, bidding her to look. She glanced at Rayburn's bag and the side pouch. The flap gaped open. A small pile of detritus lay on the floor. The kitchen was a bit of a wreck. She hadn't put Gray's gear back in its place.

The whistle again—so much closer. Three notes. Two high, one low, syncopated. Dooo-ta-do.

Why hadn't she heard a horse? Or people talking? Who would be coming alone?

Allison unzipped the case in a flash, her heart thumping.

More plastic pipe, slightly larger in diameter, shorter lengths, a few inches each. More beaver chews in spots, some sections smooth. And four corner pieces, three connector tubes jutting from each.

Dooo-ta-do.

This time, loud and close.

She zipped up the case, scooted across to Rayburn's backpack and crammed everything back inside with a jab of her fist.

Dooo-ta-do.

More than human, it was a demanding call. But no second-rate ornithologist would be fooled.

Allison scooted to the door, stepped outside.

The smell hit her—and anger instantly blossomed.

Devo.

With an impish grin on his face.

In his hands he held a rope. The rope was lashed to the wrists of a young man carrying a large, boxy backpack.

"So glad you're here," said Devo. "I brought you a present."

Tuesday Afternoon

Brett Merriman drove through downtown Meeker between the school and the county building and stopped at the main highway. Trudy admired his gentle hands on the steering wheel, his soft style overall. Her mouth was dry, and her head was buzzing, sorting through all the information, but Merriman made the day feel as normal and relaxed as the Fourth of July.

Merriman dropped her off at the motel. She asked him to wait. She picked up three phone messages—all from Jerry. She called Jerry from her room.

"Don't wait for me," she said after the preliminaries.

"You sound like you're in a rush. Everything okay?"

"Not great," said Trudy. "It's more complicated up here than you would have thought."

The pause on the line grew heavy.

"Are you going to be here with us?" said Jerry.

"Don't wait for me," said Trudy. "Just go ahead."

"The meeting is tomorrow night," said Jerry. "We're a team."

"Maybe," said Trudy. "Team" wasn't the word that came to mind. "I think you ought to go slow. Learn more first. Find out what you're getting into." She tried to say it without sounding like a preacher.

"What's going on up there?"

"I've got to go," said Trudy.

"Do you need help?"

"No," said Trudy. And thought to herself: not your kind of help, not at this point anyway.

Outside, Merriman was standing beside his pickup.

"Can I show you what this is all about?" he asked.

"What do you mean?"

"It'll take an hour," said Merriman. "Or two or three."

"Do you think Stewart Exby would tell me what he knows?" said Trudy.

"He's not somebody who talks for free," said Merriman. "A lawyer, you know."

"Three hours?"

"Less if we hustle."

The pickup gained speed as they left the town limits, heading west. Merriman followed the road south, toward Glenwood Springs. He pointed across the valley to the west, telling her about a marker in the middle of a farm that indicated the spot where Nathan Meeker had been caught and killed in 1879.

"Some obvious similarities," said Trudy.

"You know it's a lynching, and I know it's a lynching," said Merriman. "I was raised to believe in the old-fashioned, all-American system of fair hearing, fair trial and innocent until proven guilty. All Ethan Bostwick has done is come out here and ask a few simple questions about our lifestyle, how we've put our towns together, what we're teaching our kids, what lessons we're passing along about how to live our lives."

The road climbed a long hill and rolled past a series of small hogback rock formations. Merriman spoke calmly. Everything was cut and dried, his comments sandwiched with sensible generalities. "You don't get any stronger as a community by giving outsiders the cold shoulder."

"What about his tactics?"

"All he did was ask questions; he didn't attack or hurt a single person."

"Just offended."

"True."

"Does he have other friends?"

"A few. More than he knows, but not enough. The powers that be in Meeker aren't worried about his network because the people who have come out to support him are the fringe types—they're not well connected through church, the chamber of commerce, or the town council."

"But how are you so sure Bostwick had nothing to do with the buffalo being shot or with… " She paused.

"With what? Josh Keating died of exposure," said Merriman. "Do you know something I don't?"

"Don't you think it's a bit odd, putting himself in that situation, ending up like that? You said he didn't even need a hunting guide."

"Odd, yes," said Merriman. "For now I'm going with what the cops say. They interviewed all the witnesses. It does happen, sad to say, that hunters drink too much and mess up in the worst way, usually with a gun in their hands hurting somebody else."

"Okay then—about the buffalo?"

"Are you asking how I know he's clear?"

"Yes."

"Because he looked me in the eye," said Merriman. "Simple as that."

The pickup rolled south and Trudy tried to relax. She considered the next steps, and wondered if she should have tried to call Allison, wondered if she could find a room at the motel when they returned. Merriman appeared content with the silence. The town of Meeker now at her back, Trudy tried to shake the feeling that she had abandoned Allison.

At the high point of the road between Meeker and Rifle, Merriman aimed the truck down a dirt road. They drove for another twenty minutes, then the road carried them uphill. Merriman pulled over at a turnout built like a ledge at the side of the road. The land fell away to the west. The valley floor was a thousand feet below. The view was sweeping. Aspen leaves past their fall prime tried to squeeze one last burst of gold onto the scene.

"Now look a bit closer," said Merriman. They were standing in front of the truck in the cool air. Merriman handed her a pair of binoculars made from cast iron, judging by the weight. He pointed.

When she focused, a towering steel structure came into view. A drilling rig dwarfed the neighboring trees. A hill nearby had been carved away. Acres of sagebrush and aspen had been clear-cut to make room. Large tanks rimmed the site. Trudy could make out some sort of industrial pit, a series of construction site trailers and a row of Porta Potties. A convoy of trucks was parked in a semicircle near two trailers, probably offices.

"To me," said Merriman. "It's like what happened to the area around Pittsburgh and the Ohio River and other places where everything was sacrificed in the name of industry. The Roan is getting ripped to shreds. From that one rig they can drill sideways and down. They pump their formulas into the rock and the underground gets all torn up and rearranged. Who knows what's happening to the groundwater."

Trudy lowered the binoculars. She could make out the gash in the hillside without magnification.

"That's one, and there are more than a thousand now," said Merriman. "All for temporary gain. I don't mean to sound preachy, but if every town would have the conversation Ethan Bostwick wants us to have, we could leave the Roan alone. Instead, people start thinking short term—the energy companies for the profits and the landowners for the leases. The greed gets sick."

"They rip the woods right down to bare dirt," said Trudy. "And put up all this steel."

"If they left tomorrow it would take a century to grow back," said Merriman. "With no idea what damage is being done below ground."

Trudy brought the binoculars back up. A monster truck with four sets of rear tires under its carriage belched a puff of black exhaust from its tailpipe. The cloud drifted sideways and dissipated.

"It doesn't seem right," said Trudy.

"It's not theoretical when you see the damage being done," said Merriman.

A question had hung on Trudy's mind since they'd left Merriman's house, and she couldn't let it go.

"Who is Austin Rayburn?"

Merriman studied her for a moment.

"What makes you seem so worried?" he asked.

"Allison called me. We talked. I could hear it. Something is off."

"What can I tell you?"

"Tell me more about Josh Keating."

Merriman pondered the request, then found a starting point.

"Josh Keating had his buffalo processed right in Meeker," said Merriman. "Sold most of it right here too. Josh Keating was a good guy—salt of the earth. Worked hard, did everything right. Fell in love with a beautiful young woman and ended up inheriting a whole other ranch west of Meeker, part way to Rangely. From what I heard, that ranch is now prime turf, rich with natural gas. Her parents died in an accident on Wolf Creek Pass, down south. Terrible, but there you go."

Merriman stopped. He took a deep breath.

"Who knows when a relationship reaches some point of irreversible darkness? Josh Keating's wife Loretta used to come to town with him—shopping or for dinner. We stopped seeing her. Nothing said about it, nobody pushed too hard. But you could tell. Something had changed. She started keeping to herself, closing in her world. The other day, after we found out Josh was gone, most of us who went out to pay our respects hadn't seen her in over a year."

"Did you talk to her?"

"About as much as anybody else. So, no, not really. We exchanged greetings; I expressed my condolences. My wife commented later on how distant she looked. Distant and different, you know, tired. She'd been stuck inside for a long, long time."

"Lots of marriages fall apart," said Trudy.

"They do," said Merriman.

"Do you know Austin Rayburn?"

"Everybody knows the Rayburns."

"A whole family?"

"Big name in Meeker," said Merriman. "The Texas Rayburns."

"The what?"

"Dad is Dallas, and the sons are Tyler, Waco, Houston and Austin," said Merriman.

"That's funny," said Trudy. "Allison's horse—one of them anyway, his name is Dallas too. I hate to ask the wife's name."

"Susan," said Merriman. "Guess she didn't want to change it to Lubbock."

"Smart woman," said Trudy.

"Everybody knows them. They own the hardware store—the only one in town, lumber and tools, electrical and plumbing. Dad runs the store with the three older sons, and then there's Austin. Boy number four. Never connected, never got with the program. Didn't finish high school, rejected everything."

"An outcast?" said Trudy.

"Except nobody cast him out."

"Did you know Austin Rayburn was on the same hunt with Josh Keating?"

Merriman considered the question as if it was the hardest question he had ever been asked.

"I've been thinking about it ever since we talked with Ethan," said Merriman. "But I can't figure it out."

"How's that?"

"Go into that hardware store," said Merriman. "It's a beauty. There's not a screw in the wrong drawer, every aisle is immaculate, and you could eat off the floor. On the walls do you know what you'll find? Elk, deer, bear, mountain goat, bighorn sheep—everything you can hunt legally in the state. There are wild hogs from Texas. They are all trophies, all immaculately mounted. Each mount has its own plaque. There's no better collection. The dad, Austin's father, has one of the highest-rated elk racks ever bagged in Colorado and it hangs right above the paint section in the back of the store. Must be six-feet long, must weigh forty pounds. You should see the foot traffic in the store, just to admire the display. The place is part hardware store, part museum, and all the Rayburns are represented."

Maybe it was merchant envy.

"All?" asked Trudy.

"With one exception."

"Let me guess."

"The whole family did it, so Austin didn't."

"Because he was angry."

"In a quiet way, I suppose."

"How did he wind up catching on with the Keatings?"

Merriman scratched his chin, nodded to Trudy. Time to go. A convoy of oil-drilling trucks was lumbering up the hill toward them, gears grinding. It was clear Merriman didn't want to find himself stuck behind them. He swung the truck around the turnout with a shudder of dirt on the bumpy soil.

"I remember Loretta Keating putting up the help-wanted ad on the community bulletin board in the store," said Merriman. "I know she interviewed a whole bunch of people who had more farm experience and general know-how than Austin Rayburn."

"So Austin was her choice?"

Merriman leaned forward, pushed the pedal down.

"Now you've got me worried," he said.

"How's that?"

"I was over at the hardware store a couple weeks back," said Merriman. "We were building office shelves for the store. I happened to bump into Austin. He mumbled something about doing an irrigation project. He was in the plumbing section. I don't know. He looked better. He looked happier but still kind of scared. We talked for a minute, and I asked him how he was doing, and suddenly he had a big smile and said he felt like he was going to be getting lucky very soon."

8

Tuesday Afternoon

"What the hell?"

Allison said it with bite.

"Caught him," said Devo. "For you."

"For me?"

"Find out who he's working for," said Devo. "Idiot here won't say a word to me."

"Why the hell did you leave me?"

"Because I saw him." Devo jabbed a thumb at his captive. "I only had a minute, didn't have any way to leave a note."

"You abandoned me."

"But we got him," said Devo like a kid who had hooked his first fish.

"We? *You* take him down."

"Call the cops. Get 'em back up here."

"You're the one who saw him."

"His backpack is full of his shit," said Devo. "You got the terrorist, you got his bombs, all in one."

Allison stepped away from Devo, an ear out for returning hunters.

"How did you catch him?"

"Surprised him," said Devo. "Then I gave him the choice of being tied to a tree while I fetched help, but he chose this. I guess he doesn't want to be lashed to a tree from now until dawn. Go figure. Are you still mad at me?"

The young, misguided man at the end of the Devo's rope was six feet tall. His shoulders were square and big, built for winning sledgehammer-pounding contests at the carnival. He wore an orange wool hat, tugged tight to his scalp, and a complete camouflage suit. The boots matched. Long brown hair curled out from under his hat. His eyes were dark brown under black eyebrows. His thin face was a week from its last shave. He wore an angry scowl. Allison gave him twenty-five years, max. She noticed he kept the rope taut, probably to stay as far away as possible from Devo's rank, deep woods B.O.

"Did you get his name?"

"No," said Devo. "A few *fuck-you's* during the fight. That's all he's said."

"Where'd you get the rope?"

"I have supplies," said Devo.

Her thoughts raced to piece together Keating being sick and Zamora being sick and Morales being sick and what it all meant with the pipes and the stitches in the tent. Pipes, connectors, cut, stitches. And dead buffalo. And buffalo wristwatch. She put her hand in her right pocket, wrapped her fingers around the timepiece.

"Who are you working for?" she asked him.

The man-kid studied her, shook his head. He had the deep stare of a zealot with just a dash of fear thrown in. No question, Devo had him scared. "Mother Earth," he said.

"Oh, please," said Allison. "Give it a rest. Who are you working for?"

"Get this ape away from me and we can talk," said the man-kid. "I'll lay it all out."

Allison didn't have time—or the inclination—to negotiate. "You're escorting him down," she said to Devo. "And you better head out now unless you want to explain this to a bunch of hunters who will be back here any minute."

"Can't," said Devo.

"Don't," said the man-kid.

Allison snapped herself around. "Then start with your name, right now," she said.

The man-kid paused, too long. "Release me," he said.

"That was your last chance," said Allison. "You blew it."

"I can't do it," said Devo, his eyes on fire with panic. "People, civilization, topside—no way, no how."

"Top what?" said Allison.

"People," said Devo. "I can't."

"You take him down, Devo. You have to. I've got my own set of woes." Her words were calm. It wasn't a fight. Allison had the leverage. Devo had forgotten. He probably didn't think she'd play it.

"Get a cell, make a call," said Devo. "Technology, you know, use it."

"Battery's dead," said Allison. It might be true.

"I can't take him to Meeker."

"To Trapper's then. Tie him up somewhere, leave one of your clever notes and a map."

"Dang," said Devo. "Shit."

"Have you searched his backpack?" asked Allison. The less fawning over Devo, the better.

"As much as I had to."

"Are you sure he's not carrying a weapon? So when you take him down he doesn't—"

"I checked his backpack," said Devo. "Loaded with canisters, nothing but these evil canisters. I'd say he could hit fifty targets a day. I'm not taking him down."

"I'm not carrying any weapons," said the man-kid.

Allison ignored him. A surge of anger rose from a dark pit of bile. Allison had peered down at it a few times. Now she sensed the pleasure that might come by letting the rage flow. She circled Devo, kept her own wide berth, and stood by his prisoner.

"Who the hell are you working for?" She practically spit in his face.

"Nice try," said Devo. "Losing it don't help. I tried."

"Tell us," she said. Allison got right in his face. "We know you're not a lone fucking wolf."

Allison was close enough to stand on her toes and punch him in the face. "Tell us," she snarled. "I can send you down the hill to the cops with Mr. Devo here or we can wait for the hunters to come back—and given what's happened to their friends, how sick they got, they will love seeing you. Now that I think about it, maybe that's the better option. A little bit of old-fashioned Western justice right here by Oyster Lake."

No reaction. A flash of concern zipped across the man-kid's face, but it wasn't enough to prompt a reply.

The guy was shaking on the inside. Allison guessed he was paralyzed by his own failure.

"Go," said Allison.

"You," said Devo.

"You owe me."

Devo gave it a moment, took a breath. "Indeed I do," he said respectfully.

"And you don't want me to tell everything I know about the last eighteen hours—do you?"

"I didn't think you would use that to—"

Allison gave Devo a look of impatience and pointed toward Trapper's. "Who the hell do you think you are? Go. Now."

Devo turned to his captive. "Guess you got more of my company."

"It's not that I'm ungrateful," said Allison.

There was some risk. Devo was at a forty-pound deficit. He would have to guard against the man-kid trying something. Devo didn't seem to be the kind to lose the upper hand.

"Did you take any video?" she said.

"A few shots of the scene where I caught him. I couldn't shoot and tackle him at the same time."

"Then just go," said Allison. "The woman who runs the lodge at Trapper's is called Nora. Get her attention. She'll know who to call and what to do."

Devo sighed. "I ain't going all the way."

Allison went into the tent, eyed the mess, and put together a quick bag of snacks. She filled a Nalgene with water and grabbed a spare headlamp. Devo added the bag to the kid's backpack and turned to the trail for Trapper's.

Allison watched them go, cleaned up the chaos in the tent and headed slowly out to Oyster Lake. She walked with casual disinterest in case she was being watched. She felt the buffalo watch in her pocket, gave it a squeeze. The afternoon air was brisk. Daylight was eating itself.

The idea had been vague and ghost-like ever since she'd found the connector hardware, but now it took shape, revealed itself in three firm dimensions. Allison climbed the lip of Oyster Lake and took in the sweep of inert rocky shore. She cocked her head like a bird eyeing a worm, praying for the sound of movement, an errant clank. Human or horse—didn't matter.

Nothing.

They would be along. She took out the buffalo watch. The wristband was designed for a thicker arm, so Allison went to the last notch and strapped it to her much smaller wrist. She took a look at the buffalo nickel and knew it would be plenty obvious.

It was time for all the crazy stuff to stop.

It was time to set the hook.

Tuesday Evening

Dallas Rayburn was pushing sixty. Bushy gray eyebrows sprouted wild and unchecked. He was fit, trim and not as tall as Merriman. His fingers were lumberjack beefy. He oozed confidence but the look on his face slipped from pleasant to serious to concerned to worried as Merriman gave him the rundown. Trudy instantly liked his genial manner. It was clear Dallas Rayburn trusted Merriman, too, and felt comfortable talking.

"First time for everything," said Rayburn. "My wife and I were both shocked, seeing Austin heading up in the woods with a rifle. But he was happy. And it's been a long time since we could say that."

"What did he say was behind it?" asked Merriman.

They were standing inside the front door of the hardware store. Mounts lined the walls. The shelves were low, walls painted white, the lighting bright. From the front of the store you could see every antelope and bear head in the place, including the enormous buffalo mount over the entry, the only mount on that wall. It was a stuffed-head zoo. Next to the buffalo was a framed photograph of the kill. Dallas Rayburn sat on the animal's back and held up its head.

"Alaska," Rayburn said. "There are some wild ones up there."

Trudy thought it was odd to try to prop up the head when you had just killed the animal—a final indignity before gutting it.

"He kept talking about investments. He had started to enjoy working out at the Keating place. It gave him a whole new lift, a second chance."

Rayburn spoke in measured tones. The pace of his speech cut against the grain of Trudy's impatience, with dusk in full bloom and her burning desire to call Allison and leave a message. Trudy wanted to drive to Trapper's—Merriman had given her a description of the terrain—and she fantasized about heading up the trail. Allison was in trouble.

"He had money to invest?" asked Trudy. She was beyond hesitation.

"I didn't get the feeling it was that kind of investment," said Rayburn. "You know, stocks or anything. Just that he'd been playing his cards right, like he'd been offered something and was about to cash in."

"Did you talk with him about the lawsuit against Bostwick's land?"

"You gotta remember we saw him only now and then. He moved out of our house as soon as he got the job driving the truck. We'd hear about weird Austin sightings. He's my son so I can say that—weird. But I did ask him about the lawsuit because I knew he'd spent all that time at the Keating's place, helping out."

Rayburn paused. He leaned down on the large counter that constituted the checkout lane. It was closing time, but a customer with *A-1 Plumbing* on his baseball cap was paying for an unwieldy load of pipe.

"He came over ten days ago. We have dinner right at seven o'clock every single night of the week and we've always said any of our sons can join us. Susan always makes plenty of food. All the boys are married now, except Austin. Susan and I were alone that night, having a pot roast. This was right before he headed up for the hunt. All the boys were heading up for one hunt or another, deer or elk, but I stayed behind. Times are thin. I couldn't afford to be away. Anyway, Austin came in like all the boys do, right at dinner time. I said to Susan later, it was like he was trying to apologize for something—but he didn't know how."

Rayburn peered down at the floor. He drew a sharp breath.

"Usually he asks for money, but this time he sat there and talked to us, asked how things were going. Although he did ask for one thing," said Rayburn.

"What was that?" said Merriman.

"He wanted to borrow one of the store's trucks to get up to Trapper's Lake. His rig was in the shop or something." Rayburn took a breath. "Sorry. I remember thinking that night when I went to sleep, the Bible is right. Redemption is there for anyone. You can start over. He had been such a black mark for so long. There were times I wished he would move away. Far away. But that night an enormous pressure lifted. I could see he had reached a new place."

Trudy gave him a second to collect himself. She processed the image of her ex-husband George being transformed, back on the good side of the barbed wire where he now resided. She wanted him to stay unredeemed.

"Any reason for it?" she said.

"Susan and I figured it was all the extra time at the Keating ranch," Rayburn said. "Maybe it was seeing what it takes to make an honest living, the hard work. Something might have clicked. But I gather you're telling me I shouldn't feel good."

"I don't know what to think and can't tell you what to feel," said Merriman. "Lot of things aren't right though, I think you'd agree."

"Nothing's been right since Ethan Bostwick started throwing hand grenades," said Rayburn.

"I don't think he hurt anyone," said Merriman.

"That was one area, though, where Austin improved." Rayburn stood up. An edge grew in his voice. "He never had much of an opinion about anything, but after working at the Keating place, he started getting backbone, started to see how the world functioned."

"The lawsuit," said Trudy. A statement, not a question.

"Exactly," said Rayburn. "He never would have done something like that prior to being with the Keatings. We didn't even know he'd given a deposition."

An unspoken unease mushroomed in the space between

Merriman and Rayburn. Clearly Merriman hadn't revealed his sympathy for Bostwick to anyone. Trudy wondered how long it would be before one of his children muttered something in the school hallway about the fact that the fiery enviro nut was breaking bread at their dinner table.

"Good for Austin," said Merriman. "Took guts, I'm sure."

"Good to see that pesky East Coast snob back on his heels," said Rayburn. "Don't you think?"

"I don't care for the feuding, actually, no," said Merriman. "I don't think it's done us a lot of good."

"You're cutting Bostwick some slack?"

Merriman hesitated. "Not really," he said. The conviction wasn't there.

"You are, though," said Rayburn.

"Not really." The second time he said it was worse, even more watered down. "I just don't think the only answer is to railroad Bostwick out of town."

"And I don't think you move into a new town and start shredding every piece of its fabric while standing on top of what you claim is the moral high ground," said Rayburn. "He's an arrogant two-bit nobody who deserves to be squashed like a bug, and I'm proud of my son being part of the effort to show Ethan Bostwick the door."

"Okay," said Trudy. "Save it for—"

"Wait a minute," said Rayburn. "You come here asking me questions that make me think my son is tangled up in something bad, and you won't tell me what you think?" Rayburn hadn't taken his eyes off Merriman.

"I'm trying to help my friend here," said Merriman. "She's got reason to believe—"

"Believe what, exactly?"

"Hang on," said Trudy. Channeling Allison, she stepped up and inserted herself in the staring contest. She went for firm but clear, far short of any tone that might cause her to tremble. "We don't need the debate right now. Not good, not healthy, no matter what side you're on. And we can't solve that one tonight."

Rayburn sucked in a sharp breath. Merriman eased off.

"But don't you think it's strange that Josh Keating stood to make a bundle out of his rights and ends up on the rocks? Dead? Just a coincidence? Maybe your son Austin has nothing to do with this, maybe it's much more complicated than it looks—and maybe there's nothing at all—but it sounds to me like Austin knew more about the Keatings than anyone around, so that's why we're here."

The intense glare on Rayburn's face cooled a degree. Trudy stepped back. Rayburn was chewing on something, and Trudy let him gnaw. Rayburn walked a slow circle, rubbed the back of his neck with his right palm.

"I don't know," said Rayburn. He sighed again, rubbed his neck, squared his shoulders. "Actually, I'm a bit surprised Sheriff Christie hasn't been along," said Rayburn. "For the same reasons."

"Austin must have known more than anyone what was happening out there at the Keatings," said Merriman.

"Happening?" asked Rayburn.

Trudy thought Merriman had blown it.

"When was the last time you saw Loretta Keating?" said Merriman.

"When I went out to pay respects," said Rayburn.

"And before that?"

"It had been awhile."

"So Austin saw them more than—"

Rayburn held up his hand as a stop sign. "That's it. That's exactly what I was getting to."

Trudy screamed *Back off!* but only to herself. Merriman blurted out a sharp "What?"

"Them," said Rayburn. "There was no *them*. Funny. I ran into Austin one day a few months back in the parking lot at your store, Brett. He was loading groceries into his truck and I said something about how much the Keatings needed, since there were only two of them. And he said, well, as a matter of fact the stuff he'd just bought was for Loretta Keating. Said they each left lists of things for him to do on the kitchen counter, and he wasn't sure how long his job out there would last. His exact words were, 'You could hear the blood boiling inside those walls.'"

"But he kept on doing things for them?" said Trudy.

"Up until recently," said Rayburn. "I have no idea what will happen now. But not much is going to change for Loretta Keating. Austin said Josh had been sleeping downstairs in a back room for a long, long time."

Tuesday Evening

Jesse Morales, Max Hiatt and Conrad Gray returned fifteen minutes after full dark, empty handed and disappointed. They had chased fresh signs in the snow since dawn and had made it most of the way to Stillwater Reservoir and never saw a mammal larger than a squirrel. "And I think it was the same damn squirrel too," said Gray. "Mocking us."

Hiatt moved into the kitchen with Morales to start dinner. They had plans for pasta. Allison quizzed them about their day and the hunt. She watched for any indication they thought someone had been mucking around with their things. She was filling a pot for water to boil spaghetti when Colin ducked into the tent, followed by Austin Rayburn.

"Ask him," said Colin.

"Ask him what?" said Gray.

Rayburn's face was within an inch of being inscrutable, but Allison caught a faint grin. The sight of Rayburn ripped at her patience like a spot tornado.

"Ask him how he did," said Colin, beaming.

"Aw, shit," said Gray. "You got lucky? We worked all day, and you got lucky?"

Rayburn made for his cot, took a look around like something was out of place and stared at his backpack extra hard.

"Not lucky," said Colin. "Real skill."

"Yours," said Rayburn. "You spotted her."

"You shot her," said Colin. "One perfect shot."

"Damn," said Hiatt. "Your first. Congrats. I was with Tyler the year he got his first, and Houston too, if I remember right. How's it feel?"

"My nerves still ain't settled," said Rayburn.

"Adrenaline, boy," said Gray. "You can ride that shit for hours. It's the best No-Doz ever made."

Colin ran through the story. Long hike, aspen grove high up, calf-deep snow, four cows and a bull. Waited two hours for them to move out of dense cover. Didn't move a "freaking little muscle," according to Rayburn. Didn't twitch or sneeze. The elk finally drifted away. The men were downwind, followed at a safe distance and thought they were spotted once. "Like they could feel us," said Colin. "They couldn't smell or see us." The elk crossed a chute, a few yards across a narrow gully. Colin had guessed their path and had Rayburn prepped and ready.

"Got her right here," said Colin, pointing to a spot under his right armpit with his left index finger. "She fell to her knees and that was that."

"Where is she?" asked Gray.

"Two quarters are right outside," said Colin. "The rest of her is tomorrow's work."

Congratulations flew. *Attaboys.* Rayburn mugged. Allison forced a smile, stayed busy with the cooking chores. She doctored some jarred sauce with fresh-squeezed garlic, cayenne pepper and a teaspoon of sugar. She poured six servings of tequila in plastic shot glasses and made the rounds, all the shots nestled in a cluster in her hands. They toasted Rayburn, and Allison made sure her left hand was up and visible. Rayburn tossed the shot down his gullet and Allison retrieved the bottle to pour him another. She may as well have smashed the watch into his face it was so close. *Was this what you were looking for?* Pistol-whipped was one thing. This would be watch-whipping. A stunned look crossed his face like he'd been smacked. He stared at the watch longer than necessary.

Rayburn tucked away the second shot and Gray took another, but Hiatt declined. "I got my nickname to live up to," he said. "One thimble full of liquor, and I'm done. Call me good."

Rayburn squashed any lingering wisps of innocence as they ate spaghetti. She glanced at him while Gray was recounting their "worthless hike in the woods," and Rayburn stared across the tent at his backpack.

Allison had shifted everything in the tent by five tiny inches and now the repaired slash in the corner was exposed and no doubt Rayburn was calculating whether that was his own damn fault, and if it wasn't, well what? Rayburn's stare bore down. His plate of pasta teetered under one hand. Allison hoped his mind was too busy to eat; he'd weaken more. Rayburn turned slowly. Allison held his scared and busy eyes and offered a smile of warmth—as much as she could fake.

Gray grabbed the tequila and passed it around. Allison took a third shot, told herself to sip if Hiatt passed it again. Rayburn waved it off. "Meet me outside in a few," Allison whispered to Colin as she filled his glass.

Hiatt volunteered for cleanup, and Morales and Gray stood up to pitch in.

Allison grabbed her coat and headed out, sucking in a shot of night air in hopes it would cleanse her anger. She stood between the horses and waited, the bitter night air like a slap in the face. The tequila had barely dinged her sobriety.

Colin slipped out of the dark.

"What the hell is going on?" he said.

"Is it that obvious?"

"Painfully."

"How so?" she whispered.

"We got an elk, and you look like you're loaded for bear."

"So it's obvious."

"And the watch, what's up with that?"

She walked him through everything. Devo. Cut tent. Pipes. Connectors. Devo again. The captive. Everything. The darkness in their horse cave was like the darkness in a coal mine. She could feel Colin hanging on every word.

"What was Rayburn like today?" she asked.

"Green. Like a lime. Like a baby. Awkward, noisy, blurted things out at the strangest times. Shook like Elvis when we saw the elk. It was goofy."

"Lucky shot?"

Colin said nothing.

"What?" said Allison.

"He couldn't even get the rifle up to sight. Completely paralyzed."

"You shot the elk?"

"He told me to drop her. He kept talking about what this might mean to his father. Talked a lot about his father. There were times he wouldn't talk at all and then there were times he wouldn't shut up. Strange dude."

"You know shooting for Rayburn's tag is completely illegal. You're putting my whole permit in jeopardy, everything. You can't do that."

"I just wanted the poor guy to be happy," said Colin. "Bad move on my part."

"Huge risk," said Allison. "Jesus, we've got enough problems."

"Impulsive," said Colin. "Sorry."

Colin put a hand on her shoulder, pulled her close. She buried her head in his chest, and he held her.

"Want to go to the ridge and make a call?" he said.

"I thought of it," she said. "I don't think they are going to come up here tonight because of a slit in the tent and some plastic pipe." But the trip might be worth it for a message from Trudy.

"Maybe in the morning," said Colin.

"We'll call in the morning. It's already too obvious, us both out here."

A burst of sharp light flashed from the tent but she couldn't see who had stepped out. The tent glow was a dull, grimy amber. Somebody was outside.

"Huddle is over," said Allison. She snuck another hug. "I'll circle around. Let's go in separately."

"Wait," said Colin. "What are you doing tonight?"

"Sleeping."

"And what's next?"

"Tomorrow morning I'm going down to see what happened to Devo. I'm going to tell Sheriff Christie what I know—"

"And what about Austin?"

"Let him stew."

"How do you know he didn't have help?"

The thought hadn't crossed Allison's mind. A shudder boomeranged up her back in a blink. Another burst of light from the door to the tent. She still couldn't tell whether the blurry shadows were moving in or out.

"Do you need any help?" said Colin.

Allison rolled it around. "Possibly," she said. Hiatt. Gray.

Zamora? Zamora was long gone and almost forgotten. No, not Zamora. He wasn't there, wouldn't come in until the next day. "Maybe not. I looked through all their stuff. Nothing out of line."

"That doesn't mean they weren't," said Colin. "What do you expect Austin to do?"

"Sweat," said Allison. "Panic. That would be great. Just some good old-fashioned panic. And if he makes a move, I'll be his second shadow, even darker than the first."

Tuesday Evening

The hotel Allison had suggested, the Rustic Lodge, was full. "Reporters," said the woman at the front desk, looking pointedly at Trudy. "And … " she added slowly with a hiss, " … out of town environmentalists. Are you one of those?"

The Blue Spruce was three blocks west, and it was full too. "Some big wig from Interior is coming in tomorrow," said the clerk. She had tight curly hair and reading glasses propped low on her Richard Nixon nose. "He's staying right here too. I guess he's got his advance team coming in tomorrow morning—whatever it is those folks do. Between the federal government and all the sick hunters and their families coming in to pick them up, the whole town is booked."

The clerk thumped a small stack of papers on the counter, *The Rio Blanco Herald Times*. "Traces of Benzene in Flat Tops Water," read the headline. "Hunters Sick in Droves."

The clerk put a black rotary-dial courtesy phone up on the counter and slid a phone book next to it, even opened it to the right section. Trudy thought about calling back to Merriman. She wanted to call Jerry and leave a message but couldn't form the words or decide what tone to take. She flipped through the book.

"Hello again." The voice came from a man who had floated in out of nowhere, like a ghost.

The big, impatient guy from Denver stood by her side.

The guy who had been with Allison.

The guy who raced off when the buffalo were shot.

Zamora.

"Hi," she said to him. She found it hard to smile.

"You're still here," he said.

"Came back, actually," she said, wishing she hadn't. "Have you seen Allison?"

"Haven't," said Zamora. "Staying here?"

"The hotel's full."

"The whole town, I imagine."

She didn't care for Zamora's carefully shaved head and couldn't imagine the work it took to maintain.

"Do you need a room?"

"No," she lied. "It's only an hour back." Or two.

"This whole thing is messed up. Cops haven't said a word," said Zamora. "What brings you back?"

"I deliver my own line of herbs over to the grocery store."

Had she run Zamora's name past Merriman? Her brain tried to put information together. Detail tidbits jumped in her head like popping corn. She couldn't grab a kernel.

"What is it with Brett Merriman?" asked Zamora.

"I'm not sure what you mean," said Trudy. How would Zamora know Merriman?

"It's hard to get a straight answer. Like he's hiding something. Between Bostwick's absence and the dead buffalo, it's possible Meeker is sitting on too many secrets. Like a landfill building up too much gas."

Trudy nodded, sensing the rising dread that chanted: *you're out of your league.*

"Here's my card," said Zamora. "It's a Denver telephone but it will come right through to my cell. If you happen to run into Allison, I'd like to know if there's anything new."

Trudy glanced at the card—simple black and white. Uncluttered. She slipped it into her pants pocket.

"Excuse me, miss?" Trudy turned to the clerk's voice. "We had a cancellation. A room is open. It's all yours."

"Do you think everything is okay up there?" said Zamora.

"I have no idea."

The clerk slapped down a registration card, set a pen down alongside it.

"Thanks," she told the clerk, then turned to Zamora. "Are you going back to—"

"No." He cut her off briskly. "I want to keep the heat on these cops. The bad water thing mostly, now that we know Josh was an accident."

Zamora studied her hard. She was going to wait until she was alone to register.

"Hunt's over anyway," he added.

She picked up the registration card, fanned it in the air. "I've got to check in," she said. "Bushed."

Zamora looked like he had been insulted, said nothing.

"Long day," she added.

"Call me if you hear anything," he said. "I know where to find you. Especially if you hear from Allison or hear about Bostwick—anything at all."

The room was gleaming and modern. It could have been a new hotel room in Denver. Her second-floor window overlooked the main highway. Throttled-down trucks produced only a muffled growl, but she cracked the window a sliver for fresh air, and their sound came ripping inside. The hotel parking lot was jammed. There were two news trucks, each straddling two parking spaces. For a small town, Meeker hummed with activity.

The bed covered an acre. The big black television begged for attention. Trudy was tired but hungry. The small Italian restaurant one door east had a postage-stamp table available. She ordered a large house salad and bread. The locals were obvious because the young waiters greeted their tables with a minute or two of pleasant banter. Visitors like herself got a brusque but polite "Welcome" and "Care for some water?" Trudy ate quickly and realized she hadn't recovered her center from the Zamora encounter. She thought of Jerry, Lilly and Brad—imagined them rehearsing their speeches and wondered if they thought she might still show up.

Back in her room, she dialed Jerry's home, her hand and heart shaking.

"We need you," said Jerry.

"Are you doing it?"

"We are signed up. We called a reporter at the newspaper too, told them not to miss the public hearing." His voice was cool, clear. "What's happening up there?"

"Too much," said Trudy.

"You're bailing on us?"

"You don't have to go through with it."

"We're committed," said Jerry. "It needs to be done. There's never a perfect time to start. When are you coming back?"

"Soon," said Trudy.

"It won't be a one-shot deal," said Jerry. "But we'd love to have you at the start."

"Did you mention my name to the reporter?"

The pause told her everything.

"So this is publicity to you, isn't it?" said Trudy, her heart sinking and a tired tear of disappointment in her eye.

"It's about doing the right thing," said Jerry. "You know that."

Trudy said a quick goodbye, didn't allow time for his pleas.

She jotted down the key things to tell Allison, dialed her mobile number.

"I'm in Meeker. Call me if you get to a cell. Austin Rayburn is on his first hunt ever. Keating's lawsuit against Ethan Bostwick is a wicked piece of work, and Austin's deposition might be the most damaging of all. Josh and Loretta Keating were split up, even though they lived together. Nobody knows over what exactly, but maybe Austin knows. Be careful, Allison. I don't think everything around you is what it appears to be, and this whole town is jumpy over the money from the Roan and all the gas. Call me if you can. Wish I could head up there and find you. Call me, please."

Trudy stood by the window. A cool rivulet of air worked its way into her room. It was oddly soothing and freezing at the same time. Campers, trucks and RVs were starting to line the highway shoulder and the streets that led to the town square, a block away.

Fatigue took second place to creeping dread.

The gleaming room was a cold alien. The bed was quadruple the size Trudy needed. She couldn't get comfortable. She stirred and stewed, raided the mini bar for a bottle of white wine. From a chair by the window she watched a late-night couple hanging out in the cold for a smoke. She envied their carefree chat. The day had been a blur. Merriman. Bostwick. Rayburn. The Roan. Something bugged her, but she couldn't place it. Something somebody had said. She reread the copies of the lawsuit and her notes from the depositions. She checked her list of hunters from Allison's camp.

She stretched out on the bed and used every mental trick she knew to open the door to sleep. She didn't let two words form together in her brain. She stared at the dancing purple and blue lights behind her eyelids, pretended she was on a space walk, imagined the bed surrounded by cats and plants. More than anything, she assigned the "What's bugging me?" question to her subconscious, told it to report back only when it was good and ready.

"*Do you need a room?*"

Zamora.

The question seared the front of her brain on a marquee rimmed with flashing lights.

Who was Zamora to offer her a room?

Something about the question. He wasn't offering to share his room. The way the question resonated it was as if he had a room, owned a spare. Like he lived in Meeker. Or had close friends who did.

It was three o'clock in the morning when Trudy spun through her notes again, scanning for references to Zamora. It was four o'clock when she remembered the courtesy computer off the hotel lobby. She woke the computer with a twitch of the mouse. Allison had said Zamora was from Denver. A visitor didn't say *"Do you need a room?"* the way Zamora said it. And, *"What is it with Brett Merriman?"* There was the other snag. The question caused her head to cloud and clutter. She flashed on Zamora at the parking lot when she had first run into him and Allison, how easily he was able to find out about the buffaloes being shot.

There was a local-boy swagger to his presence.

"What is it with Brett Merriman?"

The question was asked so matter-of-factly. No different from asking for the local time.

The search engine stared blankly. She'd seen the power of the web. Her herb business did simple micro-blog blasts to let her customers know about the farmers' markets—where she would be and what was fresh. She'd done enough web surfing to be dangerous—and to know public records were there for the digging.

But "Terry Zamora + Meeker Colorado" returned only goofball combinations. Rio Blanco County's website, with all the public records, returned a messy list of options. She played with the confusing series of drop-down menus but generated a lot of nothing. She threw various combinations of words at the main search engine again and spotted nothing active or real.

His business card. Trudy went back to her room, retrieved the simple card from the dresser, and punched in the ten digits with the Denver area-code engine. Up popped sites from businesses offering to cull every scrap of personal information on "Terry Zamora." The "White Pages" listed phone number matched a "T. Zamora" on Bellaire Street in Thornton, Colorado. The question kept ringing in her head.

"*What is it with Brett Merriman?*"

Tuesday Evening

Devo stood with his mute captive on the shore of Trapper's Lake where the trail tipped down an embankment to an oval dirt parking lot. They were a few hundred yards from the lodge.

"I'm going to lash you to the dumpster in the lot. Then I'm going to go down to the lodge and leave a note. If they find the note tonight, you should be okay. Otherwise, it'll be the first hunter or hiker in the morning, and you might be a bit chilled."

"Don't."

Devo swung his headlamp so the beam smacked the kid in the face.

"Well, fuck me," said Devo. "Your mouth works."

The kid had been growing increasingly pathetic, whimpering on the hike down, so it wasn't hard to tell what he had been thinking. "Don't" was his first word.

"Don't," he said again.

"Then tell me who you're working for."

"Just don't," said the kid. "Don't take me down there."

"Talk to me," said Devo. It was well past sunset. Due to the kid's slow pace, it had taken three times as long as normal to reach Trapper's. "If you talk to me now I'll take you to the lodge, sit you down by a roaring fire and bring you hot chocolate."

The kid bowed his head and issued a soft sob.

"Talk to me," said Devo. "Who put you up to your crap?"

The kid took in a measured breath as if ready to talk. Here was a classic case of not-tough-enough, Devo mused. This kid wouldn't last three days in the wild.

"I don't know who."

"Bullshit," said Devo. "You gotta be working for someone. You couldn't do this yourself."

"Not someone," said the kid. "The *Earth*. I'm doing it for the Earth. Mother Earth."

"Oh, Christ," said Devo. "Spare me the crusade, okay? I know all about noble causes. I don't care if you're getting paid or not, I want to know who in the hell is helping you pull this off."

The kid went mum.

"Dumpster time," said Devo, giving his leash a sharp yank and taking a few steps down the trail.

"There's bears," said the kid. "What about bears?"

"Most bears will leave you alone," said Devo. "You have to stay cool, which for you won't be easy."

He yanked on the leash again and the kid stumbled after him. Several times the kid had threatened to lay down, and several times Devo reminded the kid he would have no problem tying him to a tree so tightly that sap would run through his veins come spring.

"Okay," said the kid. "I'll take the lodge and the fire."

"Your name first, and who put you up to this."

The kid sighed. "Fuck it," he said. "Can we talk in the lodge?"

"I don't do indoors," said Devo. "Talk here or else the dumpster will be your friend. Let's start simple. Where are you from?"

"Gypsum."

Devo only knew the exit on the highway, not too far east on the other side of the Flat Tops.

"Good start." Devo stepped closer. "Now let's try your name."

"Drew Addigan."

"I hope you're telling the truth."

"Lodge and fire?"

The kid was desperate for warmth. Devo despised his frailty.

"You were racing all over the Flat Tops awhile ago. Are you giving out now? It's a beautiful night. Keep talking."

"You gotta agree," said Addigan. "Something's gotta be done to stop what's happening on the Roan."

"Who are you working for?" said Devo. "I don't care about your reasons. Who?"

Devo gave an angry tug to the leash and started jogging down the trail, light bouncing on the well-groomed path ahead of him.

"That guy Bostwick," muttered Addigan. Devo stopped so suddenly that Addigan nearly crashed into him. "That's who. He's got a whole network trying to help him. I guess he's the most hated man in the White River Valley because he's got a cleaner, greener way of doing things."

"Never heard of him," said Devo. "Bostwick? I've been out of touch."

"Ethan Bostwick," said Addigan. "He's got all sorts of ideas to make life miserable for the energy companies. You should be on our side—you want to protect all of this here, don't you?"

"I don't think you save something by fucking it up," said Devo.

"It's temporary."

"And you made a bunch of people sick."

"For a good cause, man."

"Don't 'man' *me*, asshole. We ain't friends. You were putting nasty shit in my water."

"To prevent them from putting nasty shit in your water for a long, long time," said Addigan. "The whole thing is going to tumble down if methane or benzene is seeping out. It's like blood from an underground wound, man. They don't even say what chemicals they're pumping down in the earth. Hundreds of chemicals. You don't know, I don't know what crap they're injecting."

Devo kept the headlamp boring down on Addigan's face. "You hurt people," said Devo. "Does that mean anything to you at all?"

"They were going to hurt everyone. It's an easy trade."

"Your lawyer can try that logic for your defense," said Devo. "So you're working for Bostwick."

"I'm working for the Earth, but Bostwick organized things."

"You met with this guy Bostwick?" asked Devo. Relaying all this back to Allison might earn back some good will. She would be proud of his work. "He paid you?"

"For the costs," said Addigan. "My time is free. I'm a member of his network."

"Network?"

"Green Up Rio Blanco."

"I've heard enough," said Devo. He gave the leash a pull, started down again. He would go to the lodge and wait for someone to walk past and hand the kid over and tell them to go to the cops.

"Bostwick," said Devo. "I gotta remember that name. Anyone else?"

No answer.

"We still have the bears-by-the-dumpster option," said Devo. "Anyone else?"

"Have you stepped back and thought about—"

"Dumpster, bears, and before I leave I'm going to the lodge, and I'm going to find the smelliest bag of trash I can," Devo snarled. "I hope it's full of fish guts. I'm going to put it on top of the dumpster where I've got you tied down. Now tell me who else!"

"I never met Bostwick," said Addigan, scared again.

"But you said—"

"I said it was his network. The guy I met with helped me with all the logistics. Bostwick's network has more support than you might think. This guy said he was a recent convert. He was older. Part of the establishment. You could tell. Big ranch on the river."

Addigan's tone was now confessional. He was nearly blubbering. Reality was settling into his bones. He knew he was in trouble.

"We met there back in a shed where he stored the canisters, and we looked at maps," Addigan said. "It's funny but I remember he told me he might be up hunting—one of the reasons we did it now was because the hunters would get sick and report it. There would be lots of people in the backwoods. Anyway, the ranch was a buffalo ranch, nice piece of land. He took me down to the river. It was one of the prettiest views I've ever seen. He said he was sick of the greed, and that things would change forever if the drilling continued. Anyway, his name was Keating."

"First name?" said Devo.

"Josh, I think," said Addigan. "Only he died—I heard he got drunk one night while hunting and they found him by a lake. He froze to death."

Addigan was still blubbering. They were close to the lodge which loomed high above them on a ridge.

Devo was struggling to sort it all out. There was still the question of where to tie Addigan so he'd be found soon—and what to tie him with. Then, the note.

"Let's wait here a second," said Devo.

Addigan stopped. Devo let the leash go slack. They could trudge up the hill to the lodge and he could find a way to tie him to the vertical supports of the picnic deck.

"Please don't tie me up." Addigan's blubbering was growing old.

"Climb this hill," said Devo. "I'll leave you under the porch and knock on the door. Then you yell and draw attention."

"It's a hundred yards straight up."

"Easy," said Devo.

"Wait," said Addigan. "Let me get some water. I'm dying."

Devo sighed. What the hell. He dropped the leash and watched as Addigan slung his backpack down. Gravel crunched on the road where it landed. Devo could use some water too. Lights from the lodge floated in the night sky, a golden hovering spaceship. The kid squatted down and plucked a water bottle from a side compartment.

Ironic, thought Devo, that they would share some bottled water.

The kid took a swig, passed it over. Devo put the bottle to his lips. Strange sensation—water from a plastic container. He tipped his head back and pointed the headlamp to the dark sky.

Devo was mid sip when he caught a flash of a canister.

It was in Addigan's hand.

It was headed straight for his forehead at a high rate of speed.

Wednesday Morning

Tracking Austin Rayburn was a snap. The biggest challenge for Allison was hanging back. A scuff or unchecked thud from Lightning could echo down the trail.

Right after dawn, Rayburn had quietly moved his pack away from the tent, as if nobody would notice, and then he had hung around for another half-hour drinking coffee and pretending to be carefree. Austin Rayburn would never win an Oscar. He was chewing up the scenery. He was overly friendly and overly helpful. When he went for an alleged leg-stretching stroll, Allison waited a few minutes and saddled up Lightning. His tracks led straight down the trail.

For the first stretch, Allison kept Lightning at a slow walk and watched the ground for any signs of Rayburn straying. The tracks suggested he was moving at a dead run. Enough snow remained to reveal if Rayburn plunged into the woods for a bivouac or a hiding place.

Where Rayburn was headed didn't matter. She would follow him to the gates of hell. Or Denver. Whichever came first.

Rayburn's strides were steady, relentless. He was pounding down the hill. Humid, tangy pine arrived on a soft morning breeze. Lightning turned the corner at the top of a long straight pitch and Allison gave his reins a gentle tug. The horse stopped. A hundred yards ahead, no more, Rayburn motored on. Allison caught a flash before he plunged down and out of sight. She waited two minutes. Once in the open crossing—low scrub and no trees—she would be completely exposed. If spotted out here, her presence wouldn't be chalked up to coincidence.

Her own uncertainty fluttered in her chest, created an odd woozy bubble that kept her breath short and her fingers tingling. In the low light, her eyesight hustled ahead down the trail and vacuumed up all the tidbits of available information. The key would be following Rayburn once he reached Trapper's, not letting him depart in a waiting truck. She would plead for a spare vehicle if that happened. Nora would come to the rescue.

The trail climbed a low ridge. Allison slowed Lightning to a crawl. The exposed spine was rock. Snow didn't last long here. Rayburn's boot pattern popped out from the soft dirt near the top of the ridge, then vanished on the hard rocks at the top. Allison climbed down from Lightning and crouch-walked, alone, to the top of the spine. She stopped.

Waited. Listened. Looked. Nothing. She took Lightning by his lead rope, guided him over the rocks.

The trail cut back along the face of a sharp pitch down a series of hairpin switchbacks. The forest was a murky thicket. Aspens huddled close, competing for shoulder room. The carpet of snow returned where shade controlled the thermostat. The sun was officially up but she knew this side of the slope grabbed the clock and yanked the big hand back an hour toward dawn. She stepped down to a prominent boulder at a gap where the trail was hit by morning sun. Lightning followed every step like a dog, sensing her caution. There was one spot of open sunlight before the trail would suck her back under the shaded canopy.

She leaned against the boulder, closed her eyes and let the heat warm her face. Lightning sighed. A five-minute pause would give Rayburn some distance and keep her outside any bubble of detection by noise.

An unmistakable click popped in her ear and she opened her eyes.

"Stay right where you are, bitch," said Austin Rayburn. "Don't move a fucking muscle."

Wednesday Morning

The Blue Spruce lobby was coming to life. A staffer was organizing the continental breakfast buffet. A few guests were checking out. Trudy stood up from the computer carrel to make way for a full-fledged cowboy in tight jeans and black cowboy hat who asked kindly if he could check his e-mail. The cowboy came with a whiff of apricot shampoo and a quick, glinting smile. Trudy took the interruption as an excuse to take a break. She enjoyed a hot bath in her room, turned off the light as she soaked to let the pieces mesh.

Nothing gelled.

No gears ground together.

It was full morning when she returned to the lobby. Couples and travelers and truckers filled the tables, sipping coffee and eating oatmeal from Styrofoam bowls and nibbling on cinnamon rolls from Styrofoam plates. Some of the eaters wore tie-dyed shirts, sported long hair. Protesters, no doubt. Trudy poured orange juice, made whole-wheat toast and drizzled honey from a plastic tub smaller than a matchbox. She sat at the counter looking out at the parking lot. A TV hung in the corner of the room, showing CNN. A report on an OPEC meeting, of all things. Trudy smiled but only inside. The breakfast room was quiet. "*What is it with Brett Merriman?*" What was she overlooking? What was she missing?

Three matching blue SUVs pulled into the parking lot, each with tinted windows. A few minutes later, the lobby was filled with men and women projecting a serious aura and well-organized vibe. Cell phones in full effect. Those who weren't leaning on the clerk's counter were talking on their phones or texting. They were well-dressed for business, poorly dressed for the mountains. There wasn't one suitcase among them. After a few minutes they shuffled back out to the parking lot and milled around their vehicles. The commotion had caused the breakfast crowd to perk up, and by the time the SUV crew was out the door, the flotsam of conversation bobbed Trudy's way, and she could make out that they had been the advance team checking on logistics. The news conference. The decision. There was liveliness to the room now and more hubbub.

Trudy poured coffee into a cup and returned to the computer. She stared at the screen for a few minutes, then gave up.

She put her things together, shook off fatigue and checked out.

"Everything okay?" said the clerk.

The same clerk from last night, same low reading glasses.

"Just fine," said Trudy. "You are certainly putting in a long shift."

"A few minutes of sleep here and there. My husband and I own the hotel and with the undersecretary coming in from Washington we wanted everything shipshape."

"It looks like he's staying here."

"That's the plan. Is everything okay with you? You looked worried."

Trudy paused. Her plan was to go to Merriman's store and bounce the issue off him.

"Did you recognize the man who was talking to me last night?"

"Sure," said the clerk.

Trudy glanced at the name tag. Bonnie. "You did?"

"It's been a few years since he was around, but yes. Terry—oh shoot—Terry …"

"Zamora."

Bonnie cocked her head, ran it around.

"No, definitely not Zamora. God, he still does the whole shaved-head thing. I thought that was a phase. So unbecoming. No, not Zamora. It's Terry Oliver."

Trudy let the name settle. At least that would explain the search engine shooting blanks. "Are you sure?"

"Positive," she said. "I can't remember exactly what it was, some strange scandal but he left town a few years ago and headed to Denver to make his fortune. He would tell anyone who would listen. How did he know you?"

Terry Oliver. Something clicked.

"He doesn't. Not really. Did he move back?"

"Maybe," said Bonnie. "I've seen him a few times. He might have changed his name for the Denver version of himself. You know how people like to get a fresh start, see if they can find a way to shake their reputations. Doesn't usually work, but they try."

Sparks popped, nothing ignited. Trudy spun through the possibilities, instantly disliking the snake for trying to shed his skin.

"Can I have my room back?"

"Let me check," said Bonnie. "What has Terry Oliver done now?"

"I don't know."

"You look like you've been told some very bad news."

Trudy mustered a smile. "Just worried. Is a room still available?"

Bonnie stepped away, clicked her computer.

"You've got it for another night," she said. "Is there anything I can do to help?"

"I need the computer again," said Trudy. "And my morning back."

Wednesday Morning

Blurry grays and greens cut through the black fog. A throb with sharp edges seized her temples. It kept time with her heart. An EKG would generate sharp spikes, each pulse the contour of a dunce cap. Flat and rigid on her back, Allison could make out soft thuds on the snow, but couldn't turn her head to find the source.

She checked her head's range of motion. She could turn her head an inch, no more. The throb from her cheek reminded her of the rock in Rayburn's paw as it came at her.

Her arms lay ramrod straight down her sides. They were lashed and cinched to her body. There was give at her elbows, but not much.

She didn't need a mirror to understand her predicament. She was in a killing device with a wicked design. The rectangular box was a cube made of the pipes, the ones she had found in Austin Rayburn's supplies.

Except for a series of pipes around the middle, like a belt, the cube was open on the tops and sides. The adult-scale Tinker Toys had been reassembled as a jail for one. You don't get to stand up in this jail. You just get to lie down.

The size of the cube was enough to have kept Josh Keating inert. He must have gained enough consciousness to realize his plight. His arms couldn't move much, most likely, but his hands had enough freedom to undo the watch and bury it as a signal that he had been aware and alert when the shit hit the fan. Once hypothermia had done its work, the pipes would be removed and they could position the body to make it look like a bad fall.

Austin Rayburn didn't have time to cut the cube down to fit Allison's smaller frame, so to compensate he had lashed her arms to her torso and tied her ankles to minimize her ability to move. She had more wiggle room, but the sides and top of the Tinker Toy coffin were still too narrow and confining to escape.

The thudding came to a stop. He was close. She peered through half-cracked eyelids. The light was blurred. She wasn't sure her eyes would focus. Her head hurt as if she had a punishing tequila hangover.

Through the slits in her eyes Rayburn slid into view, upside down. He was a dark cloud blotting out the sky. He was on his knees, his gaunt face a foot above hers. From what little she could tell, her vision still coming around, she was on a slope, her head higher than her feet.

"Well, well," he said. "You've come around. Maybe you'd like to make a call. I've got your cell phone right here."

"This won't work," said Allison. Each utterance was a struggle. Each sound in her head triggered a fresh jab of pain.

"What won't work?"

It wasn't her cheeks. She now knew she was down to her underwear. He had left her bra on too. How considerate.

"This," she said.

"What do you mean work?"

"Won't work."

"Of course it will."

"Not cold enough." She hoped.

"Not *now*," he said. "Now" was a three-syllable word, long and dragged out. "Maybe you'd like to use your phone to get the forecast. Give me a break."

His knees cracked as he stood up. His face disappeared. From upside down she watched a motion as if he was hurling a rock. She heard a soft knock against a distant tree.

The blurry blotches on the fringes of her peripheral vision were the pipes.

The light through the dense trees indicated midday. She pinged her internal clock for a readout, got nothing back. Her throat was dry. Her toes were out of touch. It was cold, but it was a tolerable cold.

"How did you do it all by yourself?" she asked.

"Do what?"

"Keating wasn't small like me. Probably double my size and then some."

"Shit," muttered Rayburn.

"He must have been a handful."

"Shut up. Just shut the fuck up."

"What did he do to you?"

"What the hell business is it of yours?"

Allison remembered the shudder in her guts as the rock came toward her head.

"There has to be a good reason. There usually is," she said. How far had Austin dragged her from the trail? Would one hearty scream be worth it? Was she up to it? "Come on, Austin, what did Keating do?"

"Your job is to shut up and freeze," said Rayburn. "Judging by the way your toes are turning blue, you're doing a good job."

When the jet aircraft she had been sitting in hit its zenith above the LaGuardia runway, it took only a few seconds to fall back to earth. She remembered a small story in the newspaper a year later, when the event had started morphing into a chapter of her life that she could ponder from a distance. The story was about the number of seconds the plane must have taken to fall, as if there might be comfort there for the friends and family of the victims, knowing how few seconds of utter terror they had endured. The article mentioned nothing about the survivors and the fact that they had those seconds to relive over and over for the rest of their lives.

But Allison had been sitting next to people who had been forced to process the possibility of death at lightning speed. Now she would have to deal with an agonizing crawl to the dying moment. She wondered if she would be lucid enough to confirm the theory that hypothermia wasn't a bad way to go. Keating had left a neatly buried wristwatch. She would scratch a happy face in the dirt.

"My horse?" said Allison.

"What about it?" said Rayburn.

"Where is he?"

"Like I give a damn."

"This won't work."

"Time is all," said Rayburn. "Time brings night."

"You got Keating's watch back, I take it." The truth was that she had no sensation on either wrist and she was guessing.

"I don't know what you're talking about."

"Who were you running to tell? The same somebody who helped you drag Keating around?"

"Fuck you."

"This is imaginative. Almost creative. Almost art. It took a lot of planning, getting all the pieces in place, smuggling them up there. Standard issue hardware-store pipe, right?" There was something stiff about her jaw, as if the joints were caked with wet cement. Her head thumped, each beat a jolt of pain. "But don't you think two hypothermia victims with a bash to the head— don't you think there might be a problem there?"

"Who says they're going to find you?"

He was close again, though she could only make out a rough

shape near her feet. Her head couldn't move up and down, just her eyes.

"You left your elk behind," she said.

"Not an issue."

"Colin's elk, from what I heard."

An angry growl filled her ears. "Goddamn it. That fucker swore he'd never tell a soul. That's my elk and I'm going back up there and hurt your cute little guide buddy for that one. I'm going back to town with my fucking kill."

A branch snapped, and he grunted again. He was breathing hard, starting to panic. She tested her elbow motion, looking to find leverage. Nothing. She tried pulling her arms as tightly as possible against her body and then slamming them out, but she only had an inch of slack to work with. The plastic cage rocked a bit. It was conceivable that she might be able to flip it, but that would only put her on her side, or worse, face down.

"It's as good as steel," said Rayburn. "Interesting approach though."

No doubt Josh Keating had tried the same thing. He must have awakened—thus the scars on some of the pipe as he tried to wriggle free.

The numbness was taking over and Allison's fingers felt as thick and useless as carrots.

Rayburn's face came into view again, upside down. He caught her by surprise and jabbed a stick across her mouth, pushed it down until her lips pinched back as far as they would go as if she was a horse gripping a bit between her teeth. She choked and gagged. A strap was tied to each end of the stick. He tucked the ends of the straps around her neck and attached them to each side to the plastic cage like a hammock strung between two trees.

"There you go," said Rayburn. "If I let you talk you might burn up a few more calories and die quicker. But this ought to hold you.

Now we can both wait and listen to the birds chirping and the tree branches rustling in the wind. Who knows? Maybe a nice elk will wander through here, and I'll bag my third trophy for the week—two elk and a busybody bitch. Wouldn't that be nice? Now you just lie there and try not to make too much noise while you freeze to death."

9

Wednesday Morning

Trudy hustled up the stairs to her room and sat on the bed. Counted to ten slowly, looking for a calm interior space. She took a quick shower, dressed and stood by the window. The hotel parking lot was filling with protesters, cars and pickup trucks sporting banners made of sheets and poster board: *Drillers Go Home. Reduce Your Carbon Footprint One Step at a Time. Don't Bury the Roan!!!*

Protesters were videotaping each other. They huddled in groups sharing coffee and nibbling on donuts. A television reporter interviewed key people across the street. News trucks were hubs of activity nearby, their satellite dishes aimed at the bleak sky.

The lobby buzzed. The hotel staff let protesters come and go as they pleased. No hassles. The alcove with the computer drew a line of anxious users like a Porta Potty at Woodstock.

Bonnie was selling breakfast tickets to all takers—eight dollars a pop. A steal. "It's past the time when we normally close the buffet," Bonnie told Trudy. "But we'll take it any way it comes."

"Is there another computer by any chance?"

"For paying guests, honey, sure. Follow me."

Bonnie's office was like a home. It included a large leather couch and a refrigerator. Trudy was shown a seat at the desk. Two antelope heads, with horn pincers, peered down at her. "Take your time," said Bonnie. "I'll be plenty busy out front. I can tell you're good people."

Bonnie left the door cracked open. From a well-positioned mirror over the wall, Trudy could see the entire front counter and the teeming lobby beyond.

During her search on the web, Terry Oliver turned out to be every bit as much a phantasm as Terry Zamora. She had started with high hopes—something had resonated when Bonnie uttered "Terry Oliver." She added the search word *Meeker* to Terry Oliver and quickly mined one strong hit—a police blotter ten years old. The police had responded to a call of disorderly conduct at a bar and arrested one Terry Oliver, age thirty-six, who was "belligerent and clearly intoxicated." And then one link turned up under *The Rio Blanco Herald Times*. The site said "obits" at the end. It was a long shot, but then the next page said you had to register and pay twenty-five dollars for online content. The price wasn't formidable, but it didn't seem fair to pay so much to peek at what was likely one snippet of probably useless information.

In the mirror, Trudy could see Bonnie leaning over the counter. Trudy went to the door and asked if she happened to have an account she might access.

"Sure," said Bonnie. "Advertisers get it for free."

Bonnie followed Trudy back, punched in the account code and password. "You got a hit on Terry Oliver in the paper?" Bonnie asked. "Was it an arrest or something? It wouldn't surprise me."

The link clicked through to an obituary.

Trudy scrolled down the page.

Bonnie let out an audible gasp.

The obit was for Hector and Lois Oliver. A few paragraphs told the story of their awful car crash on Wolf Creek Pass, and how their wreck hadn't been found for weeks. Trudy's heart ached for them. "Loretta Keating's parents, right?" she said.

"You came all the way from Glenwood Springs, and you've already got our community figured out," said Bonnie. "I thought I knew a lot too, but apparently not everything."

Trudy had to start at the beginning of the sentence to grasp it all: "In addition to their only child Loretta Keating, of Buford, survivors include Terry Oliver, Hector Oliver's son by a previous marriage."

"Holy holy," said Bonnie. "No wonder he's been hanging around like a nosy tomcat mainlining nip. He's about to cash out big time if they sell the family ranch. And if the feds give them permission."

Wednesday Morning

His nose knew.

He was inhaling chemicals.

The light behind his eyelids was too bright, manmade bright, ugly bright.

The surface he was lying on was too soft.

He cracked his eyes open, anticipating the worst.

Devo was surrounded by a white curtain. The room was quiet except for a low-frequency electronic buzz that nagged his ears. He hopped from the bed, and a dull ache began pounding his head. An IV drip was tethered to his left arm.

He found the gap in the curtain and stepped into the empty room, which had eight-times more floor space than the bed.

Devo was surrounded by the stuff of death, the epitome of anti-progress.

The room was too perfect, too white. It was like a movie set. Behind his IV drip stood a bank of monitors and gauges. Strands of wire ran from a machine to spots on his chest, held in place by white plastic tape where patches of skin had been shaved. *Shaved!* Devo ripped them off in disgust. He dragged the IV drip on its rolling stand to a washbasin. He needed to pee like an over-hydrated moose, and he used the washbasin. Charles Bukowski said it best: Sometimes you just have to pee in the sink.

A mirror told him what he didn't want to know.

A giant white bandage engulfed his forehead. It squashed down his hair, which had been clipped and shaved as well.

Fuckers!

Devo pondered his reflection in disgust. He needed to get the hell out of here.

The door opened behind him.

"Mr. Devo," said a stocky woman in a white uniform. Her lips were bright red and her hair was short, shockingly gray. She wore thick glasses. "Your alarm went off."

"I gotta go."

"You gotta get back in bed. You are going nowhere." She was strikingly pale and unwell.

"Who brought me?"

"The ambulance. You lost a lot of blood."

The room wobbled, and his vision was soft and oily around the edges. "Not that you could afford to lose much of anything."

"Where are my clothes?"

"I'm not sure what we saved. We had to cut you out of your wrap."

"I need them back."

"You need to get back on your back and rest. I'm going to get the doctor."

"Where am I?"

"Meeker."

"I'm not supposed to be here. I need to get back to the woods."

She departed. Devo scoured the room and found a Ziploc bag in the top drawer of his dresser. Camera, four hand-carved fish hooks, pieces of twine and rope. He turned the camera on, pressed *eject* only to see a vacant carriage, a baby bird's empty mouth waiting to be filled. *Cheep-cheep.* His stomach seized, the light flickered and a strange sadness of failure overwhelmed him. Failure of the mission, failure of Allison's trust.

Addigan was gone.

The evidence was gone too.

The door swung open with a low buzz. The nurse returned with a large white plastic bag in her grip and a doctor in tow. He wore a white business shirt and khaki slacks. He was boiled clean as a newborn. He wasn't past thirty, but was already pudgy and soft. His fingernails were perfectly trimmed, his round wire-rims were shiny gold, his cheeks radiating pink.

"Doctor Peter Kober," he said. "How do you feel?"

"I've been better."

"Pain level?"

"Manageable."

"The nurse says you want to go, which you must not. You have serious deficiencies of minerals, and your bone density is at a critical level. You have strange sores in unusual places. We're waiting on test results."

"I need to go home," said Devo. "Those health problems are a part of the process of devolution, the transition. I can't stop the process."

The nurse raised the bag over the bed. The contents spilled out. "Your clothes," she said. "I couldn't really clean anything but I wouldn't be surprised if there are some nasty bugs that call this home. They might be the source of your sores, although we did spray it. Bug spray and other kinds of fumigation. The ambulance workers had to mask up in your presence, if you know what I mean."

Devo reached into the bag and slowly pulled out the deer/raccoon/beaver/rabbit skin garment that had been patched and adorned with feathers. The garment was in two pieces, top and bottom. He had sewn a maze of pockets and pouches into the lining of the jacket, and a few inside the pants.

"You weigh 115 pounds," said Doctor Kober. "A good forty or fifty pounds below your ideal weight. You have a nasty crack on your skull that wants to bleed."

"How long have I been here?" The name of the day would be meaningless. He did not live by the calendar.

"About fourteen hours, give or take," said Dr. Kober.

Devo's hands worked pockets open. He had planned ahead for this possibility. "So it's morning," he said, experiencing an elevation in his mood. "I take it they didn't find the kid who whacked me."

"They found only you," said the doctor. "It was a man out for a post-dinner stroll. You were damned lucky. You could have died right there of hypothermia."

"I have to go back now," said Devo. "It's who I am. In fact, I'm wondering if you and I can cut a deal." Hot lava rocks of pain tumbled down the fissure behind the crack in his skull. He winced.

"This isn't a bargaining situation," said the doctor.

"I don't want anyone to know I was here," said Devo. "I don't want anyone to know I needed help. I'll stay another day here and won't complain about anything if you promise not to tell a soul about me."

The nurse smiled a big beaming smile conjured from the depths of her heart. "Isn't that quaint," she said.

"What?" asked Devo. He reached into a jacket flap and fingered the video card. He grinned, pulled the card out of its hiding place as if lifting a bullet out of a wound with surgical forceps. "What's so funny?"

"I'm afraid it's too late for that particular deal," said the nurse.

"The man who found you at Trapper's, the medics, the police," said Doctor Kober. "It's not every day they deal with a celebrity. I'm afraid the word has already gone out. Reporters are waiting to interview you."

"Apparently your YouTube channel is at the top of the charts," said the nurse.

Devo studied the video card with satisfaction. He had separated the evidence from the camera before he had been bushwhacked. At least the pictures had the guy's face and his ugly demeanor. The video would show the backpack too, as well as the contents of the backpack, and the pool where he'd poured the poison.

"A throng is gathering outside the clinic," said Dr. Kober.

"Fans," said the nurse.

Devo rolled it around in his mind. He couldn't quite understand what they were saying. "In Meeker?" he said. "This is my first time here, but it's not that big a town, is it?" Could they all be devolutionists? Did he have a flock already?

"They're in Meeker," said Dr. Kober. "But they happen to be here to send a message to the undersecretary."

"The who?"

"Undersecretary of the Interior. He's making a big announcement later today," said the nurse. "Whether to expand the drilling, the leases, or whether it's time to stop and check to see if it's all that safe."

Devo held the card up. His eyes couldn't focus on it. The inside of his skull throbbed like a bass drum. He needed help.

"The latest video?" asked Dr. Kober.

"No," said Devo. He stretched out down on his side, let the cool cotton pillow soothe his bearded cheek. He clutched the card in his palm. "It's a blank."

Wednesday Morning

Wind scolded the tree branches enough to make them flail. The branches were angry, so was she.

Allison gagged. Her windpipe was wide open to the sky but her breathing was choppy and irregular. Her tongue felt odd and thick. Her teeth had gnawed on the wood jammed into her mouth, but it was a green stick and it was too soft to shatter and spit out.

She could touch her thumb with her pinky finger and detect that the muscles were working, but she knew the blood vessels on the surface were contracting. Her body was pouring its energy into keeping the vital organs warm. Thoughts didn't gel. She felt immensely tired. She hadn't heard Rayburn's huffing presence in a long time.

She pictured herself from overhead in her mind's eye, looked for a weakness in the plastic-frame coffin, but foresaw only a corpse in women's underwear. There would be no scars on her body, just another frozen idiot in the woods.

She wriggled, seeking leverage. She felt nothing. The strap around her ankles yielded a touch. She pulled her head up enough to see motion at the end of the plastic cage, a busy blur of feet and toes. She kept wriggling. Since Rayburn wasn't telling her to stop, he must be away. Allison ran through the possibilities. He was busy covering his tracks. He had gotten impatient because she was taking too long to die. He had grown bored. He'd decided to just leave her and come back in the morning to take the pipes away and dress the corpse.

She might live through the day, but the nighttime cold would finish her off. Shivering, confusion and soon she'd have blue ears, blue fingers, blue toes, blue lips.

Devo.

The thought gave her a boost. Was it possible that he would come back from Trapper's and find her? Would he spot something on the trail, a disturbance in the snow where things didn't look right?

She wriggled more. She squirmed and yanked and jabbed at the straps, heard guttural barks and strains that were most likely hers, given that there were no other options. There was a desperate quality to the voice she didn't know she possessed. She squeezed her ankles together, jerked them apart. Her lips stung, her throat ached. She squirmed, sensed more give on her bonds. Another grunt. Straining. Twisting. She realized she could roll to her right and turn the entire plastic jail on its side. With the shift in weight and change in the stress points on her bonds, she felt an inch more wiggle room in her left arm. A bit. A bit more. And another bit more. Just enough. She couldn't throw a fastball, but her left arm had a respectable range of motion. Some leverage.

She watched her fingers circle around the plastic pipe. The fingertips were an inhuman grayish-blue. When they touched the pipe they returned no sensation, no information about the texture of the plastic. For a second she thought it might be a matter of delay, like audio sync in a badly dubbed movie. Surely the information would be along any second. But no. Her fingers were as good as dead.

She rolled onto her shoulder and stared into the woods, trying to detect motion, trying to see if Rayburn was around. Empty cold forest—nobody. Nothing.

She reached behind her neck with her fingers to see if she could feel the knot where the gag was tied. Her fingers registered nothing. She could not tell if she was touching anything, let alone a knot. The fingertips were shot.

"Help!" she called. Her tongue worked behind the bit. "Hey!" she shouted. "Over here! Somebody!"

She shivered. Waves of pain rippled up and down her body. She gagged. Her mouth was bone dry and sour from her own bile. She stared at her free arm, watched it reach outside the plastic coffin and grab the earth, watched the hand seek a perch in crusty leaves on the forest floor. The arm belonged to somebody who was trying to help. Good arm, desperate arm, thinking arm. She worked to roll over, worked to rock the plastic-tube box. The arm kept clawing. It was fixated and determined. She watched the ground move under her, the coffin of pipes edging along the ground toward a hefty stick like a baseball bat a yard away. Her skull raked against something hard, and a disturbing jerk of pain throttled her head like a bare-knuckle sucker punch. In spite of the pain, it was encouraging to know that some of her nerves still functioned.

The arm wouldn't give up. It crawled an inch at a time. She couldn't feel anything, but she saw the fingers suddenly grip the stick and hold it up. It had the quality of an optical trick. She could see the fingers gripping it, but felt nothing.

The stick came down on the plastic tube with a meek tap. It came down harder the next time, but the blow wasn't good for a dent of any significance. The cage might as well have been made of steel.

On the next backswing, the stick caught a rock and issued a satisfying wallop.

Bang.

Bang.

Bang.

She slammed the stick, heard the bang on the rock. She watched her wrist flail but felt nothing in her grip. The fingers were robot digits and robots had no feelings. Frustration clogged her throat. Anger made her squirm in a rage, the plastic cage rattled, and she kept hammering the stick until she floated in a hazy world filled with clouds of bitterness and confusion and anger for ending up like this, for being trapped, for losing the upper hand. Bang. Bang. Bang.

She felt herself beginning to float as she had floated in the water after the jet went down, but this was a delicious deliriousness enveloping her. She didn't feel cold. She didn't feel much of anything. She continued in a rhythmic, hypnotic, mindless buck and roll, flailing at the rock, hammering the cudgel, stick up, stick down, stick up, stick down, bang bang bang.

She heard a heavy thud on the earth. She twisted her neck around. A branch snapped. Two branches. A thud sounded from overhead, and it carried power and weight.

She craned her neck back like a tourist gazing up at the Empire State Building, and a horse head blotted out the sky.

Lightning.

He neighed with authority.

"Lightning."

She tried to mouth his name as a form of praise but her jaw was numb.

The horse was standing beside the cage. His head descended and his teeth went for a clump of grass. He ripped the tuft with his teeth and began chewing it. His lead rope dangled within reach. Allison watched her arm move toward the rope, watched her hand grab the rope, but her fingers felt nothing. Lightning's head turned around as if in surprise, and his ears shot forward.

"Git," Allison moaned. "Go." She hoped her grip was firm. But Lightning didn't move.

Allison worked to shake the fuzzy cobwebs clouding her brain. Grabbing the lead rope didn't work. It tugged his head down and that was all.

"Come here," she gasped. "Come around."

Lightning looked at her curiously, as if to say he had done his thing, he had been alerted by the sound of her hammering, he had been drawn to the sound, and now Allison should do her thing. The horse pivoted around as Allison held the lead rope, stood broadside to her, and snorted. If only she had taught him to sit like a dog. That might have come in handy, better to reach his stirrup. But he was slightly downhill, which helped.

Allison strained her numb arm and reached for the stirrup, watched her fingertips touch the square leather loop. She rocked the cage and strained, shoulder and chest aching, until she saw her fingers slide around the stirrup.

She clucked as if sitting in the saddle. "Let's go," she said, catching her breath. Trying to maintain her grip. "Giddyup."

Lightning knew this wasn't right. This was not the correct procedure.

"I know," Allison said. "Come on. Walk for me."

Her shoulder throbbed as Lightning took a step forward, the plastic cage moving along the ground like a sled. "Go," she said. "Giddyup."

Lightning moved forward and the cage followed. Allison felt her exposed flesh scraping leaves and dirt. "Go," she said. She clucked. Her arm screamed. She stared at her grip on the stirrup to make certain it stayed put. "Good boy," she murmured. The cage jerked and banged against the earth, Allison's view became a montage of sky, trees, horse, arm, ground, snow, stirrup. She focused on the stirrup. "Giddyup," she said breathlessly. "Walk for me, boy."

Lightning moved faster. They crossed a clearing where sunlight broke through. Allison clung to the stirrup, her arm extended like a water skier flipped on her back skimming along the choppy surface of a cold lake. Her shoulder burned, it hurt, but that was a good thing—she wasn't frozen solid. She stared at the passing sky. Trees came and went. Thick clouds, light and shadow, the crackling sound of whipping branches and tumbling rocks, the odor of plowed mud, shorn bushes, and shredded leaves. She closed her eyes and said, "Walk for me," in a husky, reassuring voice. "Good boy."

Lightning stopped. "Go!" Allison commanded. She felt an odd tug. The cage was caught on a tree trunk. "Walk," she said. She felt Lightning heave, heard the plastic pipe scraping against frozen bark. "Go!"

The cage was jammed too tightly among the sprawling roots of the tree.

Allison writhed inside the cage, rattled the pipes, tried to help shake it loose.

"Go!"

Lightning strained like a mule. Allison willed her grip to stay locked on the stirrup. Lightning whinnied, tugged, yanked. "Go," Allison said. "Just fucking go!"

The plastic cage exploded.

Allison closed her eyes and felt the pieces fly away from her body, felt Lightning pick up speed, felt her body slithering along the forest floor like a tin can tied to a bumper. She could no longer hold on. Her fingers ceased to function. She released the stirrup and skidded with exhaustion face down in a pool of sunlight and dirty snow.

She heard the sound of horse hooves near her head. She willed herself to flip onto her back before a thousand pounds of shank crushed her skull. The clop of hooves came closer, yet Allison could see Lightning standing motionless on the far side of the clearing.

The footfalls stopped.

"Allison."

The voice was like a quiet rain, reassuring and calm—and Colin's face accompanied it.

"My god, what in hell happened?"

Wednesday Morning

Meeker hummed. The main road through town was a stop-and-go, bumper-to-bumper parade of vehicles as protesters poured in from all over the state and, judging by the license plates, Wyoming and Utah too. The town square evolved as the main encampment. Families and friends and hangers-on who enjoyed a good uprising were clustered around the park. Everyone knew each other. An air of confidence clipped through the throng, as if they had already won.

Trudy walked the five blocks to the grocery store, where the parking lot was jammed with activity. Inside, the store was so busy they might have been giving money away.

Merriman was sacking groceries as if he were one of the hired help.

"Trudy," he said, "can you believe this? Most people come in to buy a few things for lunch, extra fruits and veggies, but it's been like this all morning."

Merriman kept a poker face, but Trudy could tell he was ecstatic.

"You can't exactly high-five 'em, can you?" she said. A couple was coming through the line. Merriman packed their beets, parsnips and carrots into a canvas bag. The man had a long, tangled, unkempt beard. The woman's face was hidden behind brown dreads.

"Do you know how many employees I have who would quit if they sell the drilling rights? They aren't enjoying today like I am." Merriman thanked the couple as they left. "They are worried that when the federal analysts see the numbers, they'll cave."

"Doesn't the federal government already know what it wants to do?"

"It's possible," said Merriman. "But if they're going to let the drilling expand and go unchecked, they have to consider that all these sick hunters might signify a major problem, especially if the water is turning foul."

"I want to go find Allison," said Trudy. Government decisions were beyond her influence. She wanted to bear down on the things she could control. "I'm worried. I thought all night about going up to Trapper's Lake."

Merriman stopped his bagging chore and stepped a few feet away from the checkout lane.

"I'd go with you but I can't leave the store. Today is big in so many ways. Do you know the route? The only problem would be finding out where exactly she would be hunting, and knowing which trail to take. There are quite a few."

"The paper said Josh Keating was found by Oyster Lake."

Merriman smiled. "Yes, good. Perfect. Just get up there and ask around. Do you have the clothes you need for an October hike? Some orange? I can get you fixed up. Hunting season and all of that."

The prospect of finding Allison was daunting. Needle in a haystack. Needle in a whole hayfield.

"Should we talk to the sheriff first, tell him what we know?"

"We could, but I think the cops have their hands full with the crowds." Merriman issued a defeated sigh. "Besides, what are we going to tell them? That the Keatings weren't getting along? I guess I was thinking about this last night too. I was talking to Ethan Bostwick. I told him about our trip to the Roan. He was glad to hear you were appropriately disgusted. But he also said he wasn't surprised to hear that the Keatings hadn't been seeing eye to eye. I don't think it would hurt to tell the cops, but it's not very much to go on, is it?"

"It's the sum of all the pieces," said Trudy. What happened to his concern? "It's the pieces that make me worried—if they all fit together, it's not a pretty picture."

"I know," said Merriman. "I can see what you see too, but I'm trying to imagine if you were Sheriff Christie, what would you do with the information?"

"Do you want to hear something else that's pretty strange?"

"What?"

Trudy walked him through the Terry Zamora/Terry Oliver saga. "Pretty peculiar, wouldn't you say?"

Merriman looked stunned, shook his head slowly. "Holy you-know-what," he said. "What next?"

"Got me," said Trudy. "The cops have to be told that much."

"Agreed," sad Merriman. "But the cops have their work cut out for them with the federal officials in town and all the protesters, and now they've got Devo at the clinic and part of the crowd is over there waiting to see if they can catch a glimpse of their hero. I guess Devo is big among the Save The Roan crowd, and I gotta say I love that guy." Merriman beamed. "You have to admire what he's doing—"

"Devo is here at a clinic?"

"Up the street," said Merriman. "I guess he got busted in the head near Trapper's Lake Lodge. There's not much of him left, either—somebody said he's a shadow of his former self."

"Where's the clinic?"

"North a few blocks, then turn right and go up another four blocks. Fourth and Cleveland. You'll have to get in line from what I hear. He's got an interesting flock, I'll say that much. And you're going to try and get in to see him?"

"He was with Allison," said Trudy. "He was right there."

Wednesday Morning

The writing was neat block letters—pretty and feminine.

"You've had a lot of notes and letters," said the nurse. "But this woman was certain you would want to see her."

Devo read the note:

"Hi. My name is Trudy. Allison Coil is my best friend. I think you've met her. I was wondering if we could talk. I'm worried about her. I don't think everything is what it seems at her camp. I don't want to put too much in writing. I hope you are feeling well enough to see me—and I hope you are feeling well."

This was a no-brainer. Key phrase: Allison's best friend.

"Bring her here, will you?"

As much as Devo wanted to sit in a chair and greet a guest like a regular person, it still felt best to lie on his back and not move. The doctors wanted to put a plate in his skull. One doctor was worried about "intracranial hematomas." Another warned that the "cerebral arteries" might have been damaged, and they needed to watch the brain, make sure it was getting the blood flow it needed. Devo hoped the searing pain would soon fade.

The woman who came through the door had a meek, quiet air about her. Devo felt instantly better, just laying eyes on her. She sat down at the foot of the bed and hitched a leg up like an old lost friend.

"Are you okay?" she asked.

"Not great," he said. "I'd rather be back up in the woods. But my head is cracked pretty bad."

Funny, thought Devo. He had supposed "Allison's best friend" would be another semi-tough cowgirl with a leathery texture sporting a few dings and dents. Trudy oozed softness and calm. The whites of her eyes were as pure and sparkly as any he had ever seen.

"You have fans outside. It's like waiting for a rock concert out there. They're all talking about your videos."

"That's what I hear. After my skull heals up we'll muster a collective. We'll go back together and show how it's done."

"Go back?"

"In toughness, in time. Start a new breed, develop a new colony with fresh genes to survive the long haul."

"I think you would have plenty of volunteers." She smiled gently.

Allison's best friend was downright encouraging—pretty in a plain-folk kind of way. It wasn't hard to picture them together, especially in spirit.

"What do you know about what's happening with Allison?" Devo said.

Trudy started right in. She spoke calmly. She began with Allison phoning her two nights ago. Devo figured the call was the same night he had struggled in the snow. The night he would rather forget. A night he hoped Allison would forget. Allison must have called from Trapper's Lake Lodge. Trudy told him about the depositions and the lawsuit.

"What was the name of the new guy in town?" he said.

"Ethan Bostwick," said Trudy. "He was the target of the lawsuit. Why?"

"Keep going," said Devo.

Trudy started a new thread about one of the other hunters in the camp: Austin Rayburn. His first hunt. He was a helper at the Keating place but Mr. and Mrs. Keating apparently were involved in a bitter feud. And then Trudy told about another one of the campers, Terry Zamora.

"Big guy, right?" said Devo.

"Bald and wears glasses, dark frames."

"That's him," said Devo. He remembered Zamora's overbearing

pushiness when they met in the woods—the day Devo turned over the batch of bad water.

"His name was originally Terry Oliver," said Trudy. "And he's a half brother of Loretta Keating. Loretta's dad had an earlier marriage and this guy Terry has been gone for a long time, and now he's back? A coincidence?"

Devo took it all in. The concern on Trudy's face for Allison was deep.

"You want to go find Allison, don't you?" he said.

"Of course."

"And every bone in my body wants to go find her too."

"She's in trouble."

"Last I saw of her, things were starting to come to a head. Might have been this Austin Rayburn guy that she was nervous about."

"So what happened to you?" Trudy asked it with so much sympathy that Devo felt like he was the sole victim in town.

"First tell me more about Ethan Bostwick. Who is he?"

"He's a lightning rod," she said. "Moved to the Meeker area not too long ago and started pushing his agenda around. From what I hear, he made people feel like they didn't know how to put their lives together. Made a few friends, made a lot of enemies."

"I don't know who's who or what's what, not really," said Devo. "But the guy who was pouring the shit in the water said he was part of a network and he said Ethan Bostwick and Josh Keating were working together."

Trudy stood up like she had been levitated. She closed her eyes for the equivalent of a long blink, then turned to stare. Devo could see her processing the details, imagining a new scenario.

"Keating was suing Ethan Bostwick. They hated each other."

"Maybe," said Devo. "Maybe not."

"But Josh Keating was the one who got sick, right before he died," said Trudy.

"Might have been," said Devo. "What I do know is that on the day he died he was as tough and fit as Teddy Roosevelt. If you ever want to read about somebody who could hack it in the wilderness, you should read up on Teddy—"

"Maybe he was faking it to add to the numbers," said Trudy. "Maybe they were working together on the plan to make the water in the Flat Tops look like it was being screwed up by all the drilling." From everything Devo could tell, Trudy hadn't heard the Roosevelt remark. She was thinking things through. "But it wasn't Keating's idea, was it? That had to be Bostwick."

"I wouldn't know."

"Who told you this?"

"A kid who was doing the legwork, carrying the stuff up, pouring gas in the drainages."

"So Josh Keating changed his mind and maybe Austin Rayburn was helping Loretta Keating."

"Her agent in the woods," said Devo.

"Allison's not so sure that Keating tripped and passed out."

"Really?"

"Back to the guy you found," said Trudy. "What exactly was the guy doing?"

"Pouring benzene into water all over the place. He had a backpack loaded with canisters. He said the canisters were stored out back at the Keating ranch. I was supposed to bring him to Meeker and turn him in to the cops."

"Did you get a name?"

Devo searched his hurting brain for the name.

"Drew Addigan," he said. "At least that's what he told me. But it doesn't matter. I can have him on YouTube in a few minutes." He held up the video card like it was a rare diamond.

"One of your videos?" said Trudy.

"All the footage a cop could ever want," said Devo. "It was all sabotage."

"Or terrorism," said Trudy. "What happens now with the video?"

"I heard the federal government folks are in town," Devo said.

"I saw their advance teams this morning."

"Do you think they'd want to see it?"

"Or one of the TV people," said Trudy. "The town is crawling with reporters."

"Or get it to the sheriff, keep it simple?"

Trudy held out her hand. Devo put the card in her palm.

"A reporter would make sure everybody saw it," said Trudy.

"Like the speed of light," said Devo.

"I've got one thing to do first." Her tone was somber. "I've got to warn a friend. I've got to tell him everything is about to change."

Wednesday Midday

Trapper's Lake, dead ahead. Colin, Merlin, Allison, Lightning. The trail hit the southern tip of the water and curved east. Another mile to the lodge. The killer pipes were cinched to both their saddles.

No sign of Rayburn.

Allison was cold deep down in places she had never sensed temperature. After Colin arrived, she had stood in her underwear at first for a minute while Colin brought her in close for heat exchange, the fastest and best thing to do. No time for a fire. She dressed stiffly with his help, fingertips and toes doing most of the whining. They had found Allison's clothes tied up in a plastic bag, hanging from a branch. Rayburn had gone to the trouble, of course, because dry clothes would have been easier to pull onto a corpse. Her corpse.

Her dying spot was fifty yards from the trail, behind a knoll in the woods. Rayburn had smudged his tracks, but the work was crude. Colin had passed the spot the first time but then realized he'd gone too far when Allison's tracks vanished. After he reversed course, he had found the location where Allison and Rayburn had tangled.

The damage from the cold was reversible. She shivered seated on the horse—her jaw, hands and chest trembling.

"You decided to check on me? Follow me?" Her jaw lacked feeling. Her tongue did not form the words well. She aimed her tongue at the right places in her mouth and forced the words to come.

"I decided to do that, then I told the others what was what. Hiatt and Gray got worried." Colin was behind her. The plan was that he would keep an eye on her to make sure she didn't list or keel over. "I guess Austin Rayburn's got a bit of a reputation as an all-around oddball."

"Or worse."

"Yes, worse. They're all packing up. They should be along in a few hours."

They both heard the raucous buzzing, an ear-splitting lawn-mower chomping the treetops, before the ultralight came lumbering into view above the lake. The sound was deafening. And familiar. The ultralight's bug-like black underbelly flashed smack overhead.

"Son of a bitch," said Colin.

"Same one as I saw that morning," said Allison. "On his way to make a Devo drop, no doubt."

"Some strange stuff going around." Colin turned in his saddle to watch the plane go.

"And it's time it all went back to normal," said Allison.

The lake slipped by, the rumbling noise fading. On the flat trail, she gave Lightning encouragement to hit second gear every now and then.

At the north end of the lake, they led the horses through the parking area and onto the road to the lodge. Colin helped her off, her toes packing a wallop of pain, which she knew was a good thing. It was hard logic to swallow, but true. She hobbled like she'd torn both Achilles and tried to stand up straight. The lodge had a fire on full throttle and Nora brought blankets as soon as she saw Allison enter. The need was that obvious. Hot toddy offered and rejected. Hot tea accepted.

Behind her, Colin and Nora consulted briefly and then Colin told her he'd be right back. She stared at the fire. Nora sat nearby. They waited.

"Did you see Austin Rayburn come through?" said Allison. Her voice sounded like hell. The old jaw was utterly unreliable in generating precise phonics.

"There's been a Rayburn Hardware truck parked around here all week," said Nora. "Two hours ago a guy stomped right through here. I know a couple of the other brothers—Waco and Tyler— but not Austin."

Waco? Tyler? And Austin. Jesus. Maybe the father was named San Antonio.

"Skinny guy?"

"That was him."

"Looked kind of pissed off?"

"Focused, I'd say. I was running a picnic lunch to one of the cabins, and he came on through, didn't say a word. We can go see if his truck is still here."

"Don't worry," said Allison. "It's gone."

"Did he do this to you?"

"Yeah," said Allison. But I got out, she thought. "He did this to me."

Colin was back.

"Can you make it to Meeker?" he said.

"In a car, yes," said Allison. "But walking or on horseback, probably not today."

"I meant car or truck." Colin said with a smile. "I'm glad to see your humor isn't frozen."

"Why?"

"The cops are slammed. They said they brought help in from Rangely and Craig. Some top-dog federal dude is in town, and the place is full of protesters. Cops want to talk to you, said they already had their squad cars on the east side of town, and they'll keep an eye out for Austin if he comes back. They know him well."

Two-hour head start? It was already too late.

"Are they concerned at all?"

"Sure," said Colin. "Deputy Durkin said he was very glad to hear you were all right."

Nora urged them to wait for "the mayhem to die down" and brought her a bowl of beef stew. Feeling the peas squish in her molars was as good a sign as any that she might live. Nora offered a hot bath, but Allison didn't want to linger. She was no colder now than on the night she had ridden home in the dark, before all this started to go haywire.

Allison headed to the tiny bathroom off the dining room before they left. It would be another good sign if her plumbing was awake. Her gait was more recognizable as human.

The woman in the mirror was witchy or bitchy or both.

The face belonged to a woman who hadn't smiled in a few days.

And it wasn't about to start now.

Wednesday Afternoon

The man inside the TV van was too young to be out of college, let alone working as a reporter for a big Denver station. Channel 9 was Trudy's favorite, the one that didn't hyperventilate—although they could work up a head of steam over a few inches of snow. Trudy always caught a bit of TV news each day in order to marvel at the complexity of life and to appreciate her own stripped-down version.

The reporter had short hair full of product, a gentle voice and sparkling blue eyes. Jace Something. Trudy described Devo and the tape. He asked her to start over again and she did, massaging the story to be as clear as possible. There was no question that the Devo reference set the hook.

"So you were with this fellow Devo? Can we interview you? We've got the satellite dish, and we can have this on the air in an hour."

Jace put the card in a slot in a machine, waited a few minutes for it to "convert" and "upload," as he put it. Trudy sat next to him inside the van, which was idling and warm. She was completely surrounded by plastic, metal and a low hum.

Jace started screening the footage—a bunch of walking-in-the-woods shots at first. The next clips were by a pond, following a man with a large backpack. They could hear Devo breathing. The breaths were steady and under control. The man in view slung his backpack off, kneeled by the pond, pulled a canister out of his backpack and poured a liquid into the water. The shot was askew, the camera planted on a tilted rock. As the man stood admiring his work, he turned in time to see a two-legged beast springing at his throat. The fight lasted only a few seconds, the audio track was grunts and groans and unintelligible utterances. Devo had rope and a plan. The last thing before the tape went black was Devo leading the man toward the camera on a leash.

"Holy crap," said Jace. "This will be on the national networks by tonight. Can we interview you by the hospital? Or go inside and talk to Devo? Can we?"

From what Trudy could tell, "we" must mean Jace, his camera and his tripod.

"I don't have the time," said Trudy. "And the hospital is a zoo."

They stood on the sidewalk outside the van. Protesters and cops milled around. Trudy held up the video card to show it to the world as Jace took a shot of it. Jace walked her through the motions. She didn't mention Allison by name, merely said that she got in to see Devo through a friend who had met him in the woods.

"A fellow devolutionist?" asked Jace.

"No," said Trudy. "Not like that. A hunting guide."

Trudy declined to talk about Devo's condition. That was private. "He'll be okay," she said. After about eight questions, she could hear a dry catch in her own voice. This wasn't easy.

When the interview was over, Jace asked if she could talk Devo into letting them into his room. Trudy said she might circle back later and check. Jace reassured her that Devo's footage would air on the four o'clock news. "At the top," he promised.

Trudy walked to the grocery store, consumed with revisiting every question she had been thrown and every answer she had given. This time Brett Merriman was in his office back by the dock.

"I assume in the last couple of hours you have not managed to drive clear home and retrieve more herbs?" he asked. "We are plum cleaned out."

"No." She smiled. "But look for me on television."

Merriman gave her a sideways glance. "What in the world did you do?"

The story took a few minutes to unravel. After she mentioned Bostwick, the look on Merriman's face went from happy-go-lucky to deep betrayal.

"Damn," said Merriman. "Fooled me. Are you sure that was the name?"

"The name didn't mean anything to Devo when he heard it," said Trudy. "It was just a name. And one more thing."

"Isn't that enough?"

"Bostwick wasn't alone on the plan to poison the water."

Merriman looked exasperated.

"Josh Keating was in on it with him," said Trudy.

Merriman sat up. The chair squeaked. "Damn," he muttered, running calculations. "But that fits."

"Fits what?"

Merriman covered his eyes with the fingertips of both hands like the see-no-evil monkey. He let out a sigh.

"I think everyone in town knew Josh Keating was only the front man on the lawsuit," said Merriman. "The lawyer Exby came up with the suit, but they needed the neighbor, Keating, to pull it off. I think Josh went along with it for awhile but then the bad blood got too thick for his way of liking."

"Which made things worse."

"Worse?"

"Between the Keatings. Mister and Missus."

Merriman stared at her, stared at his desk, stared at her.

"So you think Loretta wanted the lawsuit."

"She certainly didn't want Bostwick to make any more headway. She probably can't stand what's happening today in Meeker, the chance the government might shut it down."

"Her family's ranch."

"Her entire family's ranch."

"Including the half brother."

"Yeah," said Trudy. "Including her half brother."

Merriman shook his head.

"But he couldn't do it himself."

"Probably not," said Trudy.

"So she turned to her favorite errand boy and offered him a piece of the action."

Trudy kept waiting for a flaw in the scenario to reveal itself. Nothing surfaced.

"From what I know about Austin Rayburn, a small share alone would change his station in life, wouldn't it?"

"Practically like starting over," said Merriman.

"So they all teamed up," said Trudy.

"I suppose," said Merriman. He could have spit blood. "A team formed in the depths of greed, where redeeming traits shrivel up and die."

10

Colin drove as if the pickup were a Maserati. The road down from Trapper's was bumpy but dry. Every jolt hurt, but Allison didn't care. When they turned west on the blacktop, it was as if they were floating on air, the tires humming.

Something still hadn't fallen into place. A knot had formed, and Allison couldn't find a way to loosen it. The knot was wet, cold and under a pressure that could have crushed granite.

The sky was pristine. The day had an hour of light left. Her toes smarted, but there was improvement in her fingers. Her chest had discovered equilibrium, felt normal. She put a hand on Colin's leg as he drove. It was a sign of confidence and thanks, nothing more. Somewhere in there all those other thoughts still simmered, but she couldn't find them now.

The road snaked down.

"Does the radio work?" asked Allison.

"It's busted."

"I can't imagine Austin Rayburn would be dumb enough to saunter right up the main drag of downtown Meeker."

Colin gave her a look. "Remember, as far as he's concerned, you're dead."

"Well—not for another few hours anyway."

"But he thinks it's all over."

He thinks.

Somewhere in "he thinks," that gnawing sensation burned. It was like the negative space in a painting, like spotting the profile of a face in a vase's outline. It was right there, but it wasn't the first thing you saw.

The road came up on the bridge she had clattered across on the day the buffalo were killed.

The Bostwick spread rolled past, and then the Keating ranch, still home to a mini-fleet of vehicles.

"What the hell?" said Allison.

Colin kept driving.

"You didn't see that?" she said.

"See what?"

"The truck—Rayburn Hardware. Turn around."

Colin found a wide spot in a straight stretch and ground the gears through a three-point turn.

He kept the speed up and drove past again.

"I'll be damned," he said.

"Let's park the truck and hike back," said Allison.

"What do you want to do?"

"Scout around."

Colin parked the truck by the bridge.

"Rifle?" said Colin.

"Bring it. Got a spare?"

Colin plucked his Browning High Wall from the gear, dug out a Winchester 94 and passed it to her.

"Binoculars?"

Colin scrounged under the seat, came up with a pair of Bushnells heavier than a waffle iron.

"You can zoom in on a tick standing on an elk's ass from three hundred yards," said Colin.

"I don't need the tick," said Allison. "Just the ass."

They walked back up the road to the main highway and then cut over toward the Keating ranch. They walked single file on the narrow shoulder.

Allison's gait had a stiff hitch. Her toes needed tender loving care. She sent them positive vibes, a concept Trudy had taught her.

Without a kayak, the road was the only approach. Since they were walking on the far side of the road from the ranch, and the land sloped away in the dusk, they were out of sight.

A pickup truck came straight at them and sailed past. They kept their heads down. Another truck came up behind them, shot past in a punch of air. UPS. For some it was just another day.

Gravel crunched underfoot. The road made a slow curve. Allison looked both ways, ducked and jogged across the road. Colin's soft footfalls followed. Allison found a fence post and sat down next to it, trying to blend in with the landscape. Colin plunked down next to her. They were perched above the Keating spread, Bostwick's ranch to the left.

The land fell steeply down from the road before it leveled off in a long field and rolled down to the White River. They could hear the water's distant roiling. The Keating complex included the barn, corral and shed. A couple of horses were in the corral, heads down and working on a fresh scattering of hay. A giant tub of water sat outside the corral, within horseneck distance. Nearby, a pen with a shed and goats, a dozen or so. Adjacent was another pen with chickens.

A pair of ducks passed in flight, their wings working the wind, following the curve of the river in tight-couple formation. Their soft calls pointed the way—away.

Four dozen buffalo dotted the terrain. Whoever had to clear the dead from that battlefield, she didn't want to know, and could not think of the equipment it would take. What did a buffalo stretcher look like?

Allison raised the binoculars, focused on the house. Curtains were drawn. Nothing moved. Parked nearby were two SUVs, two sedans, a van and the Rayburn Hardware truck. The east side of the house sat in shadow in the gathering dusk. She studied the back kitchen window for a minute, thought she caught a light shift inside—a passing shadow.

A low rumble warned of a truck on the highway, and they both laid flat. The truck rolled past—and they sat back up.

"Whatcha got?" asked Colin.

"House. Lights. Shadows."

A door slammed across the field with a staccato whack. Allison focused on the corner of the porch in view. The sun was nearly done for the day, but it had found one last gap between cloud and earth to bathe the house in a late-afternoon glow.

A man drifted into the frame, stood for a minute scanning the road. He was bundled up. He gripped a white mug in his left hand. His narrow face, underneath green camouflage baseball cap, was unsure and unsteady.

"Austin Rayburn!" hissed Allison. "What the hell?"

Rayburn sat down with his back to them and placed the mug on the porch rail.

Colin put his eye to the rifle scope.

"One shot," he said. Colin's whispered voice had bite. "You gotta be on familiar terms to come out of the woods and go straight to somebody else's house."

"Not just somebody," said Allison. "The wife of the man you killed."

"Looks to me like a fresh set of clothes and he's all cleaned up," said Colin. "Came straight here and took a shower."

"Like he belongs."

Rayburn sipped his coffee. Most of mankind would relax on the porch and watch the sun go down from a comfortable chair, but Austin Rayburn had put his back to the beauty and gazed at the scrubby field.

Another door slam.

Rayburn didn't react. He was expecting the company. His mouth moved, saying something to somebody. In the gray and brown afternoon, Allison and Colin could not have constituted anything more than minor smudges on the dull canvas.

But Austin Rayburn turned and stared straight at them.

A pair of legs came into view. Jeans, boots, the flash of a gesturing hand. The porch roof restricted their view. Rayburn turned his head, said something, turned his head back to stare again.

The boots moved off. Allison could see a man cover the gap between the house and the line of vehicles. His head was down. A pickup blocked her view, then another, then a van like a small RV. At the next pickup, before the Rayburn Hardware truck, the man climbed in.

Car door opened, slammed shut. The tight crunch of metal on metal snapped across the field.

Allison spun the binoculars back to the porch. Rayburn remained seated.

The pickup growled, backed around and shot up the driveway, dust churning in its wake.

Allison realized the problem, and Colin whispered "fuck" to echo her thoughts: they had been spotted.

If the pickup turned left at the top of the driveway and headed toward town, no worries. If it turned right, they would be exposed in seconds.

The return path was no escape. Their truck was too far away. The embankment across the road, too steep to climb.

The only route was down into the field—into the open.

Which was no escape.

The pickup rolled to the top of the hill and gathered speed.

"The binocular lenses must've flashed in the sunset," said Allison.

Rayburn stood up and continued to stare in their direction. He appeared frozen with anticipation.

The truck turned in their direction.

Allison stretched out flat. Colin did the same.

"Won't work," said Allison.

The truck engine screamed. The truck wasn't on a trip to church. It was gunning right at them.

"Sitting ducks," said Colin. "We stay or go."

"Go!"

Allison rolled under the fence rail, stood up and ran, the binoculars bouncing off her chest.

Colin pounded the ground next to her.

Breath came hard.

They were halfway down the slope. The truck skidded to a rattling halt. Allison heard the screech of power steering. She glanced back. The truck wheeled around and shot back the way it had come, pressed to the speed limit.

Allison began to look for cover behind the barn or the horse corral.

Her legs churned with angry complaints of evil and wrong-doing. Her knees and thighs burned with each stride.

Rifle heavy in her hand, Allison lifted the binos from her neck, passed them to Colin as they ran. He tossed them aside.

Rayburn leaned casually on the porch railing, as if he were observing nothing more alarming than a game of horseshoes, and then he swung his legs over the rail. His right hand gripped a handgun.

Allison hit the ground, her face skidding in the dirt as a crack of gunfire split the air.

She looked up.

Colin brought his rifle up and stood as still as a sleeping horse. He was thirty yards from the house. Rayburn froze.

Colin's rifle was a stiff branch silhouetted against the pale sky.

Walking forward, Colin kept the rifle aimed at Rayburn's heart.

Allison levered herself upright on dying legs and raised her rifle.

"Put the gun down, Austin." Colin said it like a jaded cop, his voice steely with authority. "Now!"

Having seen Colin drop an elk from 300 yards with a single shot, Rayburn probably understood that his scrawny chest was the equivalent of the broad side of a barn.

He bent at the waist, set the gun on the ground and turned at a dead run as the truck came shuddering down the road and skidded to a halt near the fence.

Colin measured the magnitude of each threat and decided to let Rayburn go. Calmly, Colin picked up Rayburn's gun, tucked it under his belt.

Allison crawled where she had fallen, her legs still angry. She spat dirt.

Colin aimed his rifle at the truck. The dimming light and angle of the windshield concealed the driver's face. The door opened with a wailing creak. The driver climbed out, stood behind the open door.

Shaved head, thick glasses.

Terry Zamora.

The rifle in Zamora's hand swiveled up and took a bead on Colin. Allison tested the weight of her rifle, checked her nerves. The barrel held steady. A fountain of anger spewed strength and resolve.

"Okay now," said Zamora, keeping the rifle on Colin, the closer threat.

Allison's mind raced to add up the horse and drive time it would have taken Zamora to leave Oyster Lake and make his way down to Trapper's and then to Buford, Meeker, Rifle, Glenwood Springs and up through the canyon and full circle to her barn and appear to be waiting for his guide to show him the way to camp. All in one freezing cold night. It was a convoluted trek, but it could be done.

Terry Zamora.

Rayburn's muscle.

She had escorted one of the murderers back to his goddamn fucked-up crime scene. He had arrived like a snow-white innocent.

"It ain't only us," said Colin. "Hiatt and Gray are coming to talk with the sheriff right now. Won't matter what happens here. Whole valley knows by now."

Zamora smiled. "Nice try."

"It's true," said Allison. "They were right behind us. We told them everything. You may as well not make it worse."

Zamora moved his gaze to an upstairs window, gave a nod.

Allison turned and looked up. The window cracked open.

"You little fuckheads aren't getting in our way," said a calm, strong voice. Female.

A pistol cocked.

Out of the corner of Allison's eye she saw Zamora move toward Colin. Her gaze stayed on the window, the barrel aimed square at her eyes, dead on—and she turned and scampered toward the porch, every thought drowned out by gunfire.

Wednesday Afternoon

"You hurt all those people," said Merriman.

"Most of them are hunters," said Bostwick "All I did was throw off their schedule a few days. No real damage."

Trudy stood off to the side, let the two go at it. They were standing in front of Merriman's house. Bostwick had been evicted. Even here, blocks from the main square, protesters were milling around. The Devo tape was all the talk—and it wasn't good. They had picked up word that the announcement would be delayed until six. Also not good.

Buried By The Roan

"You give us a bad name," said Merriman. "You made it harder to talk about what's right."

"We got all these people angry, all these people fired up to send a message," said Bostwick.

"And it didn't work." Merriman practically barked it. "You've been exposed. It was stupid attempt at a hoax. Stupid."

Trapper's Lake was uppermost in Trudy's mind. Finding Allison. But it was already dark.

"You know the chemicals and shit from their drilling are seeping into the groundwater," said Bostwick with a note of disdain.

"Maybe," said Merriman. "But nobody will listen now."

"They can't link me to it."

"Devo did."

"Some crazed survivalist whacko? I know nothing. I did nothing," said Bostwick. "Who are they going to believe?"

"You dreamed it up and hired the kid."

"Nobody got paid," said Bostwick. "They did whatever they did because they believe in the cause."

"Like burning down ski lodges," said Trudy.

"I don't have a problem with that," said Bostwick. "It's a counterpunch for what the ski areas do to the forests."

"Shee-it," said Merriman, long and slow. "Good riddance."

"I guess talking about this is going to make everything okay." Bostwick pointed his finger at Merriman and started shaking it. "You know something? You got to take action. You've got to fight. You've got to make a stink, get noticed. You've got to get your hands dirty. You can't sit back and hope they'll get it, because the big corporate boys will roll over everything. They've got giant vacuum cleaners, and they come to town ready to suck the dollars right out of your wallet and screw the environment. They always have and they always will."

Merriman shook his head. "You and your stunt have set us back years. Made us look like a bunch of crazed freaks when there

327

are lots of regular town folk who want to make sure the Flat Tops are protected."

"And you were making so much progress," said Bostwick, spitting sarcasm. Smarmy anger isn't pretty, thought Trudy. "No wonder the Roan was getting ripped to shreds. The valley was next, and you know it."

"Come on," said Trudy to Merriman. "I've got to go."

"What are you going to do?" said Bostwick.

Merriman shrugged. "I don't think we have to do much of anything."

"Going to the cops?"

"No need," said Trudy. "But we'll make sure Devo tells them everything he knows."

"I think they have some questions for you about the dead buffalo," said Merriman.

"I had nothing to do with that!" said Bostwick.

"Yeah," said Merriman. "After they talk to the kid on the video, and after they talk to Devo, I'm sure your credibility will peak at an all-time high."

Wednesday Afternoon

The footage wobbled more than he remembered, but it was clear enough. The footage had been broadcast three times in its entirety. Reporters had talked to political experts and anyone else with an opinion. Topics ranged from the ramifications for the federal government and its decision to whether or not milking the Roan for its natural gas had the chance of upsetting international energy politics. A man in a crisp suit sat at the news desk with the anchors in Denver. He represented the Colorado Oil and Gas Association and predicted, shockingly, that the tape would calm fears of pollution from drilling. "We have extremely high expectations for safety," he said.

A reporter in Meeker interviewed protesters on the streets. Most people said that while it was unfortunate some of the water was being purposely poisoned, there was still no doubt the drilling was doing damage.

And then came Trudy. Devo admired her stage presence, her poise, her simplicity. When the time came to assemble a larger group to undergo devolution, he would have to send her an invite. The reporter talked to Devo's fans outside the clinic and followed this with a few of Devo's greatest hits—how to barbecue squirrel, how to build a deadfall, how to clean deer hide. All the clips were mere snippets and went by in a blink. All the newscasts zipped from story to story like a drag race. The anchorwoman had a strange look on her face when the story ended. She had rouged cheeks, dark red lips, fake blue eyes and a starched pointed collar on her pink blouse. She sat in front of a glam shot of the mountains—absurdly colorful—behind the news desk.

Her red lips puckered, her blue eyes laughed—straight at Devo. There goes another whackadoo.

"And what can you do?" Devo shouted out loud to his empty hospital room. "You can read a teleprompter. You are the poster child for modern civilization. The freaking poster child!"

The news flipped to a live shot of a room somewhere in Meeker. The words on the screen said "Rio Blanco County Building." The camera focused on an empty podium, then pulled back to show a somber reporter gripping a microphone and pressing on an earpiece.

"We expect the undersecretary in a minute. We have confirmed that he has seen the videotape taken by the man known as Devo. We have no idea what that means in terms of his decision. Okay, here he comes—"

Devo spun his legs off his bed, ignoring the white-hot flash of pain in his skull.

He dug through the drawers for his clothes. His aching head prevented him from dressing as fast as he'd like, but his clothes seemed to welcome him back.

He took a deep breath and snapped off the television just as some old man in a dark suit was starting to lay out his case.

On a tray next to Devo's bed sat a sandwich on a green plastic plate. Inside the white bread—processed meat, plastic cheese and bland mayonnaise. Next to it, a stack of baby carrots machine carved from whole carrots.

Devo dumped the food in the toilet and pissed all over it.

He poked his head out the door.

The hallway was empty.

With the whole town hanging on every televised word, Devo found the rear exit, stood for a minute to get his bearings, ducked behind some bushes and tried to think of anything he might be able to scavenge in town before heading back. He'd need a place to take cover tonight. The hike back to Trapper's alone could take a long time.

Wednesday Afternoon

Allison ran down the porch toward Colin, legs like deadweight blocks.

Colin fired and the sound ripped thick in her chest. Zamora's hand jerked up. His rifle fell to the ground.

Zamora grabbed his hand, buckled to his knees and let out an angry howl. The rifle rested out of reach, but he stared at it hungrily. He took two short steps on his knees. Colin's next shot turned the weapon into a spinning top in the dirt.

Allison gave Colin a tug on his jacket, pulled him back under the overhang, out of sight from the window above. Colin kept his rifle locked on Zamora.

"Fucker!" yelled Zamora.

Zamora started to stand but didn't make it. He looked back as if to judge the distance to his pickup and fell again to his knees. Blood ran from his wrist. He cradled his hand and let out another low bawl, then stood and took a few tentative steps.

"I'm going inside to get some ice and something to wrap him up," Allison said. "Can you call 911?"

"My phone hasn't been near a charger in many days," said Colin. "Dead."

"Mine too," said Allison. "I'll call from inside."

"Don't," said Colin. "Someone's in there."

"I've got to," said Allison. "No choice."

"I need help," said Zamora.

"Don't," repeated Colin.

Allison scooted past a window and refreshed her memory of the downstairs layout.

The front door was unlocked. Allison opened it slowly, raised her rifle and kicked it the rest of the way open.

Listened.

Nothing.

Allison stepped inside, rifle leading the way. Rage had her senses on fire. She felt like she could see through walls.

Footsteps creaked on the floorboards overhead, and her heart lurched.

She could see a wooden staircase, which ascended off a hallway that led to the rear of the house.

The dining room was empty. She peered into the empty kitchen, noted the back door by the stove. She kept the rifle in her right hand and with her left gathered dishtowels, a large bowl and three trays of ice cubes. She scooped up the supplies in an unstable bundle. Muffled footfalls thumped above. Allison opened the back door, followed wooden steps down to the ground and hugged the wall as she made her way around to the front. Colin stood guard. Zamora was in agony, still in the dirt where he'd gone down.

"There's a phone in the kitchen," said Allison. She dropped the supplies. "These should help. I'll be right back."

"Don't—" Colin stopped himself.

Allison retraced her route to the rear, maintaining a delicate posture as she climbed the steps.

The door was open a crack. Had she left it that way? She waited, heard nothing. With the muzzle of her rifle she pushed open the door another inch.

Two.

Slow.

A sharp metallic click from inside.

Three inches.

Gunfire erupted and the door exploded.

"Allison!" shouted Colin.

The ringing buzzed her ears.

Another shot slammed the wall above her shoulder.

"We have to take Zamora to a doctor!" shouted Allison. She backed down a step. The ringing in her ears briefly smothered all other sounds. "He's bleeding bad!"

"He'll live," said a cool, calm voice.

Loretta Keating.

Zamora, Rayburn and Loretta Keating—had the whole mourning scene been an acting job?

"What did Josh do?" Allison asked.

Another shot. This one sailed through the open door.

"Are you okay?" shouted Colin.

"Yeah!" shouted Allison. She counted the shots. The last one would have been six, including the round from upstairs.

"Something to do with your neighbor Bostwick?" said Allison.

No reply, but no shot either.

"What did Josh do to you?" said Allison. She desperately wanted to prod Loretta into talking.

"He ruined *everything*."

Allison waited for Loretta to fill in the blanks, but she didn't take the bait.

"What did he do?"

"He messed with everybody and everything." Allison took a step up, her back pressed against the wall. She thought she heard a heavy sigh.

"Messed with?" said Allison.

"He started to *sympathize*." Loretta mocked her husband. The hatred was thick. She might be out of bullets, but she wasn't out of steam. "He started to *sympathize with Bostwick*. He screwed up the whole plan."

"What plan?"

Another step up. One more to go. Back to the wall, rifle up. She wished she had a periscope to see around the corner.

"It wasn't my idea," Loretta said.

"Then whose?"

"Goddamn it," Loretta said. "The idiot out there with the busted hand. My half brother. The *loser*."

Half brother? She'd been right in the middle of one big family-built cabal. What the hell?

The final step. Could she risk a look? She poked the muzzle into the opening. No reaction. A few more inches. Still nothing.

Allison followed the tip of her muzzle around the open door and into the kitchen, ready to shoot.

Loretta Keating stood on the far side of the butcher-block.

Allison's eyes locked on the black barrel of the Smith & Wesson .38 in Loretta's hands. Her arms were straight out, elbows locked, barrel shaking. Loretta's long hair was loose and wild. Her face was tired and strung out.

A shudder rattled Allison's chest. Her windpipe functioned as well as clogged hose. The world closed down in a hazy wobble of strange light and the tip of Loretta's gun.

"Your half brother is hurt bad," said Allison. The words were a blurry mumble.

Tears ran down Loretta's cheeks. Her grip tightened.

A soft click.

Loretta squeezed again.

Another click.

Loretta tossed the gun on the table like a dead fish.

"He'll live," she snarled.

"We've got to get him to a doctor."

"Good," she said. "Good for you."

"I'm going to make a call." Allison stepped over to a wall phone, its long gray cord twisted and tangled to the floor. "What the hell happened? What the hell happened between you two?"

Phone off the hook now, dial tone like a foghorn.

Rotary dial—911.

"What happened?" said Loretta Keating. "What happened? Funny. Yeah."

One ring.

"What happened?" she asked again, mulling the question. "That's it, actually."

Two rings.

"Josh decided he didn't want anything to happen. He said he wanted to keep everything the way it was."

Three rings.

"We had a gold mine here. My family's ranch. Solid gold."

Fresh tears.

Four rings.

"Josh wanted to keep things the way they were."

A male voice in Allison's ear: "Rio Blanco County Dispatch."

Allison covered the basics—shots fired, man hurt, send ambulance and cops.

Loretta slumped over on the counter and sobbed.

The open door blew shut. The windows rattled.

"Josh Keating didn't trip and die," said Allison. "Did he?"

Loretta Keating sobbed harder.

Outside, Colin had Zamora's hand wrapped in a big towel with the ice. The towel was already turning red. Allison walked Loretta out under gunpoint, though it was probably overkill. She sat down on the edge of the porch. Her fire was out.

"Cops are on the way," she said.

A cold wind struck her face. Her feet prickled in pain. Her heart banged as she walked around to the front of the house, rifle up and ready.

Where would Austin Rayburn have run? The river was too far. A grove of cottonwoods downriver was a blip on the horizon. She doubted Rayburn had the stamina for that kind of sprint. There were no outbuildings on this side of the ranch house, no real place to hide unless he was lying flat over on the bank down by the river.

Allison studied the clusters of buffalo. A few loners munched russet clumps of grass. About half were lying down. Whatever ancient residue might have stirred from the nearby gunshots, there was no visible sign of concern. Allison peered through the scope on her rifle, still a bit unsteady. She took a chest-deep breath, felt her heart tap the brakes. She aimed the rifle from buffalo to buffalo, the scope bringing her close up to their matted, mangy hides.

"What are you ... " said Colin.

"Just looking," said Allison.

Through the scope, a buffalo stood, kneeling first on its front legs and then straining to its feet. The buffalo shook its head like a wet dog, jogged around in a tight circle and there was Austin Rayburn, crouched over in a hiding position at first and then fully erect. He was staring at the buffalo, holding out a hand like the beast knew sign language.

The buffalo lunged at Rayburn, narrowly missed his hip and Rayburn turned, his legs digging and churning. Allison dropped the scope, gave the stringbean no chance. The angry buffalo turned and chugged, issued a throaty grunt and gave chase so quickly Rayburn looked like he was stuck in first gear. The buffalo was closing in when Rayburn reached the chest-high fence and vaulted it, knees and elbows clawing their way across in a mad scramble of frantic flesh and bone. Rayburn dropped back to earth on his hip and shoulder. Allison winced at the awkward landing. The buffalo, head down and loaded with grim determination, veered suddenly and let Rayburn go, no interest in bashing its head through the wood fencing.

Rayburn sprinted for the gray river.

"What the fuck?" shouted Colin.

"Rayburn's running," said Allison.

Rifle in hand, Allison hopped the porch rail and landed with a hard thud, unleashing a jolt of agony from her sore feet.

Allison ran.

White River, dead ahead.

Rayburn stumbled, his legs not in it. Maybe he'd hurt himself clamoring over the fence. He glanced back as he ran.

He reached the riverbank, looked up and down, deciding. Neither direction offered escape. The riverbank was dense brush and the odd, craggy bush. Allison slowed to a walk, raised the rifle on Rayburn as he turned. She flashed on the plastic coffin cage.

"Come with me," said Allison. "No troubles and no shot-up limbs like your buddy Zamora."

"It's Loretta's and Terry's land," said Rayburn. He was huffing. The words came with a snarl. "They've got a right to milk it."

"And I suppose that gives you a right to kill people who get in your way," said Allison.

Rayburn backed up another step, boot heels in the swirling, freezing water.

"The official report says it was an accident," he said. Another step back.

"Some of us know different," said Allison. "Come out of the water."

Allison was close to the riverbank now. She studied his panicked eyes.

"You little bitch," said Rayburn. "Your little boyfriend found you, saved you?"

He was up to his knees now.

"Just come with me," said Allison.

"That land is worth millions. Who knows?"

"Get out of the water," said Allison.

Rayburn plunged down like he'd stepped in a sinkhole, his hat floating off.

"Aw, shit," muttered Allison.

Rayburn shot to the surface and let out a heaving gasp, his head barely above water and his arms flailing. Allison sensed the weight of the clothes on his body, the drag. The current pulled him out toward the middle of the river. The water here was gloomy and drab. Rayburn went under again, bogged down and no doubt heading into deep shock.

Rayburn screamed something unintelligible. The message was clear.

"Swim!" Allison shouted when he resurfaced.

There was no response. Rayburn disappeared again. The hat floated aimlessly.

Allison tugged off her coat, dropped her rifle and scrambled along the shoreline keeping an eye on the spot where Rayburn last went under.

She dove headfirst, the cold smacking her like a punch in the face, every cell and fiber attacked and frozen with a mean-spirited wrath. The cold dug for her bones and searched for the switch that would flip consciousness to goner status. She wondered if she'd smell jet fuel on the surface, imagined she might see bobbing suitcases there, too, and other flotsam. Was that salt water she tasted? The cold wanted to crush every pocket of air in her body. The subsurface water jerked her along, yanked her down. She could feel the current's energy, reached her hands out in front of her, into the black.

She broke to the surface and spied the hat but no Rayburn. He'd been swallowed whole.

Allison dolphin-kicked down. She figured she had a minute, no more, including the fight back to shore. If she had a minute, Rayburn had less. Allison swam, fingers numb, boots heavy, chest reeling from the merciless cold, face on fire from the sheer pain of the stinging water. She broke back to the surface and heard him bellow, spotted a swirling eddy of churning water where he must have thrashed, and Allison plunged straight down, feeling her hand bump something. She grabbed Rayburn's jacket and pulled, scissor-kicking with all her might back up toward light.

He came to the surface flailing. Allison felt like she had dragged a dripping wet laundry bag up a long flight of stairs.

Rayburn tried to yell, but instead coughed and spewed water and tackled Allison around her shoulders and pushed her back under. He was somewhere out beyond desperation. All his survival instincts were in full rage, fueled by pure adrenalin. Allison kicked him in the shin underwater and broke free, wriggled back to the surface and popped him hard in the cheek with as much force as her heavy, soaking arm could deliver.

Rayburn slumped, and she caught him, stretched her arm over his scrawny chest and flipped him on his back. He half floated, half sunk, and she looked for her bearings, her legs pumping like those of a fat, tired, frozen frog toward shore, her minute about to expire.

Wednesday Night

The Keating ranch appeared on fire from the swirling lights of cherry tops. The scene was eerily quiet, like a fireworks show minus the thunder. Allison stood on the porch. She had already made two extended trips to the dining room where Sheriff Christie had established an interview base camp.

One of the deputies drove Colin up to the road to retrieve his truck. The plastic pipes were photographed like missing links from an African archaeological dig. The police interviewed Colin and Allison separately, then chatted informally with them together. Their stories matched. There was nothing to fudge. When Allison mentioned Devo for the fifth time, Sheriff Christie stopped her.

Zamora and Rayburn had been raced to the hospital in the same ambulance—one for a shot-up wrist, the other for hypothermia and several other ailments. Loretta Keating had been escorted to a police car, handcuffed and deflated.

Allison sat in a fleece blanket on the couch by the fire while Colin washed her clothes and ran them through the dryer. She had hot soup, felt a slight return to normalcy. An emergency medical technician tried to coax her to take a precautionary trip to the clinic to get her vitals checked but other than still-warming fingertips, she primarily felt fatigue.

Dressed in her revived clothes, she stood on the porch with Sheriff Christie. Colin sat on the rail nearby. Red and white lights bounced off the buffalo that had drifted close—a strange mesh of nature and man.

"I suppose you didn't even know Devo was in the hospital," said Christie.

"Devo? In a hospital?" said Allison. The image didn't compute.

"But he slipped away—out the back door we figure."

Sheriff Christie talked about the segment of Devo's videotape that had appeared on the news, and the fact that Ethan Bostwick was in jail for questioning on a conspiracy to poison the water in the Flat Tops. "So now we can ask Bostwick about the buffalo that were shot—the first time we've seen him in days."

"Did Devo have anyone with him?" asked Allison.

"I guess he did, but that's how he wound up in the hospital. Devo got jumped. But he had a video of the guy, and we've already got a bead on him—it's just a matter of picking him up. His name is Drew Addigan. He's part of some loose network of planet-hugging radicals over by Gypsum. He'll turn up."

The intensity of the scene at the ranch house started to ebb. One cop car peeled away, then another. Muffled squawks of radio banter burst from each squad car as its driver climbed in. The scene had attracted a gang of neighbors and crime-scene gawkers, all held back behind yellow crime scene tape. As the police cars departed, their lights illuminated the row of civilian cars and pickups in the driveway. The remaining gawkers were down to six. They formed a huddle, shifting on their feet, shaking their heads and absorbing each new scrap of information with equal parts shock and dismay.

News was reaching the gang via a short, slender man who was walking with a cane but didn't rely on it much. His gait was sturdy.

He might have been seventy, but looked spry. He wore an un-buttoned leather waist-length coat. Beneath, a suit jacket with a white shirt and a black bolo tie like Wyatt Earp. The man delivered tidbits back and forth to the gang by sidling up to every cop that came within striking distance of a conversation. The cops knew him. He seemed to wander unchecked, but didn't have any official capacity within the crime scene territory.

The man never smiled. He was all business. More than once Allison realized she was taking the brunt of his ferocious glare.

"If Devo was in the hospital was he badly hurt?" said Allison.

"Doctors said he might have needed surgery, but even without the skull fracture he was dangerously underweight," said Christie. "He doesn't sound to me like someone who can survive the winter unless he's already laid in a ton of food, or unless he's figured out a way to hibernate."

"Sheriff?" Deputy Durkin came through the house and snuck up behind them. "I think you might want to see what we found in the barn."

Allison signaled Colin, and they tagged along.

Sheriff Christie was escorted by Durkin and two other deputies. Allison walked behind Christie. The man with the cane was confidently following a few paces back.

The barn sat eighty yards off from the house. Industrial-strength lights had been set to full stun, the Dutch doors pulled back and wide open. Another wide arc of crime-scene tape. Sheriff Christie let Allison slide under and follow. A few steps later, she turned to look. The man with the cane decided not to follow.

Allison was exhausted. The idea of draining the town tequila supply in a one-night assault made perfect sense.

The barn was neat and sharp. It had the sweet barn smell of animals. The front area consisted of high storage shelves and extra-large cabinets. Stairs to the right led to a loft. The stalls were in the rear, beyond a tack room.

Durkin led them inside the tack room to thick wooden shelves where two other deputies crouched over three old wooden peach crates. One deputy had a camera and was giving the crate the same paparazzi pummeling that the plastic pipes had received.

"Canisters of liquid benzene," said Durkin. "Fifty-three canisters here, and judging by the empty crates, half the supply is gone."

"Holy crap," said Colin. "But—but Keating got sick."

"Or claimed he did," said Allison. Loretta Keating's charge that Josh Keating had "started to sympathize" rang in her head, but Loretta might not have known to what extent it was true. The Keatings were two snarling dogs tied to the same stake.

"Josh Keating and Bostwick were working together?" said Colin.

The question was greeted by shrugs and uncertainty, stoic cops with their "go-figure" stares.

"They might not have been friends," said Allison. "But they agreed on protecting the valley, and Keating might have faked a bout of poisonous water to fatten the total of sick hunters."

Outside the tack room, the man with the cane, who must have decided he couldn't be left out of the loop, chatted in familiar, easy-going terms with a deputy. The man came up to the deputy's chest. The deputy had been at Oyster Lake, the one with the sideburns and stiff manner. The man with the cane lit a fat cigar, puffed it without touching it, blew smoke wherever he pleased. He glanced inside where Allison and the others were gathered around the crates, then headed off back into the night. Alone.

Allison gave Colin a look. It was time to go home and collapse. Every bone cried for sleep.

They followed the cigar smoke back toward the house, walking across a square pool of light from the barn. The man walked slowly, arrogantly, one hand in his coat pocket and the other fooling with his cane. Colin said nothing. There was nothing to say. The questions could wait. The answers could wait. Allison imagined Devo scrambling across town and following the river back to the Flat Tops, diving into the wilderness, the cold and the caves. She hoped he would be okay, reprimanding herself for sending him down the hill without her.

"Hang on."

Allison stared at a print in the soft mud around the horse corral. The print was made where water had seeped from the tub. It was a beauty. It came with three matching pairs of lefts and rights before the ground returned to hard pack. Each set of prints possessed a round dot off to one side. Allison didn't have to squat down to confirm the match. The octagons shouted *hello*.

"You don't know the guy with the cane, do you?" she asked Colin.

"No, but he seems to know everyone. Why?"

"I'll tell you in a second."

Sheriff Christie and the deputies were behind him, lugging crates of canisters.

"I've seen that look before," said Christie.

"Who's the man with the cane?" said Allison.

"Stewart Exby," said Christie. "Why?"

"Who is he in terms of the Keatings?"

"Their lawyer."

"Is he a hunter?"

"You should see the trophies in his office."

"Do you have the ballistics on the bullets that killed the four buffaloes?"

"Yes, but no weapon or motive."

Stewart Exby had reached the house at the edge of the light. He was moving toward the parked cars. His slow, methodical gait hadn't changed.

"What kind of gun are you looking for?"

"A .375 Magnum. 270 grain."

Allison nodded. "Lots of weight. You would need to pack a punch from that distance."

"But you'd have to be one helluva shot to keep it that accurate," said Christie.

"What are you saying?"

"I found your buffalo killer," said Allison. "He's driving away right now."

Allison stepped around the muddy spot. Across the field, a car moved up the driveway toward the road at a crawl, headlights carving a triangle of white into the night, bloody hands on the wheel.

Allison put her arm around Colin and headed to the house. The porch was a gathering point for a gaggle of neighbors, friends and cops. The work was over. Low chatter bounced around indecipherably. Allison hoped to steer clear of the group and head straight to their pickup.

Out of the edge of the shadows, one woman walked their way, hands stuffed into her jacket, her distinctive long hair flowing.

Trudy.

Allison broke free of Colin, her head filling with wonder, her throat swelling with joy.

Trudy.

Allison ran as fast as her tortured legs would allow.

Wednesday Night

The federal government's team had cleared out right after the news conference. Bonnie, whom Trudy seemed to know well, was more than happy to offer Allison and Colin a pair of rooms. Allison took one. Trudy kept her own.

They huddled in Trudy's room. Bonnie helped them order food—the downtown cafés were still open and making money off the protesters who lingered. Cheeseburgers for Allison and Colin, veggie burger for Trudy, a giant chef salad and a basket of onion rings to share. They had stopped for tequila, red wine and beer to handle the alcohol needs of Allison, Trudy and Colin in that order. They were well into their supply of drinks when the food arrived.

The news came on TV, and they ate as they absorbed the overview of events. The U.S. Secretary of the Interior called for more studies. Devo video or no Devo video, waiting was the better option. "The drilling can be postponed. The Roan and the valley have only one chance for us to get it right," said the undersecretary. The announcement was greeted with an unsettling mix of wild cheering and obnoxious boos. Cashing in on the jackpot from the drilling rights would wait for another day.

"Brett Merriman's the happiest man in town," said Trudy. "But he can't show it."

"Sometimes the quiet ones win," said Colin.

They were all stretched out on Trudy's bed. The room smelled gloriously to Allison of grease and meat.

The news switched to "early, sketchy" reports of a "shoot-out" at a ranch southeast of Meeker, "the same location where four buffalo were slaughtered." The reporter was young but calm and unexcited. He was standing outside the Rio Blanco County sheriff's office in downtown Meeker. "One man was wounded in the shoot-out," he said, "and another was pulled from the river with hypothermia. The two are hospitalized. While police haven't released their names, 9 News has learned that one of those arrested is buffalo rancher Josh Keating's widow, Loretta, along with the son of a prominent Meeker businessman. Austin Rayburn, son of hardware store owner Dallas Rayburn, may face attempted-murder charges for an incident that occurred earlier today in the

Flat Tops Wilderness. There will be much more to sort out overnight. Police are still keeping most of the details to themselves."

Trudy hit mute on the TV—they were going back for reaction from the celebrating protesters who felt they had won the day.

"So Josh Keating faked it," said Colin. "It sure didn't look fake to me."

"And none of the others were in on it," said Allison.

"Not judging by their reaction," said Colin. "But why?"

"It planted the seed," said Trudy.

"It added to the totals," said Allison. "And meanwhile the whole town thinks Josh Keating is their point man, their ramrod. But he's consorting with the enemy."

"But Loretta Keating knew," said Colin.

"I don't know if she knew her husband was collaborating with Ethan Bostwick," said Trudy. "But if he told her he was opposed to selling the rights on the family ranch, maybe that was the trigger right there, the flashpoint. They own hundreds of acres, and the rights to drill on those acres could have been worth millions. Austin Rayburn told his father the Keatings had been living separately for a long time. Being told you don't have access to the family fortune might have been enough."

"And then the half brother comes sniffing around for his share of the family pie," said Allison.

"And Loretta Keating suddenly had help—more than enough," said Trudy.

Allison sipped her tequila and rested her head on the pillow.

"Did you talk to Jerry?"

Trudy looked at her with a tired and faraway expression.

"Yes," she said. "The phone was ringing when I walked into the room."

"And?"

"He said it was rough."

Trudy had filled her in with Jerry and The School Board Saga earlier.

"How rough?"

"He sounded sheepish. Even humbled."

"Really?" asked Allison.

"I guess the school board and the district have been pretty aggressive on this whole issue. When they saw the preview story in the paper about Jerry's campaign, they were waiting with a load of information about what steps they had already taken. They let Jerry, Lilly and Brad speak, and then they unloaded right back on them. Jerry said they should have done their homework." Trudy offered a feeble smile.

"You were right," said Allison.

"I don't think you go in with guns blazing," said Trudy. "I think you need to respect the work that's gone before."

"You're not asking for much, are you?" said Allison.

"Not to me," said Trudy. "Not to me."

"And so?" asked Allison.

"And so what?"

"Where do things stand with Jerry?"

Trudy paused and took a breath. "That was rough too," she said. "I told him he would always be a friend, you know? He said he would keep carrying my basil in the store. We'll be okay."

Allison stood and stretched. She hugged Trudy for a full, silent minute.

"Break it up," said Colin. "We don't have all night."

"Get some rest," said Trudy. "Remember—rest. We'll go back tomorrow, and I'll make us a feast—squash soup, beet salad, eggplant parmesan, the works. I've got it all planned out."

Allison led Colin down the hall, carrying her drink. She flipped on the lights in their room, let him get two steps in the door and planted a tequila kiss on his lips. She walked him over to the bed, moaning as she backpedaled, feeling his tongue on hers, inhaling his sweat, sensing the deep ache of desire resurrect itself from the grave.

The ache started in her heart and radiated across her chest.

It was the fun ache, the good ache.

"I'm a mess," said Allison. "I'm sure I smell like death."

"I think I got you beat."

"Care to get cleaned up first?"

Colin smiled.

"First?"

"Before—you know."

"No, I don't. Before what?" asked Colin, playing dumb.

She stood, took off her shirt.

"Try to guess," she said.

"I'm thinking hard."

She wriggled free of her jeans half way to the bathroom. The number of thoughts in her head was reduced to precisely one.

A tent, sleeping bags and a fire would have been the preferred setting for what was about to happen next.

Tonight, a motel room would have to do.

Acknowledgements

Many thanks to my late, good friend Gary Reilly, one of the finest prose craftsmen I have ever known. I will miss your eye, your insight, your encouragement.

Thanks to my wife, Jody Chapel, for all her support through the years and to daughters Ally and Justine Chapel. During one July drive to go camping in Paonia, Justine helped me think through the best way to wrap up the plot. At the time, she was thirteen. Thanks to all the masterful editors and wordsmiths—Catherine Lutz for copious edits and careful, inspired analysis, Cindie Geddes for her hard scrub of the copy and Tanya Klein for a final, deep polish. Thank you to Mirte Mallory for her upbeat stewardship of the whole project. Colorado Division of Wildlife officer Frank McGee generously provided a closed reading and fact-checking. Thanks to Christy McGee, too. Mark Graham and Stephen Singular, both fine writers, provided stellar support and insights. Ralph Beall is responsible for Devo, but may not know it. On a related Devo matter, thanks to Les Stroud for the television series *Survivorman*. Todd Hartman's "Beyond the Boom" series for *The Rocky Mountain News* served as a major source of information and inspiration. Much of the research for the sections about Devo's survival skills relied on Bradford Angier's guide, *How to Stay Alive in the Woods*. In addition to my own trips, I drew heavily from Al Marlowe's *A Hiking and Camping Guide to the Flat Tops Wilderness Area* for detail, though some locations are amalgamations and imagination. Thanks to the Short Story Book Club stalwarts—Ted and Susan Pinkowitz, Dan Slattery, Parry Burnap and Laura Snapp for their early feedback and analysis. Mark Eddy, Abby Smith and Margaret Lake read early drafts and provided spot-on comments. Longtime friend and novelist Barry Wightman provided rocking support and a keen writer's eye. Allyn Harvey deserves thanks for, well, everything. Allison Coil wouldn't be out there if it weren't for the original, Renee Rumrill. Thanks to multi-talented Nick Zelinger for a perfect capture-the-mood cover. And, finally, thanks to Rocky Mountain Fiction Writers. What a fantastic group.

Do not Miss Allison Coil's adventures in *ANTLER DUST*

The first of the Allison Coil Mystery Series

"A deliciously cool read ... functions on two fast-paced levels: that of a mystery as well as keenly observed social commentary."
— *Great Falls (Montana) Tribune*

"Mark Stevens is a natural-born storyteller."
— Stephen Singular, best-selling author of *Unholy Messenger*

"Allison is a standout protagonist."
— *The Denver Post*

"Prose and plot sing in perfect harmony."
— *The Aspen Times*

"You won't find a fresher, more satisfying new voice."
— Stephen White

www.antlerdust.com

People's Press
Minds Wide Open

Published by People's Press
www.PeoplesPress.org